Payback

Alan Dunn

THOMAS DUNNE BOOKS
ST. MARTIN'S PRESS  NEW YORK

THOMAS DUNNE BOOKS.
An imprint of St. Martin's Press.

www.minotaurbooks.com

Library of Congress Cataloging-in-Publication Data

Dunn, Alan, 1954–
    Payback / Alan Dunn.—1st U.S. ed.
        p. cm.
    ISBN 0-312-31099-4
    1. Private investigators—England—Fiction. 2. Winter resorts—Fiction.
    3. England—Fiction. I. Title.

PR6014.U544 P39 2003
823'.914—dc21   2002034687

First published in Great Britain by Judy Piatkus (Publishers) Ltd.

First U.S. Edition: January 2003

10 9 8 7 6 5 4 3 2 1

I'm fortunate to share my life with many wonderful people, some of whom have graced the 'thank you' pages of my previous novels. If you've read these you'll be familiar with my wife Jan, my sons Mike and Pete, and my extensive extended family; my thanks, once again, go to them all, to my agent Diana Tyler and to all at MBA.

The past year saw me studying at St Martin's College, Carlisle, where I enjoyed the company of a band of lunatics on the English Drama and Media Studies PGCE course. They've now been unleashed; be afraid, be very afraid. This book is for them, and for those who guided me along the winding road to teacherdom, especially, Fiona, Dave, Ron, Iain and the English department at Ullswater Community College.

But there are three others who deserve particular praise. Sophie, Tim and Amy have endured my dragging them to every village hall in Cumbria to play in a folk band. They've put up with my bad jokes and cooking. They've even said they enjoy my impersonation of Mark Knopfler. For all this, but most of all because they're lovely people, I thank them.

Chapter One

I can't sleep, though I'm aching with tiredness.

There's a book spread-eagled on the arm of the chair, but I can't read.

The mug on the table beside me is full of cold tea, its surface thick. There's no sound of traffic. I can hear the clock ticking wearily, telling me life goes on, slowly, slowly. It's just after three thirty, the lowest dark of the morning.

I'm sitting in my ex-wife's house, in her chair. The central heating clicked off hours ago. I'm wrapped in her thick towelled dressing gown, I can smell perfume on it and I bury my nose in its collar, inhale deeply. It's a cloying, musky fragrance. I don't think I ever bought perfume for Sara, not before, not during and certainly not after our marriage. I suppose John must have given it to her. John. Her new husband.

I close my eyes, rotate my neck one way then the other, hear the crepitus of tired muscles. I stare at the phone, will it to ring, but it remains silent out of spite. I need to occupy myself, find work to do. But it's too late and too early to switch on the vacuum cleaner. I've already done what little ironing there was, and the washing basket is empty. Sara must have spent days tidying up. She knows me too well.

I push myself to my feet, pad across to the television and switch it on, volume low. There's a photograph on the

1

wall, a photograph of Sara and Kirsty. There'll be new prints on display shortly, new gilt-framed photographs of the bride and groom at the wedding, on honeymoon. Perhaps there'll be a group photograph and Sara will describe the event to visitors.

'Yes, that's John's mother, she does very well for her age. You know my mum and dad, and my sister. That's Marge from the office, and Jackie. John's relatives, I swear I can't remember all their names. Oh, yes. And Billy was there. We didn't think he'd come, but he behaved himself very well. Is he seeing someone? Well, there was a girl, a young girl, Jen, just finished training as a doctor. But she decided to go off to Canada for a year, I'm not sure if they've agreed to keep the relationship going. But enough of Billy . . .'

I'm sure there'll soon be a photograph of the two of them with Kirsty, Kirsty between them, tall as her mother and far more beautiful. And then, in six months' time, when Sara's baby arrives . . .

There's a nature programme on television, all soft-focus and long-lenses. The commentary's treacle-thick and growling, it has to be American. I switch channels, flick from a games show to current affairs, find but then discard a black-and-white gangster movie; I'm in no mood for Bogart. I switch off.

It was a stupid thing to say. 'Ring me when you get to the hotel, just to let me know you got there safely'. She should have laughed, and said there was no need. She should have known I'd work it all out. Twelve hours for the flights, allow three hours for clearing the airport and transfer to the hotel, adjust for the time difference. She should have known I'd stay up, waiting for her to call. She should have rung by now.

'So who looked after Kirsty when you were on honeymoon?' the visitors will ask.

'Billy again. He's really been so civilised. I mean, Kirsty said there was no need, she could stay by herself, but Billy and John and I agreed there was no way . . . And Billy's flat – more of a bed-sit really – is just too small. So we decided he could stay in the house with Kirsty. At least we had no worries about it being clean for us coming back!'

I walk over to the window, twitch the curtains open. The cherry tree at the end of the garden is being whipped by bitter, black winds, even the lamp-posts are swaying. The mirrors that were once path and road are swept by miseries of rain, rain that claws at the windows and etches the glass.

I let the curtain close, shiver, decide to switch on the fire. I don't like winter. The seasons seem to lag behind the calendar; I don't mind September and October, they still carry traces of summer. November and December are bright with the optimism of Christmas, there's still a hustle of life in the air; it's as if everyone wants to horde the sense of well-being before they hibernate. January's bad, but predictably so; it heaves and smothers the world. I always expect the worst from January, but it never lives down to its potential. Then comes February, short and hard, fast and eager, darting like a sneak thief. It's armed with ice daggers and it likes to hurt. February's the worst month, and it's on the streets already.

It's different for Jen. Her winter's full of snow and blue skies, mountains and ice-rimmed rivers. She goes skiing, tells me stories of people I don't know, people I'll never meet. She sends me an email (usually manages to attach a photograph) every week. But they're getting shorter, and last week she said she was going away, she didn't think she'd be able to contact me. She said she'd try to phone. I told her where I'd be.

I settle down in the chair again, try to think of Jen. I close my eyes, but I can't see her face. Her body, yes. But not her face.

'Dad? Dad, wake up.'

I struggle back to the surface. Kirsty's there, peering down at me, wrapped in her dressing gown. There are times when she looks so much like Sara it hurts. I must

3

look ill or worried, she crouches down and her hand reaches out to touch mine.

'Are you all right?' she asks.

I'm coming round. There's a dim light showing round the curtain, a faint smell of burnt toast escaping from the kitchen.

'What time is it?'

'Just after nine,' Kirsty answers. 'And there's a call for you.' She must have answered the phone before it could disturb me, I pick up the receiver from the table beside me. 'Hello?' I say, but there's no answer, no tone. I look down at the floor, see a coil of cable not attached to the wall point.

'Oops,' Kirsty says, her hands fly to her mouth. She hurries into the kitchen, explaining as she goes. 'I came down about four, the light was on but you were asleep. I unplugged the phone. You looked so tired and ...' She returns with the cordless phone from the kitchen, '... I made a policy decision. Sleep was the priority.' She hands me the phone and my glare makes her step back.

I start speaking straightaway. 'Sara? I thought you were going to ring me as soon as you got there. Is everything okay? Was the flight delayed?'

There's a deep belly laugh from the phone. 'I always knew you'd flip, boss, but I didn't think it would come so soon.' It's a voice I recognise, dipped in a Yorkshire accent.

'Sly? I'm sorry, I was expecting Sara ...'

'Getaway! I'd never have guessed.'

'I was asleep ...'

'I know, Kirsty told me.' Either he's not letting me finish my sentences, or I'm incapable of normal speech. I shake my head, try to clear the debris of almost forgotten dreams, unpleasant dreams, unfulfilled, wanting dreams.

'I'll make a cup of tea,' Kirsty says, glides into the kitchen.

'You busy?' Sly asks. It's not an innocent question. Sly

4

works for me sometimes, he's good at his job, a top class electrician. He can turn his hand to other tasks as well, he's tall and strong and black and he can make himself look evil. He doesn't need to put on an act to play the part of the heavy. I can't remember whether he owes me a favour or I owe him one, but I suspect it's the latter.

'Can't complain,' I reply. 'I've a backlog of work, sites to survey, quotations to prepare, systems to install, but the weather's been against me. Why are you asking?'

'Oh, just wondering.'

'You never "just wonder", Sly. It's not in your nature or your name. What are you after?'

'Company,' Sly says, and I can hear a voice behind him. 'Let me speak to him,' it says. I hear the click and rustle of the phone being passed over.

'Billy Oliphant,' the woman's voice says, 'I haven't seen you for over a month. Have you gone off good cooking?' Sly's wife doesn't take prisoners.

'Paula. How are you?'

'I'm well, the kids are well – except they keep asking when you're going to come and see them – and Sly's got a proposition for you. And the answer you give when he finally gets round to asking, is "yes".'

She passes the phone back to Sly. 'Ask him,' I hear her say.

'Come on then, Sly, out with it.' My voice sounds weary.

'Okay, okay. I don't know, everybody picks on me, everybody bullies me. Anyway, here's the deal, boss. I've been working up at Forestcrag Village; have you heard of it?'

'Forestcrag? Who hasn't?' Kirsty brings me in a mug of tea, puts it on the table at my side. I pick it up, put it down again on a coaster, ignore her raised eyebrows.

'Well, they close down every winter for two or three weeks, get all the maintenance work done in one go. And I've been up there doing eighteen-hour days. There are three hundred lodges up there, Billy, and they've all been repainted, cable TV and computer links installed. The Tesseract has been . . .'

'Hold on, Sly, hold on. The what?'

'The Tesseract. It's the big dome in the centre of the village, except it isn't shaped like a dome. It's got four sides, but they're curved and they sort of overlap. It's made mostly of glass, and when you look at it, it seems to change shape. It's weird. Anyway, that's where the pool is, and the shops and restaurants, the cinema, the sports centre and . . .'

'Okay, okay, I get the idea.'

'You asked! So it's been emptied, remodelled and re-themed, new slides put in the pool, the works. I tell you, Billy, I've never seen . . .'

I hear Paula's voice again. 'Sly, *please* get to the point.'

'Yes, Sly, get to the point. Kirsty's here, she's already late for school. I'll have to chase her out of the house.' I hold my hand out, shake my wristwatch at her. I mouth the words 'Get dressed', nod my head to make it a gentle request rather than an order. She stays where she is, says softly 'Free periods.'

Sly's hurrying along now. 'This is the story, boss, a two bird story, just imagine you're the stone. Here we go with bird one. The work's all finished, dead on schedule. There's a reception tonight, to say thank you to the main contractors.' He pauses. 'That includes me. I'm invited to stay two nights, bring the family, try the facilities. The lodge holds eight, there are six of us. I thought you and Kirsty might like to come along, fill the extra places.'

It's kind of Sly and Paula. It's kind of Sara, she and Paula still see each other, and it's her hand behind all this. I can even hear her voice. 'I'm not sure how Billy'll take all this, the wedding, looking after Kirsty, staying in the house again. Keep your eye on him, will you?' But I can't match their kindness with my enthusiasm.

'I don't know,' I say, 'I've a lot to do. I'm sure Kirsty has lessons . . .'

'Free periods all morning, Dad, only General Studies this afternoon and I'm already good enough at that, it won't hurt me to miss it. Honest. And tomorrow's Saturday.'

She's in on it as well. Everyone I know is conspiring against me.

'I don't really feel I'd be good company, Sly.'

'Hold on, boss, hold on. Bird two, I haven't told you about bird two. The big boss, Morland's his name, David Morland, he's having problems. He knows I do security work, asked if I knew a good private investigator. I said no, but I knew a fair-to-middling one, and I told him about you. He wouldn't say what his problem was, but he wants to meet you. And that's it. Come with us, mix business and pleasure. Kill both birds. You'll enjoy it, Kirsty'll enjoy it. You're not really going to say no, are you?'

I don't want to go. I don't want any more work. I just want to be alone with Kirsty, to spend some time with her. I want to talk to her, listen to her. My mind's made up. That's when I look at my daughter. Sometimes she looks so worldly, so mature, it frightens me. But every now and then, in an infrequent, unguarded moment, I see the gauche teenager she really is. That's what she is now, a young girl desperate for a new adventure. Even if she and Paula and Sly and Sara have dreamed up this whole thing, I can't let her down. She catches me looking at her, she pleads silently, raises her eyebrows and smiles, nods eagerly. I can only mimic her approval. 'Yes,' I say. I want to go on, I want to say that it's against my will, that I know what's going on, that I'm not happy at being manipulated like this. But I don't get that far. Kirsty hears that one word, that affirmative, and leaps into the air. 'Yes!' she says, 'I knew Sly would persuade you. I'll have to pack, get my swimming stuff together. And there's going to be a dance tonight, I'll take something smart. Casual, I don't want to be overdressed. But smart.' She strides for the door, then turns back. 'There's something I made in design at school, you haven't seen it Dad, but it looks great!' She launches

7

herself at me, hugs me, kisses the top of my head. 'Thanks, Dad,' she whispers, runs away again. I can hear her leap the stairs.

'You're coming?' Sly asks tentatively. He can read my uncertainty.

'So my daughter tells me.'

'Women,' Sly says. 'I'll pick you up at one.'

The receiver goes down. I think of what he said and it disturbs me. Women. My daughter is less and less a girl, more and more a woman. As if I didn't have enough troubles.

Chapter Two

I'm using the spare room. I didn't think I'd be able to sleep in the double bed Sara offered me, it wouldn't have been right; too many unresolved memories. I haven't unpacked my clothes, it takes only a few minutes to transfer some into the overnight bag Kirsty's found me. I stroll across the landing, knock on her door; her voice invites me to enter.

'This is really great, Dad, do you realise how exclusive that place is? Expensive isn't the word. Wait till I tell them at school.' The suitcase on her bed is already half full, and she's intent on emptying her entire wardrobe into it. She catches my silence, slows her excitement, turns to face me.

'It doesn't matter, me missing a lesson today,' she says. 'I'm up to date with everything, coursework, essays, you name it.' She adopts a Mockney accent. 'I'm a good girl, I am.' She sees me looking at the clothes, both in the case and on the bed. 'And I'd rather be prepared for every eventuality.'

'We're only going for two days,' I remind her.

'You're so one-dimensional, Dad.' Before I can figure out what that means she reaches low into the depths of the wardrobe, brings out a plastic carrier bag and hands it to me. 'Here, I've got you a present. I was going to keep it for your birthday, but it'll be more use now, and ... well, it might distract you from the amount of stuff I'm taking.'

I slide my hands into the bag but keep watching her face.

Despite her attempt at diffidence she's eager, excited. I can feel the smoothness of paper, pull out something heavy wrapped in brown paper and tied with string.

'I made it myself,' she says. 'Designed it as well. It's all me.'

I try to feel the contents through the paper. It's something I learned as a child, to take my time over unwrapping presents. Kirsty and Sara were always the opposite, they'd tear at parcels, throw the paper aside in their haste to get at the present itself. I usually slide my fingers into a gap, try to remove the Sellotape without harming the paper. It takes me all morning to open half a dozen presents at Christmas.

'Come on, Dad,' Kirsty encourages me. I'm busy trying to undo the knot, though the string's tied so loosely that I could slide it off the parcel in a single loop.

'It's something to wear,' I tell her. That's not a clever guess since she admits to making it herself; she's doing a design course in textiles and I can feel some type of cloth inside. But it's heavy. 'And it's going to be useful to me now!'

She's sitting cross-legged on the bed. She nods, and the movement travels down her body and makes the whole bed vibrate.

'Dad, Sly said he'd be here about one and it's nearly ten now. That only gives you three hours to open it. Don't you think you'd better speed up a little?'

I ignore her. 'It's heavy, too heavy to be a sweater. Outer wear? A coat, it must be a coat of some type.'

'You must have peeked!'

'No, I'm just applying logic. And you said it would be useful, and a coat would certainly be useful in this weather.'

'Okay then, Mr Clever. What colour is it?'

I close my eyes, hold my hands over the parcel. 'It must be unusual for you to mention the colour. Unusual for me, or unusual in general? But it's useful, so it can't be too garish. And it's definitely a coat, I could tell by the way you were annoyed when I suggested that. So it's a winter coat in . . . red. Yes, red. Or green? Yellow, perhaps? No, not green, that's too conservative. Red or yellow.'

'Give it to me! You're impossible!' She's quick, she grabs the parcel from me before I can lower my hands. She rips the paper away and holds out a bright yellow duffel coat. It has buttons, not toggles, there's no hood and it has deep pockets.

'I'm just so good,' I say.

'You're your daughter's father, that's all.' She hands the coat to me. 'Go on, then, see if it fits.'

I push my arms into the sleeves, they're just the right length. It fits across the back with enough room for me to wear a thick sweater beneath, it hangs halfway down my thigh. I turn one way and then the other, stroll over to look at myself in the mirror.

'Wow,' says Kirsty, 'it looks good. It really suits you.'

'It does,' I agree. 'And it fits perfectly. I'm impressed.'

'Do you like it?' She's a little girl again, eager for praise.

'Kirsty, it's wonderful. It fits, it's just the right style, and it's different enough to appeal without being completely wild. Thank you.' Her room isn't large, we meet in the middle and hug. I even manage to kiss her on the forehead.

'Go on,' she says, 'I've got to get dressed and get the rest of my stuff together.' She extracts herself from my arms and returns to her packing. She has her back to me. 'You know, you're almost good-looking when you smile.'

I'm at the door, I can feel a grin stretching across my face. Kirsty has an annoying habit of making me feel good.

'I can see why Mum fell for you.'

11

Chapter Three

I've never seen Sly's car before. I didn't know he had one,
I assumed he used his van for family as well as work. I
should have known Paula wouldn't let their brood rattle
around inside a long-wheelbase Transit. Sly jumps out of a
large, dark-windowed vehicle, the hybrid offspring of
sports car, minibus and jet aircraft. Rain slides off the
force-field of its polish. Kirsty, watching from the window,
can only say 'Wow,' and no other word will do as well. I
hurry to open the door.

'Hiya, boss.' Sly winks down at me, throws his coat
hood back. He holds out his huge hand to engulf mine,
squeezes gently in case he damages my fingers. 'How you
doin'?' he asks, and I'm sure he really wants me to answer
honestly.

'Better for seeing you,' I reply. 'But not as good as I'll
be when I see Paula and the kids.'

He accepts the compliment. 'You ready? It's damn cold
out there, make sure you've got something warm to wear.
Forecast's not good.'

I pull on a fleece, top it with Kirsty's coat. Sly looks at
it, raises his eyebrows, tilts his head to one side.

'And what does that look mean, Sly Rogers?' Kirsty's
appeared at the door, hand on hip, pretending to be
annoyed at his reaction.

'Sorry, Miss.' Sly bows slightly. 'I didn't know the boss

had company. I was expecting his daughter, Kirsty. Little runt of a girl she is, no meat on her at all. Quite the opposite to an elegant, well-dressed, good-looking young lady like you.'

'Is that meant to be flattery? Or is it just a poor attempt to distract me from the fact that you don't like the coat I made for Dad?'

'Oh. *You* made the coat? Right.' He pinches his lips, half closes his eyes, sticks out his chin. He looks as if his head has been squeezed by an invisible vice, and it's clearly Kirsty who's applying the pressure. 'Well, I'll admit it's not the type of thing *I'd* wear. But allowing for the fact that I've no dress sense, I'm colour blind, and I buy clothes 'cos they're comfortable, that probably means it looks great.' He holds out his hands in reconciliation, pale palms uppermost. 'Bright, but great.'

'I think I could grow to hate you,' Kirsty says, 'if I didn't like you so much.'

'Kirsty! It is you! I only realised when you started insulting me.' He steps into the hallway, she meets him halfway and disappears inside his hug. When they separate he looks across at me again. 'Perhaps it's the model that's at fault rather than the coat. Yeah, it's the model. No style.'

I'm hoisting my bag onto my shoulder, struggling with the far greater weight of Kirsty's suitcase. 'You only ever had a small amount of style, Sly, and you used all that up when you asked Paula to marry you.'

'Ooh!' Kirsty and Sly chorus together.

'God knows why she said yes.'

'I'd tell you,' Sly says, grabbing Kirsty's case from me, 'but I'm too modest. And I don't want to give you an inferiority complex. Is this it, then? Are you ready?'

Kirsty reaches for a small black jacket.

'Don't you want to take something a bit more substantial?' I'm being the anxious father again.

'No,' she says, 'this'll do. I'm not planning on doing any hiking this weekend.'

13

She's out of the door before I can object. In the cupboard under the stairs there's a waterproof coat and a pair of wellington boots. I roll and fold them into my bag. Just in case. Then I slam the door behind me and rush through the rain to the car.

Sly's at the rear, forcing Kirsty's case into the boot. I throw him my bag as I pass. 'We've saved a seat in the middle for you,' he says, 'so you can keep the kids occupied.'

I open the door and climb in to a chorus of 'Hiya, Uncle Billy.' Paula's in the driving seat, her eldest son, Gav, on the bench beside her. Next to me Julia's sleeping in her car seat, while Kirsty's jammed in the back separating twins Tim and Jo. I lean forward and kiss Paula on the cheek, her hand rests for a moment on my shoulder. 'Good to see you,' she whispers. Then Sly's bulk fills the remaining place in front of me.

'Everyone belted in?' Paula asks. There's an arpeggio of assent, then we're off.

'Uncle Billy,' Gav says, leaving the book he's reading and turning round in his seat, 'Dad says there's an indoor football pitch and we're gonna play, do you want to play as well? I'm gonna be Kieran Dyer, he says he'll be Sol Campbell. You can be ... you can be that goalie, the French one. Or Alan Shearer.'

'I've always thought I was more the skilful creative type, Gav. Can't I be David Ginola?'

'Na,' he says, 'you haven't got enough hair.'

Gav has the wary, witty repartee of a ten-year-old. The twins are a more amenable eight: Jo has her mother's elegant good looks, she glances at me from long-lashed eyes; Tim is a fidget, eager for attention, Kirsty's busy trying to occupy his attention by playing 'I Spy' with him. The car settles down for the journey.

'Nice wheels,' I comment.

'A necessity,' Paula replies. 'Norm found it for us. I was a bit doubtful at first, I thought it was too flash. But he

14

looked at it, checked on the availability of spares. He managed to knock quite a bit off the price for us.'

'How is Norm?'

'I saw him last week,' Sly says, 'he seems okay. Says he's got a spot of arthritis. He's got a garage full of hula-hoops; apparently it's going to be the next big craze. Like yo-yos a few years back. Offered to let me in on the ground floor.'

'I take it you said no.'

'He's still got a few thousand straw hats left over from last year's heatwave,' he giggles. 'Yeah, I said no. Why can't he just stick to what he's good at, cars?'

'Because,' Paula suggests, 'it's more fun being a wheeler-dealer. He knows the motor business inside out, it isn't exciting any more. That's what he wants, excitement.'

'He could look after the twins sometime,' Sly says, 'he'd soon want to go back to something quiet like tightrope walking or breeding alligators.'

'Kirsty seems to manage quite nicely,' Paula says. I look around, the back seat occupants are singing and doing what looks like a modern version of the hand-jive.

'I just hope she can keep it up,' Sly says, peering forward, 'this could be a long journey. Good job this beast's got four wheel drive.'

The wind has changed direction and strength and the rain is thickening into sleet. We're heading north, out of the city, into the weather, and the traffic's crawling in a blaze of white and red lights. Inside it's warm. Kirsty and the kids are still singing. I can hear Gav reading aloud to Sly. Beside me Julia stirs slightly, licks her lips, then opens her eyes. She looks straight at me, but contentment slides her back to sleep. I can sympathise with her, I feel almost contented myself. I'm relaxed, it's a pleasant experience after weeks of being on edge. Perhaps it won't last, but while it does ... I close my eyes, though I know I won't sleep.

'Boss? Think we might have a problem.'

15

It's dark outside, except ahead of us where the headlights shine on a wall of snowflakes. Sly and Paula have swapped places, he's driving very slowly and she's breastfeeding in the passenger seat. I turn to look behind me. Kirsty smiles at me, one arm round each sleeping twin.

'Where are we?' I ask, stretch to shake away my dreams.

'I *think* we're close to Forestcrag road, but I could be wrong. It normally takes about forty-five minutes to get there, but it's almost three hours since we set off. We haven't been much above ten, fifteen miles an hour since we left the dual carriageway. Good job I had your snoring to entertain me.'

'Do you want to turn back?'

'I can't imagine it'll be any better. But that's not why I woke you. Look, up ahead.'

I lean to one side, squint past him. Not too far off there's a pair of flashing blue lights. 'Police. Perhaps the road's blocked?'

'Could be. But it doesn't look right, one of the lights is too low. Hang on, I can see better now. Yeah, look boss. It's a police car all right, but it's off the road.'

I undo my belt, push myself forward so I can see better.

'Two cars,' Paula says. 'No, one car and one van. A security van.'

She's right. The police car has two wheels on the road, two in the ditch. Behind it the van is sideways on, its front bumper crumpled and digging into a flat tyre. It's not a police van, though it has the look of one. The small windows have metal grilles across them.

'I'd forgotten,' I say. 'I should have known. Where do you get to if you don't turn off at Forestcrag? Keep going over the moors? Garthdale Prison. They must be taking someone away, that's why there's an escort.'

'Do you think they're all right?' Paula asks. 'I can't see anyone around.'

On Paula's cue a figure appears, a plump policeman swaddled in standard issue bad weather coat and fluorescent jacket. He waves to Sly, urges him to pass by.

'Ask him if he's okay,' Paula urges.

Sly winds the window down, though only halfway. The snow flurries through the gap. 'Anything we can do to help?' Sly asks.

'Thank you, sir, but no one's been injured. The car skidded, the van nudged us off the road. We've radioed for assistance, it should be here shortly. Now if you'll just move along. And watch out, there's ice underneath the snow.'

I push my head forward. 'Sure it wasn't just bad driving? Perhaps you fell asleep at the wheel.'

The policeman's confused. 'I beg your pardon?'

'You always had problems walking a straight line, never mind driving one.'

'Who's that? Who's that inside there?'

'I can recognise your voice, Danny Bateman, even if you don't remember mine.'

The torch beam lights up the inside of the car, catches me full in the face.

'Billy? Billy Oliphant?'

'The one and only. And can you point the torch in a different direction, you've already fried my eyeballs.'

'Billy, I don't believe it. What the hell . . .? What are you doing now? I thought . . . That is, I never dreamed . . . How are you?'

'Good,' I say, 'good. Keeping up. This is Sly, by the way, Sly Rogers. And his wife, Paula, their family. And my daughter Kirsty's in the back there. We're on our way to Forestcrag for the weekend.'

'You must be doing well, then,' Danny answers. He's an old acquaintance, once I would have called him a friend. He's a good driver, experienced. Conditions must be bad if he's spun off the road.

'Transferring a villain?' I ask.

'Only an awayday. His mother's being buried tomorrow. The Governor must have been in a good mood. Pity he didn't check the weather forecast.' He glances round. 'I could have told him this lot was on the way. Like all the brass, never bothers consulting the ones who *really* know.'

'Sure we can't give you a hand? We've got four wheel drive.'

'No, it's okay, I've told them what we need. Including a snowplough. It's quite warm and cosy inside the van, we've got the cards out. And let's face it, there won't be much traffic about tonight. Go on, you'd better keep going or you'll end up stuck in a drift. I reckon we've got a whole weekend of this to look forward to.'

'Okay, Danny, best of luck.'

Paula whispers something just as Danny begins to move away. I call him back. His coat and hat are almost white now.

'Sorry, Danny. I don't suppose you know how far it is to the Forestcrag turnoff?'

He turns and smiles. 'Half a mile to go, I reckon. Should take you no more than an hour.' His sense of humour's as bad as it always was. He waddles round the van and waves without looking back. We pull away.

'Old friend?' Paula asks.

'I was his boss. Seems like a whole different life now, as if I was somebody else. Most of the time I don't miss it.' I have to smile, thinking of Danny padding back through the snow to the van. 'Like now.'

'Well I hope somebody comes to rescue him soon,' Kirsty chips in. 'it must be cold in that van.'

'He'll be all right,' I say, 'the engine's still running, they'll be warm. And you heard what he said, they're playing cards. They've probably dealt the poor old lag a hand too, he'll be sitting there with his cuffs on trying to hide his cards from Danny. If they gave him any money to come out with he won't have it for long, not with Danny playing.'

The view forward's like a migraine. I don't know how Sly's managing to drive, the car's beginning to slip a little and the snow's getting deeper. I doubt we'll make it if we have to go up a hill. I can see the canyon walls of pine trees on both sides of the road, they must be sheltering us from the worst of the wind, when we pass a firebreak there's suddenly a bank of snow to one side, as high as the car.

'I don't like this,' Paula says, softly, in case the children hear.

'It's not too bad where the wind can blow the snow away,' Sly says, 'but it's just building up deeper and deeper where it's sheltered. I'm sure the turn's somewhere around here.'

A solid white sign looms out of the more fragmented, darting whiteness. No words are visible, but two artificial arcs of snow-clad wall show us where the road should be.

'Here we are then,' Sly sounds relieved. 'I recognise this bit, it's only a mile from here.'

The tyres slither as he turns the wheel. The car slides, corrects itself, then we're pulling up a long, slow hill. Sometimes there's wheelslip. Sometimes I can hear the bottom of the car scrape on thickened snow. I expect to hear howling from a distant wolf pack.

'Not far now,' Sly mutters, 'not far now.' The road bends, first to the right, then to the left. We must be close to the edge of the pine forest, I can feel the wind trying to catch the car, trying to push it off the road. I can hear it, not whistling, but groaning, then roaring.

'Mum, I'm frightened,' Gav whimpers.

'So am I,' Paula answers.

'So am I,' I whisper to myself.

'Look,' says Sly, 'there, straight ahead.'

Those of us who are awake stare over the snow settling deep on the sloping bonnet. I can't see anything at first, but then find a patch of whiteness brighter than the rest. It disappears as the snow blooms on the windscreen, then the wipers cross and it's revealed a little brighter than before.

'It must be the Tesseract,' Sly says, 'they've got it lit up.'

The road crosses a treeless tract of what must be moorland (I can't actually see anything, just judge by the lack of trees and the sudden blast of wind and snow). The snow's banked up in waves, a peak to the left, a long sloping bank to the right. I assume there are walls, that they're keeping the snow off the road; if the blizzard continues it won't be long until it fills the gap between the walls with snow. Then we're back in the trees, descending again. For a moment the snow stops, the wind dies, and we can see ahead of us. There's a huge block of building made of glass, something vaguely distorted, not quite a cube, shining in the middle of the forest. There are ribbons of lights leading away from it, and other smaller warmer lights in what look like houses. Then the snow closes round us again.

'Almost there,' Sly says. We're moving slowly now, he's worried in case the car slides downhill. I can see a building ahead, lights shining at all windows, a barrier in front of it reaching across the road.

'They're obviously expecting us,' I say.

'We haven't seen tyre tracks,' Paula mentions. 'Perhaps we're the only ones who came. It *is* this weekend, Sly, you haven't got it wrong?'

Sly touches the brakes and we slither to a halt a few feet from the barrier. 'No, I haven't got it wrong. And we *were* meant to be here earlier, so I'm not surprised there was no sign of other vehicles or their tracks. But I'll just go and wake the security people up, and then we'll be off to find our cosy little cabin in the woods.'

Through the window of the lodge I can see a distant bank of television monitors. The people sitting in front of them seem reluctant to brave the weather. 'I'll come with you,' I say. I'm curious to see the security set-up; I might be able to take some ideas away with me.

Sly and I climb out together. The snow on the ground is knee-deep; in the air it feels like grit, I half close my eyes and swim through the harsh wind to the door of the lodge. Sly's close behind me, we push through together and find ourselves in front of a counter. There are two men there, both dressed in green sweatshirts and slacks. They're looking intently, urgently, at a bank of twenty or so monitors. One of them is keying numbers into a computer, the other is swearing under his breath.

'Sorry to keep you, sir,' the first one says, 'we'll be with you in a moment.'

'Having a problem, Sam?' Sly asks.

The man turns round as Sly peels back the hood from his coat. 'Sly. Good to see you, I'm surprised you got through. Just give me a minute.' He turns back to the monitors. 'Damn! No response from sixty-two through to sixty-eight. Seventy-four, seventy-six and seventy-seven are snowed up. How do they expect us to find someone just by using cameras?'

There's a radio on the desk beside him, it crackles into life though I can't hear what it says. He picks it up. 'You've found her? Where ...? Asleep under a bed? And they hadn't looked? I've a good mind to throw the fuckers in the lake! Thanks, Jimmy, call off the search. You can come home now.'

Sam turns round to face us. 'Sorry about that, Sly. About half an hour ago a guest rang, said her six-year-old daughter had wandered off into the snow. We've got every security guard in the place out looking for her, I was just going to call out the cooks and reception staff. Even David Morland is out there with his boots on.'

'The big boss,' Sly explains to me.

'And it turns out the girl was asleep under her bed. And the bloody parents hadn't even searched the lodge before calling us out! Jesus Christ!'

'You having problems with the monitors?' I ask.

Sly does the introductions. 'Sam Ellis, head of security. This is my friend Billy Oliphant. He's in the security business as well.'

We look each other up and down, thinking the same thoughts. Do I recognise your name? Should I know you? If

I've met him before I can't remember him, and the security business isn't large. Most of the local operators have been involved with the police force in one way or another, but security on a site this remote, this large, is probably quite specialised. Perhaps he's been imported, perhaps he's experienced in this type of project. We nod at each other, reserving judgement.

'The problem's with the cameras. We've over a hundred scattered round the site. Some, quite a few, just aren't working. Could be the cold, could be the poles knocked down by the wind. Others are snowed up, even though they're hooded. The system's well designed, it's been working for a year now with no trouble at all. I suppose it's just that the weather's exceptional, and it's so bad I can't get anyone to look at them.' He grins at Sly. 'I don't suppose you and Mr Oliphant want a bit of work while you're here?'

'We're into relaxation,' Sly says, 'and anyway, the family's outside in the sledge. Do you know where we're staying?'

'Sorry,' Ellis says, 'I'm forgetting myself. We've got everyone staying as close to the Tesseract as possible, you're at ...' He consults a clipboard lying on the desk, '... let me see, yes, fourteen Simonside. We're also letting everyone keep their cars beside their lodges, I've a feeling the car park'll be impassable if this keeps up.' He hands Sly a key, presses a button on the desk. I can see the barrier in front of the car rise slowly into the air, complaining at the weight of snow and ice it has to carry.

'There was an accident close to the site turnoff,' I say, 'a police car on prisoner escort duty ended up in the ditch. No one was hurt, but they've sent for a snowplough. It might be worth asking if it can be diverted onto your entrance road, otherwise I can't see anyone else arriving and no one'll be able to leave.'

'No need, Mr Oliphant, no need. First of all, we've got everything on site you could possibly need. And second, we've got our own plough and tractor unit. Used it a lot last winter. Don't worry, we'll look after you. Like Sly says, you just go and relax.'

If I was a normal, straightforward customer I'd think he was trying to reassure me. But I'm not, I'm an ex-policeman who knows just a little about security management. I prefer to believe he's putting me in my place. It's his operation, he's in charge, and he doesn't want any interference from someone who obviously can't appreciate the problems associated with managing security on such a large site.

'Come on then, boss,' Sly says, throwing the key in the air and catching it neatly.

'What type of tractor unit?' I ask.

'Pardon?' Sam Ellis has already returned to his monitors; even more of them are showing a picture blanketed with snow or crazed with interference.

'If it's a four wheel drive Land Rover, or even a bog standard John Deere or Massey Ferguson, it won't cope. You're going to need something big. If I were you, I'd be on the phone to the Council now, tomorrow might be too late.'

He doesn't even bother to turn round, he's playing with his keyboard again. 'Thank you, Mr Oliphant, for your advice. I'm sure we'll bear it in mind.'

Sly takes my arm, guides me back into the snow. 'Relax, boss. It's his problem, not yours, not mine.' The words are coated with a frosting of steam, and the wind catches them, flies them into the night.

'Yeah, you're right. I just want to make sure Kirsty gets to school on Monday.'

Chapter Four

'Wow,' says Kirsty, 'this is the biz. Look at this, Dad.' She's holding open the fridge door, there's no room for us to add anything around the food and drink already in place. 'Champagne. Real Champagne, Dad, not just fizzy wine.'

'The bath's *huge*,' Gav yells as he rushes past, 'there are *two* shower rooms, and you should *see* the size of the television. And the fire, look at the fire, a real fire with real flames!'

'I want the top bunk,' cries one of the twins from a distant bedroom.

'No, *I* want the top bunk,' the other counters.

'I'll go and sort them out,' I offer.

'Let them argue,' Sly says, 'if they kill each other that's two less mouths to feed. Anyway, they know they'll be taking turns. They're just after attention.'

Paula's propped in a huge armchair, feeding the baby again. 'I could do with a cup of tea,' she suggests quietly.

Kirsty's the first to move. 'I'll put the kettle on and make the tea,' she says, 'then I'll calm the kids down. You two,' she nods at me and Sly, 'could get the cases in from the car?' She's thinking clearly, logically, so we do as she says. Five minutes later we've unloaded the car, another five minutes and we're warm in front of the fire, mugs of tea in our hands, a huge cake on the coffee table beside us.

'Well,' says Sly, 'is it nice, or is it nice?'

'I like it,' says Kirsty. She's reading a story to the twins.

'It's great,' says Gav, 'and have you seen the snow? It's huge, it's already up to the windows.'

Paula looks as if she's about to fall asleep, curled up in the chair with her feet tucked beneath her. 'It feels good,' she says, 'to be in pleasant surroundings with people you love.' She feels for Sly's hand and smiles at me. It makes me feel good, included, and that was Paula's intention.

Sly takes the floor again. He's reading from a brochure left ostentatiously on the table, a brochure embossed with his name.

'It says here we're invited to a short reception at 8pm in the nightclub. There'll be a few speeches, then the gaming tables open, and there's music for dancing. Tomorrow there's a chance for everyone to try out the pool and the other attractions, the sports centre, the gym, the spa, lifestyle centre, the lake . . .'

I have to interrupt. 'You're joking, of course.'

'Perhaps the lake won't be open. Ice skating? I'm sure there'll be lots of other things to do. Then at night there's a disco. That should suit you, Kirsty. A gourmet buffet and complimentary drinks. Sunday morning we recover, Sunday afternoon we drive home.'

'If the weather lifts,' Paula points out.

'Let's see what's likely, then.' Sly points the remote at the television, flicks knowledgeably through more channels than I can recognise. Eventually he stops. 'Tail end of the news,' he says as the figure on the screen summarises the day's events.

'But in the North the country is at a standstill. Public transport has ground to a halt, workers are being advised not to attempt their journeys home. Ambulance, police and fire service vehicles are, in many places, unable to leave their bases. Several towns and villages are without electricity, and the Meteorological Office states that we have not yet seen the worst of the weather. That's the news tonight, now over to the weather desk.'

The weather forecaster has an easy job. Even I can see that, with low pressure squatting over the country and a wind coming down from the Arctic, there'll be no relief over the weekend. I suppose that, if I have to be cooped up in a luxurious lodge for a few days, there's no one I'd rather be with than my daughter and some good friends. But even in their company I feel alone. Sly and Paula have each other. Kirsty has the children to play with, to look after, and a whole weekend of adventure to look forward to; perhaps she won't want to spend her time with her father. That leaves me with only myself as an old, too familiar companion. If only Jen was here.

'There's a note from David Morland in here,' Sly mentions, waving the brochure at me. 'He says he's looking forward to meeting you this evening.'

'Great,' I say.

'Dress is informal,' Sly continues, 'which is just as well, given the weather.'

'I'm not moving from here,' Paula says, grabbing the brochure from Sly's hands. 'I'll be babysitter. And tomorrow? Tomorrow I'm having the full treatment at the spa. Massage, manicure, pedicure, facial, I'm going to have my legs waxed and my skin moisturised. And then, after all that hard work, I might need to relax. So tomorrow, Sly and Billy, *you* are in charge of the kids.'

'I'll stay with you tonight, Paula,' Kirsty offers.

'You will not! You can get out and enjoy yourself, you've already done your bit on the way here. Now then, I'd love to see the clothes you've brought. I feel so out of touch with what's going on these days. Why don't I help you unpack . . .'

'I just hope you've got something other than that coat to wear,' Sly says to me, 'or I'll deny I know you. But first . . . which shower should I use?'

Chapter Five

I always choose my clothes carefully, though the commandments prompting my choice are few. I don't wear brown shoes with a dark suit (though my one dark suit is used only for weddings and funerals). I hate it when my shirt collars bend like bananas. And I match items with similar colours. That's enough for me. I wear the clothes I like until they wear out, then I buy more the same. That's why I'm wearing black trousers and shoes, a fawn-coloured double-breasted jacket, and a white shirt with button-down collar and a vibrant – for me – yellow and black tie. Hanging in the hall above a pair of walking boots is my new coat; not only is it bright, but it's proving very warm. If I'd ever pretended to like it, that pretence is being replaced by genuine approval.

I tidy my room then go into the lounge and wait for the others to appear. The children are watching television; Paula's sitting in the corner reading. It's eight o'clock, we're meant to be at the reception, and there's no sign of Sly or Kirsty. Paula glances across the room at me. I realise she's looking at my fingers, they're drumming the arm of my chair. I stop.

'Sure you don't want to go?' I ask Paula. 'I don't mind staying in.'

'No, it's a hot bath and an early night for me.' She returns to her book.

I could stay behind with Paula. I'm sure Sly and Kirsty

27

wouldn't mind, they'd be good company for each other. I could have an early night, write a letter (a proper letter, not an email) to Jen. I could try to tell her how I'm feeling, what I'm feeling. About her. About life. I've just about persuaded myself that's what I'll do when Sly appears. He was lying when he said he had no dress sense. His polo-neck shirt looks as if it's made of silk, and it's the same muted grey as his trousers. His jacket is darker – though not black – and long, almost like a Regency dress coat, but essentially modern. He looks good and he knows it, he struts into the room like a fashion model and pirouettes in front of Paula.

'Man, I feel hot tonight,' he says, though he can't manage the American accent the phrase demands.

'You need to be, ' Paula says, 'it's still snowing.' I can see the smirk on her face; she can't hide the pride she takes in Sly. Even I can see that many women would consider him handsome. I feel small beside him.

There's a nervous cough from the far end of the room where Kirsty has entered. 'How do I look?' she asks.

'Let's have a look at you,' Paula says, prompts her to come forward. She takes three or four steps towards us.

'What do you think?' she asks.

I haven't been sure what to expect. I'm not naive, I know that girls mature earlier than boys, earlier than girls used to when I was a teenager. I'd been prepared for the outrageous: the skirt too short, the blouse with the low neckline, the heels making her taller than me. It had been difficult for me to sit back and allow Kirsty (with Paula's help) make her own choice of what to wear. But I needn't have worried.

'You look beautiful,' I say. Sly whistles his approval. 'Oh, yes,' Paula whispers.

She's chosen a black dress, its hem just above the knee, and a matching black jacket; everything sparkles with an inner sheen. Her hair is tied back in a tight pony-tail, her make-up is subtle and mature. Sly steps forward and offers her his arm. Together, the effect they create is even more startling, they're like an exam question, 'compare and contrast'; they're negative and positive, take one of them away and the other suffers from the loss.

'I got it wrong before,' I say, 'you're *both* beautiful. I feel like a caterpillar beside two butterflies.'

'A chrysalis,' Paula says, 'not a caterpillar. Your beauty's within.'

I shake my head. I have to smile, and my smile broadens, it becomes a laugh, a laugh I can't control. Sly looks at Paula, Paula looks at Kirsty, and they begin to laugh as well. But they can't see my vision of the dull chrysalis that's me, as I am, splitting to reveal the same me in my staid jacket and well-worn slacks, my cheap shirt and garish tie, blinking in the light reflected from Sly's broad barrel chest and Kirsty's shining, excited eyes. I'm no butterfly, I'm a moth. I shun daylight but I'm fatally attracted to brightness, to shining, glorious beauty. I wipe the tears from my eyes.

'Are you okay, Dad?' Kirsty's beside me, her arm round me.

'I've never felt worse,' I manage to say, and they all begin to laugh again. I breathe deeply, swallow, hide my head in my hands.

'Should we go?' Sly asks.

I can't cry off now, the moment's passed. 'I don't want to be back too late,' I say, 'we've all had a hard day. And from what you've said, there's another late night tomorrow.'

'We're not far from the Tesseract,' Sly says, 'see how it goes. If you want to come back early, if Kirsty and me want to boogie on down, I'm sure you'll find your way.' When he says 'boogie on down' he does a sort of shuffle, a bend at the knees and swagger of the chest. I think it's meant to be part of a dance, but it makes him look like a pouting, self-important pigeon.

When I open the door there's a wall of snow swept up against it almost half my height. The wind and snow have grown up and become a blizzard. I close the door again.

29

'I'm not going out in that,' I say, 'we'll be soaked before we get to the road.'

'I brought these.' Sly pulls a set of overalls from the coat rack, reaches into a cupboard and brings out a huge pair of wellington boots. 'I'll go first, I'll make the trail. I can carry Kirsty – she can put her jeans on under her dress, take them off again when we get there – and you can follow in my footsteps, Billy. It's not that far. Come on, get your dayglo coat on.'

Kirsty's already disappeared to find a pair of trousers and outdoor shoes. Sly shrouds himself in voluminous overalls and a woolly hat, a huge coat and his boots. I remember the coat I brought for Kirsty, go to find that. Five minutes later we set out.

It feels strange to be outside. It's cold, so cold it penetrates my clothes and sucks the energy from me. The flakes of snow are being driven in all directions by an angry wind, their random motion upsets my already precarious balance. Sly's forcing the path, kicking his way through the drifts. Kirsty's giggling, arms round his neck, legs supported by his arms and hands. And I can only shamble along behind them, follow their hunch-backed passage. There's no one else around. The roads and paths are lit, but the lights are low level, only a metre above the ground. Some of them are already topped by snow, their faint glow dulling with each additional flake. But ahead the Tesseract beckons, its walls bright as ice. It looms over us like a palace; I feel like Kay being brought to the Snow Queen.

Sly was right, it doesn't take us long to reach the main entrance. We shuffle around the huge revolving doors and find ourselves in a vast, dimly lit auditorium. There are no people to see us remove our outdoor clothing. There's a warm breeze in the air, a forest of trees and plants and a scent of flowers that feels natural. I can hear water flowing. Gently sloping footpaths wind away in many different directions, and a signpost signals their snake-like destinations. Most seem to lead to restaurants; one heads for the pool, another for a shopping mall, a third for a bowling alley and games room. There are signs pointing to a reception area, theatre, cinema and 'Ronnie Roe-deer's play area'. Different colour signs, presumably indicating that the facilities aren't in the Tesseract itself, show that somewhere in the forest there's a boating lake and a sports centre, a place to hire bicycles, and several woodland walks.

Sly has a look of ownership about him. 'Impressive, eh?'

'Big,' Kirsty says.

'Ostentatious,' I offer. There's a map beside the signpost, it shows the network of roads, paths and lodges, the lake, a mountain with a waterfall, the boundaries of the site. 'It's like a big garden. A wilderness tamed. Outdoor holidays for those who aren't prepared to make the effort to go outdoors.'

'Dad, that's being cynical. You haven't even seen it properly.'

'I don't need to. It's a holiday camp for the rich with a big fence to keep people out and to keep people in.'

'It is expensive,' Sly agrees, 'that's why the facilities are so good. And I certainly couldn't afford to come here if I was paying. So let's enjoy it while we can, I doubt there'll be another opportunity.'

Kirsty takes my arm. 'Yeah, Dad, it'll be cool.'

'Okay,' I say, 'I'll behave. I promise.'

'Great!' She claps her hands together, jumps up and down, then remembers she's not a young girl but a sophisticated woman. She pulls herself together. 'Which way do we go?'

'The casino,' Sly says, points at the map, 'touch the label.'

At the side of the map is a bank of signs. Kirsty finds that labelled 'Casino' (a hand of cards), and touches it.

A deep, polite voice surrounds us. 'You wish to find the casino? Please follow the yellow waymarkers.' Lights set into one of the paths glow yellow.

'Should we go?' Sly asks.

'Onward to Oz,' I answer, leaving Kirsty to thank the signpost for its politeness.

I recognise some of the foliage around us. There are several different types of palm, banana plants, Yuccas and rubber plants, all carefully planted to give the illusion of an impenetrable bank of sub-tropical jungle. It needs only speakers filled with the screech of monkeys and squawk of parrots to complete the mockery.

'I can't understand it,' I say, 'people come here, to one of the most beautiful wild places in England, and they spend their time in a giant greenhouse pretending they're in a jungle.'

'Dad,' Kirsty says, 'you promised.'

'I'm only telling you how I feel. I'm allowed to do that, aren't I?'

'I know how you feel, you don't need to tell me. You've already told me. Even if you don't say another word, you're still telling me. Please, Dad.'

'Sorry, love.'

The Tesseract isn't a cube. The frameworks of its walls and ceiling are made from ribs of steel, they run into one another in long curves so they seem almost organic. Sometimes they double back, creating swellings or indentations in the glass skin hung between and around them. It feels as if the structure was grown rather than built. It's difficult to keep a sense of direction, there's no fixed viewpoint where I can anchor my vision. When we round a bend in the path and find a pair of doors ahead of us, we could be facing any direction. It must be easier during the day, I tell myself, when the sun shines and imposes a more rigorous geography on the building.

There's a curvaceous, art-deco sign, 'Metropolitaine', it says. When Sly opens the door I can hear soft conversation and a muted jazz trio.

'Let it be live music,' I pray.

There's a slow slope downwards to a woman lounging behind a counter in a dark hallway, she wakes up as we come closer. 'Can I take your coats?' she asks.

Sly hands her a plastic bag containing his coat and overalls. 'Do you take wellington boots as well,' he asks, holding the offending articles up to her.

'They're the biggest ones I've had this evening,' she replies, 'but not the only ones.' She takes Kirsty's waterproof as well, lifts her eyebrows as I hand her my duffel coat.

'A present from my daughter,' I warn her.

'I was just going to say how nice it was,' she whispers back. I don't believe her.

Kirsty can't pass the toilets without going inside to check her appearance in a mirror. There's a curtain at the end of the hall, it's holding back most of the sound, but I can hear applause following the completion of the trio's song.

'When we get in,' Sly tells me, 'I'll introduce you to David Morland. He'll want to talk about whatever he wants to talk about, then we can start enjoying ourselves.'

'We could always miss the talking, start on the enjoying first.'

'Boss! All I ask is that you listen to him. If you don't like what he says, tell him. If you can help him, if you want to help him, all I can suggest is, charge top whack. Forestcrag isn't short of money.'

Kirsty reappears. She looks the same as she did when she went in, and I'm tempted to point that out to her. But I curb my tongue in time. I find myself doing that more and more. It's not holding back from saying things I ought to, it's stopping myself offending people by voicing thoughts I should never have had in the first place.

As we approach, the curtain's twitched aside (automatically, I guess, there's a sensor beam at floor level) to reveal two doormen in DJs. For some reason I expect to be searched for guns or drugs, but they smile and wave us through. Presumably anyone who's driven through blizzards and waded through snowdrifts doesn't need an invitation to get into the party.

The room is shaped like a scallop shell. At its lowest central point is the small stage where the jazz trio's sliding into Glenn Miller's 'Serenade in Blue'. In front of the stage is an empty dance floor; radiating out and up are clusters of tables, each surrounded by a circle of chairs and crowned with a low-shaded light. Close to the walls are the gaming tables, roulette, dice and baccarat. The room is sparsely populated. Although there are dealers at each gaming table, there are no customers. The guests – and I can count no more than forty or fifty – are congregated close to the stage, their small numbers belied by the volume of their conversation. No one seems to notice us, but as Sly leads us towards an empty table a waitress appears at our side. She waits for us to sit then places two bottles of wine (one white in a cooler, one red in a wide-necked carafe) in front of us.

'Can I get you a drink?' she asks. 'Compliments of the house.' Sly asks for a whisky, Kirsty glances at the wine, then at me. 'Mum lets me,' she says. I nod, ask for some iced water.

'I've never been in a casino before,' Kirsty announces. She's looking around, but there's little to see in the semi-darkness.

'You've played the slot-machines at the fair,' I say. 'It's the same principle but with the opportunity to spend far more.'

'But it's more glamorous, Dad.'

'Don't you believe it,' Sly says. 'Glamour's just a front. See the guy down at the front, in the white tuxedo? He's a plumber. I've nothing against plumbers, but they're hardly glamorous.'

'It's all pretend, love. Like us getting dressed up to come out tonight. Nothing's done without a reason. This place is done up the way it is to encourage people to spend money. Not tonight, perhaps, everything seems to be free. But there's a reason for that as well. Sly says it's a thank you to the contractors who've worked here, and to the locals who put up with crowded roads and inconvenience, or who supply goods and services. But Forestcrag needs to make a profit. They carry out two weeks of concentrated mainten-ance, two weeks when they close and have no income, but the contractors *have* to do the job in that time.'

'That's right, Boss, the penalty clauses are huge.'

'So this free weekend is a bonus, a little extra for the workers. But it's counted and costed, it's part of the business, and it works. If something goes wrong in the future and this boss, this Morland person, rings Sly, I bet you Sly'll jump and get up here straightaway.'

'Too true. The money's good and it's regular. Two weeks' work here is like two months' anywhere else.'

'So there we are. In business, in life, nothing is ever done for nothing.'

'Never?' Kirsty's got that look in her eye, Sara's look, the one that means she's been listening and she's about to start arguing.

'Not in business, no.'

'But you said "in life" as well.'

'Yes. Well, that's life as a metaphor for . . .'

'For itself, Dad, it can't really stand for anything else. But what about love? Are you saying that love is the same? That it's always tied with conditions?'

I want to say yes, because I believe that's the truth. Love is never honest. Love always hides things that are left unspoken and are therefore often misunderstood. Love can't exist without a framework of respect and dependency, of trust and support. Sometimes love relies on deceit and antagonism, sometimes it's confused with sex, sometimes it becomes a short but complex word trying to attach itself to a meaning, any meaning. But I'm sure Kirsty's too young to know about this type of love. I'm ashamed that I know so little about her. Sara hasn't told me whether she's had any boyfriends, and if she has, I don't know (and could never ask) how physical her relationships have been. It's that old father-daughter complex, the refusal to believe that a girl can become a woman. At least I can see that, I'm not blind to my own shortcomings. So perhaps that's what she's talking about, the unconditional love a parent can have for a child. A father for his daughter.

'No, Kirsty, you're right. It is possible to love people regardless of their faults, without caring about the hurt they can cause you. You're right.' She's near enough for me to squeeze her hand, the light isn't so low she can't see me looking at her. And when she returns both the pressure and the glance, I begin to believe that such a love can travel in both directions.

'Hey you guys, this is him, this is the big boss.' Sly's guiding our eyes towards the stage where a round, middle-aged man has taken the place of the trio. He's rocking nervously forward and back, his belly fighting the waist-band of his trousers. He's sweating under the lights, the top of his head and his fleshy cheeks are glistening; he looks as if he needs to shave three times a day.

'Ugh,' says Kirsty, 'oily.'

'To look at, yeah,' Sly says, 'but just wait.'

I've watched, listened to, many speeches. Formal and informal, public and private, the way people speak to an audience has always interested me. It's probably because it's something I can't do, no matter how well prepared I am. I get nervous. I imagine – no, I'm certain – that I'll make a fool of myself. I've tried to find out what gives an individual the confidence to speak to and hold an audience, to the extent that I can tell before they start whether someone's going to be good or not. It doesn't matter what they look like, how they're dressed, they can even seem nervous as they're standing, waiting to begin. What counts is that moment just before they begin, when they hold the microphone or lean into the lectern, when they look out at their audience. I know before David Morland begins that he'll be good.

'Ladies and Gentlemen. Welcome to Forestcrag.' His voice is warm and dry as a doctor's handshake. When he says 'welcome' he sounds as if he means it, as if he expects you to believe he means it.

'Thank you all for coming this evening. Some of you have had journeys which have taken a little longer than you expected. Some of you may enjoy a slightly longer stay than you originally anticipated. Your numbers are certainly a little less than we planned for.' He smiles, his eyebrows dance up his forehead, and there's a ripple of amused laughter. 'But you may rest assured that your enjoyment this weekend is, always has been, and will continue to be, of paramount importance to every member of Forestcrag staff here this evening.'

'I still think he's creepy,' Kirsty informs me. 'That's not sweat, it's insincerity.'

'Shh,' Sly hisses before I can.

'Some of you will be familiar with the attractions and services we have to offer. Others will be enjoying the Forestcrag facilities for the first time. Some of you have worked here – worked, I must add, to a particularly high standard, under great pressure of time – and you deserve the opportunity to luxuriate in the Forestcrag experience *you've* helped create. Some of you are our neighbours. Perhaps that's the wrong word, when we opened three years ago you were neighbours, now I hope I can say you're our friends. You may not have had the opportunity to visit us since our last guests' weekend; if so, then I trust you'll notice the improvements in the accommodation and service we offer.'

He's not speaking from notes, and I'm sure he's managed to make eye contact with everyone in the room. But Kirsty must have been looking away, she's not impressed. 'He's trying too hard,' she says. I still disagree. He's not trying hard, he's finding it easy. Perhaps a little too easy, he's saying too much, speaking for too long. He may know he's good, but he's not as good as he thinks.

'Most of our essential staff managed to reach the site before the really bad weather began. I hope you've noticed that your lodge refrigerators and cupboards have been well stocked, but if there's anything you lack, let us know and we'll make sure you have that item. Free of charge, of course.'

37

Kirsty suddenly pays attention. 'Free? Did he say "free"? What a nice man.'

'You may, however, wish to dine out. Our "Blue Piano" restaurant will be open every night for you to enjoy gourmet meals if you wish. Those of you with young children may prefer "Billy's Burger Bar". Or, for a snack at any time of the day, you could try "La Baguette". Free of charge, of course.'

Kirsty's grin is in danger of permanently creasing her face.

'All the Forestcrag attractions are available to you, free of charge, throughout the weekend. As are your drinks this evening.' He holds up a glass, raises it, and we all do the same in return. He puts the glass down and applauds us, we applaud him, loudly, enthusiastically. He holds up his hands, we're quickly silent.

'Thank you, ladies and gentlemen, thank you. There is one more thing I ought to mention. There are gaming tables at the back of the room. These are available for your use this evening, and are —' we all anticipate his generosity; he seems to let us down '— not, alas, free of charge.' There's a murmur of disappointment. 'Yes, I'm afraid that if you lose your money tonight, it stays lost. But, in an effort to soften this blow, my staff will give each of you an envelope containing £100.' The intake of breath is collective, it could move heavy curtains. But David Morland goes on. 'This money is counterfeit. You cannot spend it outside this room. What is more, if you do make a profit from your gambling, the fake money you win will be taken from you as you leave.' He pauses. I wonder, at some time, he's been an actor. When he continues each word is enunciated slowly and carefully. 'It will then be added to the money the house has gained from you, and a cheque will be issued to the value of that total, made payable to the local Medical Centre's equipment fund.'

The applause is wholehearted.

'Please enjoy yourself, ladies and gentlemen. In fact, I

insist that you do so. I intend visiting every table to make sure you're doing precisely that. Thank you for your time and your attention.' He jumps down from the small platform of a stage and, in the middle of enthusiastic applause, begins to gladhand the room. He seems to know everyone's name, he laughs and slaps backs, punches forearms, kisses one or two women. Before the applause dies down, waiters and waitresses are passing amongst us offering embossed and sealed envelopes. Kirsty's the first to tear hers open, she fans the notes out in front of her.

'I can't believe this,' she says, 'this is so amazing. Thank you so much, Sly, for inviting me. This is going to be the best weekend of my life.' She grabs his head, pulls it down and kisses him on the forehead. 'And now I'm going to spend some fake money. Anyone want to join me?'

I hand her my envelope, unopened. 'Lose this for a good cause,' I say. 'I think I'd rather wait for the trio to come back.'

'Spoilsport,' she says. It's obvious Sara hasn't told her about all my vices, nor about the efforts I've made to overcome them.

'I'll make it up to you. I'll have a dance with you later, if you want.'

Sly rises to his feet. 'You think that's something for Kirsty to look forward to? Come on, good-looking, I'll go with you. Let's see if a little of the Sly Rogers good luck rubs off on you.' He pulls her seat away, allows her to stand, then takes her arm to guide her up the room. I'm just about to change my mind, to follow them (watching could surely do no harm, be no temptation) when there's a cough behind me.

'Mr Oliphant, I presume?'

David Morland looms over me, one hand outstretched, the other clutching a large brandy glass. I shake his hand, it's damp, its clasp too eager to impress with its firmness.

'Your presumption is correct,' I say, 'please, sit down. And let me say I'm impressed.'

He smiles. 'By my little speech?'

'No. I thought you could have said what you said more effectively in half the time.' I suppose I could have lied to him, but I don't need any favours. I'm surprised he doesn't seem dismayed by my honesty.

'Yes, you're right,' he nods. 'It's a fault of mine. That old saying, "always leave them wanting more", I never could get my head round it. I just can't stop when things are going well.' His smile is larger than his mouth and lips should allow, it curves under a broad nose and its corners reach for his ears. 'So what impressed you? If it wasn't my speech, it certainly can't have been my good looks.'

Why do I feel he's trying to win my approval? The refusal to be annoyed with me, the smile, the self-disparaging comments? What does he need me for? I decide I might as well continue telling him the truth. 'I was watching you work the room, I noticed the way you've memorised people's names. Even the contractors' relatives, people you probably haven't met before and won't meet again. But they'll remember you knew who they were, they'll remember you. It's good public relations. I suppose you know my daughter's name as well?'

'Kirsty? Yes, I know her name. And Sly's wife Paula. Four kids, Gav, Tim and Jo the twins, Julia the youngest. It's a useful trick, I've something of a freak memory. It's helpful in my business. I tend not to forget names. But let me return the compliment, I'm impressed with you.'

'Which of my many talents?'

'I know about you, Mr Oliphant. I checked you out as soon as Sly mentioned you. You're good at your job. And now I've met you, I respect your honesty. I like the way you watched me, saw what I was doing. You knew I was playing a game, flattering people, making them believe they're important.'

'Is showering me with praise meant to have the same effect?'

David Morland nods to himself, considers the question.

'I'll be as honest with you as you've been with me. Yes, I did intend flattering you. But I memorise and regurgitate names just in case I need a favour sometime. I do it with everyone, it's a habit, a learned skill, most people can learn it if they try. But you, you saw what I was doing, no one else did. Being a good watcher, making deductions from what you see, is a talent. A gift. I recognise talent when I see it. You have it. It's a talent I could use.'

It's flattery of a subtle kind. Just as I recognised his skills, so he claims to have recognised my talents. But I also told him about his verbosity, while he hasn't claimed knowledge of any of *my* shortcomings. At least, not to my face.

'Let's form a mutual appreciation society,' I suggest.

'Let me tell you why I wanted to meet you,' he counters. 'But not here. I'm a little warm anyway, I could do with some fresh air. Do you mind?' He rises to his feet and, curious, I follow. He leads me out, through the curtain, into the main area of the Tesseract. It's noticeably cooler than the casino, night-club, whatever hybrid we've just left. He lights a cigarette, the need for fresh air less urgent than that for nicotine.

'I have a problem,' he tells me.

'Most of my clients do.'

'I'm being poisoned.'

'Try patches.'

'Patches? What ...?' Then it hits, but his laughter's false. 'Patches ... Poison ... Cigarettes ... very good, Mr Oliphant, very droll. But seriously, this isn't something to joke about.'

'So you think someone's trying to poison you? Do you have any evidence? You don't look ill.'

'No, not me. I'm sorry, I do tend to personalise every-thing that happens in this place. *I'm* not being poisoned. But my staff are.'

'Same questions, Mr Morland. Evidence? Suspicions?'

'Okay. Staff sickness rates are increasing, in percentage terms, year on year. Forestcrag is owned by Arden

41

International, we have similar sites in this country and abroad. Comparisons show absence through sickness is greater here than in any of our other operations. But it's only the staff who are suffering, customer illness isn't a problem. And, what's worse, it's key staff, people who know the ropes, who are being targeted.'

'And you suspect . . .?'

'Since it's only staff involved, I believe someone's contaminating the food in the staff restaurant. But I don't know who, or why. A personal grudge? The opposition playing dirty? That's where you come in, Mr Oliphant. I'd like you to work undercover in the kitchens, something mundane, veg prep perhaps. We could swap you around shifts, get you working with everyone at one time or another. You'd just have to keep your eyes open, report back, tell me what you see.'

We're heading towards one of the walls. I can see the snow still falling, but it's being churned and shredded by a wind whose violence is increasing. The building seems to shift slightly, but there's no accompanying complaint from the steel superstructure. The lights don't seem to have flared or dimmed and Morland doesn't seem to have been affected, so I have to assume it's something to do with the way I'm looking at the glass walls and the snow beyond.

'It might take some time, Mr Oliphant, but I can assure you that you'll be well rewarded. Sly will have mentioned, I'm sure, that we pay top rates. And for a job such as this, requiring very particular talents, we can arrange a particularly attractive package. I anticipate at least two weeks, let's say five thousand a week with a bonus of five thousand on successful prosecution?'

That is attractive. I could whistle at a figure like that. But I need to know more. 'You already have security staff, have you told . . .?'

'The security system here isn't designed for matters such as this. They don't know about the problem. No one except three or four senior executives knows about the problem. That's the way it will stay, you'll report directly to me.'

We're heading back into the centre of the Tesseract, he stops to lean on the rail of a small wooden bridge over an artificial stream. He's speaking as if I've already taken the job; he shouldn't be so presumptuous.

'Some of your staff will already have seen me, they'll know I'm not a carrot peeler.'

'Why? Because you're friends with an electrician? That's all they know, Mr Oliphant. If they recognise you, well, you asked me to get you a job. Problem solved?'

I move on. 'Have you done the logical thing? Reported it to the police?'

He's staring into the water, as if it deserves his attention more than I do. He doesn't look at me when he speaks. 'The local police objected strenuously when we submitted plans for this venture, Mr Oliphant. They said they wouldn't be able to cope with the extra work it would bring. After all, we're the largest village for almost twenty miles in every direction and our population changes every three or four days. Do you know how many times we've had to call them in the three years we've been open? Once. And that was a false alarm, a customer rang them direct, thought she'd seen a bear. The only other contact we have with the police is when they send delegations to learn from our security systems. I'm on first name terms with the Chief Constable. I don't want to bother him and his over-stretched force with a problem I can solve myself.'

He's as talkative in private conversation as he is in public discourse.

'I take it that means no, then. And what about medical tests? Urine samples, stool samples, blood samples? And what exactly are the symptoms of this poisoning?'

This time he looks at me when he replies, though it's clear he feels his explanation is unnecessary. 'The symptoms are sickness, diarrhoea, headaches. Nothing serious, but enough to keep important people off work for a week or two. And we've paid for all the tests you've suggested. They came up negative.'

'Why do you want me, me in particular, to look into this for you?'

'Because you ask the right questions. Because you appear to be thorough. Because Sly recommended you, because you have a good reputation – and yes, I have asked around. I know a little of your background, Mr Oliphant. Despite your untimely exit from the police force there are some of your ex-colleagues still willing to speak up for you. Off the record, of course.'

The prospect interests me. It is, I'll admit, a combination of two factors. The first is the money. Five thousand a week is interesting enough in itself. Then there's the chance to do some investigative work, rather than installing security cameras and window alarms. I feel a sense of excitement at the prospect, and I realise I haven't felt that way for some months. Perhaps I need to get away from the security business, devote all my time to private investigations. It's a nice thought, even though I know that most PI work involves the humdrum and the everyday, divorce matters or tracing missing wives, sitting in a car at three in the morning with only binoculars, a camera and a cold bacon sandwich for company. But the daydream's pleasant enough. And having to take instructions from the verbose Mr Morland would certainly be sweetened by at least ten, probably fifteen thousand for a fortnight's work.

'I'm tempted,' I tell him.

'You're meant to be.'

'I can start in a week. Say ten days, I've some outstanding jobs to clear up.' I've been running through them, working out which are now urgent, which should have been done a fortnight ago. Ten days should clear them, as long as the weather lifts and lets me out. As long as I work at least twelve hours a day. As long as Norm and Sly can clear the decks to help me. As long as Kirsty doesn't mind looking after herself. It's too much.

'Better make that a fortnight,' I say, 'when I add things up . . .'

'You'll start on Monday. That's the deal, Mr Oliphant.'

'I've other commitments.'

'Get rid of them. I'll make it seven thousand a week for the inconvenience.'

'Am I that good?'

'No, but you're here, you're recommended, and it would take too much of my time to find someone else. That's my final offer.'

It's a lot of money, far more than I'd earn from the customers he wants me to discard. But some of them are regulars, almost friends. They could spread the word about me. Yes, I could earn money working for Morland, but it could also be the last money I earn.

'I have friends,' Morland anticipates my objections. 'Do this well and they'll know about you, I guarantee. They're good friends. Wealthy friends. Business from them would more than make up for your potential losses. Whichever way you look at it, wherever you start from, you come to the same logical conclusion. You have to take the job.' He's finding it hard to read me, probably because *I* don't know what I'm going to do. 'Look,' he says, pulls three leaves from a tree overhanging the water. He walks along the upstream path, no more than five yards, drops a leaf into the water. He walks another five yards, does the same; he repeats his action. He arrives back at the bridge just as his first leaf is passing beneath it.

'No matter where you start,' he says, 'the conclusion is the same.' The second leaf floats past us. 'It's just a matter of when.' The third leaf, yellowed where the others were bright green, autumned with a touch of red, twists and turns in artificial eddies but arrives on cue. 'You'll say yes. Might as well do it now and save us both time.'

His need is obviously great. If his competitors are the source of his problem they could slip the news to the press. The publicity wouldn't be good. Even if they weren't involved, they could have found out about it. Either way, Morland would have to show he was doing something about it, doing something positive. I'm tempted to be greedy, to ask for more. Then I see one of the leaves. It's the last one and it's caught in a whirlpool. Just for a moment it appears to be heading back upstream, against the current. It's fighting the stream's determined efforts that it should proceed in obedient fashion to its pre-ordained destination. And then it disappears. I bend to look more closely into the shallow water, but I can see no sign of the leaf. I feel rather sad; its colour, its individuality, its persistence in refusing to follow its companions, all combined to endear it to me.

'I've changed my mind,' I say. 'I'll do the job for you.' I seem to be playing with people's hopes more and more, leading them one way then changing direction at the last moment. 'I won't need two weeks to clear my backlog of work. I'll need three.'

I once saw a print for an old advert for Fry's 'Five Boys' chocolate. Its wrapper showed five drawings of the same round-cheeked boy's face in different states of emotion. The first, with the boy on the verge of tears, was labelled 'Desperation'. Then came 'Pacification', 'Expectation', 'Acclamation' and finally 'Realization – it's Fry's'. Morland's face (perhaps a distant relative was the model for the fat-faced boy) runs through a similar range of expressions but in reverse, and ends with 'Thwarted and Displeased'.

'You're making a mistake,' he says.

'If you can't find anyone else I'll be pleased to help, but only after I've honoured the contracts I already have.' Even before I finish he's walking away. He can't be used to people telling him 'no'.

Before I follow him I look back at the stream. There's no sign of the leaf where I last saw it, but further downstream, in a deep pool, three leaves are moving lazily, languorously. Two are green; the third is yellow-red. Despite its adventures it ended up in exactly the same, pre-determined place as the others.

Chapter Six

When I get back to the casino the trio's playing again. Sly and Kirsty are back in their seats. It feels warmer, as if the thrill of gambling has generated heat.

'Dad, that was great,' Kirsty tells me, giggling with wine and excitement, 'we were almost a thousand pounds up, but then we lost it all again in only a few minutes.'

'Losing a thousand pounds is great?'

'You know what I mean!' She nudges me gently with her shoulder and I glance at Sly. He gives me his 'it's nothing to do with me' look.

'I want to dance,' she announces, 'will you dance with me, Dad?'

I can't remember dancing with Kirsty before. When the opportunity's arisen – at weddings or birthday parties – I've felt she wouldn't want to dance with her father. I'd waltz her round the room when she was very young, but her feet didn't reach the ground then. It's not that I can't dance, but the band's playing medium tempo jazz, not fast disco; it demands more than moving from foot to foot in time with the music. But I'm clearly not being given the opportunity to refuse, Kirsty's already on her feet and taking off her jacket.

'She's only had one glass of wine,' Sly whispers across at me. Then he looks past me, and raises his eyebrows. He mouths 'Wow,' and I turn quickly.

Kirsty's jacket is high-necked, and although she's undone some of the buttons as the evening's grown old, I'm not prepared for her revelation. The top part of the dress is loose, it scoops low at the front in a restless curtain which threatens to part. At the back it's almost non-existent, its straps cross over and back several times but there's no material there until the small of her back. If it were anyone but my daughter I'd probably say how good she looked. No, I'd do more than that, I'd react just as Sly has done, as every other man in the place will probably do when she reaches the dance floor. But she *is* my daughter.

'Come on then, Dad, what are you waiting for?'

What can I do? Order her to put her jacket on again? Tell her the dress is too revealing? Refuse to dance with her? Then I notice the light shining in her eye. It's nothing but a reflection, of course, but her eyes and face seem illuminated from within. She brushes a strand of hair away and sucks her bottom lip into her mouth for a brief, beautiful moment. She used to do that when she was a little girl, when she was excited, when she was concentrating on something special. That's when I realise I've been doing her an injustice. She's not drunk, she's only been enjoying herself and wants to keep doing so. And she wants to involve me. I'm not sure if she knows how beautiful she really is, but I know that her beauty's deeper than the dress and the body within it. I don't really want to dance. I want to take her away, I want to tell her I'm sorry for all the things I've done which have hurt her and Sara, for the times she's cried and I wasn't there for her. But that isn't what *she* wants. At the moment she wants to dance with her father. And dancing with her suddenly becomes the most important thing in the world.

'Lead the way,' I say. And she does, waving her hands and swaying her hips, threading a path through the tables and down onto the dance floor. As I follow I can sense heads turning to look at her, but she's oblivious to them. Only when the plush carpet gives way to wood, when she crosses into a new territory, does she hesitate. She realises she's the only one there, her self-confidence has led her this far but she needs help to go further. Then I join her, hold out my arms. She moves gratefully into them, her right hand resting on my left, her left hand on my shoulder. The music's an up-tempo 'Lover, Come Back to Me'.

'What do we do?' she whispers.

'Start together,' I reply, 'finish together, and smile in the middle. And let me lead.'

She has a natural sense of rhythm, just as I'd expected; Sara and I danced well together. I guide her in a variation of quickstep, more a sort of slouch than an elegant slide, but it suits me and it clings to the music. She soon finds it too easy and we modify the steps, widen the turns, add hesitations and variations.

'You're good,' she says.

'I owe it all to Mrs Cook. My geography teacher, she taught some of the sixth formers to dance. She was gorgeous, I had to fight my way to the front of the queue to be her partner.'

'Was she good at geography as well as dancing?'

'Is Rome the capital of Spain?'

Soon we're joined by another couple, but they can't manage as well as Kirsty and me. I see someone approach the pianist. He winds down the tune and Kirsty and I spin into a bow and a curtsey. Then the music starts again but the volume's doubled, it's amphetamined Jerry Lee Lewis, raw and raucous, and the floor's suddenly filled with rock 'n' rollers.

'I like this!' Kirsty mouths. I'm too busy breathing to reply, spinning her under my arm, turning, catching her as she comes back to me. I'd forgotten how good dancing was. Sara and I just didn't go out together in our latter days, and Jen . . . Jen dances against a rhythm rather than with it, as if she's fighting it. Dancing with Kirsty is easy, natural. She's grinning wildly, and I'm doing the same, feeling the sweat bead on my forehead.

One more song and I'm relieved when Sly appears at our side. The band ('trio' doesn't seem the right word now, the double bass has been discarded and replaced by an electric guitar and the pianist's playing electronic keyboards; all three musicians are singing) is sticking to standard rock and pop and seems to be arranging their songs in chronological order. I surrender my place as they move into early Presley, I'm pleased to sit down and dab myself with a serviette.

If I didn't know Sly so well I might be jealous. He and Kirsty move as if they're joined together, they're slinky and sexy and they look each other in the eye as they dance. But the look is one of enjoyment, exuberance even, they know they have an audience, they know this is a performance. The other couples are watching them, unable to compete; those still sitting at tables are watching them; even the musicians are watching them, grinning their pleasure, aware they're contributing to something special. Band and dancers conspire in a last coda of dementia; Kirsty's hair is whipping from side to side, her hips thrusting. Sly's strutting, one fist raised high; and the drums rise to a crescendo then stop in a crash of chord and cymbal.

There's applause, the band join in. Sly bows. Kirsty's embarrassed, she tugs at his arm, pulls him away from the dance floor and back to the table.

'That was warm work,' she says as she slides into her seat. It's her turn to use her serviette as a towel.

'Where'd you learn to dance like that?' Sly asks.

'It's in the genes,' I answer on her behalf.

'I didn't know you had black blood in the family.'

Kirsty's quick to speak; is she worried I might take offence at Sly's joking? 'I really enjoyed that,' she announces, 'thank you Sly, thank you Dad.'

There's a movement at her shoulder, a young man coughs and smiles. 'Excuse me, I wonder if you'd like to dance?'

She spins in her seat, looks him up and down. He's

wearing a suit, though it's cut in a style I suspect would be called modern. His hair is almost as blond as hers, and he seems poised, confident and, as far as I can tell in the dim lights, good-looking. I'm surprised when she turns back to look at me.

'Do you mind?' she asks softly.

'No, not at all. Please, go and enjoy yourself.'

'I'd love to dance,' she says as she rises to her feet. 'I'm Kirsty.'

'Philip,' the youth replies, 'Philip Plumpton.'

Sly and I watch them head for the dance floor. I lean towards him.

'I feel old,' I confess. 'It's not because I'm constantly tired. It's not because my body aches when I wake up, not because I'm losing my hair and putting on weight. Those are slow things, they creep up on you and become part of you so you don't really notice they're there. But I look at Kirsty, I look at that boy, young man, call him what you like. Then I realise there's a generation gone by and I haven't really noticed it. It's the sudden shock of looking at my daughter and having to come to terms with the fact that she's almost an adult. I don't think I'm ready for that.'

'I think it's worse with girls,' Sly says. 'They move so fast. One day sitting on your knee, next draped round a strange bloke's shoulders. They kiss you on the cheek in the morning, that night you catch them mouth to mouth with some spotty youth you've never seen before.'

'I don't think I want to know that,' I tell him.

'Then there's the clothes. You're used to white cotton knickers and suddenly you find skimpy leopard-skin pattern thongs lying round the house.'

'Thanks, Sly, but . . .'

'And the friends? Every male in the neighbourhood's on the phone or on the doorstep, and they all seem at least ten years older than her. And they've got cars! That's the worst things, cars, people can get up to all sorts of things in cars.'

'Sly, you're not helping me.'

'I mean, I had three sisters, all older than me. Some of the things they'd get up to.'

The dance has finished and Kirsty's being escorted back to the table.

'I think it's time we left,' I say. Kirsty doesn't seem to object, and that surprises me. I pick up her jacket, don't give her time to change her mind.

'I have to go as well,' the young man says politely, 'I thought I'd better see Kirsty back to her seat.' He smiles at Kirsty. 'See you tomorrow?' he asks. 'In the pool?'

'Yeah, that'll be cool,' Kirsty smiles back.

'Cool?' Sly mutters, 'It'll be bloody freezing.'

We head for the exit. The dance floor's beginning to look crowded and all the gaming tables are occupied. Kirsty links one arm in mine, pulls Sly towards her with the other.

'I've had a lovely time,' she says, 'thank you both for making it such a good start to the weekend. I've a feeling I'm really going to enjoy myself.'

Chapter Seven

My watch tells me it's seven thirty. I'm normally awake earlier, about seven, but I switched the alarm off the previous night. There's something unusual about the morning. No, not something; some *things*. First there are the strange noises to filter out. I haven't forgotten where I am, but the sound of children sleeping, their easy, peaceful breathing, is so distant a memory it becomes new. And I can hear Sly's occasional splutter of snoring, Paula's lighter, more sonorous accompaniment. They're in different rooms, some of the doors are closed, but I can still hear them. I try to put them to one side but can't. And the reason they refuse to leave me is that, behind them, there's nothing else. Only silence. No sound of wind, no storm, no traffic, no voices. No birdsong. Oh, there's the subdued grumble of a heating system, a gurgle of water in pipes, a rumble belonging to the refrigerator. But these are constants, they exist in homes everywhere and filter themselves out of existence because of that. Beyond them there's nothing.

I roll out of bed (the lower of two bunks in a cupboard with pretensions of grandeur) and stand, stretch, yawn. There's a narrow window, I twitch aside heavy curtains and have to squint into the brightness. There are no shrubs, no pathways, no distinguishable features. Instead there is a rolling, curvaceous world of smooth white. Trees are cones, but their broad bases merge into the general carpet of shadowless frost. There's no sun, no blue sky. Where they ought to be there's simply more grey-white, an endless variation of shape and form and texture but all covered with subtle gradations of pale and chalk and milk.

There's no movement, no sign of there ever having been movement. No footprints, no tracks of bird or animal. Just stillness, and silence, and a complete absence of life.

'Scary, isn't it?'

I hadn't heard Kirsty come into the room. She comes up close and leans on my shoulder, I can smell the perfume she was wearing the night before.

'I don't think I can remember ever seeing anything like this,' I say. Both of us are whispering.

'Perhaps we've been kidnapped. Aliens have come in the night and taken us away to a different planet, a planet made of ice.'

I squeeze her hand, and there's a warm, welcome response.

'Or we've died. And this is the doorway to heaven, all white and silent.'

'Shouldn't there be hymns?' I ask. 'And St Peter?'

'Hell, then. Why should hell be hot and fiery? Cold can be just as painful, you can have a freezing Arctic desert as well as a burning sandy one. Or it could be a halfway house, a sort of limbo, neither heaven nor hell. Somewhere you have to wait to be judged.'

'I don't think I want to be judged, love, not just yet.'

'Look!' She grips my shoulder tightly, stretches out a finger. 'I can see something, someone. Over there.'

There *is* someone approaching, labouring to pull one foot then the other through glutinous drifts of snow, breath clouding.

'What do you think, Dad? Angel? Devil? Or alien?'

Identification is difficult. The figure's shrouded in heavy coat and hood.

'I don't know, but it's heading this way, so I'm going to put some clothes on.' Only then do I look at Kirsty, realise

54

she too is wearing only a nightshirt. 'I'd suggest you do the same. You never know, it might be that boy you were dancing with last night, come to collect you for an early start.'

She flounces away. 'No, I said I'd meet him at ten.'

I dress quickly in layers, T-shirt, shirt and pullover, then wait by the door for the crunch of snow and heavy breathing. Then I open the door quickly. The person on the other side is standing in a wedge of snow, his gloved fist is already falling but there's no longer a surface for it to meet. It completes its arc and the figure almost overbalances, would fall into the room if I didn't hold out my own arm to support it.

'Jesus Christ,' the man says, 'how did you know ...?'

'Don't let the heat out,' I say, 'come in and drip on the carpet.' I recognise the man's voice. Sam Ellis, head of security, is making a personal call. I close the door behind him.

'You're up early,' I say. 'Overseeing the snowploughs? Showing them the way to my front door?'

'Very funny, Mr Oliphant.' He's not taking off his coat, his boots or his over-trousers. It looks like he's not planning on staying. 'I've come to take you to see Mr Morland.'

'Oh, thank you. But I don't think I have any reason to see Mr Morland. I saw him last night, I don't need to refresh my memory.' I'm not normally antagonistic, but I dislike people sending for me; I don't like being summoned by third parties.

'Mr Morland needs your ... skills,' he says, though he has difficulty in forcing that last word from his mouth.

'My skills? With a snow shovel?'

'Your experience as a private investigator.' He's lost the word 'skill', he finds it easier to cope with 'experience'.

'Did Mr Morland explain to you that we'd discussed his employing me to investigate certain matters, but ...'

'Mr Morland told everyone,' Ellis interrupts, 'that you were a detective. He didn't say what you were meant to detect, mind, and I pointed out that our existing security systems . . .'

'He told everyone? Who, exactly, is "everyone"?'

'All the staff. Last night, after the party. He gathered us all together. Told us to spread the word.'

'What word?'

'That you were here. That you were a PI. That you'd be around, watching. He told us we'd better behave ourselves. He said you'd be able to go wherever you wanted, speak to anyone you wanted. He said you'd look at the place, then consider what to do, but that would probably involve an undercover team.'

'To investigate what?'

'*I* don't know. *I'm* only the head of security. No one tells *me* anything.'

It's clear that Ellis is Morland's messenger boy, and that Ellis doesn't like the role. I could refuse to go with him, aggravate Morland further (he must be fairly annoyed with me to have spread the lie that I was going to work for him). I'm tempted to send Ellis away, to tell him that if Morland wants to see me he should come himself rather than send a lackey. That would annoy both of them in almost equal degrees. But before I can say anything Gav and the twins are peering round their door, Kirsty's appeared eating a slice of toast, and from Sly's room there's an imperious 'Everything all right?' I don't want to involve Sly, Paula and their kids in a slanging match; that leaves me no choice but to visit Morland.

'Everything's okay,' I shout back to Sly. Then it's the kids' turn. 'Go and get dressed,' I tell them, 'warm clothes. Kirsty'll help you. When I get back we'll build snowmen!' I nod Kirsty in their direction. 'Well,' I say to Ellis, 'I'm curious. I'll have my breakfast when I get back.' I wait for him to say there's plenty of time for me to eat, but he doesn't. I'm beginning to dislike him, even if he is just a lackey. 'I take it Morland's office is somewhere in the Tesseract?'

'Yes,' he says, 'but I'm to take you to the staff quarters. That's the message I got.'

'Staff quarters? Why there?'

'Look, Oliphant.' He's losing his patience. 'I didn't ask. Mr Morland said to get you, I'm here doing as I'm told.'

'Couldn't he just have phoned me, invited me himself?' The phones are internal, they let you contact other lodges and the site facilities. Is Morland so arrogant that he won't use a phone?

'The phones are down,' Ellis admits.

I can't resist it. 'And the security cameras?'

'The same.' He feels obliged to go on, to offer an excuse. 'It's the weather. There was a blizzard last night, didn't you know? The phones and cameras rely on the same circuitry, there was a blow-out, an overload, something like that.'

'Something like that?' It's amazing how effective, how annoying, repetition can be.

'Yes! I don't know what it was, the technical guys'll be able to sort it out. We've already put a call in. They'll be here as soon as possible.'

'I suppose I'd better come and see what Morland wants. Even though it is inconvenient.'

I knock on Sly's bedroom door, wait for him to call me in. It takes a moment, long enough for me to conjure up a reason for the delay, smile at that reason, then remove the smile from my face.

'Come in,' Sly yells.

'Sorry to interrupt your, uh, sleep,' I say gravely. Paula's eyes flicker open. She's trying to stifle a laugh.

'It's okay,' Sly growls, 'I'll get my own back.'

'I've been summoned to the staff accommodation, to see my friend Mr Morland. I don't know why, Ellis tramped through the snow to get me and he doesn't know why either. There's been a problem with the internal phones and security cameras, he might want my help with that. The kids are awake, Kirsty's helping them get dressed, I've promised them adventures in the snow. And that's it. I reckon you've got ten, fifteen minutes before they come and interrupt you. Enjoy yourselves.'

'Hold on,' Sly says, sits up and drags the quilt with him, 'if it's a problem with electrics I might be able to help.'

Paula clutches at the quilt as it moves across her. 'No you will not,' she says, 'Morland knows you're here. If it was something you could do, he would have sent for you. He didn't, so it isn't. Come back here.'

'If I need help, I'll send for you. Bye.' I close their door. Ellis is getting impatient, he's standing beside the door, tapping his boot.

'I'm just going outside,' I shout through to Kirsty, 'I may be some time.' She opens the door and looks at me. 'Okay, Captain,' she says, salutes then returns to her charges. I put on a fleece, a pair of tracksuit bottoms over my trousers, then lever myself into wellington boots. If they weren't so tight I'd have worn extra socks. It only needs the addition of coat and hat and I'm ready at last. 'Should we go, then?' I ask Ellis. He hurls open the door.

Outside it's still and cold, cold like jumping into a moorland stream, cold so it snatches at your breath and taunts you to breathe it back in. Ellis retraces his steps, I flounder after him, using his track, desperate that the deep snow shouldn't overflow into my boots. After five minutes I'm sweating, but I daren't undo my coat or take off my hat. My gloveless hands are thrust into my pockets but they still feel cold and numb.

'Is it far?' I ask.

'Not normally,' he mumbles back at me.

There are other lodges almost buried in the snow, no sign that anyone has attempted to clear any paths. Here and there lights shine from windows, I see curious faces disappear as we pass by. This is all new to me. I've never experienced weather like this, snow like this, cold like this. The previous night's blizzard has sculpted the forest into foreign shapes. A drift might hide a bush, a rock, an electric light, perhaps even a child's abandoned bicycle. Or it could be nothing more than a whim of the storm, an empty hummock caused by a temporary collusion of wind and snow. Sharp-edged waves have been razor hardened by frost, their downward curves forming tunnels of crystal surf. Everything is new and fresh, fragile and impermanent. I want to stretch out and touch, see, feel before it disappears. But Ellis is struggling ahead of me, heading up a small slope to a high wall of white which can only be snow-laden trees. Round one corner I can see a building, a long rectangular block of brooding utility, quite unlike the elegant wooden lodges. Ellis lumbers up to a door, takes out his keys and, after some awkward manipulation (his gloves are thick) hauls the door open. I follow him inside.

'Staff quarters,' he says as he pulls down his hood.

'And this is where Morland said he'd meet me?'

'That's what he said. On the radio phone.'

'So where is he?'

'Waiting for us somewhere? How the hell do I know.'

I don't rise to the bait. Ahead of us is a long corridor, doors opening off it at regular intervals. There are no windows. To my left is a staircase which I assume leads to an upper floor with the same arrangement of rooms.

'Hello!' I shout. 'Anybody here?'

There's a rumble of feet from upstairs. 'This way,' Morland's voice calls. I follow its sound, unbuttoning my coat as I do so. It's not as warm as the lodge was, but much warmer than being outside. Morland's standing at the top of the stairs, waiting for me.

'Billy, thank you for coming ...'

'I hear the whole world thinks I'm here to carry out an investigation for you.'

'Pardon?'

'You heard. As did all your staff last night. Ellis told me. Apparently I'm to be allowed entry to all areas and all people, I can ask anyone anything I want. Or perhaps Mr Ellis was wrong.'

'No, he wasn't wrong. That is ... But there are more important things now, I need your help ...'

'Well you won't be getting it. I don't know why you said what you did, but if you think I'll change my mind, you're wrong. Very wrong.'

'Look, Billy ...'

'Mr Oliphant,' I remind him.

'Mr Oliphant. Okay, okay, I'm sorry. I wanted to frighten my staff, it seemed like a good opportunity. And I didn't actually say you were working for me. All I said was that you were here, which was true. That you were a private investigator, which is also true. And that you could have access to them for questions, which would have been true if you'd taken the job on. Yes, it was wrong of me, I apologise for that. But I thought ...' He tails off. He knows that thinking is the one thing he didn't do.

'Have you two quite finished?' It's a woman's voice, more pleading than angry. It comes from further along the corridor. I look up. The voice's owner is wearing a floor-length dressing gown, one hand is holding it closed tight at her neck, the other is making sure it's closed across her thighs. She looks frightened. Her hair is shoulder-length, brown, untidy with sleep. She isn't wearing make-up. I'd put her in her mid thirties, about the same age as me. The skin beneath her eyes is dark, swollen, it looks as if she's been crying.

'I'm sorry, Eve,' Morland says. 'Mr Oliphant, this is Eve Marton, our computer manager. She's the one who found the body.'

This is moving too fast even for me. I want to go out, come back in, start again. I look at Ellis but he's already shaking his head, shrugging his shoulders.

'Body?' I say.

'Eve found him,' Morland explains. 'She heard a noise and ... Perhaps I'd better let her explain.'

'He lives in the room next door,' Eve Marton begins, 'at least, last night he was, I don't normally stay, but because of the snow I had to and ...'

'Whose body?' I ask.

'Eric. Eric Salkeld.'

'Where?'

Morland takes over. 'The room next to Eve's. He's dead, I've checked. But we haven't disturbed anything. Do you want to look?'

I don't really want to look. Whoever this Eric Salkeld is, if he's dead, it's beyond my control. It's a matter for a doctor and an undertaker, perhaps the police.

'I heard a noise,' Eve Marton explains, her voice faltering. 'I knocked on his door but there was no answer and then I noticed it was open. I went in and ... he was there.'

I push past Morland. Eve Marton slips into her room as I pass, I'm surprised how tall she is, even without shoes. Or perhaps it's just that I'm forgetting how short I am. The next door is slightly ajar. I touch it with my foot and it swings open.

The room is small. It has a window at the far end. Beneath the window, in the right hand corner stretching towards me, is a single bed with a quilt. The surface is rumpled but it hasn't been slept in. In the far left hand corner is a basin, a mirror above it. There's little else in the room; a small desk, a cheap, narrow wardrobe. And, hanging from a coat-hook between the basin and the desk is the body of a man. Tied to the hook – and looped around his neck – is a length of plastic clothes-line. He looks dead. His eyes are open. When I reach for his wrist the skin is cool. There's no pulse.

'Have you telephoned the police?' If my voice sounds weary it's because I don't know who the man is, but I can sympathise with him. It looks like suicide and I can imagine the despair he must have felt to take his own life.

'No, not yet. I wanted you to look first, I knew you'd been in the police, you see. And then there's the publicity, I don't want any bad publicity.'

'You'd better ring them now,' I say, 'I assume you've

got a mobile. And I assume *he* was a member of staff. What was his job?'

'Payroll Manager,' Morland replies, brings a bulky radio-phone from his coat pocket and shifts it from hand to hand, 'he was a quiet man, kept to himself. He was living here, not many management staff do that. But he was.'

'Not much of a room,' I say. 'Hardly first class accommodation.'

'It's not meant for management,' Morland defends himself. 'I mean, sometimes they do use it, when they need to work late. Or, like Eve, when she couldn't get away because of the weather. Mostly it's people like lifeguards and shift-workers, new staff who haven't been able to find places to stay.'

'Phone?' I prompt him.

'Who should I ring?'

'Give,' I say. He hands the phone to me. 'Can't afford a proper mobile?' I ask.

'Mobiles don't work here,' he sulks, 'no masts. Company policy, won't give permission. Gives the place an extra air of isolation, they say. Bloody pain if you ask me.'

I ignore his whinging, punch in a familiar number. It's the same with the police as everywhere these days, no matter who you want to speak to you go through a central switchboard. The phone rings twice, then informs me I'm being placed in a queue. So I wait.

'I imagine they'll be busy,' I tell my audience. 'The weather's bound to have affected things. There'll have been road accidents, people stranded in the snow. It's not surprising it's taking a while to get through.' I wait for another two minutes. The music is pleasant, something classical but not demanding. Then, finally, there's a reply.

'Hello,' I say, 'I want to report a death in what might be suspicious circumstances, probably suicide but I can't be sure yet. Yes, my name's Billy Oliphant, I'm a former police officer, and the death occurred at Forestcrag Moorland Holiday Village. My number?' I look up at

62

Morland, repeat the digits he fires at me. 'Yes, I'll hold the line.'

I wait for another few minutes, then repeat all the information I've given. The constable on the other end of the line is polite but obviously under pressure. I listen carefully to what he has to say, then I disconnect.

'When are they coming?' Morland asks.

'They aren't,' I reply. 'The road leading to the road up to the village is blocked. The whole of the county's at a standstill. We're lucky we still have electricity; lots of villages and several towns don't. The snowploughs are giving priority to motorways and major roads and they're even having problems there. The forecast is for more snow tonight and high winds.'

'So what do we do.'

'I told him I was an ex-policeman. He spoke to his sergeant. He suggested that, since I knew procedures, I do a basic report on scene of incident. Ask questions. Make notes. Take photographs. Let them know what I find. And sit tight. That's it. Any objections?'

No one says anything. They're pleased to be rid of it, pleased someone else is taking the responsibility for dealing with their problem. Part of me says I don't want to do it, but part of me welcomes the opportunity to be back in the old routine, the safe, familiar, regular format of police investigation. It won't be difficult, and there isn't really anyone else who could deal with it. So I fall back on well-known, well-remembered habits.

'Okay then, Ellis, I'll need a camera, preferably thirty-five millimetre SLR with a selection of lenses and films, black-and-white if you have them. Paper, preferably a notebook, and pens. Plastic bags, small freezer bags will do. Morland, I need to know who slept in the building last night. And Miss Marton, I'd like to take a statement from you as soon as possible.'

Everyone moves at once. Even the small feeling of power that generates is exhilarating.

Chapter Eight

It's a small, lonely way to die. Most suicides are like that.
Sometimes there's a grand public gesture, the leap from a
high building after making sure the whole world's watching. But most of the time it's a private, quiet affair: in a
lonely car with a hose-pipe attached to the exhaust; a
whisky and paracetamol cocktail in a dingy hotel room; or
a pile of clothes left on a cold grey beach. It's something
I've contemplated myself; hasn't everyone, at some time?
What would be the quickest, easiest, most painless way of
killing yourself? It depends on what's available, of course,
and whether it's been a long-term plan. Some suicides think
ahead, they take great pleasure (if that's the right word) in
killing themselves neatly and effectively. For others it's a
rush job. They make a decision, they use what's at hand. It
looks as if Eric Salkeld was one of the latter. He found a
piece of plastic clothes-line, put it round a hook on a wall.
And that was it.

It's a method I know well. I've seen suicides before, but
most of them have been in prison cells using belts or
shoelaces, items of clothing – yes, even underpants or
trousers – to constrict the neck. It doesn't need a hook high
on a wall, it's not like judicial hanging where the neck is
broken. Just something tight to restrict breathing. Light-
headedness leads to unconsciousness and then death. It's
that easy.

Eric Salkeld's body is slumped against the wall. I move closer. I can see the red mark around his neck where the plastic cord has rubbed against the flesh. He's wearing pyjamas, blue and white striped, so conservative they're from a different time. Only the bottom button of the jacket is done up, most of his chest is visible. It's not cold in the room, so I don't expect to learn much from his body temperature. But I touch him, above his heart.

'Mr Oliphant?' It's David Morland's voice.

'Come in.'

'I'd rather not,' he says.

I open the door. He's holding a camera in his hand, a dozen films in the other.

'I had Ellis get these from the shop,' he says, 'it's a good camera with a flash, costs over a hundred, though it's not an SLR. And we don't stock black-and-white, but there's a range of other films here, different speeds.' He hands me a bag. 'Paper and pens, plastic bags,' he explains. He's eager to please. Does he feel some obligation towards Salkeld? Guilt, perhaps?

'I need to ask you some questions,' I say, 'after I finish here. Please don't go away.'

The camera's adequate. There's not that much to photograph; the body from different angles, the room from both ends. Close-ups of Salkeld's neck. In the lack of a proper forensic investigation there's little else I can do. I can't leave the body hanging there waiting for the storm to blow over, the snow to melt, the police to get through. I put the camera down, go back to the door. Morland's still there, a dishevelled and wet-looking Sam Ellis, and Eve Marton. She's dressed now, jeans and a sweatshirt, sensible shoes.

'I need a hand to get the body down,' I say.

'Not me,' Morland backs away, 'I couldn't do that.'

'I've a penknife in my room,' Eve says, 'I'll cut the rope if you and Sam can take the body.' Sam Ellis nods his agreement, takes off his coat and over-trousers. He's beginning to get warm.

It needs all three of us. Salkeld is heavier than he looks, his body is unwieldy. Eve has to take some of the weight as we stagger across to the bed with him. She isn't frightened by his body, when we lie him down she makes sure his arms and legs are straight.

'At least he hasn't pissed himself,' Ellis mutters.

'He will,' I say as we step back, admire our work. There's a small pocket on the front of Salkeld's pyjama jacket, I dip my fingers into it.

'No suicide note?' Eve Marton asks.

'I haven't found one yet. Sometimes there isn't one.'

'How about this?' Sam Ellis says. He reaches down to the floor, just below where the body was hanging and picks up a computer disk. He hands it to me. It's unlabelled.

'A message, perhaps, but no way of writing it or reading it. Not in here, at least.'

'But Eric had access to computers,' Eve says. 'He spent most of his time working with them. Most of his spare time as well, he really was dedicated to his work.'

This is going well. A body with a possible computerised suicide note. The person who found the body is co-operating, sounds intelligent and might be able to read the note. I might still get back to help the kids build a snowman. 'Let's have a chat,' I say to Eve Marton. 'In your room? It's probably more comfortable than being in here.' I let her lead the way. 'I don't need to mention that you shouldn't touch anything,' I tell Ellis and Morland.

'Can we go yet?' Morland asks. 'I could do with a coffee.'

'Are there no facilities here?'

'Well, yes, there's a kitchen. But I thought I could go back to my office, freshen up. And I haven't had breakfast yet ...'

'My heart bleeds. I'd suggest you make yourself coffee in the kitchen here. You could bring me a cup of tea ...' I raise my eyes at Eve Marton, she nods her head. 'Make that two teas. And biscuits, if you can find any, I didn't

66

have any breakfast either. If there's anyone else around, please don't tell them about Mr Salkeld's death. I'll try not to be too long.'

Eve Marton and I go into her room. It's the same size and shape as Salkeld's. She's already pulled the quilt neatly over the bed. There are bottles and tubes on the dressing table, arranged in order size. A towel is folded below the basin, toothpaste and brush stand in a glass. There's a book on the bedside table, closed, pristine. I squint at it, notice the author, Graham Greene, but not the title. At least she has good taste in writers.

'You're being a bit hard on him,' she says, sits on the bed and points me into the only seat.

'On David Morland? Me? hard? That's not being hard, Miss Marton. That's just getting my own back for several small injustices. I take offence easily.'

'He's not very happy.'

'Happy? A strange concept, happiness. Difficult to define. And very comparative. He may feel unhappy, but I don't think he's as unhappy as Salkeld was.'

She swallows, nods, dabs at her eyes. 'Poor man.'

I look round the room. 'You don't actually live here, then? It's just temporary accommodation?'

She takes a deep breath, pushes Salkeld out of her mind. 'That's right. This block is used as temporary quarters, usually for new employees, until they can find a place to live. But, as David said, the rooms can be used by other staff if the need arises. Working late, bad weather.'

'But Salkeld did live in his room?'

'Yes. At least, he was doing, for the past few weeks. He didn't always, I think he had a home somewhere. But when there was a lot of work to do, he moved in here. He told me that. I didn't know him well, but sometimes we talked.'

'Did he mention any family?'

She seems surprised. 'No. Why should he have done?'

'No reason.'

'We only talked about work. He wasn't . . . he didn't say much about anything really.'

'His room doesn't look lived in. Not exactly homely.'

'No.' She's not being impolite, it's as if she's thinking of something else. 'I can probably look on that disk for you,' she offers.

'I was going to ask you anyway. You are the Computer Manager, aren't you?'

'Yes. I look after applications, though, not software development. If anything goes wrong I still have to call in the experts. It's more of a training role than anything else.'

'Does that mean you have to work with all other departments? I imagine most of them will use computers in one way or another.'

'Yes, I work with department managers.'

'Including Eric Salkeld?'

She's quiet again. Not refusing to answer, just thinking of her words carefully. She's made an effort to compose herself since I first saw her. She looks tired, but not distraught. She's wearing a little make-up, though I think it's more to give her confidence than to impress me. She's too tall, too well-built to be described as beautiful; but her face is attractive in the way some middle-aged women's faces are, as if they have stories to tell. She looks as if she's trying to decide what story to tell me.

Eventually she gathers herself together. 'Eric was a strange man. He kept himself to himself. I don't think he was popular with his staff – he only had two or three assistants, data input clerks really – but he was, as far as I know, good at his job. And if anyone had a problem about pay, he'd sort it all out for them. And he usually did it himself. He's been with Forestcrag since it opened, but he only moved in here a few weeks ago. After New Year, I think. He didn't have many friends.'

'Were you his friend?'

'No. No, I wouldn't describe myself as a friend. The only dealings I had with him were professional. I didn't . . .

I know it sounds hard, but I didn't like him. He gave me the creeps.'

I try to picture the body on the bed. Eric Salkeld was in his fifties, grey-haired, with a paunch. He was as tall as me. I can't imagine Eve Marton being intimidated by him.

'What did he do to make you feel that way? Did he make advances? Did he touch you?'

'Oh God no, nothing like that! I could have coped with something like that. No, he was too solicitous, always asking how I was. And he was quiet, I'd turn around and he'd be there, looking at me. And he stood too close. There was nothing definite, nothing you could say "*that* really annoys me." It was just him. The way he was.' She puts her head in her hands. 'It's so easy, isn't it, to talk about him in the past tense.'

'How did you find him?'

'Something woke me, a noise, I think. I lay in bed for a while, then I heard it again. Not a groan or anything like that, just a thumping sound. It must have been his heels on the floor, or his hands on the wall, something like that. I got up, looked out in the hallway. His door was slightly open, I listened but I couldn't hear anything. I knocked, there was no answer. So I pushed the door open. I didn't even know it was him staying next door. I just . . . I saw his body. Hanging there.'

'Was he alive?'

'He wasn't moving. I didn't know what to do.'

'Did you scream?'

'Scream? No, I didn't scream. I probably swore. Then I went in, I felt his neck for a pulse, held my cheek to his mouth to see if there was any breath. But it was obvious he was dead, just by looking at him. So I sent for help.'

'Sent who?'

'Sam Ellis. I knew he was staying over, he'd told me the night before. He was downstairs, when I knocked on his door he was just getting ready to go out.'

'You didn't tell him what you'd found?'

'No. That is . . . I didn't know what to do, what to think. I just said I had to speak to David, I knew Sam had a radio phone. I told David, I was actually out in the corridor, Sam didn't hear me. Then David asked – told – Sam to fetch you.'

'Without telling him what it was about. Then I asked him to get me all sorts of stuff. So he's in charge of security but no one bothered to tell him about all this. No wonder he's been a little bit sulky this morning.'

Eve's looking at me. 'That's why he doesn't seem to like you?'

'Let's just say our relationship didn't get off to a good start.'

There's a knock on the door. 'Yes?' I shout.

'It's your tea,' David Morland calls.

'We're just finishing,' I answer, 'could you bring it in?'

David Morland does as he's told. There's a teapot on a tray, two mugs, milk in a carton and sugar in a bag. I pour. Eve takes her mug.

'I'll have a word with Mr Morland now,' I tell her, 'then perhaps we can look at Salkeld's disk.'

'I'll wait outside,' she says, swaps places with her boss. He sits on the bed, unsure of what to expect. He's sweating, nervous.

'I don't think I can tell you much,' he begins, 'Sam woke me up . . .'

'You weren't sleeping in this building then?'

'No. My office has a small suite attached. I spent the night there.'

'Alone?' I don't really need to know this. I don't even know why I asked the question, unless it's to find out how far I can go with him.

'Yes, I was alone.' I have no reason to disbelieve him, but I wonder if he'd give the same answer even if someone had been sharing his bed. It's enough that he answered without blustering.

'How well did you know Eric Salkeld?'

'Not very well. He's been here since the site opened, but I didn't appoint him. I don't suppose I've spoken to him more than two or three times, just in passing.'

'Do you know Miss Marton well?'

'Eve? Well, yes, of course.'

'Of course? Isn't she a departmental manager, just like Eric Salkeld? Why should you know her better than him?'

He's on comfortable territory, I can see him relax. 'There are hierarchies of management, Mr Oliphant. Eve is close to the top. Salkeld wasn't. Payroll is a fairly low-grade function in all organisations, a necessary evil. Finding a replacement for Salkeld won't be difficult. I couldn't say the same if Eve were to leave, she has skills and talents which are particular to this company and its computer systems. My time is valuable, Mr Olphant, I have to distribute it according to priorities. Eve and her computers are a priority. Eric Salkeld wasn't. That's why I didn't know him well.'

I've never believed that first impressions are always right. Experience has taught me that many people live by deception, and not all of them are criminals. The first time I saw David Morland speak I could appreciate his skill. But that was a public display, a veneer, and when he spoke to me personally I saw the cheap material hidden beneath that glossy surface. Disliking David Morland was, from that moment, simple, logical even. But now it's becoming easier to cultivate that dislike, to encourage its growth into a luxuriant aversion to everything he says, everything he believes in. Eric Salkeld was unimportant to him when he was alive, and his lonely death has the potential to be nothing more than inconvenience. All he's worried about is the way that it might affect his business.

'Not exactly homely surroundings, are they?'

'They aren't meant to be. They're a stopgap. The rent we charge . . .'

'You charge people for living here?'

'Of course. Only for those who choose to stay here

71

rather than find local accommodation. We don't charge when it's a one-off, when the person staying has been working late, for example.'

'How long had Eric Salkeld been living here?'

'I don't know. Eve mentioned that he had, otherwise I wouldn't even have known that.'

'So you don't know why he chose to live here?'

'No. Sorry.'

I led him through the bare bones of the body's discovery. His story ties in with everything Eve Marton has told me. Then I look at my watch, it's almost ten o'clock.

'Thank you,' I say. I hope my politeness is cold enough, formal enough to register with him. I hope he appreciated that I'm doing this because no one else could, not because I want to help him.

'What happens now?' he asks.

'Eve Marton and I look at the computer disk we found. We get Salkeld's body moved somewhere cold. I don't suppose the local GP was amongst your guests last night?'

'She was invited, but she didn't come. One of her nurses is here, though. She's probably in the Medical Centre.'

'Her nurses? You mean you don't employ your own?'

'Good God, no! We contribute to the cost of having them work up here at weekends, but we don't employ them ourselves. That would mean having to assume responsibility for them. But if they're provided by the local GP, she gets an NHS fee every time one of them treats someone, and we get a service which is actually better than our customers get at home. Clever, eh?' He really believes I find his intrigues admirable. I try to think of a way to puncture his pride.

'A nurse might be helpful, just to look the body over. Could you arrange that? And a large fridge for the body? Given the weather, an unheated outhouse would do. Do you think you can manage that?'

'I'll get Ellis on it straightaway.' He stands up, ready to scatter demands.

'Might be better to do it yourself, I've a feeling Ellis is going to be very busy dealing with the other problems the weather's brought.'

'But . . .'

'And I'll need to stay in touch with the police and with Ellis, since on-site security's his pigeon. I'll need your radio-phone.' It's his badge of office, a symbol of authority. He doesn't want to give it up. I reach across behind him and take it anyway. 'Thank you,' I add, 'keep me in touch with any developments. Let me know where you've moved the body and when the nurse can view it.' I don't expect there to be developments, and if there are, it'll be me instigating them and I won't be letting him know unless I want something from him. I'm making it clear I'm in charge. I open the door for him but speak to Eve Marton outside.

'Where can we read this disk?'

'There are computers all over the site, but Eric's office might be a good place to do it. There might be something there to help you . . . You know. Find out a little more about him.'

'Let's go, then.' Morland is still sitting on the bed. 'Come on, David, get yourself going. Oh, and can you get a radio-phone to Sly as well? I might need to speak to him. Have him ring me as soon as he gets it.'

Then we leave.

Chapter Nine

The place is beginning to wake up. First I hear children's voices riding on the still air. They take me back to a winter of my youth, one of snowfalls and carol singing, sledges and icicles, bright sunlight and clear, sharp shadows. I feel comfortable with the memory, though I'm sure it's a false one. It's probably crept into my brain, been absorbed by osmosis; it's the result of too much exposure to Hollywood films and Raymond Briggs cartoons.

There's also the familiar noise of shovels slicing through crisp snow. Someone's managed to persuade the limited workforce that pathways should be cleared, though I'm sure the snow's too deep for motorised snowploughs to work their way along Forestcrag's roads. I follow Eve Marton, she's forging her own pathway with little regard for the profligate way she's expending energy. She's like an icebreaker, but still I struggle to keep up.

'Have you worked here long?' I throw at her.

'Since it opened,' she answers.

'In from the beginning, then?'

'Yes.'

'Started about the same time as Salkeld?'

'Yes.' Conversation doesn't seem to be her priority at the moment. I try again.

'Where are we going?'

'Admin offices. They're on the other side of the car park. Not too far.'

It appears that the designers decided to keep the decorative and the functional separate. The main building – the Tesseract – is surrounded by lodges skilfully grouped in natural hollows and glades so that none has a view, from the front windows at least, of any other lodge. The Country Club (why they couldn't have just called it a sports centre, I don't know) is, according to the brochure, well-cloaked by trees and disguised as a Swiss mountain lodge. But the car park is nothing but a wide expanse of flat land, cleared by bulldozers, with the excess soil and peat formed into high banks to prevent it being seen by residents. Entrances and exits are gaps in the bank. The staff accommodation is at one end; the admin block at the other end. And, if the limited view I have can be believed, the two buildings are almost identical.

'Was there an offer on,' I ask, 'two for the price of one?'

'Don't judge by appearances, Mr Oliphant, everything inside is state of the art.'

I want to believe her, but if the security system's an example of 'state of the art', I've a feeling her computers are going to be powered by clockwork.

By the time we reach the door I'm cold and wet. The lack of any wind disguises the bitter edge to the air, and my fingers and toes feel as if they're turning black, ready to drop off. But once inside (the door, to my relief, opens on production of a security swipe card) I can remove my damp clothes and reassure myself that frostbite hasn't yet attacked my extremities.

Eve Marton leads me along a corridor. It runs the whole length of the front of the building, doors open off it. I see one with her name on it, but she ignores it, passes on instead to one labelled 'General Office'. The door isn't locked; it opens to reveal a large, open-plan room with about a dozen desks, each with a computer terminal. There are filing cabinets and cupboards, wall-planners and charts, graphs with upward sneaking lines in red and black. It seems no different to any other office anywhere in the world.

'Everything is on computer,' she says proudly, 'we're a paperless office. Payroll, personnel files, sales and purchase ledgers. Where we have paper, we scan it then destroy it.' She wanders over to a desk in one corner, a desk looking out at all the others, and switches on the computer. I position myself at her shoulder, watch her fingers rather than the screen. She's going to try reading the disk in an ordinary windows environment. I'm rather pleased that the words 'windows environment' rise so clearly to my mind – I'm not computer friendly. I have the disk in my pocket, I hand it to her. My feet are complaining again, they thought I was going to remove my wet socks. But the time isn't quite right yet.

Eve Marton's clearly proficient in her work. She doesn't look at her fingers as they tap-dance over the keyboard. I can understand what she's doing, reading the disk from drive A. What I'm not prepared for is the message that comes immediately onto the screen. I read it over Eve Marton's shoulder.

Dear Mr Oliphant,
If you're reading this then you'll have succeeded in one of your aims. The fact that, in doing so, you've caused my death will probably not affect you at all.

As soon as I heard that Morland had hired you I knew you'd find me out. I don't claim that what I've been doing was particularly clever; anyone with a bit of common sense and a knowledge of computers could have done it. But I was quite proud of the fact that I'd managed to keep it secret for so long. I suppose one of the reasons I'm telling you this, rather than just waiting for you to uncover me, is because I don't want you to have the satisfaction of detecting my fraud. And the suicide? Pride, I suppose, and fear. I don't think I could survive in prison. I've heard and read about what goes on. A man like me would be torn to pieces, physically and mentally. It's easier this way, kinder.

There is one more reason. It's to get my own back on that sanctimonious, hypocritical bitch Eve Marton. I could have done her job. I mean, Mr Oliphant, it's obvious she hasn't been doing it well, otherwise I wouldn't have got away with this for so long. She's too busy sucking up to Morland, probably literally, to pay proper attention to computer security. She pretended to be my friend, yet secretly she wanted rid of me. But I was too clever for her. Anyway, this will be a something of a puzzle to you since you don't know yet what I've done. So I'll tell you.

Forestcrag employs about 800 staff, that's over 400 whole time equivalents at an average salary of just over £9000 pa. No, I know it's not much, particularly when bastards like Marton are getting far more than that, but that's the way it is here. The wages bill is almost four million a year. What I've been doing, from the beginning, is running two sets of payrolls. The first is for what everyone ought to be paid; that money is drawn from head office, every month, into a pay disbursements account. The second payroll disk performs the same calculations, but everyone's gross pay is 3% less. And I pocket the difference. That's almost £125,000 a year. You won't find it, of course, I've covered up that information. I may not benefit, but I'll make damn sure Forestcrag won't get it back.

There were one or two little problems I had to sort out. Access to contracts of employment, for example, so I could amend all local pay scales. Audits were sometimes tricky, but a few dummy employees here and there did the trick. You have to realise, Mr Oliphant, Forestcrag's run on a shoestring; the management believes in 'multi-tasking', getting staff to be proficient in more than one job. All I had to do was say I had experience in

77

computerised personnel records. And, like I said,
computer security is so lax here, it was easy. And every-
one thought I was so diligent, working such long hours to
make sure everything was just right. When really I was
making sure there were no silly mistakes.
So there you are, Mr Oliphant. I'm sorry if I've
spoiled your fun. The two payroll disks are in my desk,
they're labelled 'Payroll 1' and 'Payroll 2'. Not very
original, I know, but I never was the creative type.
There's nothing else I can tell you, except that I want to
be cremated. And I'd like to have something by Judy
Garland or Dusty Springfield playing.
Eric Salkeld

'Well,' I say. 'He doesn't seem to have liked you very
much.'
'The bastard!'
'Is he right?'
Eve spins in her seat. She looks as if she's about to cry,
or shout, or storm out of the room. 'Is he right about what?
Me being a hypocritical bitch? Who cares? About defrauding Forestcrag? How the fuck do I know? I was reading as
fast as you were, taking in as much as you were. I'd have to
check the two disks, compare them. Even then, I'm a
computer manager, not an accountant. I don't know what to
look for.'
'Perhaps we should find the disks first,' I suggest.
'Yes. Find the disks.'
It's not difficult. Salkeld's desk has two drawers, Eve
opens the top one first. Sitting on a pile of paper are two
floppy disks. She takes them out, examines them. 'Payroll
1, Payroll 2,' she reads.
'He didn't believe in making things difficult,' I say.
'Do you want to look at them now?'
'Why not?'
'They'll run in payroll manager. All I need to do . . .'
There's an icon on the screen with a green 'pounds' sign.

She double clicks on it and the screen requests a password from her. I watch her fingers but they're too quick for me.

'Hold on,' I say, 'you have access to the payroll software?'

'I have access to all software – I'm the computer manager.'

'Is that normal?'

'It is here. Someone's got to be able to deal with glitches when they happen, and to do that you need access to the programs. For access you need a password.' She explains it as if I'm stupid.

'I assume it's a different password to the one Salkeld would have used?'

'You assume correctly, Mr Oliphant. Every user has an individual password. That password gives access to a limited range of applications. My password gives access to all applications. But everywhere anyone goes, they leave footprints. I can tell which software application's been used, when it's been used, and who's been using it.'

'Unless someone knows someone else's password.'

'Yes. But letting someone else know your password isn't permitted.'

'That's all right, then.'

She turns round in her seat and glares at me. 'Are you suggesting that the system is open to fraud?'

'No, we already know that, Salkeld's kindly pointed it out in nice large figures with lots of zeroes.'

Even from behind I can see her blush. I can also hear her soft-muttered 'Bastard!' again. But I forgive her, she must be worried, primarily about her job. Once Morland knows how much the company's been taken for a ride he'll have to sack her. Money talks, and here it's pointing several fingers at Eve and shouting 'It's her fault!'

There's a menu on the screen, Eve puts the first disk into the computer and selects 'read'. The screen fills with numbers.

'What does it mean?' I ask her, bending close. The

79

perfume she's wearing is having difficulty cloaking the smell of nervous sweat.

'How the fuck do I know? Like I said, I'm no expert on software, on the way it's used. I solve problems, get things working again. I can't possibly know everything about every piece of specialist software in the building.'

'Let me look,' I say. 'Is there somewhere you can get a cup of tea round here?'

She climbs out of her seat. 'There's a kitchen along the corridor.'

My question carried the suggestion that, while I looked at the figures on the screen, she might like to make some tea. Hidden in her answer was the statement that if I wanted tea, I'd have to go and make it myself. We appear to be at an impasse. Perhaps I need to be more direct.

'Okay. You make the tea and I'll see if I can make sense of these figures.'

She doesn't move. 'I suppose you're an expert in payroll?' she says like a little sulking girl, weight over one leg, hands on hips. I decide to pull rank.

'No. But I'm the nearest thing you've got at the moment to a policeman, and I'm acting under the instructions of the managing director. I'm also very curious to find out what's been going on here. But I've been up too long, I don't really need to start a petty argument with someone who appears to have been culpable in losing her boss a considerable amount of money, and I really could do with a cup of tea. Please.'

She whirls on her heels and stomps noisily towards the door. I examine the screen. I know a little about payroll, most people do if they think about it. After all, no one ever wants to pay too much tax or national insurance, so they always check their payslips to make sure everything's all right. There are columns here for hours worked, hourly pay, gross pay, different types of deductions. I scroll down to the bottom of the page and look at the total, scribble it down on a pad of paper. Then I take out the disk and replace it with its twin, look at the equivalent cell. There is, as Salkeld said there would be, a discrepancy. The difference between the two figures is almost £100,000.

I'd like to know where the money went. Salkeld's pocket, yes, that's obvious, but how? Credit transfer to a secret bank account? That shouldn't be too difficult to find. Perhaps several accounts, that way there wouldn't be large, single amounts going out. But even then, it's difficult to hide £100,000 pounds a month when the average pay is more like five or six hundred. Then I realise, with relief, that it's not my problem. What I know is enough to tell Morland, enough to keep him occupied until the snow clears and the police can get through, enough to satisfy my own limited curiosity. I can even, with justification, ignore the small gnat-bites of guilt which have been irritating me – Salkeld's suicide note was addressed to me personally. After all, David Morland was the one who'd lied when he said I was going to work for him. Let the insects plague him instead.

Eve's coming back, carrying two mugs of tea. She hands one to me, hot and steaming. 'I've brought separate milk,' she says, fishes three small catering cartons from her pocket and places them on the table. 'Sugar as well. I thought you might like a biscuit.' She leans back on the desk next to mine, leaves the peace offerings to me. 'I'm sorry,' she says. 'This isn't easy for me.'

'It's okay. Understandable reaction, in the circumstances.' I take a biscuit, pour one of the cartons into my tea. I gesture towards them, politeness can be infectious.

'No thanks, biscuits make me fat, sugar rots my teeth and milk makes me puke.' I feel guilty at the way I'm destroying my body, but hunger and thirst take precedence. While my mouth is full Eve takes a deep breath, disposes of the small talk. She's been thinking what to say. 'I know this looks bad, very bad. But I can probably claim it's not my fault. Lax security, that is. I have to work within criteria laid down for me, I have to work within budgets.

Everything I do is dictated by company policy.'

'Perhaps they might learn from this sizeable mistake, then.'

'So there's no doubt?'

'No doubt. Salkeld was siphoning money away, the police – when they get here – will find out where it's been going.' I sip from the mug, the tea's so hot it almost scalds my lips. Eve doesn't appear to be suffering, perhaps she microwaved my mug. Petty revenge?

'I can't understand why the company's accountants didn't figure it out. That much money going missing, surely . . .'

'It wasn't going missing from the company, Eve, it was being stolen from the employees. But – this is just a thought, it should really please Morland – the company has a duty of care for its staff, and it hasn't carried out that duty. Those staff who've suffered should be able to sue the company for their loss of earnings.'

Eve grins. 'He won't be very happy.'

'Perhaps, when it all comes out, you might keep your job and he'll lose his.'

'People like Morland never suffer, he'll hide it, find someone else to blame. I've been here too long anyway, it's time to move on. I'll offer to resign, get a good reference in return. I quite fancy going abroad.' She looks past me at the window. 'Go somewhere warm and sunny. Get away from the bloody awful weather.'

It's starting to snow again.

Chapter Ten

'Now what?' Eve asks as we stand by the door, ready to brave the snow again. My feet are still cold and wet, all I want to do is get them warm. I want to tell Morland what's happened rather than phone him. I want to see the expression on his face. Then I want to leave him to sort out the mess himself, while I go back to the lodge and find Kirsty, Sly, Paula and the kids. It's ten thirty, they're probably wondering what's happening.

'Morland's office?' I suggest. 'I take it he doesn't share space with the lesser mortals in *this* building?'

'He'll be in his suite in the Tesseract,' Eve replies. She's calm now, still looking tired, but capable of a smile in her conversation. She talks as we walk. She'd like to go abroad, Australia perhaps, or the Mediterranean, start up again before she gets too old. She has no family, no ties. I say the usual encouraging things at the usual moments, offer bland encouragement.

The main path leading to the Tesseract has been cleared, though the falling snow is doing its best to recover its territory. There are a few people about, rolling and fat with clothes. Most of them are heading into the Tesseract.

'Just point me at Morland's office,' I tell Eve, 'there's no need to come in with me.'

'I'd like to know what he says, how he reacts, if you don't mind. I might be able to help.'

'Help me? Help Morland? Or help the company?'

'A bit of everything, I think. And help myself as well. I've a feeling I'll be the first name out of the hat when they're choosing a scapegoat.'

She leads me up a long, wide curving ramp. It heads for, then runs parallel to, a large glass wall. Beyond the wall is a balcony, a viewing area looking down on the pool complex. The executive suite is through a door at the end of the ramp. Its internal walls and ceiling are curved, it's like stepping into the inside of a doughnut. There's a reception area with sofas, small tables well-stocked with magazines, a desk where a secretary would normally sit. There are two doors marked as toilets, three further doors which, presumably, house Forestcrag's 'executives'. One of the doors is open. Eve gestures me towards it.

Morland is standing beyond a desk whose centre would only be accessible if he climbed onto it. It's occupied by a radio-phone, nothing else. Morland is looking down at the pool from a large window, his back to us. There's a smell of coffee and cigarettes in the air.

'Well?' he says without turning round. 'I hope he had a good reason for killing himself. Do you know how long it's taken me to find a secure, cold room for the body? And to get it there without any of the customers seeing it? Jesus Christ!'

I could get to dislike this man. I pull a seat up to his desk and sit down, Eve does likewise. I place my own phone on the floor, it's too cumbersome, too uncomfortable to leave in my back pocket. I take off my boots. I remove my wet socks. Warm air is being ducted into the room, I look round and find two floor vents close to a wall. I wander over, place my socks over the vents and pad back to my seat. Then I put my feet up on the table. I say nothing. I'll win this game (that's all it is, a power game) because I want nothing from Morland, but he needs a great deal from me. And so we wait. Eve leans forward in her seat, it looks as if she'll speak, I raise my finger to my lips and she settles back.

'Well?' says Morland again.

I turn to Eve, my voice is a stage whisper. 'How long do you think it'll take my socks to dry? At least an hour, I reckon. I'll just go and get a magazine to read, while we're waiting. Do you want one?'

Morland spins round. 'All right, Mr Oliphant, what's going on?'

'My mother always said it was rude to turn your back on people when you were talking to them, and I suppose the same applies if you want people to talk to you. And anyway, I wanted to see your face when I told you the news.'

He looks worried. 'The news? What news? Was there nothing useful on the disk?'

'Useful? Yes, it was very useful. It helped me find out, oh, many interesting things. Would you like to hear them?'

'You're toying with me, Oliphant.'

'That's because you're behaving like a child, Mr Morland. I'd suggest you sit down, put your pompous face away in a drawer, and listen carefully.'

He considers storming out of his own office, but that isn't really an option. He can swear at me, but he risks making me more resolute in my awkwardness than I am. He's already found that being impolite only annoys me. So, after some brief and angry reflection, he has no choice but to sit in his high-backed executive chair and listen to me.

And I tell him everything.

He doesn't react well. I forecast ulcers, perhaps a heart attack, within five or ten years. After all, he smokes, he drinks, he's overweight and I can't imagine him exercising. As Eve suggested, he attempts to blame her for everything. She accepts some of the responsibility, but points out that she's spoken to him in the past about computer security. She reminds him, politely, that she has copies of the memos she's sent. That doesn't really calm him. He shouts and swears, then he sulks into silence.

'Hold on,' he says eventually, 'the company hasn't lost anything because of this, has it.'

'Apart from its reputation, you mean? Or perhaps it didn't have one to begin with.'

He doesn't care what I say, what I think. He looks at me as if I'm the drunk grandmother at a wedding, telling embarrassing stories about all the family.

'Have you been back in touch with the police?' He hasn't quite finished with me yet.

'No. I thought it would be polite to tell you first. No, I'm sorry, forgive me. I forgot, "Polite" is a word you probably don't understand.'

He's refusing to rise to the bait, it's too obvious. I need something more subtle, something to lie on the water and tempt his greediness. But he's thinking now, ignoring me. If he contacts the police himself he can spin this, if not to his advantage, then at least to minimise his discomfort. I watch his face, I can tell he's come to that conclusion. Now he just wants rid of me. I've outlived my usefulness.

'Thank you, Mr Oliphant, for your help in this. I'll take over now, I don't think there's anything else you need do.'

If the circumstances were different, if Morland had been anyone other than Morland, I'd have been pleased to let him do as he wants. If he'd tried reverse psychology, insisted that I ring the police and report my findings, then perhaps I'd have flung the phone at him and told him to do it himself. But he's used me, and I don't like being used. So, out of pure spitefulness, despite the fact that it will involve me writing reports and filling in forms, I decide *I'll* phone the police and tell them what's happened.

'It's okay,' I say, 'I'd rather finish the job myself. Make sure everything's parcelled, packaged and tied. After all, we don't want any inaccuracies creeping in, do we?'

That's the line I've been looking for, the cast was perfect. Morland's face begins to turn red. He leans forward, pushes himself out of his seat. He looks as if he's going to throw himself across the desk at me. 'Are you implying that I won't tell the police the truth?' He's forcing himself not to yell, restricting himself to a barely controlled growl.

I take my time answering him, it's more rewarding that way. And then I nod and say, simply, 'Yes.' The desk is too wide for him to reach me, it would make him look silly if he ran round it to attack me. That's when the phone rings. He scowls at me, as if the sound has rescued me, picks up his phone and presses the 'answer' button. It keeps ringing. I reach for the phone I've been using, the one on the floor at my feet, the one which made the sound.

'Hello?' I smile sweetly at Morland as I speak. 'Yes, this is Billy Oliphant.' I listen. I listen for a long time. I don't reply. Morland's aggravated by this. 'Who is it?' he asks impatiently, but I ignore him, he's shrinking, retreating to the very limbs of my consciousness. I'm concentrating on what the voice on the other end of the phone is telling me.

'Okay,' I say, 'I'll come straightaway.' I stand up, put the phone into my pocket, pick up my socks. They're still wet, but I pull them on.

'Well?' says Morland.

'That was Sly,' I say, 'thanks for letting him have a phone. He just wanted to tell me that my daughter thinks my being here is just a figment of her imagination. If you don't mind, I'll go now.'

'And I can ring the police?'

'Yes, you can ring them. Tell them it was suicide. Tell them the suicide appeared to have been committing fraud on rather a grand scale. Tell them I'll be in touch sometime over the weekend.'

I try not to notice the triumph in his smile. Instead I concentrate on forcing my feet into boots as wet as my socks and far colder. I don't want to leave Morland thinking he's won his argument, thinking he's been able to bluster and bully and browbeat me into submission. I want to say more but I can't.

I can't tell him I was lying about it being Sly on the phone, that it was really the local doctor's nurse on the phone. I can't say she's found some marks on the body, marks she feels aren't consistent with suicide. I can't say any of this, because if Eric Salkeld didn't kill himself, then someone murdered him. Someone then tried to disguise the murder as suicide. Someone fabricated a suicide note on a computer disk. Someone had access to Salkeld's computer. Someone had information about a payroll fraud which may not have involved Salkeld at all. The reason I don't tell Morland isn't that I don't want him to know, it's that I don't want Eve Marton to know. She found Salkeld, she found the disk, she has access to most of the computers on site. She could be the Someone I'm looking for.

Chapter Eleven

I ring Sly as soon as I step out into the snow. 'Yeah, boss?' he answers.

'How did you know it was me?'

'Who else would want to ring me, boss?'

He's right. There's crisp excitement in the air. Families are building snowmen together, rolling huge snowballs. And I'm about to drag Sly away from his wife and children.

'What are you doing?' I ask.

'Waiting for you to ring. I'm at the pool, everyone else is in the water. Kirsty's helping out with the kids, so's that youngster she danced with last night. He's like a little puppy, boss. If she said "hold your head under the water for ten minutes," he would.'

'So you're actually in the pool?'

'No, everyone else is. I'm on the balcony, watching them. Never was fond of the water, not total immersion anyway. And Paula says I'm getting a cold, best to keep out. But, like I said, the real reason I'm just sitting watching is that I'm waiting for you to ring. Something's up.'

'How do you know?'

'You've been away two hours, boss. When Sam Ellis dropped my phone off he wouldn't say a thing. Made me suspicious. You want me to come and meet you?'

'Yeah. Apparently there's a garage at the side of the

Tesseract, beside the kitchen service area. Meet me outside there.'

'Okay, boss.'

He's about to sign off when I remember something. 'Sly!'

'Yeah?'

'You don't happen to have a spare pair of dry socks with you?'

I head for the temporary cold store, my mind clouding over. A few minutes before I'd uncovered a fraud and managed to insult David Morland several times. I was feeling pleased with myself. But now I'm faced with the prospect of investigating a murder. I don't want to do that. It's bad enough trying to cope with suicide; taking your own life is a desperate thing to do. But murder? I never could come to terms with murder. I could never see myself wanting to take someone else's life and couldn't imagine anyone else wanting to. When I was in the police force, I didn't want to be armed. I had weapons training, like everyone else. But that didn't mean I had to like it. Some did like it, some carried their guns with a worrying bravado I couldn't understand. They tried the usual arguments on me. 'What if someone threatens you with a gun?' 'What if someone threatens your wife, your daughter, a member of the public?' I had to tell them I couldn't see myself in that position. They never asked me to train to be a marksman, though my range scores were good. They must have known I'd say no.

Murder? A killer on site? I decide not to think about it yet, to wait until I meet the nurse, find out what she has to say. It may be prevarication on my part, it may even be delaying the inevitable; but if this is murder, there's only one person on site capable of dealing with it, and that's me. I don't want to think about that until I have to.

Sly's waiting for me as I huff around the corner to the garage. There are huge waste-bins and wheeled racks, all ice-coated, floundering in deep snow. Steam rises from a

90

snow-capped steel chimney. Somewhere inside, in one of the kitchens, a tuneless voice is accompanying a strident, tinny radio. Sly sees me, waves. He's well muffled against the cold, only his eyes are visible through layers of hat and scarf. He hands me a plastic bag.

'Socks,' he says. I take them from him and knock on the garage door. 'It's me,' I call, 'Billy Oliphant.' I can hear the noise of key in lock, then the door opens into a gap where there's a wedge of snow missing.

The head which appears is large and round, smoothed with powder and bright with rouge, eye-liner and mascara, blusher and toner. It's topped with a fur hat, a garish red scarf matches the face's lipstick and can't hide the first of several dewlaps. 'Come in,' commands a matronly voice. We do as we're told.

There are no windows but it's well-lit inside. At the far end four or five lawnmowers are almost covered with a tarpaulin. Someone has draped a cotton sheet over a work-bench, and below a second sheet is the outline of a body.

'Oh-oh,' Sly says, 'dead people.'

'And you are . . .?' the nurse asks.

'I'm sorry,' I explain, 'I should have done the introductions. I'm Billy Oliphant, this is Sly Rogers, he sometimes helps me in my security business. Sly this is . . . Catherine? Is that right?'

'I prefer Cath. Cath Watson. Nurse to the bumped and bruised, tick-bitten and wasp-stung. Most of the time I deal with people falling off bikes.' She throws a glance at the body. 'This is a little beyond my experience.'

The nurse, like Sly, is wearing layers of clothes. She needs them, the garage feels colder than outside. But even several thicknesses of clothing can't alter her outline. She's not particularly fat, just large. Her body is in proportion to her head. And while both Sly and I are wearing functional, outdoor clothes, she looks as if she's ready to go out for dinner. Her coat is made of grey gabardine, long and flowing. Her boots are black chisel-toed leather, gloss-

91

polished. She stands with arms crossed, black handbag hung in the crook of one elbow.

She nods with carefully considered wisdom before she speaks, delivers her judgement. 'When I said this was beyond my experience, I did mean immediate experience, of course. It's a good job it's me here and not one of the others.'

'The others?' I ask her.

'There are four of us on a rota. By rights I should be at home now, if it wasn't for this awful weather. But the others don't have my knowledge, my interests. My experience.'

'And what are they?' Sly asks.

'Criminology. Murder and so on. That's the interest, of course, not the experience. I read all I can about it. That's why I thought there was something up, soon as I saw him.'

'And the experience?' I find myself echoing the stress she places on the word.

'I've been around.'

I can sense rather than hear Sly's snigger. I try to ignore it, wait for further explanation.

'I worked in casualty for a while, as part of my training. We'd get all sorts in there, criminal injury, the lot. Attempted suicides. And I went out with a police officer for a while – a long time ago, I'll admit, but you don't forget the things you learn. From people like that, I mean.'

This time Sly tries to cover his laugh with a cough. Cath looks at him questioningly, and that gives me the opportunity to pinch myself.

'I keep up to date with the journals and, as I was saying, after a while you get to know when something's not quite right. And this isn't right.'

I feel something like relief. She may be old enough to behave like a matron, but (despite her assurances to the contrary) she seems to have had no real experience of forensic medicine. So she's learned from books, probably watches a lot of television, and applies that knowledge accordingly. She believes Eric Salkeld's been murdered because she wants to believe that, because it's exciting, beyond her normal experience. So I prepare to humour her.

'This was Eric Salkeld,' I tell Sly, 'his body was found in his room this morning. There was a computer disk beside his body, a sort of electronic suicide note. He seemed to have hung himself. But Mrs Watson thinks differently.'

'Cath,' she says again, 'call me Cath. Yes, look, I'll show you.' She rolls across to the table. 'I'm not surprised you didn't notice yourself. After all, he did have his pyjamas on when you saw him.' She pulls the sheet away with a snap and flourish, like a magician, to reveal Eric Salkeld's naked body.

Sometimes a corpse can look ridiculously healthy, as if it's about to spring into the air and begin dancing round the room. But Salkeld's body is pale, definitely lifeless. His skin is patched: in places it's translucent, veins traced in pale blue on legs and arms; elsewhere, on stomach and thighs, it seems to have taken on a heavy, substantial opacity.

Cath moves round the body. 'Not a hairy man,' she says, 'except for his ears and his eyebrows. Funny how hair migrates round the male body as it ages.' I check to see if she's looking at me, but her comments are directed at Salkeld. She's right, he has little hair: that on the sides and back of his head is untidy, it straggles around his ears and down his neck, an anaemic, sandy colour; his chest is smooth and bare, even his legs look smooth; a stunted thicket of knotted whorls shelters in his groin. Even alive he would have looked ill.

'Here,' she says, positioning herself beside the head, 'you can see the mark on the neck where the rope was tightened. But there are similar marks here,' she points at his wrists, 'and here,' she moves round and touches his ankles.

I look more closely. The skin at Salkeld's neck is red and broken, the pattern of nylon rope can be seen in places. At ankles and feet the marks are less apparent. But they are there. Sly bends down, looks back at me and nods.

'His arms and legs weren't tied when you saw his body?' Cath asks.

'No.'

'And the hook on the wall, the one he was hanging from, how high was it?'

I hold my hands out in front of me, I'm trying to remember. 'How high is a coat-hook normally positioned above the ground? Five foot?'

'So it's not as if he climbed up somewhere on a chair and fastened a noose round his neck, then jumped. It looks to me as if someone tied his arms and legs, put the rope round his neck, then pulled his feet off the ground. They waited till he was dead, then removed the ropes from wrists and ankles. And there you are, instant suicide.'

It seems horribly plausible. It's an answer. But it may not be the only answer. It might even be the right answer to the wrong question.

Sly takes the initiative. 'Are there any other signs on the body? Signs of a struggle? I mean, if someone did truss him up, how did they do it? Was he unconscious? Any signs he's been hit on the head?'

'There's nothing I can see, no bruises, no contusions to the temple or anywhere else on the head for that matter. And I can't smell drink on him, so it's unlikely he was drunk when someone strung him up.' Cath has already decided this was murder.

'So the cause of death is asphyxiation?'

'Well, it certainly looks like it to me, though it would need a post-mortem to confirm it. But even then there are problems.' She opens her eyes wide and moves into declamatory mode, begins her lecture, points at the body as she speaks. 'Suppose there's a fracture in the thyroid plate, as a result the tongue, soft palate and larynx are pushed backwards, blocking the airway. He suffocates. That still doesn't tell us whether he hung himself or somebody else hung him. But there were definitely, close to the time of death, ropes round his wrists and ankles, and they weren't there when he was found. That makes me suspicious, Mr Oliphant. Very suspicious.'

She's enjoying herself, playing the role of detective and pathologist combined. It would be easy to laugh at her earnest expression, her swaddled bulk, the triumph in her voice. But perhaps she's right. Perhaps Eric Salkeld was murdered.

'Thank you, Cath,' I say. 'Do you have a radio-phone?'

She pats her rump; anything could be hidden there. 'Part of the job, Mr Oliphant. Never go anywhere without it.'

'Good. Just in case I need to get in touch with you in a hurry. Are you the only one with a key for this place?'

She reaches into a coat pocket. 'Two keys, one's held in the grounds department, the other in the main key bank. I told Mr Ellis I wanted both of them. After all, we don't want anyone interfering with the evidence.' She waves two keys in front of my eyes.

'You keep one,' I tell her, 'I'll hold the other. Just in case I need to come back when you aren't available.'

'Fine by me, Mr Oliphant. You look the trustworthy type.'

Sly plays the gentleman. 'Do you need a hand to get back to your lodge?'

'Lodge? They don't give me a lodge. No, I've a camp-bed set up in the medical centre. It's not far, I can go in through the kitchen here and out at the main door. I've everything I need on hand, a radio, plenty of books. I'll read up some more on hanging, see if I can find anything else which could help us.' Her mask suddenly cracks and she giggles, she reminds me of one of the good fairies in *Cinderella*. 'This is so exciting, Mr Oliphant. Let me know if there's anything else I can do to help.'

She closes the door after her, leaves me with Sly and the body. Sly wrinkles his nose – though there's no odour from the body that I can smell – and covers it again with the sheet. 'I don't like bodies,' he says. 'They just lie there,

95

don't say anything, don't move. But at the same time they're mocking me. "You'll be like this one day," they're saying, "enjoy yourself while you can." Don't they affect you that way?'

I feel cold, shrug myself deeper into my coat. I can feel the warmth, feel the love Kirsty put into making it. 'No,' I say, 'I don't feel uneasy. Death's inevitable, it doesn't seem worth worrying about the where and when. But I don't think either of us is due a visit just yet.'

Sly nods at Salkeld's body. 'I wonder if he knew.'

'If it was suicide, yes, it's part of the deal. Choose the time of your own death.'

'And was it suicide?'

'If it was suicide, we need to explain the marks on his wrists and ankles. If it was murder ...? Let's assume it was, for the moment. Someone tied him, put the noose round his neck. Pulled his feet off the ground? Kicked them away, perhaps, let him panic and struggle, kicked them away again if he managed to support himself. Then what? Untied his hands and feet, wrote a fake suicide note on the computer. The murderer knew about the payroll fraud. Perhaps he or she was involved in it.'

'Any suspicions, boss?'

'Only the obvious one. Eve Marton was staying next door to Salkeld. She found the body. As far as I can tell she has access to every computer system in the Forestcrag set-up. Motivation? Who knows? She was blackmailing him, he was blackmailing her. It would fit.' The trouble is, I don't want it to fit. I like Eve Marton, she's intelligent, attractive and she can see through Morland. She's also taller than me, probably stronger than me. She'd have no problem heaving a semi-comatose Eric Salkeld onto a coat-hook. I just don't know, I feel out of my depth. I don't want to take things further. I'm not a policeman any more, I don't have the knowledge, I don't have the back-up needed for an investigation like this. I don't need help, I need someone to take the burden away entirely, someone to pat me on the head and say 'you've done very well for getting so far, now we'll take over.'

I have no choice. I press familiar buttons on the radio-phone. 'Hello, I need to speak to the senior duty officer. The name's Oliphant. I'm ringing from Forestcrag Holiday Village. Yes, the duty sergeant will do for the moment.' I wait.

'Hello, Mr Oliphant? Desk Sergeant here, Chief Superintendent Warrington needs to speak to you, hold the line please.'

Chief Superintendent? And I haven't even told them yet that the suicide might be a murder. Has Cath spoken to Morland, has he passed the message on? Or do they have information on Salkeld that makes the matter suspicious? It must be something like that, Chief Superintendents don't speak to people like me unless there's something very wrong or they want something very badly. It can't be the latter because I've nothing to offer them. I'm beginning to worry.

'Hello, Mr Oliphant, Alan Warrington here.' His voice is like treacle, dark, thick and smooth but with a potential for stickiness. 'I'm pleased you rang, we were about to contact you. How are things at Forestcrag?'

They were about to contact me. Something's up. 'It's cold, snowy. Much the same as outside, I'd imagine.' For some reason I can't bring myself to say straight out that he might have a murder on his hands.

'You're probably better off there than anywhere else,' he says, then stops. I'm expecting an explanation but there's none forthcoming.

'If there's a problem,' I say, 'why not tell me what it is rather than dance round it like this?'

'Yes, Mr Oliphant, I'm trying to find the best way of explaining matters to you. We're in the middle of a full scale emergency out here. Virtually every road in the county is blocked. There've been power cuts. My men are stuck in drifts or stuck at home or stuck at work, but wherever they are, they aren't moving. There's another storm forecast for tonight. There's no chance of us getting through to you, getting into Forestcrag for several days.'

It can only mean they know something about Salkeld, or the person who killed him. 'So what do you want me to do?'

'Lie low, Mr Oliphant. Stay indoors.'

'What? Superintendent Warrington, what the hell are you talking about? I'm stuck here, I've got an unexplained death on my hands which looks as if it could be murder, and you're telling me to lie low! What's going on?'

'A death? Someone's died in Forestcrag? I wasn't aware that ... Just a moment.' I can hear him shouting, then a muted conversation, and finally something that might be a shuffling of papers. Then he's back on the line. 'Mr Oliphant, I think we're talking at cross-purposes. I didn't have the paperwork at hand, at least, not all of it. You told us – let me see – yes, we were informed of a suicide, a Mr Salkeld? Eric Salkeld?' He's reading as he's speaking, I can tell. 'And you now feel that it may not have been a suicide?'

'The nurse on site,' I explain, 'suspects Salkeld was murdered. She may be right, I'm not sure, I haven't done any further investigation. I rang you to inform you of that fact, to find out when you'd be able to send a team in. It's more than I can cope with, you need a post-mortem, a forensic team, an interview team. Three or four officers would do.' This is getting, if not worse, certainly more peculiar. He didn't have the Salkeld paperwork beside him. So why was he ringing me?

'There's something here about payroll fraud as well? Is that definite?' At least the file's complete that far, Morland's made his phone call.

'As far as I can tell, given the lack of resources at hand. But the fraud came to light because of a suicide note, and if he was murdered ...' There's no need for me to go on, no need for further explanation.

'I'm sorry, Mr Oliphant, as I explained, I didn't have the file at hand. You do seem to have a problem there.'

I'd like to think that the word 'you' is being used in its widest, plural sense. But I suspect that it's being used in the singular, directed at me in particular. And there's worse.

'So when you were talking to me, you didn't have the Salkeld information at hand. But you said you wanted to talk to me. Why? What did you want to talk to me about?'

I'm trying to make sense of this and getting nowhere.

'Please calm down, Mr Oliphant. I'll explain.'

'I think that would be a damn good idea.' I move closer to the door, the signal seems to be weakening. I open the door slightly, I feel as if I'm granting the radio waves easier access.

'You have a greater problem than you think, Mr Oliphant. I have a second file on my desk dealing with an entirely different matter, but you're also involved. I understood, mistakenly, that you were ringing about that second case. Let me get you up to speed.'

I hate that phrase. People who use it are only slightly better than those who wiggle their fingers in the air to signify quotation marks. Warrington is unaware of my feelings, he keeps talking.

'On your way to Forestcrag yesterday you saw the aftermath of a minor accident. There was a police car involved, on escort duty. A private security firm was doing the transfer. You stopped and spoke to the escort officer, Danny Bateman . . .'

'You're telling me things I already know, Superintendent.'

He doesn't like that, he doesn't like being interrupted. I can hear the intake of breath. He's wondering whether he ought to be rude to me. He decides against it. He'll go in the opposite direction.

'Danny Bateman is dead, Mr Oliphant. He was killed by the prisoner he was escorting. The driver of the van was a witness. The prisoner was quite calm until Danny came back to the van after speaking to you. He mentioned your name, said you were going up to Forestcrag. Then the prisoner went wild. He'd been released from his chains – standard procedure after an accident – and attacked Constable Bateman. He managed to get hold of his nightstick. He beat him about the head, fractured his skull. He also attacked the van driver, left him unconscious. Then he escaped.'

'Jesus Christ!' I didn't know Danny well enough. He won't have been in tears when I was kicked out of the force. But he was a good, solid policeman. He had a wife, kids, perhaps even grandkids now. He was probably due for retirement in a year or so. 'I'm sorry,' I add, but it doesn't seem enough. And Superintendent Warrington hasn't finished.

'The prisoner's name is Harry Simpson, Mr Oliphant. You were his arresting officer five years ago. Remember him?'

The name is too familiar. 'Robbery with firearms. GBH. We wanted him for murder, we thought we had him, but he got away with manslaughter. I thought he was in Rampton.'

'He was cured.' Warrington's voice is dripping with cynicism. 'No longer criminally insane. Transferred up here. And now he's killed Danny Bateman.'

I can't say anything. Warrington's waiting for me to speak, waiting for a reaction, but there's nothing there. I find Sly at my side, ready to catch me if I fall. Can I look that bad?

'You okay, boss?' Sly whispers. I nod, but he stays where he is.

'Are you still there, Mr Oliphant?'

'Still here, Warrington.'

'Mr Oliphant, Harry Simpson only became violent when he heard your name. The van driver thinks he heard him saying something about "getting the bastard," and I have reason to believe the bastard he wants to get is you. I believe you're in danger. And there's nothing I can do to help you for at least forty-eight hours.'

'Hold on,' I say, 'if you know all this you must have been out to the van driver. Why can't you get someone in to help, it's only a mile and a half down the road from the accident?'

'We know about it in the same way we know about Salkeld, Mr Oliphant. A passing farmer found the driver, took him back to the farm, the local doctor managed to get out to him. He'll be okay. But there are trees down all around you, roads blocked.'

'A helicopter. You could fly some of your men in.'

'All grounded because of the weather. Cloud base is too low, and there's worse weather coming.'

'So what do I do?'

'Lie low, Mr Oliphant. Keep out of the limelight. If he's coming after you, first of all he's got to get there. Then he's got to find out where you are. Then he's got to do something. He's not armed, Danny Bateman's gun was still strapped in his car. I think you'll be okay.'

'Thank you for that small piece of reassuring advice, information and opinion. It's really heartening to know you think I'll be okay. But you're the one sitting behind a tidy desk in a warm office with a cup of tea and a chocolate digestive biscuit. You're not the one he's trying to kill. Thanks for nothing.' I disconnect, look up at Sly. He seems very large, very reassuring.

'Problems, boss?' he asks.

I begin to laugh. Someone wants to kill me. I'm standing in a freezing cold garage with a dead body. I'm looking for a murderer, a different murderer's looking for me. The pressure's building and I'm the release valve. Then Sly asks me if I have any problems. I feel like hitting him or hugging him, I don't know which.

'You all right, boss?'

Behind Sly I can see the outline of Salkeld's body. Death is so permanent. I take a deep breath. 'No,' I say, 'I'm not all right. But I *am* alive. I just hope it's a long-term situation.'

Chapter Twelve

We head into the Tesseract. There's an air of normality about the place, children are running around, coffee bars are open. It isn't crowded, too few people made it through before the snow. But those who are there make the place seem busy, almost friendly. Sly's leading me towards the pool viewing area, I'm telling him that part of the phone conversation he missed, filling him in on the details of Salkeld's murder. Or suicide. I'm not quite sure myself which it is, I'd like his opinion, but when I finish speaking he says nothing.

'Well?' I ask.

'Difficult,' he says. 'If I was you, I'd leave it alone. Leave it for the police. The snow won't last for ever, they'll get here. And Eve Marton won't be going far anyway.'

It would be easy to do that, so easy. So tempting.

'But I'm not you. And you normally do the opposite of everything I tell you anyway. So it doesn't really make much difference what I say.'

'And the Harry Simpson threat?'

Sly pushes open the door to the viewing area. There's a high-pitched cacophony of scream and echo, yells of excitement. Parents shout warnings and scolds, children ignore them. And flowing around and over and beneath this babble of human discord there's the tumble and splash of water. There's water in pools, cascading down slides, arching from fountains, bubbling in Jacuzzis; there's water slopping and speeding, rushing and rolling, water paddling round islands, diving from cannons, water roiled and carved into waves and foam.

'If the police can't get here, what makes you think Harry Simpson will?'

We sit down on the balcony. It's hot, I take off my coat then bend down and remove my boots and socks.

'Determination?' I'm trying to put a face to the name. What did I do that made him hate me so much? Lock him up? That wasn't my decision, it was the judge's, the court's, the jury's. Harry Simpson. Did I do anything else to him? There were days, bad days, when being the good, honest, decent cop would get too much. All it needed, when cynicism, frustration with the due course of the law took over, was a word with the right person. Then a prisoner – sorry, a suspect, the accused – could have an accident. Fall downstairs while struggling. Hit his head on a doorframe. Even indulge in self-mutilation. As long as it was out of the view of the video cameras. Most villains didn't complain, they knew there'd be worse to come if they did. Had I subjected Harry Simpson to that treatment? I couldn't remember. The name and the crimes he committed were familiar, but there was nothing beyond that. The crimes themselves were impressive enough; if he indulged himself in robbery with firearms, GBH, if we suspected him of murder, then he was unlikely to be the quiet, level-headed type. He'd killed Danny Bateman simply because he's heard my name mentioned. Would he let a few miles of snow stop him from finding me? Catching me? Killing me? Was he that determined?

'I don't think I could dislike anyone that much,' Sly says, 'not enough to wade through drifts of snow to get you.'

The noise below us increases in volume. Paula's there, and all Sly's kids, they've seen us and are trying to attract our attention. Sly waves at them.

'What if someone hurt Paula? Or Gav, or Tim, or Jo, or

103

Julia. Would you still feel like that?'

'There'd be an opportunity sometime, boss. I wouldn't say "Oh, some idiot's hurt my family, I must take revenge now." If I needed to take revenge, there'd be a time. I'd wait. It would come round.'

'Perhaps this is Harry Simpson's moment.'

'Well, it might be best if you did as the Superintendent said. Lie low till the snow melts.'

'But I've a possible murder to investigate.'

'See! You don't listen to a bloody word I say!'

'Are you coming swimming, Uncle Billy?' It's Gav, immediately below us, hands cupped into a loud-hailer. Sly looks at me.

'Are you going swimming?' he asks, 'I brought your trunks and a towel, they're down by the pool. And I can see Kirsty over there in the water, she seems to have attracted a small entourage.'

I follow Sly's finger. Kirsty's with a pack of young people, boys and girls, about six of them. They all seem about her age – that is, the boys are too large, too male, and the girls are unaware of the effect they're having on those boys.

'It would be a pity to spoil their fun. It would probably cramp Kirsty's style, having her old dad floating alongside her. And besides, there's so much else to deal with at the moment.' I don't want Sly to agree with me, I want him to force me down into the pool. I want to spend a little time with my daughter.

'No one, not Eve Marton or anyone else, is going to get off-site in the next hour. And if you want to stay hidden in case bogeyman Simpson's coming after you, well, it's pretty anonymous in a swimming pool. You can't remember his face, why should he be able to remember yours? Come on, boss. Relax. Just for a while.'

'Sly, there's one more thing. If Simpson does come after me, if he finds me and I'm with you and Paula and the kids ...'

Sly cuts me off. 'I've already thought of that, boss. First thing I thought of. What do you want me to say? That you'd better go, get away from us? Just in case a madman appears on the doorstep? No way, boss, no way.'

'If he does get through, Sly, I'll go. I'll have to, for all of you, for Kirsty as well. If I do . . .'

'We'll deal with it when – if – it happens. And don't worry, I'll look after her.'

We've come to an agreement, the best we can manage under the circumstances. There's nothing better I could hope for than to have Sly looking after Kirsty.

'Well,' I say, 'the water's waiting. And the kids.'

It takes us no more than ten minutes to get down to the changing rooms and swap outdoor clothes for swimming costumes. Despite Sly repeatedly telling me he hates water, despite the cold that his sneezing warns is imminent, he decides to join me in the pool. It's the first time I've seen him dressed in so little. He's taken his shirt off in the past, when we've been working together in hot weather, but he's normally worn a vest. His arms and legs are muscled, I'd expected that, but so is his chest, even his stomach. He has wiry curls of dark hair all over his upper torso. He looks like an athlete, and he's wearing a pair of proper swimming trunks. I stand beside him in my shorts and suck in my stomach, wonder why my arms are so slender, why the hairs on my chest seem so anaemic. Then I follow him into the pool itself.

The new perspective makes it more difficult to appreciate the size of the place. From above, from the viewing balcony, the different pools and slides were easily visible. From below, within the complex itself, the main pool seems surrounded by a jungle of exotic plants; paths curve away, stairs climb, portions of slides are visible. I think I know where everything ought to be; if I walk to my right I should find the bottom of the tallest water splash. But the top of the same slide is away to my right. My sense of direction has gone exploring without me.

105

I'm about to start searching for it when Tim and Jo launch themselves at me. They're wet, they seem to have a surplus of arms and legs, and they drag me into the water. It's a sloping entrance to the pool, like a tiled beach, and the water's warm. If Sly and Paula had been conniving to find a way to help me forget my problems, they've found the right answer in setting the twins on me. Their attempts to drown me may not have been deliberate, but they work well as a team and their effectiveness is unquestionable. They both seem to want to occupy the same space, and that space is inevitably in my possession. In the end I give up, accept that I'm their sea-horse, and carry them round the shallows on my back. I head into slightly deeper water to throw them off – they're both wearing armbands – and then let them chase me and catch me so we can repeat the process. When I feel the skin has been torn from my knees I cry for mercy and usher the children back to their parents.

Sly puts down his book as we approach. 'You're a born child-minder, boss,' he smiles, welcomes the twins into warm, wide towels.

'I think I deserve a rest,' I say, lower myself into a plastic seat.

'Don't bet on it.' Paula draws my attention to the gaggle of young people heading towards us. Kirsty's waving at me. She's with two girls, about the same age as her, I'd guess. They're wearing bikinis, they sway gracefully as they walk. The boys behind them are trying to look at the water, the plants, other people in the pool, but their eyes keep returning to the rear view of the girls in front of them.

'Hiya, Dad!' Kirsty bends over me, kisses me on the top of the head. 'Isn't this a fantastic place? Have you tried the big slide yet? It's awesome, really great, I'm so enjoying myself.' She steps to one side, introduces the others. 'This is Amy and Claire, and Phil – I think you met him last night – Ben and Will.'

Each of them nods at me in turn. Amy's small, dark-eyed and smiling, while Claire's taller, wide-shouldered, red-haired. The boys are ape-like, bristling with hormones and scanty facial hair, not sure how to control the new muscles they're developing.

'Hello, everyone,' I say. I've never had the opportunity to associate with Kirsty's friends before, I'm not sure what to say to them, how to greet them.

'This is my Dad,' Kirsty says, 'he's a detective.'

I roll my eyes. 'Security consultant,' I correct her. I don't really want to be reminded of the responsibilities associated with being a detective.

Kirsty's insistent. '"Detective" sounds better, more romantic.'

'Are you being a detective now?' asks Amy, a joke in her voice.

'He can't say,' Kirsty winks at me, 'confidentiality and all that.'

'I *can* say,' I insist, 'I'm *not* a detective and I'm simply sitting here trying to enjoy myself.'

'He's working undercover,' Kirsty says in a ridiculously loud aside.

'I bet it's a murder.' Amy's voice is melodramatic. She looks round at her companions. 'I think we should be seriously concerned, we've all seen the films. The murderer always looks for groups of people, like us, and picks them off one at a time. There's always an even mix of good-looking girls in bikinis – that's us – and hunky boys.' She puts a hand on her hip, head on one side, glances at Philip, Will and Ben. 'Well, you can't have everything.'

'I'm the more mature type,' Phil announces loftily. I can't tell if he's joking. 'I'm into British genre films, you know the stuff, Hitchcock, Carol Reed, things like *Brighton Rock*, *The Third Man*, *Room at the Top*, *The Loneliness of the Long Distance Runner*.' I have a feeling he may have recently completed a Film Studies module at university.

'Have you seen that one *Pretentious Crap*?' Will asks.

Ben pulls the conversation back onto course. 'Those

slasher films,' he says, 'have you noticed it's always the girls who get it first.' He's the tallest of the three boys, he needs a shave. 'And it's usually the short dark-haired dip-head who's first of all.'

Amy pretends to be affronted. 'Is that me? Are you suggesting I'm a dip-head?'

'It's okay, Amy,' adds Will, shorter but more well-muscled than his friend, 'you're quite safe. The first one to go always has big boobs.' He backs away, willing her to chase him, and she doesn't disappoint him. The others urge them on, then they follow, eager to miss nothing. Only Kirsty stays behind.

'Go on,' I say, 'join them.'

'Is everything all right, Dad? What was the problem this morning?'

I could tell her it was nothing, but I try not to lie to my daughter. 'Someone found dead, love. Suicide. They just needed me to look into it.' What I say isn't a lie, it's just not all the truth. Or perhaps it is the truth. That's the real problem. That's why I can't settle. That's why I need to work at things, sit down somewhere quiet, think. And I can't do it here. It's helped me, seeing Kirsty with her friends. I won't feel so guilty now if I spend more time on the case. 'Look,' I say, nodding in the direction of the water-splash, 'they seem a good bunch of kids. I'm quite happy to potter about by myself, relax, see what else is going on. There's no need for you to hang around. You've got a key for the lodge, you're not the stupid, immature type. You go off with your friends. Enjoy yourself!'

'Are you sure?' She's already half-turned to follow them.

'Go! And don't do anything I wouldn't do.'

'Yes, Dad. Anything you say, Dad.' She runs off, waves back at me.

'They seem a nice bunch,' says Paula, peering over the top of her book.

'Very grown up,' adds Sly lasciviously. He's dried the twins, so they're naturally keen to head back into the water.

'You're not turning into a dirty old man, are you?' Paula suggests.

'Always have been. I thought that was why you married me.' Sly reaches his hand out. 'Would you care to join me and our children in the water?'

Paula rises to her feet. 'I'd be delighted. I've another hour to spare before my treatment at the Spa.' She and Sly follow the twins. As they reach the water his arm sneaks round her waist and she moves closer to him. Then his hand moves down, inside the elastic of her swimming costume, and squeezes her behind. She jumps away, squeals with what I suspect is delight, and begins to splash him vigorously.

'I'm going to get changed,' I call to them, but I'm not sure if they hear me. 'See you around.' There's no reply, no response. 'Yeah,' I tell myself,' see you around.'

Chapter Thirteen

I'm hungry. When I check my watch I find it's almost twelve thirty. The day's been too long. I find an area with tables and chairs, potted trees and shrubs play passionless music; a sign tells me I'm in a 'food court'. There are four or five different shops, each selling a different type of food, but only one is open. I'm pleased the limited number of staff on site have been placed in the sandwich boutique rather than 'Take-away Tacos' or 'the Big Burger Bar'. The queue is short, the service prompt, the tea served in a pot rather than a polystyrene beaker, and the meat in my baguette tastes like chicken. There are few people about, I have no problem in finding a table to myself.

I occupy myself with my thoughts. There's a possibility that two murderers are loose, and one of them has me as his target. Why don't I feel worried? Why am I not in hiding? It's because I don't believe Harry Simpson could find his way to Forestcrag, not through last night's storm, not through the snowdrifts. He could, of course, have found somewhere to hide, somewhere to gather his strength before waiting for better weather. He could even have made a superhuman effort and be on site at the moment. But even if that's the case, he doesn't know where I am. He probably doesn't even remember what I look like – I certainly can't put a face to *his* name. He's probably weak, he has no weapons. There are, in short, too many random variables, there's too little concrete information. Yes, I should be careful. Just in case. But that doesn't mean I should dig a hole in the snow and hide away. Especially when there are more worrying things to think about.

Eric Salkeld is dead. The nurse thinks he was murdered; the computer disk says he killed himself. I can choose to believe it was suicide, to believe the disk, to believe that Salkeld was the only one involved in the payroll fraud. Or I can assume it was murder, that the disk was a plant, and that the murderer's motive was to pin the blame entirely on Salkeld. Eve Marton is a suspect; she's computer literate, she's tall and probably quite strong, and her room is next door to Salkeld's. She had the opportunity, the ability and the motivation, if she was somehow involved in the fraud, to kill Salkeld. But so could anyone else. Eve Marton could have been asleep while the murder occurred, the murderer could have prepared the disk beforehand and left it at the scene of crime. What I really need to do is get access to the computer system, find out which account or accounts received the missing money. Then I can tell the police and they can find out who opened those accounts. But even then the names will probably be false, so that won't really help. Backtrack. Think again, Billy. Salkeld was murdered? So investigate the murder. I've a suspect already, Eve Marton. Accuse her of the crime? Not yet, I don't know enough to do that. So I should find out more. So how do I do that?

'Excuse me, are you Billy Oliphant?'

The woman who's interrupted my thoughts is leaning on the table opposite me, looking intently at my face.

'It is, I swear it. Billy Oliphant.'

I don't recognise her. She's smaller than me, in her late twenties or early thirties, hair died bright yellow blonde and cropped short. She's wearing tracksters and training shoes, a loose-fitting sweatshirt.

'I'm sorry,' I say, 'I have an appalling memory for faces. Have we met before?'

111

'Oh, yes,' she answers, and her smile and her nod don't bode well. 'But I do seem to remember you were either drunk or nursing a hangover. I looked different, of course, I had longer hair in those days, brown hair.'

She could be describing me at any time in a five year period which ended only when I was kicked out of the force. It's a past I don't want to discuss.

'I'll put you out of your misery. Nessa. Nessa Clifton.' She holds out her hand; I stand up, perform the necessary politeness. Her grip is firm. 'You still don't remember me, do you?' She sits down as I do.

'I'm afraid not. Look, I'm sorry ...'

'That's all right, there's no need to apologise. Your memory's the first thing to go. As senility approaches. And I did have a different last name then.'

I'd been going to tell her I was too busy to talk, but the grin on her face seems suddenly familiar. Perhaps it's wish fulfilment, she is, when I look more closely, attractive. 'Go on then,' I say, 'give me a clue. We old people need help in matters like this.'

'We were on a course together. Something to do with team building. To be perfectly honest I was prone to having a glass too many myself in those days, I can't remember too much about the course itself. But at night? There were four or five of us, we ended up putting the world to rights.'

The scene seems familiar. The company, the drinking, the discussions, they were always more valuable than the course itself. 'I think I can remember,' I tell her.

'I knew you would. Mind, I can't think of any other names. God, I must have been stewed most of the time.'

'Yes, the specifics aren't too clear.' I want to change the subject, I don't like talking about those days. I don't like the person I was then.

'I was rounder in those days, a bit more flesh on me.' The woman sitting in front of me has the sharp, well-honed look of an athlete, the nylon tracksters cling to prominent calves and muscled thighs. I find myself

112

wondering about her upper body, sheltering beneath the baggy sweatshirt.

'I must have made a good impression, for you to remember me.' I'm not sure how sarcastic my comment is; perhaps I'll let her decide.

'Oh, I wouldn't have known you if Morland hadn't told us all you were here. The name was familiar, then when I saw you there ... I had to look twice. You're looking better than you did then.'

'I must have looked really bad.'

'You did. You just couldn't see it. I suppose being kicked out of the force helped?'

'You don't hold back, do you? But yes, it made me realise how things had deteriorated.'

'You and your wife split up, I heard.'

I'm beginning to wonder if she's been reading my biography. 'Bad news travels far.'

'Yeah. Same thing happened to me. Divorce. He was too jealous.'

'Jealous of the Force?' It's a situation I can understand, even sympathise with. There's something special about police work, something that excludes outsiders. Sometimes it becomes more important than your home, your family.

'The Force? Shit, no. I'd left by then, couldn't stand it. Sexist bastards. Made my life hell. I just told them to stuff it. Then I looked at myself, the person I'd become. I was unfit, overweight, drinking; but at least I could see I had a problem. So I did something about it, took regular exercise. Then I started helping out in a few local gyms, began to train seriously. Running at first, though I was never quite good enough. Same with swimming. But then someone suggested triathlon, I took up cycling and ... well, I was good at it. It began to take over. I spent too much time training. So he left me. He's got kids now, serves him right.'

'So what are you doing here?'

'I'm a fitness trainer. The pay's naff, but the facilities

are good. I can train all I want. I'm good, one of the top five in Britain. But I can get better. I've been to one World Championship, I've been pre-selected for the next. And the Olympics, that's what I really want.'

I'm impressed. I tell her so. She says thank you, gets ready to rise and leave me to my thoughts again. But I won't let her.

'Did you know Eric Salkeld?' I ask.

She raises her eyebrows. 'Past tense, Billy? So the rumour's right. He topped himself.'

'Rumour?'

'It doesn't take long for news to get round. Everyone knows Eric hung himself. And no, I didn't know him. He was the person you went to if there was a problem with pay, but that isn't the same as knowing him. I don't think anyone here *knew* him. He kept himself to himself.'

There's not much else I can ask. I suppose I ought to go back to his room, carry out a proper search. I could even have a look through Eve Marton's stuff, strictly illegal, of course, but who would know? Trouble is, that would mean getting a pass key from Morland or Sam Ellis, and I don't know if they'd let me have one. After all, I'm not a policeman, my investigations aren't official, and neither of them likes me much. But there might be other ways of getting in.

'Do you live on site?'

'Yeah. No point in paying for a flat I wouldn't use. Like I said, I use the facilities here to train, it takes up most of my spare time. So it's handy just to slide into the pit . . .'

'Same building as Eric Salkeld?'

'Same building as all resident staff. Why?'

'Would you mind letting me in? I want to have another look round. I don't have a pass key and I don't want to bother Mr Morland for one.'

'Sure, I was heading back anyway. I just need to put some more clothes on.' She gets up, I follow. I find myself making small talk.

'So what's it like, working here?'

'Crap. Staff turnover's huge, they have to bus cleaners in from miles around. They treat you like shit. Pay's bad, conditions of service are worse. I mean, you get used to the good life in the Force. But here? No pension, no trade unions, management policy of active confrontation over everything, profit's all they ever worry about. But at the same time you've got to be polite to the guests, smile nicely, scrape and bow.' Nessa's leading me down to the main pool entrance, but instead of going in she unlocks a door marked 'staff only'. 'You know,' she continues, 'I was helping one bloke with a work-out session and he made a pass at me. It happens, you get used to it, shrug it off. But this one was persistent, so I said I'd report him. Didn't stop him, though, he offered me money to have sex with him, two hundred quid. So I did what I said I'd do, I told Morland. He said I should have taken the money, *he* would only have offered fifty.'

I whistle my surprise. 'And you're still here?'

'Like I said, I need the job, I need the facilities.' She grins at me with a mouth full of clean white teeth. 'But the guy who propositioned me had a slight accident, fell off one of the benches while he was working out. I was passing at the time, carrying some small weights. And you know what, one of them dropped on him. Bruised his balls something rotten.' She switches on the lights. 'Welcome to my private gym.'

It's a small room with a blue curtain running along one wall, well equipped with benches and weights, a running treadmill and two static cycles, a pile of safety mats and several items of multi-gym machinery that wouldn't look out of place in a torture chamber. A coat and over-trousers are thrown over the back of a plastic chair, a pair of boots nestles beneath.

'Very nice,' I say. 'It can't really be just for you, though?'

Nessa makes a noise somewhere between a grunt and a laugh. 'This is Forestcrag,' she says, kicks off her training shoes and pulls on her trousers, 'there's no such thing as an employee perk.' The boots come next. 'See that curtain? Behind it there's a big sliding door, it opens onto the pool. The original idea was that people could swim, then come in here and do a few exercises, nip back out into the water. But there were always too many kids running about, so now they only open it for special early morning or late evening sessions. Not today, of course, there's not enough demand and anyway, there aren't enough trained staff in. But I must admit, I do tend to use it more than anyone else.' She stands up, stamps her feet firmly into her boots. 'I'm ready if you are.'

Nessa locks the door behind her and leads me back through the complex. We exit by a different door set in a large glass wall, close to where the Tesseract stream flows out into a small lake. The surface is white with snow.

'Must be cold for the lake to freeze over,' I say. It certainly feels cold, especially after the luxury of an hour indoors.

'Yeah. It's shallow, though, only four feet deep. Artificial. Built with a huge plastic pond-liner.'

'A fake lake.'

'Yeah. But nice ice.'

She pushes on ahead of me. There are footprints puncturing the snow, but she doesn't try to place her feet in them. Instead she kicks a fresh track and, even though I benefit from this, I have to shuffle in a half-run to keep up with her. The exertion makes me pant, crystals of frost form on my eyebrows, and the cold tugs at me, holds me back. Nessa doesn't seem affected.

'Isn't this wonderful?' she yells back to me.

'Yes.' It would be rude not to agree with her.

'It makes it all so real. I mean, everything else here is fake. The whole idea's ridiculous, tearing up the wilderness to make a small town and then trying to disguise it as wilderness. But a few inches of snow and it reverts to its wild state.'

There are places where I'm up to my thighs in the few inches of snow, but that in itself is a reason not to argue. I just want to get to the staff residences as quickly as possible.

'There are places where it's still wild, Billy. Just a few hundred yards away, as long as you know the right direction, the forest opens out onto moorland and crag and rock. That's where I go running, out on the moors. I can take you out for a jog later, if you want.'

I know she must be joking, but I've lost my sense of humour as well as my sense of direction, and my voice is becoming a whinge. 'Have we far to go?'

'What?' Nessa seems impatient. 'No, it's just here, round this hedge.' She strides down a small bank, I slip and slide in her wake. Then we're at the door of the staff residence and she's pressing key to lock and we're inside. I feel exhausted, I have to lean against the wall.

'You okay?' Nessa asks.

'No. I don't know why, it's not as if it's far. I just feel . . . shattered. Physically exhausted.'

'It's the cold. Or rather, it's moving from hot to cold environments then back again. And the effort of tramping through snow, don't underestimate that. Then add the fact that you've not got the right clothes. I mean, your boots aren't waterproof, your trousers aren't windproof, and as for your coat! It might pass as a fashion statement, but as a means of keeping you warm and dry . . .?'

'You managed.'

'I'm fitter than you are. It's my job *and* my hobby. And I'm properly dressed.' She dismisses the subject of my abject failure to cope with the weather. 'Anyway, you know where Salkeld's room is. Mine's along here. Underneath his, actually.'

'He was directly above you?'

'That's what I said.'

'And did you hear anything last night?'

'Nothing. Mind you, I do sleep soundly. It takes a bomb

to get me out of bed in the morning.'

'Eve Marton discovered Salkeld's body, she spent last night here, because of the weather. She had the room next door to him.'

Nessa curls up her nose. 'She's a cow, Eve Marton.'

'You don't like her, then?' Perhaps my sense of humour's coming back. Nessa ignores it.

'No one likes her. She's a stuck-up bitch, thinks she knows everything.' Her voice doesn't seem angry. Her tone is matter-of-fact, as if she's stating the obvious. 'He probably woke her up, gurgling or something, trying to strangle himself but not doing it properly; he looked as if he was that type of person. Eve Marton probably heard him, went to see what was happening. I can just imagine it.' She adopts Eve Marton's voice, it's uncannily accurate. '"Eric, you can't do *anything* right. Put the rope here. Spread your legs and dangle. Oh, you're hopeless, come here, I'll hang onto your legs, then we'll get it over with as quickly as possible. After all, I do need my beauty sleep."'

'You're a born mimic, Nessa.'

'No, it's just that she's an easy target. You got a key for Eric's room?'

'Actually, no. I was hoping it would be open. And if it isn't, I thought I could force the lock, I've got a credit card ...'

'Put it away, Billy. It's a good job I'm here. Follow me.' She moves down the corridor to the door of what must be her own room, uses a key to get in, motions me after her.

The place is a tip. Clothes are escaping from open drawers, they're frozen by the room light; socks and knickers, T-shirts and blouses, they all huddle together in heaps on the floor. The bed's not made. There's a makeshift washing-line strung across the room, each end nailed to a wall, and from it hang shorts and tracksuits, sports bras and headbands. There's a litter-bin overflowing in one corner. The bedside table is cluttered with tea-rimmed mugs and half-full glasses, open boxes of tampons and contraceptive pills, a clock, a bowl containing several condom packets. There's a damp, musty smell. I see this (absorb would be a better word, the mess appeals to all senses) in one glance round the room. Nessa catches the look of disgust on my face.

'I'm not much good at tidy,' she says. 'No time. 'Scuse me.' She pushes me to one side, opens the drawer in the table, but whatever she's looking for isn't there. I'm in the way so she moves me again, I trip on a book hidden beneath a shirt while she digs in a box full of CDs. I pick up the book, for something to do while she's busy, it's a tatty copy of *Travels with My Aunt*. She looks up, sees me with the book in hand. 'I'm terrible,' she explains, 'I find authors I like and I have to read everything they've written. Scrape the clothes away and you'll probably find another dozen by the same writer hiding underneath.' I confirm the statement by noticing two more books and a loaf of bread in a plastic shopping bag.

'Not that you have the time to read,' I point out, but the sarcasm escapes her.

'Yes!' she cries triumphantly, taking a key-ring from a pink, fluffy handbag. 'One of these should fit,' she says, holding them up and jangling them for me. We head back out into the corridor and she anticipates my question.

'If you lose a key they charge you a tenner. And when we looked at the keys . . .'

'We?'

'Me, some of the girls staying here a while back. We found there were only a few different types. So we had some cut, and I got to keep them 'cos I've been here longest.' She holds out the keys for me to examine. They're for three-lever mortise locks, I could probably have breathed on the door and it would have opened.

'Come on then,' I say, 'let's see what's inside.' We head back upstairs.

The door opens on the second key. I lead the way. The room feels warm and dry. The bed's been made. I hope

119

whoever did it hasn't removed Salkeld's belongings. I begin with the wardrobe. There are two suits, several pairs of trousers, a dozen shirts. On the floor are two pairs of shoes, one brown, one black. There are shelves in the wardrobe, one contains socks (paired), another underpants (laid flat), a third, pullovers (stacked neatly). At least Salkeld was methodical.

'Jesus!' Nessa's leaning over my shoulder. 'What was his hobby, folding and filing?'

'Some people can't help it,' I say. 'It's like an illness.'

'Well this one was definitely sick.' She closes the wardrobe door. 'Desk drawers?' she suggests.

'That's exactly where I was heading.' Before I do so I run a hand along the top of the wardrobe, not because I hope to find anything, but because I don't want Nessa to think I'm blindly following her instructions. Anyway, there's nothing there, not even a layer of dust. Salkeld must have been fanatical about cleanliness.

The desk drawers reveal little. There are pyjamas and vests, various creams (I think they're for eczema) and medicines, some inhalers; in a small wooden box there's a wedding ring and some cuff-links; a few postcards; a short washing-line and some pegs, I check the walls to find out if, as in Nessa's room, there are nails to hold the line up, but I can't see any. There are pens, paper and envelopes, a book of word puzzles, a small radio.

'Did you ever hear the radio?' I ask Nessa.

'Yeah. Not loud, mind, and never music. Always voices. Never loud enough to disturb me, anyway.'

'How long had he been living here?'

'Two or three weeks? There was talk, gossip, about some marital break-up. But that was just from new staff, I could have told them he used to stay regularly this time of year. Pressures of work, I imagine. Not that I used to talk to him. He was a loner. Shared nothing.'

I get down on my knees and look under the bed; there's nothing there. There's nothing under the mattress, behind the wardrobe or the desk. The flooring's some kind of vinyl, glued down, if I could lift it I would, but there'd be nothing underneath. Salkeld seems to have lived his life in a vacuum. He's been dead for less than a day and already there's nothing left of him but a few items of clothing. He had few possessions and no personality.

'Sad, isn't it?' Nessa says. 'If this is all he had, I'm not surprised he topped himself. Come on, I've had enough. There's nothing here.'

She seems eager to leave and she's right – there's nothing there. I climb to my feet, Nessa's already left the room and is heading down the corridor. I lock the door behind me and, since the keys are already in my hand, try the first one in the door of Eve Marton's room. It opens easily.

'Hey,' calls Nessa, hurrying back towards me, 'you can't do that. That's Eve's room.'

'That's why I'm going in,' I tell her.

'But don't you need a search warrant or something?'

'Only if I get caught.'

Eve's travel bag is neat and square on the bed. There'll be nothing untoward in there, I'm certain of that.

'Billy, what if someone comes?'

'Then we'll hear them. Or even better, you can go and keep watch at the top of the stairs.'

'I'll stay here, thank you.' She moves close as I open the wardrobe doors.

'Well, well,' I say, reach in and bring out a coat-hanger. Slung beneath it is a shiny black basque made of latex, fishnet stockings attached to it by suspenders. Slung over the hanger is a pair of elbow length gloves. I hand them to Nessa, she wrinkles her nose in distaste.

'And that's not all.' I bend down, produce a pair of stiletto-heeled boots. 'Quite a kinky little madam, our Miss Marton, eh?'

'It's got nothing to do with us.' She pushes past me, puts the hanger and its contents back in the wardrobe. I let her

121

do so, put back the boots myself, lie them on top of a plain brown cardboard box.

'I think we'd better go,' I say, back out of the room and lock the door. I hand her the keys, lead her back into her room.

She seems pleased to be back. 'Want a coffee or a tea? Has to be black, mind.' She examines the floor and the clothing on it, picks up a blouse. There's a mug beneath it, empty, but with a ring of brown close to the rim.

'Nothing for me,' I say.

'What d'you think, then?'

'About what?'

'The gear, Billy! I mean, it's strange but . . .'

'If it's what turns her on, Nessa, as long as it doesn't harm anyone else, it's got nothing to do with us. We shouldn't even have been in there.'

She raises her eyebrows. 'I was only following you.' She giggles. 'Christ, I was nervous. It gets the adrenaline going. And it's amazing what you find.'

'Amazing, but irrelevant. Just forget you saw it.'

'Irrelevant? How do you know? I mean, perhaps, it *is* relevant. Maybe . . .' She tails off.

'Perhaps, nothing, there's no "perhaps", no "maybe". Just someone with sexual preferences a little different to your own.'

'Yes, I suppose so. And you're right, we shouldn't have been in there. But every time I see her, I'll imagine what she looks like. God, I won't be able to look her in the face!'

'I think I'd better go now,' I say. 'Thanks for letting me into Salkeld's room.'

'You're welcome. I'm sorry . . .'

'It's okay.' I find my coat, it's still damp. I need to get back to the lodge, dry out, think what happens next.

'See you around, Billy?'

'Yeah.' I leave her room, trudge along the corridor. She's wondering what's happened, why I'm suddenly so abrupt, but I can't tell her. I open the door and step out into the cold. I think I know the direction of the lodge, there's a rough track funnelled in the snow and I follow it.

There's too much to think about. Did Salkeld see Eve Marton dressed like that in her room? No, that can't be it, she was only there for one night. But if she hadn't known she would be staying, why did she have the whole regalia with her in the room? Something was wrong there, something to go back to. Perhaps Salkeld saw her somewhere else, in a special club? If so, it must have been back in town. Let's say he saw her. He recognised her. He blackmailed her? And then she took her revenge. But how did the fraud fit in? Was she implicated in that as well? There are still too many possibilities, too many permutations. I could rearrange the facts to point in many different directions. Eve Marton might be innocent of everything except enjoying the feel of rubber against her skin, and that's no crime.

My slow, shuffling, snow-kicking gait may not be effective, but it's persistent; I can recognise the car almost hidden beneath a loaf of snow, the lodge beyond a welcome destination. I know what I'll have to do. Have a bath, drink some tea, dry off my clothes. And sometime later, when it's dark, when no one's about, I'll make sure Eve Marton's not in her room. Then I'll go back. My fingers close around the hard, cold metal of Nessa's key, the one I sneaked from her key-ring. I'll go back and see what else I can find, look in the boxes in the wardrobe. Just in case.

Chapter Fourteen

'Dad! Where've you been? We were just going to send the St Bernard out to find you.' Kirsty and her new friends are clustered round the table playing *Cluedo*. I try to remember their names as I lever myself out of my boots. There's Claire with the red hair, and Amy. Then there are the three boys, Phil – I met him the night before – Ben and . . . What was the last one called?

'I met an old friend,' I say, 'we ended up talking.'

'What's her name, boss?' Sly's voice carries from the kitchen.

'How do you know it's a woman?'

'You don't have man friends, 'cept for me 'n' Norm. We're the only ones who can put up with you. So who is she?'

'Her name's Nessa,' I say, 'I knew her in the force.'

'I like your coat, Mr Oliphant,' says Claire. I look at Kirsty.

'I didn't say a thing,' she protests.

'Uncle Billy,' shouts Tim, 'Uncle Billy,' echoes Jo, 'we built a snowman!'

'Will you lot shut up!' Gav's lying on the floor, his head a few feet from the television, intent on watching an old black-and-white film; I can recognise Robert Mitchum in a fedora.

'Professor Plum,' says the boy whose name I can't remember.

'It's got eyes 'n' a nose ...'

'... 'n' a mouth 'n' buttons on its tummy ...'

'So who's Nessa?'

'... in the library ...'

'I can't hear a thing!'

'No, really, I like it, Mr Oliphant.'

'Do I know her?'

'... with the revolver.'

'Ladies and gentlemen!' I yell above the tumult. The silence is immediate and rewarding. 'I'm going to have a bath!'

The bath is large, the water hot and plentiful; I choose a small plastic bottle of liquid marked 'soothing' to create more bubbles than I could ever need. Then I begin the ritual of submersion. First I stand in the water (having judged, by waving my hand in it, that it won't remove the skin from my body) and inhale the steamy perfume. Then I kneel down and lower my bottom onto my heels. This lets my hands swish the water around, making sure there are no hot or cold spots, and I decide whether to adjust the temperature by adding more water. If all is well I hold onto the sides of the bath and push my legs towards the taps, then allow my bottom to descend slowly. This is the time when the most delicate parts of me are immersed – if the water's too hot they soon let me know. The final act is when I slide forward and allow the water to cover me entirely, up to the neck; that's when the sweat begins to break out on my forehead.

I've read that having a bath uses far more energy than showering, and that the hot water causes the body's blood supply to go into overload, with great potential for heart attacks. Personally, I feel that this functional stress is more than countered by the relaxation the bather enjoys; at least, it is if the bather can remain in his bath long enough to relax. It's clear that I'm not going to be allowed this privilege.

The noise I can hear is the phone ringing. I'm tempted to let my head sink beneath the water so I can't hear anything, but I suspect my breath would run out before the phone

125

stops. To make matters worse, the phone is on the other side of the room, lying in the pile of clothing I discarded only a few minutes before.

I push myself out of the water, climb out of the bath, pad across the room and grab the phone. If it had a neck I'd throttle it.

'What do you want?' I ask.

'Is that Billy Oliphant?' The voice belongs to Sam Ellis.

'No, this is Bum, Fluff and Scratchitt, Solicitors. Bum speaking.'

'Oh, I'm sorry, I must have . . .' His voice tails away. It takes a long time for any stimulus to reach his brain, and even when it gets there he's unsure what to do with it.

'Yes, Sam, it's Billy Oliphant here. You've just got me out of the bath, so whatever you want had better be important.' I'm beginning to get cold, I climb back into the bath, making sure I don't drop the phone in the water.

'I've some information to pass on. David Morland said I should get you to come and see him, but I thought I could tell you on the phone . . .'

'Just as well, Sam, because nothing's going to get me out of this bath for at least an hour now. So why don't you just tell me what you want to tell me, then we can all go back to enjoying ourselves in our pleasant, innocent little ways.'

'There's a car been broken into.'

I nod. My chin sets ripples dancing down the bath and back again. Surely Morland can't want me to investigate that as well. No, Ellis said he was only passing on information. Does that mean the theft is less important than what was stolen? 'Go on,' I say, 'get to the point.' He's got more information, but he wants to tell me the whole story. He wants to confess. He needs absolution.

'The car belongs to Sir Charles Plumpton.'

I wonder if he's a landed Sir, or a parvenu Sir, or merely a political appointee Sir. Is that why Morland wants me to know? Would have been quite so concerned if it had been an ordinary punter who'd suffered?

126

'So, poor Chuck Plumpton's car's been broken into. Is he a local Sir?'

'Sir Charles owns all the land round here, Mr Oliphant, except for the site itself and the access road.'

'So Sir Charles yells because his car ... is it a Range Rover?'

'How did you know ...?'

'Couldn't be anything else. So he's had a window broken and something nicked. What was it? A multi-load CD player? Lap-top computer? Golf clubs? It had better be something good.'

'It was a rifle. A high-powered rifle and ten rounds of ammunition. And they didn't even have to break a window, Sir Charles must have left the car unlocked. Swears he didn't, mind you, but between you and me, he's a bit of an old dodderer. Anyway, Mr Morland thought you'd better know.'

The water suddenly feels cold. I can feel a shiver like a whirlpool snaking through the water. 'Tell Morland thank you.'

'Don't you want to know where the car is?'

'No.'

'You are going to look at it, aren't you?'

'No. I'm no forensic officer. What good would it do?'

'So what are you going to do?'

'Think. Is there anything else?'

'No. I've done as I was told. I thought you would at least have wanted to look at the scene of crime. I mean, why would anyone want to steal a rifle? Especially here, when we're all stuck on site? No one can get in, no one can get out, what's he going to do ...?'

I cut him off. I already know the answer to his question. Why would anyone want to steal a rifle? To shoot someone. Who would want to shoot someone? Harry Simpson. And who would he want to shoot? Me.

Chapter Fifteen

I don't need this. One thought crowds all others from my mind. It muscles in. Even if I'd wanted to think about Eve Marton dressed in her latex, she stands no chance. The shadow of Harry Simpson (nothing more than a shadow because I still can't give him a face) bullies and threatens its way into my consciousness. The light glints on the grey gunmetal of his rifle. He lowers it, points it at me, laughs, squeezes the trigger.

He doesn't even need to do that. It's not a shotgun, some blunt farmer's machine for shooting rusty crows; it's not a groom-polished weapon brought out every August for a ritual massacre then put back in the gun cabinet for another year. It's a rifle – a powerful rifle according to Sam Ellis – so all Simpson has to do is hide away and wait. He probably doesn't even need a telescopic sight. Just line up the figure in the V-notch and fire. Would that give him enough pleasure? Or would he want to make me suffer? Would he want me to know in advance what was going to happen? Did I hurt him that much?

The water's beginning to cool; the window's darkening with approaching night. I should get out of the bath or run more hot water, I should draw the curtains; I do none of these. I'm incapable of movement. I'm incapable of coherent thought. I know I ought to do something, but I can't imagine what that something might be. I'm helpless and want to remain so. I want someone to tell me what to do. I want someone, anyone, to pull the plug from the bath, to raise me to my feet and wrap me in a warm towel, to fetch a new mug of tea. I want someone to tell me everything will be all right, don't worry. For the first time in two days I think of Jen. Jen in Canada, Jen sending me emails, letters, phone calls, Jen feeling so close but being so far away. Too far away.

Despite the hubbub of noise coming from the room next door I know I'm alone. No, not quite alone. Just behind me is the rasping breath of Harry Simpson, while beckoning me on is the crooked finger of poor dead Eric Salkeld. Who needs companions like this?

'Dad.' It's Kirsty's voice at the door. 'Sorry to interrupt you, is it all right for me to go out with Phil and the rest of them? There's a disco on tonight and I'm invited to Will's house beforehand for something to eat.'

I hear the words but they don't penetrate beyond the outer edges of my consciousness.

'Are you all right, Dad?' There's concern in Kirsty's voice, and that forces a reaction.

'Hello,' I call through the door. 'Sorry, I was dozing, love. I'm pleased you woke me. What time is it?'

'Almost four. Did you hear me asking about tonight? About going out? It would be all six of us, and you and Sly and Paula if you want. There's a disco. It probably won't be too loud for you if you come early on.'

The volume warning clearly modifies the invitation; she doesn't really want me there. That's good, it means I don't have to make an excuse for not being near her.

'You go and enjoy yourself,' I tell her, 'I might pop in and see you for a few minutes. What time does it finish?'

'Late. But it doesn't matter, we can stay at Will's. It's just him and his dad in a lodge as big as this, there's plenty of room.'

I'm too engrossed in my own worries to listen to what she's saying, but I nod as any good father should.

'Sounds okay to me. Enjoy yourself.'

'Thanks Dad,' Kirsty echoes. Then they're gone.

By the time I'm dressed they've left the lodge. Gav is pleased, the twins less so. Normally I'd sit with them, play with them, but not now.

Sly sits down beside me, dabbing at his nose with a succession of paper handkerchiefs. 'Anything I can do to help, boss?'

'I'm moving out,' I say quietly. 'There's a gun, a high-powered rifle, been stolen from some idiot's unlocked car. It might just be an opportunistic theft, but it might also be Harry Simpson. I can't gamble on it not being Simpson, I can't risk you and Paula and the kids, or Kirsty. So I'm going to move out.'

Sly can appreciate a logical argument when he hears it. 'Where will you go?'

'Staff accommodation. I'll clear it with Morland, tell him not to spread it around. I'll be okay, it's just till the snow clears and the police get through. I haven't said anything to Kirsty, if she asks where I am, just tell her something came up. Tell her I'm pretending to be a detective.'

'Okay, boss. Anything I can do?'

'I don't think so. Unless you want to throw my stuff in a bag for me while I ring Morland?'

Sly's already out of his seat and heading for my room. I ring Morland, cut through his niceties. 'I need a room in the staff accommodation block,' I tell him, 'because that idiot Plumpton carries a rifle around in his car and then leaves the bloody thing unlocked.' I override his attempts to interrupt, explain about Harry Simpson. That quietens him, he doesn't want to think about a mad gunman on the loose in Forestcrag. 'No one,' I insist, 'is to know about this except you and me. Do you understand?' He assures me he does, and we agree to meet at the residence in twenty minutes. I don't relish struggling through the snow again, but I feel better knowing that Morland is less fit than me and has to travel twice as far.

'Here,' says Paula's voice behind me, 'you'd better take these to keep you occupied.' She hands me four or five paperbacks.

'You heard?'

She nods. 'Sly tells me everything.'

'It's only a precaution, Paula. Just in case. I'm sure nothing'll happen.'

She doesn't say anything else, just comes up to me and hugs me. I'm halfway to persuading myself I'm being silly when Sly appears with my bag. I can't back out now.

'Take these,' Sly says, throwing me his overalls, 'they should keep you dry for a while. And this.' He passes his anorak across, it's well-padded, lined with fleece.

'But . . .' I begin to protest.

'I've still got a coat. You never know, you might have to go outside again. You'll need to keep warm.'

'Okay,' I say.

'I'll keep the phone beside me,' Sly gestures at his pocket. 'Ring me even if there's the slightest suspicion that there's a problem.'

'I will.' This is like saying goodbye to a friend you think you won't see for years. I can already hear the strings playing long, sweet, sad notes in the background, I can see the steam and smoke clouding the railway platform. I have to bring the scene to an end. 'Right, I'm off.' I pick up my bag, shrug myself into Sly's voluminous anorak, and step out into the gloom. It's beginning to snow again.

Chapter Sixteen

The door of the staff residence is open, Morland's waiting for me inside. He has a key, he leads me down the corridor and opens the door of a room remarkably similar to Eric Salkeld's. There's a plastic bag on the bed, I open it to find tins of beans and packets of pasta, a loaf of white bread, tea, powdered milk, margarine and other staples.

'A present from you?' I say. 'I'm flattered.'

'Don't be. I just want you out of the way. I'd prefer it if you were off the site completely, but since that's impossible, I'd suggest you stay hidden. The kitchen's next door. Keep quiet, keep your curtains closed, and nobody needs know you're here.'

'Thank you for your concern over my well-being.'

'I don't give a fuck about you, Mr Oliphant, and I've no doubt you return the compliment.'

I could take the time to explain the meaning of irony, but I'm sure he's well educated enough to recognise it on his own. He clearly feels a need to say how much he dislikes me, and he's telling me now in case I'm not around to-morrow.

'You're wrong,' I tell him, 'I do care about you. If someone was going to kill *you* I'd try to stop them. That's because I want to see you being sacked when the board of directors finds out how you've been mismanaging the company, losing them all that money. Would you mind closing the door behind you when you leave? There's a terrible draught in here.'

He slams the door, and I hear him stamping down the corridor. Then there's quiet. The building's grim, prison-like; it seems to discourage any contact with other humans. It's easy to believe that Eric Salkeld could have killed himself if he'd lived here for two weeks, and I can't imagine Nessa or Eve Marton spending time in their rooms unless they need to sleep. That's good. It means I don't have to restrict myself to sitting moping in my room. Armed with the key I took from Nessa I pad down the corridor and up the stairs. I listen at Eve's door, there's no sound, no sliver of light shining beneath. I knock softly, dart back to the stairwell; if Eve's in, I don't really want to meet her. There's no answer, I return, knock louder. Still no response. I open Eve's door, make sure the curtains are closed then switch on the light. I leave the door open; if anyone comes into the building, I want to hear them.

I open the wardrobe. The latex suit is still hanging there. At the bottom of the wardrobe are two cardboard boxes and a black canvas bag. I take them all out, put them on the bed, open the first box. It's filled with magazines, their titles include 'Rubber', 'Bondage' and 'BDSM'. They're no worse than other pornographic magazines I've glanced through in the line of duty; their content doesn't excite me. I put them back, close the box, open its twin.

There's a pair of handcuffs and a small vibrator, a mask and studded leather collar, several small pincered clamps; they're the clichés of sado-masochistic sex, the things young men snigger over. But at the bottom of the box, curled and intertwined in one corner, are two pieces of red plastic rope, the same as was round Salkeld's neck. I take them out; each is about six feet long; that's more than enough to tie wrists and ankles tightly. I wind them up again, put them back in the box; that's when I notice, taped to the lid, a computer disk.

When I started work as a policeman there was no need to

133

know much about computers. Now it seems that every time I find something valuable, it's encrypted as a series of ones and zeroes, locked away in a box that can only be opened by electronic means. But this time I'm determined not to be beaten. The black bag is a familiar shape and size, I unzip it to reveal a laptop computer. It raises an interesting question. If it was there when I was interviewing Eve about Salkeld's death, why didn't she suggest reading the disk on it? Why did she take me all the way over to the office block? There's no doubt I'll have to talk to her again.

I flip the computer lid open, switch it on, wait for the familiar software to load. Then I put the disk in the floppy drive. I may have taught myself to use computers, but what little I know is knowledge I can easily apply. I press 'start', then 'run', then select drive A and press return. In front of me there appears a list of computer icons, at least fifteen of them, each with a number. I double click on number one, the computer clicks and hums, then a photograph appears on the page in front of me.

It's a figure wearing the outfit I've just seen in Eve's wardrobe, the whole thing, mask and collar, latex basque and stockings, gloves and boots. It's strange, there were similar photographs in the magazines; they didn't disgust me, but they didn't arouse me either. This is different. I can feel the first stirrings of an erection. I know who this is, I've seen her, talked to her, I've even acknowledged how attractive she is, but she didn't have that effect on me then. The difference is that here she's dressed for sex. She's become less of a person, less of a woman, even, and more of an object. People, men and women, can do many things, but dress them up in a certain way, say as footballers, and they become limited in their potential, someone dressed as a footballer becomes nothing but a footballer. Eve Marton is dressed for sex and, even though the type of sex she might want doesn't appeal to me, I react to her photographic availability.

I feel flustered. I close the file, click icon number two.

It's the same figure, this time with her back to the camera. Eve's buttocks are slim, almost masculine, a thin ribbon of fabric separating them. The photograph has been taken with a cheap camera with a weak flash, there's no detail in the background except for what seems to be a single bed receding into the distance, and curtains pulled across a window. I look up; it's Eve's room, there's no doubt about that.

Photograph number three has the figure clutching at her latex crotch with a gloved hand, one long finger reaching down between her legs.

In photograph four the figure's sitting on her chair, legs wide open. There's no titillation, no pretended enjoyment. It must be difficult to express any emotion when your face is wrapped in a latex mask.

I'm about to look at photograph five when I hear the outside door open. I move quickly, eject the disk and put it back in the box. I switch off the computer (it doesn't matter that I haven't closed the files, the next time Eve switches the damn thing on she'll think she didn't shut down properly) and close the lid. I put the cardboard boxes back in the wardrobe, close the wardrobe doors, check the room – nothing disturbed – and switch off the light. Then I check the corridor; there's no one there. The person I heard (is it Eve or Nessa?) must be taking off boots and outdoor clothes. There's no sound of footsteps. I peer out of the door, again, no one's there.

This is worrying. There's no reason for silence. Whoever came into the building has stayed downstairs. If it was Nessa, why should she keep so quiet? It could be that the new arrival has come to see me. But no one's meant to know I'm here.

I sneak to the top of the stairs and peer down, but there's nothing to see, no clothes, no boots. I slide down, one step at a time. I can feel fear coursing through my body. The intruder, whoever it is, will be able to hear me coming; my traitorous heart must be announcing my presence.

I'm bent double, anxious that my head should be able to see along the ground floor corridor before my feet appear down the stairs. There's no one there. I can't see any open doors except that at the far end, the kitchen door, and there's no light in the room itself.

I could go back upstairs. I could hide in Eve Marton's room. That would be the logical thing to do. I'm at the stage in the horror film where the murderer with the knife/axe/chainsaw is lying in wait. The audience knows. 'Don't go on,' you can hear them whisper. 'He's next for the chop,' the back row boys say to their nervous, head-turned girlfriends. But the rules don't allow for turning back. The trouble is, in my own film I'm always the main character and I know, with supreme confidence, that the hero always survives. But I've just been touched with the suspicion that I might be in someone else's film. I might only be one of the bit part players: the blue-clad officer beamed down from the *Enterprise*, the unnamed talkative girl with the deep cleavage, the boastful boy unafraid of the darkened mansion; all they have in common is that their destiny is death. And if someone else is directing, I can't go back. I can only go on.

I hug the wall, thin as paper, so flat I cast no shadow. I lean against each door I pass but feel no vibration of life beyond. I'm becoming hysterical, there's a bubble of maniacal laughter trying desperately to rise from my depths. Another door creeps alongside me, I discard it and move on to the next, and the next. Only two to go on each side and no sound, no sign that there's anyone else in the building. Where can they be?

I reach my own room, key in hand. Then I hear the noise of a door opening behind me. The toilet, the shower-room, it isn't locked. Anyone could get in there. That's the only place to hide.

I have a choice. I can turn round and confront whoever it is. Or I can escape into my own room. That's no choice at all. I fumble the key into the lock, twist it, push hard on the door and throw myself into the room. But my pursuer's behind me, I push at the door but it's blocked. I've always felt that surprise is the better part of valour; get your retaliation in first. So I pull the door open and throw a huge arc of a punch at the body behind it.

I feel a huge, meaty fist grab my wrist, there's strength and power in it, I can feel my muscles jar all the way down my arm.

'It's okay, boss. It's only me.' The words transform the huge silhouette into Sly himself. I want to throw myself into his arms. Instead I yell at him.

'What the hell are you doing, padding around like that? Jesus Christ, Sly, it's bad enough having to hide away here without you . . .'

'Boss . . .'

'I don't want to know. You nearly gave me a heart attack, I was upstairs, I heard you come in. I didn't know who the hell you were.'

'Look, boss . . .'

'And then you disappeared. I nearly shit myself . . .'

'Billy! For fuck's sake, shut up!'

I don't know what shocks me most, Sly swearing or him calling me 'Billy'. The combination succeeds, but only for a brief moment. My mind figures out that something must be wrong for him to come here in the first place, and then for him to speak to me like that. Something's wrong. Something bad has happened.

'What is it? Is Kirsty all right?'

'Kirsty's okay, boss. Please, sit down.' He pushes me onto the bed, switches the light on. I can see his face, it's worried, old-looking. For the first time I notice the few grey hairs at his temples.

'There's been an . . . accident,' he says. The last word is reluctant.

'An accident?'

He shakes his head. 'No accident, boss. A girl – you've met her, she's one of Kirsty's new friends – she's been shot.'

137

'Shot?' All I can do, it seems, is repeat Sly's words.

'Shot. Killed. She's dead, boss, shot through the head. It was the little lass, Amy. She and Kirsty came back, she was going to try on some of Kirsty's clothes. There was nothing she liked, she was on her way back to her lodge from ours, going for her own stuff. We heard the shot, at first I thought it was a car back-firing, but then I remembered there weren't any cars moving. I had a look out of the front door. I could see her, she was only about fifty yards from the door, lying in the snow. I thought she might have just fallen over. I thought the noise might have been a branch breaking. I ran out to see to her. The snow was turning red, boss . . .'

I'm off the bed, pulling on my outdoor clothes. 'You don't have to tell me, Sly. I can look for myself, I'm used to this.'

'Red snow. It was melting, boss, must have been because of the warmth of the blood. But then the blood started freezing with the cold of the snow.'

'Come on, Sly, take me.'

'It was a head shot. She was dead, must have died straightaway.'

'It's okay, Sly, it's okay.'

He looks up at me, covers his mouth with his hand as if he wants to stop the words coming. 'She'd borrowed your coat, boss, your yellow coat. She wasn't going far, you see. It was dark, but the coat stood out. Bright yellow. So easy to see. So easy to aim at. I mean, with the collar up, struggling through the snow, it could have been anyone. But the coat made it certain.' Sly doesn't want me to see his tears. He turns his head away, brushes his face with his sleeve, swallows. He closes his eyes then opens them again, but there's a shine of sorrow there, a deep, liquid incomprehension. He finds the power to speak again, but his voice is small.

'Whoever it was killed her,' he manages to say, 'whatever bastard it was . . . He thought it was you.'

Chapter Seventeen

The first thing I see is a circle of shadows, each merging into the next, surrounding a fragile pool of warm, yellow torchlight. As we slide and slip a little closer the shadows resolve, become individual recognisable figures. I can identify Morland and Sam Ellis, the large, rounded figure of the nurse, Cath Watson. Paula's there as well, I'm grateful she's had the sense to leave Kirsty to look after the children. But there's someone I don't know, a tall, elderly man, bare-headed despite the cold. There's an air of calm. They could be a tableau from a Wright of Derby painting, an exercise in the play of artificial light on human faces. But, close to them, I see that no one would choose this scene to paint. There's a lack of differentiation in the faces, they're all coloured with the same haunted, bloodless expression Sly was wearing minutes before. They're sharing the same posture, staring down at the ground in front of them. They move when I labour up the slope towards them, but only to create enough space for me and for Sly to join their circle.

My coat was far too large for Amy. It must have reached almost to her knees; even as she lies in the snow it seems to be covering her. Protecting her. But not her head, it had no hood, and that was where the bullet hit. She's lying half on her left side, half on her front, as if some force has thrown her to one side. The right side of her head is unrecognisable. Blood is still oozing into the snow.

I look around. Between our position and Sly's lodge the snow is trampled into a rough track, but elsewhere it's smooth. The path from the lodge curves round the base of the slope, Amy must have decided to take a short-cut. She was hit on the right side of the head. She was climbing the hill. That means the shot was fired from ... Over to the right the trees thicken, they close together. They would provide a good hiding place, but anyone using it would have to stay near to the front of the copse. There's no distant sightline.

No one has spoken. I shuffle toward the thicket. The snow is less deep than elsewhere, but still difficult to wade through. It's easy to find the firing position. First there are footprints disappearing through the trees. Then there's the depression in the snow where the murderer was lying, two deeper hollows show the positions of his elbows. I take off my gloves, brush the snow away, hoping I can find what I need before my fingers grow numb. I brush against something hard, something metallic; I dig deep and circle the cylinder of metal, hold it up to examine it. Then I go back down the hill.

'There are tracks up there,' I say to Sam Ellis, 'it looks as if they lead down to the main path, but you might follow them for me, just to make sure. See if there's anything recognisable in the footprints.' If he's unsure about the job, worried about trailing an armed man, he doesn't show it.

I point at David Morland. 'I need to speak to, what's his name, Sir Henry Plumpton? No, Charles, that's it. There's a shell case here, if it matches the gun stolen from his car ... Well, at least we'll know a little about the murder weapon. Even if we don't know why his lordship was stupid enough to keep a rifle and ammunition in the boot of his car.'

'I think you should watch what you're saying,' Morland says, 'there's no need ...'

'There's every need, David.' It's the old man speaking,

his interruption silences Morland far more effectively than I could. 'I'm Charles Plumpton,' he says, 'and you're right, it was stupid. I've no excuse. And now there's a young girl dead because of my stupidity.' He takes a handkerchief from his pocket and dabs at his eyes. There are tears there. I'm beginning to regret what I said.

'She's called Amy,' I say, still using the present tense. It makes it easier for me. 'Does anyone know any more than that? Are her parents here?'

Plumpton speaks again. 'Amy Ross. She's a friend of my son's, goes to college with him. She was staying with us for a long weekend. I don't know her parents, don't know where they live. My son might know, but ... you know how young people are.'

'Was she staying in the same lodge as you? She'll have luggage, a purse, address book and so on.'

'Yes. Yes, of course. Why didn't I think of that?'

'Do you think we should move the body?' Sly whispers, ever practical.

'Yeah. Could you sort that out for me? Get her into our temporary morgue. Morland will help.'

Morland's already at my side. 'We need to keep this quiet,' he says, 'it could cause panic. People might try to get off site, but that would be too dangerous. The weather's going to get worse. I really don't see ...'

'I agree,' I tell him, 'as few people as possible should know.' He looks surprised. 'You're right in what you say, we don't want to cause panic. But it'll come out, Morland, and soon. You can't hide murder for long.'

'I need time,' he says, and despite the cold he's sweating. 'I need time to think how to deal with this. Damage limitation, that's all I can work on. God knows what effect it'll have on business. What's the angle? A lunatic?'

He's thinking aloud, and his thoughts are all selfish. I feel like hitting him, but it wouldn't do any good. Sly comes up behind him, grabs his shoulders, turns him round.

141

'You 'n' me,' Sly tells him, 'have to get this little girl away from here. Let's talk about how we're gonna do it.'

'I'm not a mortuary attendant, I've far too much to do . . .'

Sly doesn't have to draw his fist back. He doesn't need to use all his strength. He could have hit Morland's face and broken his nose. Instead he aims for the solar plexus and Morland collapses, doubled up, wide-eyed, fishing for air.

'Watch your step everyone,' Sly announces, 'it's very slippy.' He drags Morland to his feet.

'It's all your fault,' Morland hisses at me; he clearly believes Sly was acting under my instructions. 'First Salkeld, then this girl, and it's all because of you. She was wearing your coat, that's why she was killed. It's all your fault.'

Paula's the one who restrains me. I could easily pull away from her gentle hand on my arm, but her words are stronger. 'Kirsty saw it,' she says. 'I think she needs you.' She looks back over my shoulder at the lodge. 'Come on, Billy. He's not worth it.'

She helps me back down the hill. As the lodge grows closer I can see a face at the window. Kirsty's almost angelic, her hair's shining gold, framed with light. But her eyes are in darkness. I raise a hand to greet her but there's no movement. Then we're past and in the meagre shelter of the porch, kicking and stamping snow from our boots. Paula opens the door, it takes an age for us to help each other out of layers of clothing. Paula's kids yell their greetings without looking up from the television; I can't see Kirsty.

'She's in her room,' Paula says, 'I'll make tea, I'll bring it in. Or coffee, I can add something a little stronger if you want?'

'Tea would be great,' I say, 'for both of us.'

Kirsty's sitting on her bed. I sit beside her, put my arm around her. She collapses against me and begins to cry. I can't stop her, don't want to stop her. Huge waves of shuddering tears wrack themselves against me, I can feel her fingers, her nails, digging into my arms. She tries to speak but I stroke the back of her neck. 'Shh,' I say, 'not yet, no need to say anything yet. It's okay, I'm here, you're okay. I'm with you, little girl, I'm here, I'll look after you.' I can feel the damp slickness of tears soaking my collar.

We stay like that for a few minutes, a few hours, a few days. Time ignores us. The avalanche of tears begins to subside. I realise this is the first time for – what, three or four years? – I've held my daughter close like this. No, longer than that, that was when Sara and I first began having problems. Kirsty was a young teenager, at the awkward stage, unable to show or accept any demonstration of affection. So when was it? When she was eight or nine years old, that's it, when she fell and cut her lip. It was during the day, I was off duty and Sara was out. That's right, I took her to the hospital and they said she needed stitches. They kept her in and one of us was allowed to stay, Sara had arrived by then, but we gave Kirsty the choice and she wanted me to stay with her. I slept on the floor beside her bed, on a mattress, I held her hand when they wheeled her into surgery and waited for the anaesthetic to take control. Then, afterwards, she felt sick and I sat on a chair and cuddled her. She fell asleep in my arms. Eight years. Eight years since I've held my daughter close. And why do I find myself doing this? Because another young girl has died. The vicarious pleasure I felt at holding Kirsty, at being there, being able to help her, evaporates. Perhaps she feels this conflict of emotion, because she stops crying, sits up, wipes her eyes and her nose on her sleeve. She's so young.

'I saw,' she says.

'There's no need, Kirsty, no need to say anything.'

She ignores me. 'I was standing by the door. I'd closed it behind me, I didn't want to let the warm out. I was hugging myself, sort of dancing up and down, you know the way you

143

do. To keep warm. We'd come back to try stuff on, get ready for tonight. I was going to sort my things out, Amy was going back to get hers. I was waving. She waved back.'

'Did you say anything? Shout anything? Did she say anything?' Suddenly I'm a detective, asking questions. I shouldn't be asking questions, for fuck's sake, this is my daughter. I should be helping her, calming her, caring for her. And instead I'm interrogating her.

'I don't think either of us said anything. No. No, definitely. At least, I don't think so. Why?' She seems surprised. Have I changed from father to policeman so abruptly that my daughter has seen the transition? I want to stop, I want to change back, but I can't. I'm looking at Kirsty, but it's Amy's face I'm seeing. What if she'd said she'd go with Amy to get her clothes for the party, the overnighter, the stopover? What if Kirsty had borrowed my coat? What if she'd trudged up the hill, laughing, anticipating the night ahead? What if . . .? That's why I keep going, that's why I drink the potion, transform myself from Jekyll to Hyde.

'So you didn't shout anything? "Don't be too long, Amy"?'

'No.'

'And she didn't shout anything to you?'

'No. Dad, she's dead. I know that much, you haven't said so, you haven't told me, but I know. I know by the way you held me.' She looks at me with big eyes. She hasn't understood yet. But she will. 'Why . . . Why are you asking me these questions? I hadn't known her long, but she was . . . She was a friend. She might have been a good friend. Who would have done a thing like that? Why?'

'That's what I need to find out, Kirsty. That's why I have to ask you questions. If you saw her . . .'

'She was walking up the hill.' Kirsty's hand is suffocating mine. 'I think . . . yes, I waved at her. She turned round and waved back. Then she kept going, she was halfway up and . . . there was a bang. She fell over. I didn't connect them at

144

first, but she didn't get up again. I was just going to go inside and put some boots on, see what the matter was, when Sly ... That's when I shouted! Yes, I shouted her name, but she didn't answer. And Sly was there. I told him Amy might be hurt, I said she must have slipped. Sly mentioned the bang, he must have heard it from inside. He told me to go indoors. He ... he only had slippers on, but he ran up the hill and he went up to Amy and he bent down. He was like that for ages, I was watching him. Then he came back, slowly, ever so slowly. I suppose ... I suppose that was when I knew. That was when I connected the noise, the bang, the shot, with Amy. Sly told me to come inside, he said something to Paula then he used the radio-phone. I didn't hear what he said. But I couldn't think why. Why kill Amy? She was harmless, she hadn't hurt anyone, she hadn't done anything. She was only two years older than me, Dad, she hadn't had time to do anything.'

It's coming now. I can feel it.

'We were so excited. She was ... she really fancied Will. She was wondering if he might ... I mean, she *really* wanted to impress him. She was talking about what she would wear. And then she was pulling on her boots, I was telling her to hurry up, not to be too long. And she asked if she could borrow your coat, she thought it was really cool. I was so pleased, Dad, 'cos I made it for you, but here's somebody else, somebody who doesn't know that, asking if she can borrow it 'cos it's cool. I said yes, of course, Dad won't mind. So she put it on, she had the collar turned up high, it was so cold. I told her, I said "you look just like my Dad," and she laughed, then we went out. And ...'

She's found it. She knows.

'She looked just like you, Dad.'

She's been speaking quickly, words and sentences have run into one another. But now she slows. She realises what she's said. She stares at me.

'She looked like you, Dad. If anyone had been watching, if anyone had seen us, they would have thought ...' Her

145

thoughts are visible, they're dripping from her mouth, coloured red.

'They would have thought it was you. I was waving to you, jumping up and down. You waved back. It's difficult to work out how big a person is, especially when it's been snowing. There's nothing to compare you with. So Amy, struggling up the slope, wrapped up in your coat ... Me waving ... It could have been you.'

I can't say anything. I can only nod.

'They thought it was you?'

I nod again. 'It's a possibility. A strong possibility.'

'Oh, Dad.' She can't think of anything else to say, she repeats herself, keeps on repeating herself, 'Oh Dad, Dad, no, Dad, oh Dad ...'

'I don't know for certain,' I say, and the very action of talking silences her. 'All I know is there's a man, a convicted criminal, escaped from that accident we saw on the way in here. I helped arrest him. He was overheard saying he'd get revenge. There was a rifle stolen from a car, here, on site. It looks as if that rifle was used to kill Amy. Amy was dressed in my coat. Add all that together and ... Well, there's only one possible answer.'

There's a tap on the door. 'Tea for two,' Paula calls, 'and biscuits and cake. Is it okay to come in?'

Kirsty springs to her feet, throws the door open. If Paula's surprised she doesn't show it, she marches in with a tray and puts it on the bed. 'Just yell if you need me,' she says, turns to leave. Kirsty throws herself into Paula's arms. I can hear her, 'Thank you,' she says, 'I love you,' she says. Paula smiles at me over Kirsty's shoulder, a damp-eyed smile, squeezes my daughter. Then she's gone and the door's closed again.

'Do you think he'll know?' Kirsty asks. 'The killer, will he know it's not you?'

'Probably. He might have been waiting around, he might have seen me arrive. If not, well, he'll certainly find out soon. There aren't many people here, no one can get in or

146

out, he'll hear talk. I don't even know how he's dressed. He could be . . . anyone. Anywhere.'

'And he wants to kill you.'

'Looks like it.'

She's going to start crying again. Her head drops, I can see her swallow, her lips tighten into a line. But then she looks up and there's resolve in her eyes. 'We'll have to hide you,' she says, 'keep you out of the way. There must be somewhere . . .'

'Been there,' I tell her, 'done that. But now he knows, or he will know, where I am. It's gone beyond hiding.'

'So you're going to give in?'

'No.'

'So what are you going to do?'

'I don't know. I haven't had time to think yet.'

Her voice is suddenly hard. 'Well shouldn't you start thinking now? While you're still alive. Whoever it is out there, he's just killed a friend of mine. I don't want him killing my father. So you'd better think of something, and think it quick.'

There are times when Kirsty is so self-righteously like her mother I want to shake her. This is such a moment. Instead I hold out my hand. 'Thank you,' I say, 'for caring.' Why couldn't I have said that to Sara? Why was I incapable of bridging the chasm between us, the chasm I'd dug with my own bare hands?

'So what do we do?' Kirsty asks.

'Pray?'

147

Chapter Eighteen

It's almost an hour before Sly comes back. 'It's getting colder,' he says, 'and windier. There's another storm on the way.' He looks unwell, he's shivering.

'Dad's staying here tonight,' Kirsty says firmly, as if he might object, grabbing his attention before he can take his coat off.

'That's okay with me,' he answers.

'I've told Paula as well, she says the kids being here isn't a problem.' Kirsty's been thinking of all objections.

'Okay! Like you say, no problem, boss.' I have to look closely at him, but there's no joke, no cynicism. He's talking to Kirsty. He called her 'boss'.

'I thought we could take it turns to keep awake. Keep our eyes open.'

'If you say so. But then what? What do we do if someone tries to break in?'

'If it's me, I'll hit him. I'm prepared, I'm armed.' She reaches down beside her. I've seen this already, I know she's serious. I just hope Sly doesn't laugh.

'There's not much in the house,' Kirsty says, 'but I found this in a cupboard. It's better than nothing.' She holds up a tennis racket, brandishes it at Sly. 'It could hurt, used sideways. Hit with the frame, not the strings.'

Sly nods. 'Good idea, angel, but I've come up with something better. How about this?' He takes a roll of material from inside his jacket, puts it on the table. 'If we'd come in the van there wouldn't have been a problem. Nail guns, knives, hammers, I've got them all. But I had a look round the gardeners' store.' He glances at me. Two bodies in the mortuary, he doesn't want any more. Nor do I; my name's already on the toe label.

'Anything useful?' I ask.

'If you can get close, yes.' He unfolds the material. Inside are three long, chrome plated spanners.

'Is that all?'

'I also had a word with our nurse friend, what's her name? Watson?'

'Cath Watson. What did she say?'

'I was after chloroform, anaesthetic of some type in an injection. She didn't have any. But she gave me these.' From a pocket he produces a dozen plastic-handled scalpels, still in their sterilised wrapping.

'Anything else?'

'I can rustle up some dangerous icicles. Snowballs?'

'I'll stick with my tennis racket,' Kirsty says. She gets up and heads for the window.

'Best keep away from there,' I warn her, and she stops immediately. I weigh a spanner in my hand. It's better than nothing.

'So what else is happening?' I ask.

'Nothing. Morland helped me with . . . with the job.' Sly glances at Kirsty, but she's back on the bed, staring straight ahead of her, tennis racket gripped firmly in her hand. 'I think there's a power vacuum. He won't do anything, he can't do anything. He's tried contacting the police but there's no signal. Could be atmospheric conditions.'

'Could be the aerial's down.'

'Either way it doesn't matter.' He raises his eyebrows at me. 'How you feelin', boss?'

'Claustrophobic. Angry. Guilty. Hemmed in. Under pressure. Worried. Do you want more? There is more, Jesus, Sly, I'm feeling every possible feeling there is. But

149

most of all, angry. Angry with myself, with Morland, with the weather and the snow and the whole fucking set-up.'

Kirsty looks up when she hears me swearing. I mouth 'Sorry' at her, speak more quietly. 'I feel lost, Sly, I don't know what to do next. I don't know where to go.' I drop my head into my hands. It's too long since I last shaved, I can feel my face's untidiness. My eyes feel red and gritted, tongue furred. I feel as if I ought to be allowed to sleep for a week, perhaps hibernate for the whole winter. When I wake up everything will be all right. Except it won't be.

Sly stands up. 'You gonna walk to your room? Or do you want me to embarrass you in front of your daughter and carry you?'

'Why . . .?'

'You need to sleep. There's nothing you can do now, it's dark, it's getting colder.'

'There's a blizzard on the way,' Kirsty offers, 'I heard it on the radio a few hours ago.'

'So you might as well rest while you can. Come on.' Sly drags me to my feet. The image of a warm bed is suddenly attractive, it summons me from the room.

'We'll protect you,' Kirsty says, brandishing her tennis racket. She's trying to smile, doing the job badly.

'Okay, okay. You win, the odds are too great.'

Within two minutes I'm wrapped up in bed. I don't remember falling asleep, but I can remember Kirsty's hand stroking my head.

Chapter Nineteen

'Time to get up, Dad. We're moving house.'

I open my eyes. There's a strange, diffused light in the room, it seems to creep in under the door and round the curtains.

'What did you say?'

'We're moving. There was a storm during the night, the power lines came down. I'm surprised you didn't hear anything, the noise was terrible. I thought we were going to be blown away. Anyway, there's no light or heat in the lodges, so everyone's moving into the Tesseract. Apparently there's a generator, but it only heats the main area beside the pool, so that's where we're all going.'

'Jesus Christ, it gets worse.'

'There's safety in numbers, Dad. Come on, the rest of us are ready. It's still snowing, we need your help to get the kids across.'

I climb out of bed, there's a chill in the air. I squint at my watch, it's just after ten. That means I slept for well over twelve hours. Do I feel better for it? The overwhelming fatigue has disappeared, but my mind? I once heard someone who had arrhythmia describing the way his heart felt. 'It goes along, lulls you into a false sense of security, then misses a beat. You can feel the absence, you wait for it to come, but there's nothing, nothing, nothing. And then, suddenly it arrives, heavy as timpani.

Or sometimes it just beats faster and faster, so fast it hurts. Then it's back to normal.' That's the way my brain feels at the moment, confused, misfiring. I try to remember who it was, the man with arrhythmia. Jimmy Gow? I went to his funeral.

My clothes feel damp, I thrust myself into them. I look around for my bag, then remember it's over at the staff residence. No matter, I can get it later, it's a good excuse – if I need it – to get out.

Out in the hall the kids are ready, so fat with clothing they'd roll upright if you knocked them down.

'Come on then,' I say, 'who wants a carry?'

I end up with a twin and a rucksack. Kirsty has another twin on her back, Paula's carrying the baby, and Gav insists on walking. It's left to Sly to carry the remaining bags. He's also breaking track, and that service is certainly needed. While I slept the snow has fallen and drifted and frozen. I glance up at the slope in front of the lodge, it's virginal, a sheen of curved perfection. The cold is bitter, biting, it gnaws at my eyes and nose, numbs my fingers. The others are clearly suffering as badly as me, they bunch up behind Sly and urge him on with groans and whimpers.

It's only a few hundred metres to the Tesseract's main entrance. We meet other crocodiles of families, too cold to greet each other, struggling through the snow in their search for warmth. 'Not far now,' I say to my twin; I'm not sure which it is, it's so well-wrapped.

There are Forestcrag staff waiting for us as we steam into the warmth. They have tea and coffee, hot chocolate and mulled wine. We pass through a funnel of seats and give our names to one of several employees sitting at tables. Then we're given instructions.

'There are mattresses and quilts in the foyer just outside the pool area, there are sufficient for everyone, please claim one each, but do not move them. This area is the warmest in the building, though there is a lack of privacy.

The pool area itself is closed. All food and beverages will be provided free of charge until the problems are resolved. We apologise for this inconvenience.'

There are several questions I'd like to ask. How are the problems being resolved? If the phone lines are down, does the outside world know our electricity's been cut off? How long can the emergency generators keep going? But the girls won't know the answer, probably David Morland himself doesn't know the answer. So I keep quiet and move down the line as the mantra begins again behind me, 'There are mattresses and quilts . . .'

It's downhill to the pool, along a path bordered with greenery. We can hear the hubbub of conversation before we see the rafts of humanity reclining on their mattresses. I'd estimate no more than 150 people, but they've spread out and staked their claims. The least fortunate are surrounded by others; better off are those whose new beds have a wall behind them. One or two families seem to have forced themselves into alcoves where two or even three walls offer a special privacy; and there are even sheets and coats hung on rails, breaking the general view of the people hiding behind them.

'Billy! Billy, over here! How are you?'

Across the sea of refugees I can see Nessa Clifton waving madly. She's carrying several large bags and handing out quilts to anyone who claims one, but she puts these down when she sees me and dances through the confusion of beds and bodies to meet me.

'I hear there was an accident,' she says, 'someone was hurt. Are you okay?'

I avoid answering. 'This is Nessa,' I say, introduce her to Sly, Paula and Kirsty, mention the children's names as well though I know she won't remember them.

'Hiya. Have you just arrived? Don't be stupid, Nessa! Yes, of course you have, you've still got your layers on. Looking for somewhere to make your home?'

'The best spots seem to have been taken,' I point out.

153

'Don't you believe it. It's always good to know someone who knows someone. I've just the place for you. Want to check it out?'

'I'll take a look,' I tell Sly, put my twin (it's Tim, he's unpeeled his hood) on the floor. 'Better make a claim somewhere round here, just in case.'

'Follow me,' Nessa says. She takes my arm, guides me through the crowds. Most of them don't even look up as we pass, they're concentrating on their own misery.

'Are you all right?' Nessa asks again. 'Someone's been hurt, at least that's what I've heard, that's the rumour. I thought it was you, but you seem okay. What's happened?'

Before Nessa whisked me away I caught Kirsty's expression, the curiosity dancing in her eyes. She'll want to ask me questions, and I don't think she'll believe the answers I can give. 'The usual stuff,' I say, 'it seems to follow me round.' It's as non-committal as I can manage.

'That's not an answer, Billy.'

'I'm not sure I can give as much as you want.'

'That always was your problem.'

She doesn't look round as she speaks, but there's an edge in her voice tells me she wants me to comment, to ask her what she means. I don't want to give her that satisfaction, I don't want that type of information; it might bring with it an obligation.

There are people scattered on the floor all around us. Nessa's threading her way between them, she reaches out and takes my hand to make sure I tread the same path as her. It brings me closer to her. 'They say someone else is dead,' she whispers to me.

'First someone's hurt, now someone's dead. It sounds as if you know the answers to the questions you're asking, you just want confirmation from me. How much do you know, Nessa?'

We're through the crush of people now, close to the entrance to the pool. There's a rack of sports clothing, a cardboard label attached to it says 'Half Price'. Nessa moves it to one side, beyond it, in a small alcove to itself, is the door to Nessa's private gym.

'How about that?' she says. 'A little seclusion for you and yours. Might let the kids get to sleep more easily.'

'Are you in your room, then?'

She unlocks the door. 'Perks of the job,' she says, motions me in.

'I'd better be getting back, before everyone settles. I don't want to make them move again ...'

She tugs me after her, I shouldn't be surprised at how strong she is. Then she closes the door behind me.

'The talk is, Billy, that a young girl's been killed. That the killer thought she was you, she was dressed in your coat or something like that.'

'Shit! I thought ...'

'It's true, then. There are no secrets round here, Billy, too many people know each other too well. Gossip spreads fast. Except this isn't gossip.'

I sit down on a bench. If the word's gone around that there's been a murder then ... No, it can't have done. There was no panic outside, no worries. Kids were playing, running around. So this gossip is limited to staff, perhaps to a few staff only.

'Who told you?' I ask.

'No one told me. I overheard a conversation. People get so used to seeing me around, I'm almost invisible. David Morland was talking to someone on his radio-phone. I didn't believe it at first, but you've confirmed it. I had to find out, I was worried about you.'

'Worried about me?'

'Yes. It was a shock to see you, Billy, you brought back memories I thought I'd got rid of. You ... that is ... Jesus Christ, Billy, I had a crush on you and you didn't even realise it! Right from the beginning of that course I was waiting for you to make a move, but ... At first I thought there was something wrong with me. And then ...'

'Whoa, just hold on Nessa, you didn't even know me.'

155

'I knew about you. And we'd met before, just after I started with the Force, I worked in the same office as you for a while, I was posted there as a trainee. I mean, I knew you wouldn't remember me, that's why I didn't mention it. And the rest of them on that course, they just wanted to screw me. But you were different, you looked as if you cared. You treated me properly.'

'Nessa, I was either knackered or half-pissed all the time. My marriage was breaking down, I was on a course I didn't want to be on, I was completely fucked up. And . . . Hold on, I never worked with any trainees.'

Nessa stares at me. 'Really?'

'Not in CID, they'd be too much of a liability.'

'Are you sure?'

'Nessa, believe me.'

'Oh. It must have been afterwards, after I'd qualified. And anyway, it was as the course went on, that was when I really started fancying you. It sounds as if you don't believe me.'

'I'm sorry, that's not my intention. I just . . . How did we get onto this anyway?'

She looks at me again, head on one side. 'Because I was worried about you,' she says.

I don't know how the kiss begins. I can't recall her moving towards me. All I know is that she's straddling the bench beside me and her mouth and tongue are wet. She tastes good and her hands are stroking the back of my neck, then digging into my shoulders, pulling us together. She bites gently at my lips, I do the same to hers. She pulls away from me, gently, when I open my eyes she's questioning me. Perhaps she's afraid I might disapprove. Although I say nothing, she must find the answer she wants. She stands up, pulls me after her. She's only slightly shorter than me and she's strong. As we kiss again her hands are inside my shirt, my sweater's bunched around my chest. I'm almost as active, tugging her T-shirt free from the back of her trousers, sliding my hands down to cup her buttocks

156

and pull her towards me. At the same time we're moving inexorably towards the rubber mats folded over each other in the corner.

I move one hand up and round. Nessa's stomach is flat, muscled. I meet her bra, tug it down under her breasts, pinch one nipple and then the other. Nessa gasps. She frees one of her hands, runs it down the front of my trousers. 'Jesus,' I mutter.

'I want to fuck you,' Nessa whispers into my neck. I can think of nothing else I'd rather do. Jen hasn't even come into my mind, Sly and the kids could still be tramping round the Tesseract as far as I'm concerned. And then there's a sound of knocking at the door. Nessa and I stop moving. Then she pulls one hand away, holds it to my lips. 'No one knows we're here,' she mouths.

There's another knock. Then a voice. 'Dad? Dad, are you in there?'

'Shit!'

'She'll go away. Keep quiet.'

I shake my head. 'She might need me. It could be something important.'

'*I* need you,' Nessa says, but she's already tucking her shirt back into her trousers. 'Later tonight,' she adds, 'when everyone's asleep.'

'It's a date,' I reply. Then, louder, 'Kirsty? Is that you?'

'Dad?'

Nessa's already at the door, she flings it wide.

'What's the matter?' I ask.

Kirsty peers into the room. She looks at me, curiosity in her eyes. She sweeps her gaze over Nessa. 'It's nothing,' she says, 'Sly asked me to find you. Find out if we should move or stay where we are.' She gestures over her shoulder. 'It seems like a good place here.'

'That's what Nessa thought,' I explain. 'I'm sorry, I should have come straight back, but I was side-tracked. Nessa used to work for the police, we started talking about the case and ...'

'It's okay, Dad. I know how it is. Do you want me to go and get Sly and Paula and the kids?'

Nessa steps forward. 'I've got work to do, I'll see you later, Billy. We can pick things up where we left them. I'd better lock up.' She ushers me out of the room. 'Nice meeting you, Kirsty.' She locks the door and leaves.

'Come on,' I say, 'let's get the others, make ourselves comfortable. We can find some mattresses, stake our claim.' I move to put my arm round her shoulder, but she slides gracefully to one side and I'm left clutching nothing.

'Dad,' she says over her shoulder, 'you'd better tuck your shirt in. You look a bit flustered.'

Chapter Twenty

The day passes in a strange state of frenetic lethargy. Sly
and Paula find ways to keep the kids occupied, insist that
they don't need my help; on the contrary, they keep looking
across at me, making sure I'm okay; I've become an extra
child. At first Kirsty helps them, but then she's distracted
by the discovery that one of her new friends (the young boy
she danced with on that first night so many years ago, Phil)
is camped just around the corner. She glances at me and
leaves with him. She wasn't seeking permission to go, it
wasn't a question, it was a statement of intent, almost a
defiance of parental authority. 'I'm going,' that look said,
'don't try to stop me.'

That leaves me propped against a wall with only my
thoughts for company. They don't sit with me in a neat
circle, each taking its turn to speak then allowing the others
an opportunity to contribute. No, they're like a classroom
of unruly children, all noise and insistence, they fight each
other for my attention. First there's Nessa promising me
that the night can't come soon enough, but behind her is the
dark, cloudy figure of Jen. Jen in Canada, so far away, Jen
whom men always find attractive, Jen who, even now,
could be in bed with ... a lumberjack? A Mountie? It's
ridiculous self-justification, an attempt to pre-empt the guilt
I'll feel if I sleep with Nessa. 'Not "if", but "when",' says
the Nessa figure with a lascivious grin on her face.

Other thoughts jostle for position. 'What about us?' cry Eric Salkeld and poor, dead Amy, while behind them, trying to hide, are Eve Marton and a hooded, gun-bearing Harry Simpson. They dance round each other, with each other, they merge into one. They should be the thoughts occupying my mind, not thoughts of Nessa but the more abstract need to solve crime. Who else is there to do it? I try to concentrate, I even search for a pen and paper to begin writing down the facts I know about the two deaths, but I'm interrupted by the memory of Kirsty, the look on her face. She's fond of Jen. She knows, she must know, what she interrupted only a few hours before. And she disapproves. She disapproves of Nessa, of me, of the very notion of us being together, having sex. And that's all it is, the release of sexual tension. There's no love involved, certainly not on my part. I realise how callous that sounds, try to look at it from Nessa's viewpoint. Is there something more than lust? She said she was attracted to me years ago. Does that make her feelings, whatever they are, any less real? What does *she* think?

This is becoming too confusing. I tell myself I don't even know what Nessa will do. She might have second thoughts. *I* might have second thoughts. Something might happen to stop our liaison, though I decide I don't want to know all those potential somethings. I feel I ought to be doing something, doing anything, but all I can do is sit and think, drift into and out of sleep.

I feel someone shaking my shoulder. I'm tempted to remain where I am, it's warm and comfortable, I'm cocooned from the world outside. But the hand at my shoulder is insistent, and I do as it asks. I crawl out. It's dark outside, I can see snow falling again through the window and can hear the distant keening of the wind. Nessa's standing above me, the door to her room is open.

'I don't think I can . . .'

'You can and you will,' she says, 'if you don't move of your own accord then I'll pick you up and carry you.'

160

She looks as if she means it and I'm in no frame of mind to argue. She pushes me through the door, closes and locks it behind me.

'In there,' she points to the shower, 'there's a razor and foam, shampoo and soap. Shave yourself, wash yourself. There are plenty of towels. Go on.'

I undress reluctantly, wrap a towel around my waist with a feeling of false modesty; when I look round Nessa's not even watching me. But it feels good to scrape the stubble away from my skin. The water's hot (whatever they're using as an emergency generator is damned efficient) and it sloughs a thin film of despair away. I scrub myself.

'Billy?' It's Nessa's voice on the other side of the door.

'Don't come in,' I say.

'I wasn't going to. I showered half an hour ago, don't need to again. Not yet. I'm just making sure you're okay.'

I turn off the shower, slide the door open a little and hold out my hand; a heavy towel is draped over it. I wrap myself up, leave the steam behind and step outside. Nessa's there, she wraps another towel around my shoulders.

'I thought you might need some relaxation therapy. That's what I'm here for. No strings, no pressure. You're going to get a massage.' She takes me by the hand and leads me back into the exercise room. She's lit candles and joss sticks, there are more towels spread over one of the mats.

'Nessa, I appreciate what you're doing, but there's no need for all this.'

'The fact that you think there's no need just emphasises the need, Billy. Lie down.' She has her hands on her hips, she's taken off her tracksuit to reveal a lycra sleeveless top. Her arms are as well-muscled as the rest of her. I do as she tells me, lower myself onto my stomach.

'I've done some training as a masseuse,' she tells me, crouching down by my side. She moves the towel a little way down my back to expose my shoulders. I can hear her as she rubs her hands together, there's an oily liquidity to

161

the sound and a faint smell of almonds. Then she touches me. It's a firm touch, her fingertips pressing into the muscles of my upper back. It's the touch of a professional. I begin to relax.

She deals with a small part of my body at a time, covers it with a towel before moving on. First it's my back, from top to bottom, then my arms. Then she starts on my feet and works her way up my legs. She kneads and moulds my backside, then covers me again and – with a touch on leg and side at the same time – persuades me to turn over.

There's no such thing as time any more. She pays as much attention to my chest and the front of my legs as she did to my back, rearranging muscles, sifting and layering them. She sings as she works, a tune without words, no more than a gentle hum beneath her breath, but it's as soothing as her hands.

I'm not sure how she manages to take off her clothes without removing her hands from my body; perhaps I fell asleep for a moment. And I can't recall the moment when her stroking and rubbing and caressing becomes sensual and sexual. I don't remember when I begin to respond to her, when I become aware that we're going to make love, when I know I don't want her to stop. All I know is that she's astride me, eyes closed, pulling my hands to her breasts and her stomach, up to her neck, and her movements are becoming faster, more urgent.

Afterwards we lie together wrapped in towels.

'That wasn't too bad, was it?' she says.

'It felt good to me.'

'Me too.' Our bodies have become a tangle of flesh and limbs, she pulls her hand loose, squints at her wrist. 'I should really be going,' she says, 'I need to do the rounds. Check everyone's okay before they settle down for the night.'

'I should get back to Kirsty and Sly and Paula. They might need me.'

'You're that indispensable?' She climbs to her feet. I

look at her in the dim light of the candles, admire the shadows cast in her groin and the small of her back, beneath her breasts. 'Bloody hell, it's cold! I'm not spending another winter in this bloody country. Where the hell are my clothes?'

'Where would you go? If you had the choice.'

'Somewhere warm. Somewhere with hills to run in, warm sea to swim in. Somewhere you can hear cicadas singing at night, somewhere I can sleep naked all year round. Somewhere with cheap wine and handsome men who are considerate enough to help me find my bloody clothes after we've made love!'

I take the hint, climb to my feet, find the light-switch and click it in time to see her pulling on my underpants. 'You may like cross-dressing,' I say, 'but I'm damned if I'm getting into your knickers.'

She looks down at herself and begins to laugh. 'I don't quite fill them in the right places,' she says, finds my socks and stuffs them down the front of the pants. 'That's better.' She holds her hands up to her breasts, flattens them, thrusts her groin at me. 'What do you think? Would I pass for a man?'

'As much as I'd pass for a woman,' I reply.

'You could,' Nessa insists, 'just tuck yourself between your legs. Here, I'll give you a hand.' She moves towards me, malice in her smile, and I back away.

'You'd need falsies, of course. And you'd have to shave your legs and your chest. But with a wig and make-up no one would know, honest, you'd be so sexy.' She stops. 'Billy? Are you all right? It's okay, I didn't mean it, honest.'

'Say that again.'

'What?'

'Say it again. About how I could look like a woman.'

She seems puzzled. 'You could, I suppose. Anyone could if they did it properly. A lot of depilation, you're a hairy man, and you'd need a good wig. But with a little padding, a little strapping ... You're not actually thinking about it, are you? I'm not really into that sort of thing.'

'Nessa, I'm an idiot! Get my underpants off, quickly. Think, Billy, think. I'll need a torch, do you have one? And the keys to the staff accommodation, I think I've still got them in my pocket. Come on, get a move on!'

She takes off my pants, finds her own clothes and dresses more quickly than I can.

'Tell me,' she says.

'The latex outfit,' I say, 'the one in Eve Marton's cupboard. I went back, looked in the cardboard boxes. They had bondage magazines inside and there was a computer disk taped to the lid. I put it into Eve's computer, the disk was full of photographs of her in that outfit, the one you found. Except they weren't of her. They were of Salkeld. He was dressed as a woman. Cath, the nurse, she noticed that his body was almost hairless. That's because he shaved himself. And you brought it all together, you made it click. I thought he might be blackmailing her, and that was a reasonable motive for her to kill him. But it was the other way round. She was blackmailing him. And if that was him in those photographs then he was heavily into bondage and ... Christ, I need to check, I need to see them again. I need to get back, see if the disk's still there, I only looked at the first few frames. There might be more, there might be evidence.'

'I'll come with you,' Nessa says. 'You might need someone to keep watch. And God knows you can't be trusted, if it wasn't for me getting into your pants ...' She grins.

'Okay. But just this once. If we find anything, if I have to approach Eve Marton, you back off.'

'Anything you say, Billy. But we're a team, you and me, a team.' She finds more layers of clothing scattered round the room, stuffs herself into them. 'Come on then,' she says. 'What are we waiting for?'

164

Chapter Twenty-One

It's the first time I've been outside for almost the whole day, and I've become softened by the rest. The cold snatches at my throat, stings my eyes. Flurries of snow conspire to blind me. I stumble, grab hold of Nessa's belt and hold on to it, happy to let her break the trail. She's carrying a heavy duty torch, though she refuses to switch it on until we're out of sight of the Tesseract. I'm pleased she's there.

The staff accommodation is a grey monolith, it exhales freezing air from the black doors of its face, though the lamps of its blind windowed eyes are extinguished. Nessa pulls me past her to fumble with the key. I drop it, I can't feel my fingers, and she has to retrieve it for me. She does the job herself, unlocks the door and pushes it open. She drags me inside, locks the door behind us. 'Just in case anyone's passing,' she says.

It's as cold inside as out, but at least the wind and the snow aren't coursing along the corridor. We go straight to Eve's room, open the door.

'What if she's taken everything with her?' Nessa whispers.

'What? That outfit? And the disk? She's no reason to think they wouldn't be safe here, double locked away. No, they'll be here, don't worry. And there's no one around to hear you, you don't have to be quiet.'

'So why are *you* whispering?'

'Habit.'

It doesn't take long to find everything, the place is just as I left it. Even the laptop is still there. Nessa takes the disk from the lid of the cardboard box. 'Here,' she says, 'you hold the torch.' She switches the laptop on and, with an easy familiarity, inserts the disk. 'Drive A,' she says, 'let's have a look. Yeah, lots of photo files. Should we start with number one and work our way through?'

I've already seen the first few, but I bend closer to look at them. In each the face is hidden or masked.

'Could be Salkeld,' I say, 'but it could also be Eve Marton. Keep going.'

'Pity we can't do a *Blade Runner*. You know, find a bit of the background with incriminating evidence like a news-paper or a clock, something that could mean only one thing.'

'The name's Billy Oliphant, not Harrison Ford. Keep going.'

'Ford's the actor, not the character. He was called ... Shit, I've forgotten! Straker? Stryker? Damn, what the hell is it?' While she's talking her fingers are on automatic, I have to pull them away from the keyboard to stop her.

'That's it,' I say. 'That's what we needed.'

'Bloody hell!' We're looking at Eric Salkeld's face. He's wearing a black-haired wig, but it's not quite straight. His make-up is well applied and he's grinning broadly, but it's still his face. The skin above the top of his latex basque is smooth, one arm is raised in triumph and there are no hairs nestling in the armpit. It could still, at first sight, be a woman. But it doesn't take the eye long to travel down the slim-hipped body to find the erection grasped in Salkeld's other hand.

'Bloody hell,' Nessa says, 'I don't think I want to see the rest.' Her fingers stop working. I pull the laptop from her hands, continue the search.

There are other frames. In one the top of the latex is

peeled down to reveal Salkeld's hairless chest, nipples clamped so severely there's blood visible trickling down his chest. In others he finds inventive uses for a mole wrench and a knitting needle. And there's a sequence showing him tying himself up using red clothes-line.

'Did he take the photographs himself?' Nessa asks. She's looking at the screen but her fists are clenched, as if she can't believe what she's seeing.

'I assume he had some remote lead. You can get them for ordinary cameras, why not for digitals? Probably operated by a footswitch.'

'So now what?' Nessa asks. 'Salkeld was ... strange, peculiar even. That still doesn't mean Eve Marton had anything to do with his death.'

'Then why is all this stuff in her room?'

'I don't know.'

'Is there anything else on the laptop? Anything on the hard drive? You have a look, I'll check the room again.'

I hand the laptop back to Nessa, she has to work by the light of the screen alone. I've commandeered the torch. It takes me into the wardrobe again, through the empty pockets of her jacket and trousers. Everything is neat and tidy. I move on to the contents of the small chest of drawers; two pairs of socks, underwear (purposeful, nothing exotic) is folded. Other clothes – two T-shirts, a polo-neck, a sweatshirt – could be fresh from Benetton shelves. There's nothing untoward, everything is in its place. The very fact that she has these clothes with her, backup in case of an emergency, tells me how well prepared, how neat, how methodical she is. Eve is a woman I can understand.

'You won't find anything,' I tell Nessa.

'There's less than nothing, Billy. No work at all. No letters, nothing on the notepad, nothing in the waste-bin.' She begins to close the laptop down.

'Eve Marton works on floppies. Easy to store, easy to carry, easy to transfer information. Secure as well. She could have hidden them in here but I doubt it. She must have them with her. It's what I would do.'

'You're peculiar as well, you mean?'

'She's clever, precise, systematic. Logical as well. That's not peculiar.'

Nessa looks as if she's about to argue and I recall the state of her room; perhaps she remembers as well, because her voice is conciliatory, it contradicts her face. 'So what do we do now? Present her with what we've found? Make accusations?'

'She'll deny whatever we say. And anyway, I don't know what I *could* say. Something's not right, we know that. But what? There's no evidence to suggest she murdered Salkeld.'

'So we forget what we've seen?'

'No, we think about it. See where it leads us. See what we can make of it. See how it fits into possibilities. See if we can make them probabilities.'

'That's a lot of seeing, I hope your eyesight's good.'

I'm beginning to feel cold, but it's a purely physical coldness; there's no shadow of hopelessness crouched over me. I'm doing something positive, having ideas. They could be the wrong ideas, they could be leading me in the wrong direction, but at least they might give me the opportunity to find out which way I'm facing.

'We'd better get back,' I say. 'I need to think.'

'I need to get warm,' Nessa says. She puts the laptop away and, in the dim light of the torch, I can see her face. 'I can think of one or two good ways of generating a little heat,' she smiles. 'Friction is a wonderful thing.'

I think back to her room with its lock and key, the mats and towels we'd left strewn over the floor, the warm water in the shower. I think of Nessa's body, the hard muscles and the hidden soft places, the curled spring dark hairs like tendrils reaching out to trap my fingers, the bleached sand grass hairs on her pale arms. I think of the sweet smell of her skin, the slide of sweat and salt kisses, the way she closes her eyes and opens her mouth, the way her tongue darts out to lick her lip free of the beaded moisture gathering there. I think of the way she rose above me, the way my hands found her breasts, the way she moved them up to the tender skin of her neck. No, it was more specific than that. It was her throat, she held my hands to her throat and squeezed them together, gently. 'I like that,' she'd said. 'Oh God, I like that.'

She's reaching out towards me and I'm feeling warm already, warm so I don't think we'll make it back to her room, and that's when the chill hits me. It starts at the back of my neck and plays arpeggios on my spine, I shiver so Nessa notices and her smile widens.

'Someone walk over your grave?' she asks, then realises what she's said. 'I'm sorry, Billy, that wasn't a very clever . . .'

'Shut up.'

She looks around, straining to catch a soft, distant sound, but it's not a warning. It's just a request for silence. The connection's been made. The faintest of possibilities, but it's something to look at, to follow up, to eliminate even.

'Come on,' I say. I don't even reach for her hand, but she follows. We're outside in seconds, and this time I lead the way. There are two entrances to the Tesseract and I'm heading for the main door, the furthest away. Nessa notices.

'Billy, where are we going?'

'The Medical Centre,' I reply, though I'm not sure she's heard me. I'm moving like a steam train, like a snow plough, kicking my way through the drifts. The wind is helping me, blowing me along, even Nessa seems to be struggling in my wake. I pay the price, of course. I'm not that fit. There's a pain in my side, a stitch, and I slow down. But Nessa's there to help, she overtakes me without asking questions. The Tesseract looms out of the white haze, a crystalline cliff, and beyond the glass I can see the flat water of the pool, its lights dimmed and fountains quiet.

Nessa finds the path to the main entrance, turns aside to the Medical Centre and pushes straight through the door. I follow, there are no lights in the small reception room but it's warm and dry. 'Cath?' I shout. It's naïve of me. Why should she be alone here, when everyone else is in the Tesseract?

'Who's that?' comes a reply from behind the door marked 'Doctor'.

'It's me, Billy Oliphant,' I shout. 'Are you okay?'

The door opens. 'Is there any reason why I shouldn't be okay?' Cath sails elegantly from the room, blinking over half-rimmed glasses. She's carrying a glass in one hand, in the other a paperback is folded open. She narrows her eyes at Nessa. 'I know you, don't I?'

'I work here,' Nessa answers defensively, 'I came to see you a few months ago.'

'And what was the problem?'

'I had a rash.'

Cath frowns, exercises her memory. 'Oh yes, I remember now,' she smiles, 'it was on your backside. Huge it was. The rash, that is. Recurrent problem, you said. Now, if you'd just introduced yourself by dropping your trousers and presenting your formerly afflicted area, I would have recognised you straightaway.'

'Have you been drinking?' I ask carefully, not wanting to offend her.

Cath looks at me. She looks at the glass in her hand. 'Oh dear. You've found me out. I suppose it's with you being a detective. How did you know?'

I suppose my expression makes it clear that I don't value her sarcasm.

'I'm having my regular evening glass of sherry. There was a study not so long ago, published in the *BMJ*, one glass of red wine a day is good for the heart. So I take mine a little fortified. Would you care to join me? I've no more glasses, but I do have several coffee cups.'

'No thanks,' I say, 'I'm here because I need your help.'

'You need my help? Tell me more.' She ushers us into the office, takes her place behind a large desk. She peers at us with eyes she's borrowed from a consultant. 'I do hope you haven't found me another body?'

I'm sure I can detect some hope in her voice that that is exactly what we have done.

'No, just an old one. Eric Salkeld's.'

'He's not up and about, is he?'

'No.'

'That's a relief, if he'd been Lazarus you'd have had to change *your* name as well. So what, precisely, is the problem?'

'I don't think Eric Salkeld was murdered.'

'That's your prerogative, Mr Oliphant. How, then, do you explain the marks at his ankles and wrists?'

'That's why I wanted to talk to you. You think Salkeld was tied up and hanged?'

Cath nods wisely.

'Could I ask you about the possibility of something else happening? How would you react if I suggested that he tied himself up . . .'

'Mr Oliphant, come come. Are you suggesting that this was insurance, in case he wanted to back out of a suicide attempt? "I want to kill myself, but I'm afraid I might not have the guts to finish myself off. So I'll tie my hands and feet . . ." never mind the difficulty of doing *that* . . . "then I'll hop over to the wall and hang myself." No, I don't think that would work. And where did the restraining cords go? Really, you haven't thought this through, have you?'

Nessa is curious, she's looking at me, waiting for me to say something.

'I don't think it was suicide,' I say.

'So you agree with me.' Cath's voice suggests there was never any other option.

'No. As I said before, I don't think it was murder either.'

'Not suicide?' Nessa sums up, 'And not murder? There's not much else left.'

171

'There is,' I say. 'Accidental death.'

Nessa and Cath remain silent. They want explanations.

'I'll have to go over the whole thing, if you've any objections, any problems, let me know. I don't really know if this will hold together, but ... Here goes. Eric Salkeld was a loner. He didn't have any close friends, no wife, no family. But he did have some unusual habits. Cath, you'll have to believe me on this, but Nessa's seen the evidence. He was into bondage. He enjoyed being tied up. Yes?'

'That's right,' Nessa confirms.

'So perhaps he goes places, when he can, where they'll indulge him his peculiarities. But not here. Here we're in the wilds, there's nowhere for him to go. So he does what he can to get his kicks. He dresses up. He ties himself up – it can be done, I'm sure it can be done – and takes photographs of himself. And then it goes wrong. He suffocates himself.'

Cath's shaking her head. 'I wouldn't have believed it,' she says. 'If I hadn't known you were medically illiterate I'd have sworn you've been reading the medical magazines. You haven't, have you? No, I can tell that. But you know, you might just be right.'

'I might?' I'd been expecting some opposition.

'Yes. I read about something a while ago, where was it?' She climbs to her feet. At the back of the room is a bookcase with magazines filed neatly in plastic racks. She bends down and begins to rifle through them. 'The doctor doesn't like me keeping these,' she says, 'she insists they're mostly anecdotal rubbish. No real evidence in them.'

'What are they?' Nessa asks.

'Sort of trade magazines, they run articles on what it's like being a doctor rather than learned papers on medicine. Tell GPs how to maximise their profit and so on. But they do one-offs, "my most memorable medical moment," that sort of thing. Far more readable than the *BMJ*. Trouble is, they don't do an index.' She pulls out several batches of magazines. 'There was one in particular, it had something

172

in it about suicide and murder and,' she looks up at me, 'sexual gratification. It stuck in my mind, I can remember thinking "that would make a good plot for a film".' She picks up and discards magazine after magazine.

'Can we help?' I ask.

'You wouldn't know what to look for. Remember, I do have a little experience in these matters.'

So we wait. We wait for five minutes, then ten.

'We could always go back to the Tesseract,' Nessa suggests, 'and if Cath finds anything . . .'

'No need.' Cath rises to her feet triumphantly. 'Didn't I say I'd find it? And here we are.' She waves the open magazine aloft, a Chamberlainesque gesture which worries me. She seems in no hurry to read the article out.

'What does it say?' I ask.

She sits down and reads to herself silently.

'Well?'

'As I remembered. Police found a mechanic – dead, of course – hanging in an inspection pit in the garage where he worked. The doctor – he's the one writing the piece – goes on about a "celebrated" case where a soldier was found hanging in the barracks. The army pathologist found a fracture in the thyroid plate and that was interpreted as the result of suicide.' She beams at me over her glasses.

'So?'

'So two months later the dead man's widow married another soldier. There had been rumours of a long-lasting affair between them and these came to the attention of the authorities. They conducted another post-mortem.' She pauses again, an infuriating habit.

'And?'

'The original evidence was confirmed, but they decided that the furrow from the rope was higher than the damage to the larynx. They decided the fracture was caused by a blow. Possibly a punch to the throat. So they investigated further, found that the widow's new husband was an ex-commando. They asked questions, found an accomplice.

The ex-commando had killed his rival with a blow to the throat then, with the help of the accomplice, strung the body up to make it look like suicide. If only he'd waited a little while to get married, there might not have been so many whispers, so many rumours.'

'I'm sorry,' Nessa interrupts, 'am I missing something? Surely it would need a post-mortem on Eric Salkeld to decide whether or not the fractured whatsit and the burn marks from the rope are in the same place. And we don't have the facilities or the personnel to do a post-mortem. Unless you count hatchet Harry from veg-prep, but his experience is limited to carrots and cabbage.'

'I don't think Cath has finished,' I point out, 'there's still the mechanic.'

'Quite. Now then, where was I? Oh yes, the doctor looking at the mechanic was wary of deciding how he'd died, given the precedent of this other case. When he examined the body he found none of the normal signs of asphyxia. The only injury appeared to be the very slight abrasion caused by the rope. All the internal structures of the neck were intact.' She glances down at the magazine in front of her. '"Death was due to cardiac inhibition from accidental vagal constriction." Oh, and they'd found a plastic bag on the floor, probably used for partial suffocation. That, when coupled with neck constriction, can produce sexual excitement. It appears that some people like to be strangled.'

Perhaps it's my imagination, but I'm sure I can detect a trace of a blush on Nessa's face.

'What's this "vagal constriction" business,' Nessa asks, trying to cover her embarrassment. I was about to ask the same question.

'Vagal constriction? Right, I'll explain.' Cath rises from her seat behind the desk, intent on impressing and enjoying her captive audience. 'The vagus nerve comes out of the brain and its branches wander round the body, servicing the organs of the neck, thorax and abdomen. It controls secretion and movement. Now then, if the vagus and accessory nerves are affected by, say, constriction, pressure on the throat, then the signals to various organs can be affected. There's a danger of asphyxia . . .'

'I thought you said there would be no symptoms of asphyxia.'

Cath glares at me, but her smooth, round face soon resumes its colourful plasticity. After all, my interruption shows how dependent I am on her knowledge.

'As I said, there's a *danger* of asphyxia. That's because the throat and larynx can, in effect, be rendered useless. Squeeze too hard and no air can pass into the lungs. Result? Asphyxia. But,' she hurries on, 'constriction of the throat can be taken so far, not enough to cause asphyxia, but enough to affect the way the vagal nerve functions. Then it would give similar feelings to those produced as orgasm approaches, brought about by an increase in the rate of heartbeat; because the vagal nerve supplies the heart. Blood is pumped around the body, the skin becomes flushed, breathing becomes more rapid, even though the ability to breathe is lessened by the constriction. But if the signal from the vagal nerve is interrupted for too long then the heart shuts down. Cardiac inhibition. Excitement can do strange things.'

I want to make sure I've got this right. 'So constriction less than that needed for asphyxiation can still cause death due to the heart closing down?'

Nessa looks worried. 'Wow. I've heard of the little death before, but that's taking things too far.'

'Come on,' I say, 'get your coats on. We need to visit Salkeld again.'

Cath is already on her way, she moves gracefully and purposefully. I'm reminded of a television programme I saw once, filming hippos underwater. 'I take it you want to check his neck,' she says. 'I'll bring the ophthalmoscope, it's all I have. It might do for his throat.'

We step out into another blizzard. The wind clutches at

the hem of Cath's coat, snaps and billows it like a sail. I grab hold of one arm to steady her, Nessa takes the other, and we scuttle round the side of the Tesseract to the makeshift mortuary. It takes us no more than five minutes. I fumble and grope at the lock, unwilling to remove my gloves, but it needs Nessa's hand to open the door for me. Then we're inside.

The two corpses can feel no colder than I do. One of the sheets is tinged with red, I have to assume that Amy's body lies beneath that. I like to think I'm hardened to death. After all, I've spent so many years in its company, investigating it, shadowing it, at times even courting it, that I should be used to its presence. But this is different. Never before have I been so involved in one death. The body lying underneath the sheet could have been, should have been, mine. I was undoubtedly the target. I'm not stupid enough to think Amy's death was my fault – I certainly didn't pull the trigger. But I was involved in the train of events which led to her death; and if, at some time, I'd done something different (I don't know what; turned left instead of right, stayed at the lodge instead of hiding in the staff residences, taken my coat with me) then Amy might still be alive.

'Let's have a look, then.' Cath is in her element. She tugs aside the sheet covering Salkeld, adjusts her glasses on the end of her nose and peers at his neck. 'This is where the rope abraded his neck.'

I bend close, pleased to have any interruption to my thoughts. The skin is reddened in a narrow stripe high beneath the chin, less so at the side of the neck. Cath turns the head to one side.

'And here, at the back of the head, there's a small patch of hair worn away. The knot in the rope, perhaps?'

I do my duty, move round to stand beside Cath and follow her directions, agree her finding. Then I lift Salkeld's arm.

'What are you doing, young man?' Cath asks. She wants me to know she's in charge.

'He's shaved under his arms,' I tell her.

It's another clue, a small sign pointing me along a path I've already decided to take. Cath, meanwhile, is pulling Salkeld's head back. When his neck is taut she runs her hands along it.

'I can't feel anything untoward,' she says, 'nothing obviously broken. Here, hold his head for me. And open his mouth.'

I hold his head in position, mouth open, and Cath shines her ophthalmoscope into his mouth.

'I'm no expert,' she says, 'I've no specific experience in this field, but I can't see any damage. No blood in the mouth. I can't see down his throat, though, and even if I could, I'm not sure what I should be looking for.'

'But on the balance of things?'

'I suspect it's as you say. I wonder if . . .'

'If what?'

'Just a hunch.' She covers the head and pulls the sheet away from Salkeld's body. She sees Nessa look away.

'Not very attractive,' Cath says, 'but it's not aesthetics I'm looking for, dear, it's function.' She takes a pair of powdered latex gloves from her handbag, snaps them onto her hands. Nessa and I say nothing, I'm sure I can speak for both of us when I say I've no idea what Cath is going to do.

'If Mr Salkeld here was doing as you suggest, then there may be more specific evidence.' She reaches across his body and lifts his penis with one finger. 'He may, at some time, have been in a state of sexual arousal.' She peels back his foreskin. 'He may have had an erection.' She bends down and examines the organ closely. I back away slightly, pleased to find that Nessa has done the same. There's an anticipatory grimace on her face.

'What are you looking for?' she asks.

'He may have ejaculated. And if so, there might have been traces of semen beneath the foreskin. Though I can't see any.'

Nessa steps even further away. 'Doesn't it dry out?' Evaporate or something? I mean, would you expect to see it so long after his death?'

'I don't know,' Cath answers, 'if this was a path lab they'd be able to take scrapings, tissue samples, find out by microscopy or even spectrum analysis.' I'm not sure she knows what she's talking about, but it sounds good.

She moves one hand to the base of Salkeld's penis and squeezes the flaccid organ between thumb and forefinger, then she moves her fingers upwards. 'Suppose he ejaculated but we can't see anything. There might just be a trace of semen still remaining in the urethra, and if there is . . .' She holds the foreskin back with the fingers of one hand, milks his penis with the other. And at the tip of the gland a small, almost translucent pearl of liquid appears. She bends down, sniffs it. Nessa turns away. I think I close my eyes.

'Not urine,' she announces. 'Of course, this isn't firm evidence. But I think it would be reasonable to assume that Mr Salkeld here was in a state of sexual excitement at the time of his death.' I open my eyes to see her let the penis flop down to hide once more in the nest of hair. Then she grins in triumph.

'I'm freezing,' Nessa announces, 'come on, let's go back.'

Cath discards her gloves. 'I think I deserve another glass of sherry.'

'I'll buy you a bottle,' I tell her.

The wind is beating at the door, trying to get in. A powder of snow has been forced through the small opening at the bottom of the door. I take the key from my pocket, raise my hand to the lightswitch. 'Bye, Amy,' I say.

Chapter Twenty-Two

I refuse Cath's offer of a sherry, make do with tea. She and Nessa split what's left of the bottle, pour the red-brown liquid straight into their mugs.

'That's only one problem solved,' says Nessa. 'Eve Marton said that, when she found the body, it was dressed in pyjamas.'

I nod. 'It certainly was when I saw it.'

'But if Salkeld was tied up, if he was ... well, I assume he was masturbating or something.'

'Not with his hands tied. Just the feeling of constriction round his neck would be enough to give him an erection. Then there'd be the thrill of his costume ...'

Cath puts down her mug. 'Costume? Is there something you haven't told me?'

'We think he might have been wearing women's clothing. A red lycra basque. And all the trimmings.'

'Oh. I see. But why change his costume?'

I decide I might as well tell her, she already knows a great deal. 'He left a suicide note, it was a confession that he'd been stealing company money. If he'd been dressed in a basque it would have drawn attention away from the crime. So whoever found him in his fetish outfit saw straightaway that he could be of use. Here's a body, why not blame him for ... well, for anything. Write him a suicide note on a floppy disk – very handy, no handwriting to match – and there you have it. The perfect scapegoat, no chance of him complaining.'

Nessa sounds worried. 'So you don't think he actually did it? The fraud, that is, fiddling the payroll?'

'It doesn't really matter whether he did or not. If he wasn't involved, then someone else was, and he was simply unlucky enough to kill himself at a convenient time for that person. And if he was involved, then he had a partner, and that partner discovered his body. Why else would that person write the fake suicide note? Whichever way you look at it, someone else was responsible for fiddling the payroll. All I need to do now is find out who.'

'It was someone big, someone strong,' Cath says. 'Salkeld was no lightweight. Someone lifted him down from the hook, untied him, undressed him, hung him back up again. Have you ever tried moving a heavy, floppy body? I have. Just lifting a patient from a trolley to a bed is awkward, even if you've got help. This would be even more difficult, there's an upward movement to unhook him, then a carry. And try reversing that. I couldn't do it.'

Once again we're silent. I close my eyes and try to concentrate.

'There can't be that many people,' Cath says, 'with the opportunity, the motive, the skills to do all that.' She's swirling the sherry round in her glass. 'I mean, it has to be someone with access to the computer system, surely?'

The alcohol, or the gale, or the excitement, any combination of these, has played with Cath's hair, moved a few lacquered strands here and there. Framing a normal face the effect might be unnoticeable, but I've come to see Cath as perpetually immaculate. She looks dishevelled, the colour in her cheeks is less red but more natural than it was earlier, her lipstick is blurred. But as she's become more human, less artificial, her common sense has come to the fore. Everything she's said has been logical, helpful, and reinforced my own thinking.

'There's only one person I can think of,' I tell her and,

out of the corner of my eye, I can see Nessa nodding. 'I didn't want to believe it, but it can only be Eve Marton.'

'So what happens now?' Nessa asks.

'I confront her.'

'Will confronting her be easy?' It's Cath's turn to look worried.

'I hope so. She's bigger than me.'

Chapter Twenty-Three

I try to avoid confrontation unless the odds are stacked heavily in my favour. That usually means I have large companions with me whose presence intimidates my confrontee. It also helps to have specific, incontrovertible evidence of wrongdoing. In this instance I have none of these. My intention is to have Sly come with me to seek out Eve Marton, but I change my mind when I find him. For a start, it's late, two in the morning, and he's asleep. The time of day wouldn't, in itself, normally stop me waking him; but he's lying with Paula cradled in one arm and a twin nestling in the other. Then there's the fact that Eve Marton hasn't struck me as a violent woman. So I leave Sly, with a touch of jealousy, to his family and his dreams.

Nessa's decided to help me with the search. The logical place to start is the Tesseract itself, though we realise we haven't seen Eve Marton for the whole day. So we begin. Together we step over sleeping bodies and apologise to those we disturb. The lighting has been dimmed, it makes identification difficult. Nessa works faster than me, peering under blankets and lifting sheets to see who's beneath. If I work more slowly, more thoroughly, I tell myself it's because I'm looking for twice as many people. Kirsty wasn't where she ought to have been, with Sly and Paula and their kids.

We cover the ground twice, checking each other's patch

then searching together. There's no sign of Eve, no sign of Kirsty. I'm beginning to develop a double worry.

'Is there anywhere else,' I ask Nessa, 'a hiding place we might not know about?'

'I've checked, I've asked other members of staff. She wouldn't be in the offices or the accommodation block. She must be somewhere in the Tesseract.'

'Who knows the place well, really well?'

'I don't know. Morland, perhaps?'

I don't really want to see him, but there seems little alternative. 'Let's try him. And how about Sam Ellis, if he's any good at his job he should be able to think of any bolt-holes.'

'I haven't seen either of them around.'

'Morland'll be in his office, hiding from reality.'

I'm already on my way, heading for the stairs to the executive suite. There's only emergency lighting, but it's bright enough to see where I'm going. I'm pleased Nessa's behind me, the psychological benefit of having a helper is often greater than the contribution that helper can make.

There's a faint light under and at the sides of Morland's door, and the sound of voices. I put my ear to the door and listen, but I can't make out what's being said, so I push, gently. The door swings open on managerial hinges.

The voices are the hissing, uncommunicative mumblings of a radio whose batteries are on the point of death. The light comes from a gas-fed lamp, turned low to conserve its energy. There's a gas heater glowing blue-red close to the desk; any heat it's expelling is localised, the room is chilled, cold. There's a figure slumped at the desk, unidentifiable in a heavy coat and ear-flapped cap. On the desk are two empty bottles of whisky, though I suspect one of them has spilled – there's a smell of alcohol in the room.

'Morland?' My voice isn't gentle, but the figure doesn't stir. 'Morland? Is that you?'

There's no danger, but I find myself approaching the desk stealthily, as if I might find something more unpleasant than a man I dislike in a drunken stupor. I feel no sympathy for him or for his problems, though I'm more likely than most to have shared his experiences.

'Morland, wake up.' I shake his shoulder without having any effect, then grab both shoulders and pull him upright in his chair. His eyes open, then close again as his head lolls forward, chin on chest.

'I need to ask you some questions,' I tell him, though he doesn't hear me. I slap his face. It doesn't help, but I derive a certain amount of pleasure from it.

'How about some water?' Nessa suggests. She's already heading for the washroom, returns with two glasses. I pull Morland's head back and dribble water down his face. He shakes his head, flaps his hands about. I throw the rest of the water at him.

'Morland! Wake up!'

His eyes fly open. 'Whasamatta?'

'I need to ask you some questions, Mr Morland.'

'Who . . .? Who the hell . . .?' His eyes may be open but they're having difficulty focusing.

'It's me, Mr Morland, Billy Oliphant. You're pissed out of your mind, which doesn't really help, but I'm hoping there's enough sense left in that pinhead brain of yours to let you answer some questions.'

'Fuck off, Oliphant.' His pronunciation is slurred but perfect, as is my aim. The slaps I gave him before were an attempt to wake him. The next is simply a desire to hurt. It's open-handed but he can't see it coming, and I've taken aim and put all my weight behind it. His head rolls to one side. He makes a noise which is a groaning, swearing yell of protest and a shocked whimper of pain at the same time. Blood flows straightaway from the cut his teeth make on the inside of his mouth.

'I need you to answer some questions, Morland.'

'You bastard!'

I raise my arm slowly, his eyes follow the motion. 'Do you want me to hit you again?'

'No! No, please, don' hit me 'gain.' He's realised how drunk, how incapable of defending himself he is.

'I'm looking for Eve Marton. Do you know where she is?'

'No. Why sh'd I know where tha' fuckin' bitch is?' He wipes the corner of his mouth with his hand.

'Your future could depend on you remembering where she might be.'

'Future? Got no fuckin' future. You've fuckin' made sure 'f tha'.'

'Come on, Billy, he can't tell you anything.' Nessa looks at him. 'Christ, look, he's pissed himself.'

'No future. Finished, I am. When they hear 'bout all this. Dead people ev'rywhere. 'N' you, Billy fuckin' Oliphant, call y'self a detective? Y've done nothin', y'know nothin', y're thick's shit. 'N' I was the one want'd yu t' work here! Tha' makes me almost's thick's you!'

'Don't hit him again, Billy, he's not worth it.'

I don't intending hitting him again. I bend down in front of him so I'm sure he can see and hear me. 'You should be swearing at Eve Marton, not me. She's the one who's caused all this, not me. Remember me, Morland. Remember my face. I'm the one who's trying to help you. Eve Marton stole money from you, she might be involved in a murder, and she's not downstairs with the rest of the people on his godforsaken site. So where might she be?' Okay, I'm not telling him everything. I don't mention that Salkeld killed himself accidentally. But I need to keep things simple in case he knows anything.

'Sh's gone?' Morland tries to laugh. 'Good luck to 'er. She could do it 's well, the bitch. Sh' knows the place, sh' told us once, ages ago. Back 'f 'er hand, sh' said. Better'n anybody.' He sweeps his hand across the desk, the bottle and radio and glass fly across the room. 'I hope sh' gets away.'

He lowers his head to the table. I move forward to prod him back into wakefulness.

185

'Leave him,' Nessa says, 'he doesn't know anything, and even if he did, he's not capable of telling you. With a bit of luck he'll drown in his own vomit.'

'But where can Eve Marton be? She can't have left the site, look at it out there.' The snow's a banshee at the window, clawing to get in and rip our souls from our bodies.

'He didn't say she'd left the site.' Nessa's working something out, she's wearing a pained look on her face. I know better than to interrupt. 'He said she knew the site well. She's been here longer than me, before it was even operating properly. I've seen her out running as well, in good weather and not very fast, but she looked as if she knew where she was going.'

'Could she be in one of the empty lodges?'

'What's the point? She'd need heat and light, she might be seen. And she'd still be around when the thaw comes, and when it does there's only one way out, and she'd know we – or the police – would be watching it.'

'So where is she?'

Nessa shakes her head again. 'I've no idea, Billy.'

'Come on. We need to find Sam Ellis.'

'If he wasn't on the floor he can only be in the kitchen. He always was fond of his stomach.'

We hurry downstairs again, through the food area and into the kitchen. Fewer than a third of the ceiling lights are switched on, and in the dimness the only person I can see is a woman in a chef's hat. She's chopping carrots, slowly, methodically, with venom.

'Mary,' Nessa asks, 'seen Sam Ellis anywhere?'

'Usual place,' comes the reply, 'warming his arse.' She jerks a thumb towards the back of the room where a rack of plates, pots and pans forms a dividing wall.

'Sam!' shouts Nessa, 'You in there?'

'Who wants me?' comes the terse reply.

I round the corner to find him leaning back on one chair, feet up on another. He's holding a mug of tea and there's a novel, spine split, on his knee. He looks at me. It's as if he's put a grape in his mouth then found it's an olive and he's choking on the stone.

'What do *you* want?' he asks.

It would be easy to offer him any of a whole range of insults. He's uncaring, ineffective, but I need his help. So I decide to be honest because the matter's becoming urgent, my mind is building a bridge between the two people I can't find, Kirsty and Eve Marton. I don't want to think about the nature of that bridge.

'Sam, I need your help.'

He seems surprised. 'Why should I help you?'

'Because no one else can. You're the only one who might know the information I need.'

He considers the statement. I hope my need is tangible, I don't want to waste any time.

'What do you want?' He's still wary.

'Where's the back door?'

He grins. 'You're looking for Eve Marton? She's got away?'

'I think so. We can't find her anywhere in the building, we're sure she won't be out in the lodges or the staff rooms or the offices.'

Nessa picks up the question. 'We thought there might be a hiding place in the Tesseract, somewhere we haven't thought of.'

'Hold on, hold on, that's two different questions.'

Nessa looks at me. 'Two questions? I thought ...'

'*You*,' he says, looking at Nessa, 'asked about hiding places. But Mr Oliphant here, Mr high-and-mighty Oliphant, Mr security-expert Oliphant, asked about the back door. Entirely different matters.'

'The term "back door",' I say to Nessa, 'has a specific security meaning. Every building, every group of buildings gathered together under a security umbrella, has a front door and a back door. The front door is the normal way in, the way most people use. The back door is used for special occasions. It's the way some employees get into, for example, an airport. It's the tradesman's entrance. It's the special sliproads police and maintenance vehicles use on motorways.'

Sam Ellis takes over. 'Some places – very few – have a back door modified as part of the front door. Prisons, for example. Some, like theatres, have back doors that should only work as exits, usually emergency exits.'

'So where is Forestcrag's back door?' My voice is quiet, needy.

'You really think I'd tell you? Even if there was one?'

I bend close to him and he backs away in his seat, but my hands are on his arms. I whisper to him, 'Sam, I can't find Eve Marton. I can't find my daughter either.' I let go of his sleeves and stand up. He too rises to his feet.

'Follow me,' he says. He leads the way across the kitchen, back out into the main space of the Tesseract. 'Over here,' he says, 'see, the site plan?'

The map is large, on one side it shows the various attractions within the Tesseract, on the other is a larger map of the whole Forestcrag site. Normally it's well lit, press a button and it shows you where you are, where you want to go and the best way of getting there. There are no lights shining at the moment. Ellis takes a torch from his pocket, holds it to one side so the reflection in the glass is diminished.

'Here's the Tesseract,' he says, 'this is the only way in. You can see all the internal roads and paths and tracks, but the only entrance and exit to the site is the one you, and everyone else, used when they arrived. Now then, suppose you were desperate enough to want out by a different route. Suppose you were reasonably well equipped – and Eve Marton's had time to plan her escape and get her stuff together – and knew the area well. Did Eve Marton know the site well?'

I nod. I have to take the joint word of Nessa and Morland that she did.

'Okay, then. To the south here, there's nothing but forest, a huge amount of forest, all artificial, row upon row of pine and spruce and other greenery. There are fire-breaks, but they lead down to the forest tracks. And where do the tracks lead?' He stabs at the map. 'Back here, back to the entrance road! Go that way and you've a long, long journey to end up back where you started.' He moves across in front of me, pushes me to one side. 'To the west, up here, nothing but moorland and upland bog. Way beyond there's an army firing range, but no habitation. In this weather it would be impassable. So where does that leave us? The north!'

I squint but can see nothing at the top of the map, it's too high and the reflections of the gaslight bounce from it into my eyes.

'Chairs,' says Sam, 'get some chairs.'

I drag three seats from the empty cafeteria, position them carefully. We climb onto our platforms.

'That's better. Look, up here, where do you see?'

It's not an ordnance survey map with familiar symbols. There's a blue line running up the map, I take it that's a stream, and near the top of the map is what's clearly a waterfall. Either side of it are rocks. I say as much to Ellis.

'That's exactly it. Those are the crags in Forestcrags. But they aren't real.'

'Oh? So what does that tell me?'

'They're real rocks, Oliphant, but they aren't real crags. There was a quarry there, hasn't been used for years and years. When they built this place they decided to make feature of it. So they put in a reservoir, there's a natural flow of water into it through the main quarry, and they made a waterfall. It looks quite nice.'

'So?'

'In summer we run rock-climbing courses there, in the quarry. There are still the ruins of old buildings there, and spoil heaps and so on. But there's one building still intact, it's an old wooden hut where the ropes and harnesses are

189

kept. I've been in it. It's only a front and sides of a building, the rest is carved out of the rock. But it's got a stove and a supply of wood in there, and old furniture even, a desk and a chair.'

'It sounds really cosy, Sam. If you're suggesting Eve Marton is hiding there, I'd have to ask why. It doesn't make it any easier for her to escape.'

'Let me finish, Oliphant. I know this site well. There's a footpath leads out, near the base of the waterfall, up the side of the old quarry, to the climbing hut. But it keeps going, further up the quarry, out over the top. Then it joins up with an old track, probably the track the quarry used to get its stone out or its men in. It's a two-mile walk – downhill, an easy slope – to the main road. And there's a farm. That's the back door to Forestcrag. The only back door.'

'I suppose it's a possibility,' Nessa says without enthusiasm.

I try to weigh the information Sam Ellis has given us. There's a farm at the end of the track. Vehicles, probably something four wheel drive. A road. Escape. If it was me I might try it. It's clear, logical. It's like Eve Marton. She could be there with a fire, a torch, sleeping bag, books to read, waiting for the weather to break. And then she'd be away. She might even have Kirsty with her.

'We'll have to go and look,' I say. I'm down from the chair before I realise I don't know where I'm going. Sam Ellis clambers down beside me.

'Thank you,' I say, 'thank you very much.' I shake his hand.

'I hope you find her,' he says ambivalently, quick to release my hand. 'Now if you don't mind, I've some tea to finish.' He waddles back to the kitchen.

'Yes,' I say to his retreating back, 'and I've got to get my stuff together, get out there.'

'Not yet,' says Nessa, grabs my arm. 'If she's there, in the hut at the quarry, she won't go, she can't go, till the weather improves. And it's too dangerous for her to be wandering around the quarry in the dark. So we have time, time to prepare ourselves, time to have a sleep.' She glances at her watch. 'It's three in the morning, Billy.'

'I won't sleep,' I tell her.

'Oh yes you will. Not straightaway, perhaps, but you will sleep. Come on.' She holds out her hand and I take it. 'Quietly,' she says, 'we don't want to disturb anyone.' We put back the chairs then thread our way through random sleeping, snoring adults, past snuffling children cuddling toys and parents. The storm is still battering at the Tesseract, but it's being kept at bay by dreams.

'I'll find a way to relax you,' Nessa whispers as we reach the door to her room. She pulls me into her arms and kisses me long and hard, takes my tongue between her teeth and bites. Then she stops. We both hear it, a noise beyond the door.

Nessa puts her mouth to my ear. 'Did I lock the door? I can't remember.'

I shrug, push her to one side. It could be Eve Marton in there. It could be Harry Simpson, eager for revenge, armed. I should back off, take Nessa's key and lock the door, wake Sly, get help. Then the noise comes again, faint but discernible, a gasp of pain, a groan. I don't really have any choice.

There are two ways of entering. The first involves me motioning to Nessa, trying to tell her that she should twist the handle so I can kick open the door. It sounds melodramatic, the type of thing police do in gangster movies, but it's quick and effective and it would get me in there quickly with the element of surprise on my side. The trouble is, I don't know what I'll be throwing myself into. The alternative is for me to twist the handle, slowly, gently, noiselessly, then open the door a fraction, then a little more, a little more, until I can see into the room. I might lose out on the element of surprise, but I might be able to see what's going on. Option two is less flashy, but it's also less dangerous.

I turn the handle so slowly I can't believe it's moving, but I make no sound. I stand to one side as I push the door open, if the occupant fires a gun then my arm may be injured but the rest of me stays intact. Little by little I see more and more.

First I see a torch standing on its end, pointing at the ceiling, its light diffused by a piece of material. I push the door further, the mattresses Nessa and I were using earlier are still in place. I push the door further still, it's open wide enough for me to edge into the room if I want to. I flatten myself against the door jamb, squeeze myself into the gap, move my head slowly round the door. In the dim light I can see two figures. One is obviously female, she has long hair and is sitting astride the other. The man's hands are grasping the woman's breasts and she's gasping as she pushes at him, forward and back, forward and back. 'Christ,' I hear her whisper, 'Oh Jesus Christ, I'm coming Phil, I'm coming.'

I heave at the door, it cracks against the frame and bounces back hard against my hand. I don't feel the pain. I step into the room and can sense Nessa behind me, peering past me. The figures cease their sliding and thrusting, four eyes stare at me, try to make sense of my silhouette in the doorway.

'Who the hell are you?' says the male voice, he pushes the woman off him, behind him, and climbs to his feet. He's young and muscular, but I have venom on my side. I could easily kill him. But I don't have the opportunity. The woman steps out from behind him. She reaches for the material draped over the torch, forms it into a T-shirt and pulls it over her head.

'It's all right, Phil,' she says, 'I can deal with this.' Then she looks at me, speaks easily, smoothly, with a maturity beyond her years. The words come close to killing me.

'I think we need to talk, Dad.'

Chapter Twenty-Four

They were the words Sara used, the words she used so
often at the end. 'I think we need to talk.' It was never a
good opening to what was usually a one-sided conversation.
I'd invariably retreat into my shell of self-pity, self-hatred,
self-defence; it didn't matter which, the important part was
my concern with myself at the expense of everyone else.
But this time it's different, this time I have something to
say. Something to say? I needed a more gentle introduction
to my daughter's sexuality. If we'd lived together it might
have been easier. I would have been more familiar with her
mood swings, the extra packs of Tampax in the bathroom,
briefs soaking to remove blood stains. I would have told her
to stop borrowing my razor and buy her own. I would have
known she was growing up, I would have met her friends,
girls I might have looked at in the street with admiration,
lust even, before I recognised them and realised they were
so young. I would have tutted at the magazines I'd found
when tidying her bedroom, magazines filled with pictures
of young men described as 'boyfs', magazines talking
freely and easily about orgasms and masturbation, penises
and sex, problems with relationships and love and parents. I
would have been aware that she was staying out late at
weekends, going to pubs and clubs (she'd be too young,
yes, but I'd know how sensible she was). I might even have
met some of her friends, friends who were, by accident,

male, and – once or twice – stayed the night because it was a long way home. They'd sleep in the spare bedroom, of course. Then I'd realise that one boy in particular (the polite one, the one who always offered to wash the dishes, the one who shook my hand when I was first introduced to him, the one who reminded me of me when I was young) stayed more often than the others. Then he'd stay to the exclusion of the others. And sometimes, at night, I'd imagine I'd heard the sound of footsteps on the landing. Perhaps, after several months, when I'd become used to the way she sat on his lap and the way his hand stroked her thigh when they watched television together, I'd find a stubborn used condom in the toilet or a pressed-out foil strip that once contained birth-control pills in the waste-bin. Then I'd be thankful that my daughter was wise, had chosen her partner well, was taking precautions to avoid pregnancy or disease. But I didn't have those advantages, I didn't have that introduction. All I had was a daughter who used to be a little girl but was now a woman, and I'm finding it difficult to cope with that.

'I'll wait outside,' I say to the floor, unable to look at her. 'You tidy yourself up. We can have a chat when you're ready.'

It's not what I wanted to say, we all know that. That's why there's a murmur of talk, sound for the sake of breaking the silence, everyone speaking at once. 'I'm sorry, Mr Oliphant, I'm so sorry, I don't know what you must be thinking . . .' 'It's all right, Billy, it's perfectly natural, I'm sure they've been sensible . . .' 'I'll get dressed, Dad, I'll be out in a minute, don't blame Phil . . .'

Phil and Kirsty are, independently, struggling into their clothes. Nessa's pushing me towards the door. 'Come on,' she says, 'leave them alone for a while. They feel worse than you do.'

'Do they?' I spit. 'Do they really?' We're outside the door, but I'm still hissing at Nessa. 'It looked to me as if they were feeling rather pleased with themselves.

Deliriously happy, in fact. Those noises I heard weren't cries of sorrow.'

'That wasn't what I meant and you know it. Stop being so bloody-minded and obtuse.' She's angry with me, and for a moment I'm not sure why.

'Christ, Nessa, I've just found my daughter screwing someone she's only known for two days! Who is he? What does she know about him? He could be . . .'

'Billy, do you realise what you're saying?'

'What?'

'How long have we known each other? What were we doing earlier? I think we beat them to it by a good few hours.'

'That's different!' I know as soon as I've said it that it isn't different. I want to – need to – tell Nessa I'm sorry. I've spoken without thinking, which is nothing new for me, but the opportunity to apologise is destroyed as the door opens. I can only look helplessly at Nessa and hope she can read my anguish. Whatever I do, whatever I say, I end up hurting someone.

'Dad?'

Kirsty looks soft, fragile. Her make-up is blurred, it's as if I've suddenly become myopic. I don't know what to say. I know what I want to say, and I think I know what I ought to say, but the two are far apart and bringing them together seems impossible. The only thing I can do, the only thing that makes sense to me, doesn't involve words. I take a step towards Kirsty and hold out my arms, and she throws herself into them. That helps. That's exactly what I need, and I realise she's done everything right, everything she ought to have done.

'Are you okay?' I whisper into her ear. She pulls away from me a little and I see her eyes are wet. She can't speak, but she nods.

'Do you like him?' I ask. 'Have you taken precautions?'

She swallows. 'Yes, twice yes.'

'Good. Good.' I stroke her hair. 'I'm not angry, love.

195

Just surprised. I didn't expect to see you there. I didn't expect to see you ...'

'Making love?'

They aren't the words I would have chosen. 'Having sex' would have been nearer the truth, but Kirsty's words must be her own. If that's what she believes, what she wants to believe, why should I shatter her illusions? Especially now.

'No. It was something of a shock.'

'We didn't mean ... That is, we hadn't planned to ... Not in there, that is. But I was upset about Amy, and so was Phil, and we needed somewhere quiet to talk and think. The door was open. I started crying and he put his arm round me and ... It just sort of went on from there.'

'It happens,' I tell her, 'don't worry. As long as you're okay.'

'I'm okay,' she replies, 'as long as you are as well.'

'I can cope, love. It's just a lot to come to terms with, that your daughter isn't ...'

'... a virgin any more?' She looks straight at me. 'I lost that qualification a while ago, Dad.'

'That isn't what I was going to say. I was going to say that you're not a little girl any more.'

'Doesn't that mean the same thing?'

'No. It means that I consider you old enough, mature enough, to make some decisions about yourself, about your body, without consulting me or your mother or anyone else. I just didn't know I felt that way until a few minutes ago.'

'You're not mad with me?'

'I'm more mad with me at the moment.'

She hugs me close again, squeezes me so hard I think my ribs will crack. 'You're a wonderful dad,' she says, 'and I love you very much.'

Over her shoulder the door opens and Phil's pensive face peers out at me.

'I love you too,' I whisper to my daughter, 'but I think your young man needs reassuring. You'd better tell him

196

I'm not pressing for a shotgun wedding.'

She whirls around, strides across to see him, kisses him, speaks to him. I can't hear what either of them says, but he looks at me, he nods, and relief blossoms on his face.

'Ever thought of a career in the diplomatic service?' Nessa says at my shoulder.

'Never get married,' I tell her. 'Never have kids. Especially girls.'

She takes my hand. 'You mean it's all right for boys to screw around?'

'No.' I'm not sure if she's joking. 'I don't think it's right for anyone to "screw around", if that means what I think it means.'

'Which is?'

'Having sex for the sake of the act itself.' I don't know how I've found myself arguing gender politics in the early hours of a snowstorm, but I feel the need to go on, for my own sake. '"Screwing around" has nothing to do with taking pleasure in another person's body, because I think it doesn't usually involve mutual pleasure at all. But . . . I'm not sure, Nessa, I'm not sure any more.' I hear myself sigh, and in the expulsion of air my body sags and hangs tired. 'All I know is that I don't know. It's different for girls.'

'Come on,' she takes my hand again, as she's done several times this night already, 'we've got a busy day tomorrow.' Kirsty and Phil have already disappeared, heading for the anonymity of the crowded Tesseract floor.

'Give me ten, fifteen minutes.' I tell her, 'I just need to have a walk around. Be by myself for a little while.'

'Don't want any company?' Is there worry in her voice, fear that I'm going to go off and do something silly? Does she think I can't find Eve Marton without her help?

'No, not this time,' I tell her. 'But I'll be back. Promise.'

She nods. 'Okay, I trust you. I'll keep things warm for you.' She blows a kiss then turns her back, disappears into her room.

The Tesseract is a refugee camp of sleeping, snoring bodies. There's a smell of unwashed clothes, of overnight travel, of stale railway carriages and crowded buses on wet evenings. A few insomniacs are reading, one boy is playing patience, but no one looks up as I pass. I think – I hope – I've done the right thing. At first I wanted to shout, to lose my temper. I wanted to scrub Kirsty, to cleanse her of the smell and taste and feel of sex, to lock her away. But that changed as soon as I saw her, as soon as I began speaking to her. And, in the end, what I said was what I wanted to say. Perhaps I've done something right after all. I'm beginning to feel happier with myself, I'm beginning to calm down, but I want to sit down, to be alone, to allow myself the luxury of my own company. But where to go? That's when I see the door and I smile, a smile which, to my surprise, turns into an audible laugh. Where else can a man go for a little privacy?

I soak a paper hand-towel in cold water and take it into one of the cubicles with me. The emergency lighting – all there is – makes the shadows deep and warm. I lower the toilet seat and lid, sit down. I wrap my face in the towel, feel it cold on eyelids and nose and mouth, smell the cheap paper smell. I breathe deeply. I'm tired. At least the toilets are quiet, the sound of the ceaseless biting wind can't penetrate this inner sanctum of privilege and safety. I feel as if the snow is drifting unseen into my head, covering my brain with fold after fold of numbing, sterile whiteness. A few years ago I read, like many other people, some of the stream of novels that had covers with snow on them, or titles with the word 'snow' in them. They had a collective romanticism, they suggested that cold and ice and the northern climes that went with them were fashionable. I read them and dreamed about them and was suffused with a warm glow of familiarity and comprehension; these books were cool. Now I know differently. Cold and snow sap the strength, they weaken the resolve, they creep and crawl into the mind and render the body incapable of movement.

They kill. And then I recall another book from my youth which dealt with that same notion of cold but told it in its true horror. What was it? Then the title came to me, *HMS Ulysses*, and I was transported from a world of white-coated pine trees to the dark, deep, desolate north Atlantic, to heaving seas and ice-rimed ships and deadly, killing cold. Even there, in the air-conditioned warmth of my cubicle, I shiver.

I hear the door open, footsteps. Two people.

'So what happened then?'

'I shrank. Literally to nothing, in two seconds flat.'

I recognise the second voice, and the cold I feel is suddenly real.

'And?'

'What do you think? She climbed off me, stood up. I grabbed something, my shirt, I don't know what, I think I was trying to hide behind it.'

'So she was standing in front of her father, stark naked?'

There's a laugh. 'You said it.'

'And what did he say?'

'Not a lot.'

'Shit!'

'That's just about what I did. I thought he'd kick the crap out of me. He used to be a policeman and he looks a bit of a thug. Apparently he's trying to find out who killed Amy, and before that he was trying to find out who's been poisoning the staff, least that's what my father told me. Dismal failure at both, if you ask me.'

'Phil! Amy's not even buried yet and you ...'

'I had her as well. Scrubbers both of them, if you ask me. But any port in a storm, that's what I say.'

'Phil!'

'That Kirsty, she's pretty good, I'll give her that. She had me going, I was just going to shoot my load when her stupid father came in. Noisy bitch, mind. Do you fancy joining us? I'll sort it out if you want. She's mad about me, she'd do anything I said.'

'Phil, you're out of it. You're sick.'

'She would, honest. Which end would you rather fuck?'

'I'm going.'

The door opens and closes, but I can still hear one person. There's the sound of a zip, now he's washing his hands. I stand up, not sure what I'm going to do, unlock the cubicle door. He sees me in the mirror, for the second time that night I'm a dark shadow. This time he recognises me. Even in the dim light I can see him go white. I can sense the smile on my face.

'Mr Oliphant! I didn't know you were in there. I wanted to speak to you, to say how sorry I was about . . . Well, you know. About earlier on tonight.'

I say nothing.

'I mean . . . You'll have heard . . . It wasn't me saying those things, it was the other Phil, the one who was in with me.' He's worried, really worried. It's time.

'It's okay,' I tell him, 'I'm a man of the world.' I shake my head. 'I know what you lads are like.' I step towards him. 'I was young once,' I put my left arm round his shoulder, 'I know exactly what you meant.'

I punch him. It's a windmill punch with my right fist, but he can't see it coming, doesn't even suspect it. It hits him hard in the solar plexus, he'd drop to his knees but I'm holding him up, so he simply folds in two. I bring my knee up into his face, hear the crack of his nose breaking. Then I let him fall to the ground. Blood is dripping from his nose and mouth, there's a rattling sound of desperate, ineffective breathing. I kick him in the ribs, kick him so hard I hurt my foot, I'll have a bruise in the morning. He's curled like a comma, a fetus, a soft cedilla hanging on to consciousness. I kneel down on the floor beside him.

'I think you'd better keep away from my daughter. You don't even have to explain why, I'll do the job myself. Just keep away.' I want him to swear at me, to breathe some small obscenity and give me the excuse to hurt him more, hurt him again. But he doesn't. I climb to my feet.

'If anyone asks, you could tell them you fell down the stairs.' I start to leave but come back again and I can see him wince as I approach. I bend down to whisper in his ear. 'No, I've a better idea. Tell them you lied to my daughter. Tell them exactly what you think of women. Tell them . . .' I can't think of anything else. I kick him again, between the legs. 'Tell them Billy Oliphant kicked shit out of you because you deserved it.'

I leave the toilets, somehow I find my way back to Nessa's room. She's asleep. I lie down beside her, fully clothed, and know that the night will be long.

Chapter Twenty-Five

'Come on, lover boy, time to wake up.'

There's a faint light showing beyond the double doors leading to the pool. Nessa is kneeling beside me, there's a cup of tea in one hand, a plate of toast in the other.

'I begged these from the kitchen, jumped the queue.' She puts them on the floor. 'Get them while they're hot.'

'What's it like outside? It looks as if the sun's shining.'

'It's grey, Billy, grey sky, grey snow, grey everything. It seems light because it's dark in here. But one of the cooks said the temperature's due to rise, there might be a thaw soon. And it isn't snowing at the moment. How are you feeling?'

'More dead than alive.' I must have slept, though all I can remember is lying awake filled with a brooding, malevolent rage.

'You look bad. Are you up to this?'

This? For a moment I can't remember what it is I'm meant to be doing. Then it comes back to me. The quarry where Eve Marton might be hiding. And if there's a thaw on the way I can't afford any delay, I have to be ready for ... for what? My mind isn't working properly. I have to be ready for the walk to the quarry, I have to be ready for the possibility of Eve Marton not wanting to come quietly, I have to be ready for ... Anything and everything? That's impossible, I wasn't even ready to be woken up.

'I'm ready,' I say, groping for the tea. It's lukewarm, despite what Nessa said, and I drink it all at once. Then I wolf down the toast despite its thin dryness. 'I'm ready,' I say again, though I make no attempt to move. Nessa offers me her hand, I take it and she pulls me to my feet. She doesn't try to dissuade me from going, at least she knows me that well.

'It's still bitter outside,' she tells me, 'you'll need to wrap up well. I've got a rucksack, I've put spare socks in it, a flask of tea, some chocolate.'

'It can't be that far,' I complain.

'It isn't. But we're both tired, you even more than me, and it might start snowing again. We could get lost. Be prepared, that's what I say.'

I've already accepted, without comment, Nessa's assumption that she's coming with me. 'Just my luck to end up with a Boy Scout as a guide,' I grumble.

'Dyb dob, come on, Akela. No, you're more like Baloo the bear with a sore head. Shift yourself.' She bustles over-efficiently around me, reinforcing my feeling of inadequacy. 'I've found some waterproof over-trousers that should fit you, and some good gloves.'

I begin to dress and realise I haven't had time to think about Amy being killed, about Harry Simpson being free and bearing a considerable grudge, about the stolen rifle. That brings the fear back. But it's illogical, I tell myself, if Simpson wanted to kill me the easiest way to do it would be to come into the Tesseract and find me. It's not as if he's going to be lying in wait for me, not out there in the cold.

Nessa's hoisting the rucksack onto her back before I can offer to carry it. It's even hung with crampons and an ice axe.

'Are they really necessary?' I ask.

'Billy, I'm prepared. Always be ready for any eventuality. If I had an extra axe and another pair of crampons I'd be taking them along for you.'

'No ropes? No oxygen?'

'There are ropes at the hut, and a first-aid-kit, but I've a small kit with me anyway. Spare clothes. Compass. Map. Emergency rations.'

If it had been me, if I'd been alone, I'd have taken none of these. I decide to offer no further comment, it would only demonstrate how unfamiliar I am with any form of country pursuit.

'I need to tell Kirsty and Sly where we're going.'

'Good idea, always make sure you've left details of your route somewhere.'

'Not that either of them is going to rescue us. Not that we'll need rescuing. Just to stop them worrying.'

'Of course.'

I'm pleased to find Kirsty and Paula awake, one reading to the twins, the other feeding the baby. They both look tired. Sly's asleep, his forehead beaded with sweat.

'How's the old man?' I ask. 'Still sniffling?'

Paula glances at her husband. 'I think it's turned to flu, Billy, he was running a temperature all last night. I'm trying to keep him hydrated but he hasn't eaten much for almost two days now. The nurse is coming to see him, but I'd be happier if he could be seen by a doctor.'

'I've heard the weather's on the change. With a little luck . . .'

'I hope so, Billy. I've had enough of this.'

I know how Paula feels. The temptation to lie down on a mattress and sleep, to be cared for and comforted, is so great. 'You okay?' I ask Kirsty.

'Great,' she answers. Her face and voice are alive with light. It'll take a while for her to realise that her boyfriend – I hesitate to use the word, but no other comes quickly to mind – isn't going to contact her again. She might even find out why, and I could be cast once again as the demon. But that's the price of fatherhood; that's the price of loving your daughter.

'Thanks for being so understanding last night, Dad,' she says quietly. 'I really appreciate it.'

204

'That's what dads are for, love.' I bend down and kiss her on the cheek. Just for a while I indulge myself in the fiction that she's happy because I've helped her, because I've acted in a way that's won her approval. But when I look at her I can see from her restless eyes that she's looking around for someone, and I know who that someone is.

'Understanding isn't the same as approval,' I warn her. 'And not everyone who smiles at you does so because they think you're wonderful.' Why did I say that? It's clumsy and it confuses her, I can see the puzzlement in her eyes. 'Except for parents. Parents always think their kids are wonderful, no matter what they do.' That helps. Why can't I just tell her? Why can't I say 'He's a swine, Kirsty, he's no good for you, he's using you'? The answer's easy. It's because I don't want to hurt her, and I'm not even sure she'd believe me. She'll find out herself anyway. That's the best way. Especially for a coward like me.

Paula interrupts my thoughts. 'You aren't going out, are you?'

'No, I dress like this all the time.'

'Dad, stop it! Where are you going?'

I touch the side of my nose. 'Private investigations. I need to go out to find someone lost in the snow, up near an old quarry. But don't worry, Nessa's coming along to look after me.'

Kirsty is going to worry, I can tell that much. For a few hours at least she'll be concerned about me. Then she'll find out what I've done to Philip.

'Be careful. You're the only Dad I've got.'

'I'll be back in a few hours, cold and damp and miserable.'

'I'll be waiting.'

The twins are becoming fractious; I've interrupted their entertainment for too long and they're pulling at Kirsty's arm, dragging her back into their story. I back away, wink at her and wave to Paula. When I look back they're absorbed in each other again.

Nessa's waiting for me at the main door, all alone. I feel there should be a farewell party, someone to say a few words, wish us well, clap us on the back, admire our bravery. The truth is, I don't know whether we'll need to be brave. From what I've seen of Eve Marton she's not the type to turn nasty, to threaten us. Even if she does, there are two of us. A horrible thought crosses my mind – what if she stole the gun? I run back through events, could she have had the opportunity? I'm still not sure how much money was stolen, would it be enough to provide her with a motive for my murder? But I'm not the only one who knows about her involvement, I've shared my suspicions with Nessa and with Cath Watson. Would she realise that? I'm suddenly more nervous than I was. I tell myself there's no need, she's probably hiding somewhere in the Tesseract, there's a good chance she won't even be at the quarry. After all, I'm relying a lot on Sam Ellis's suppositions, and he could be wrong.

Nessa leads me out into the snow. She said there might be a turn in the weather, but I can't feel it. The cold is still harsh, gnawing incessantly at feet and fingers and face. It's not snowing, but everything is a uniform glaring grey. There's no wind, the earth and sky and trees are still and silent, overpowering in their shared melancholy. Within a few minutes we're out of sight of the Tesseract. The path (I think there's a path, though there's no way of being sure) winds between hidden lodges weighted with white. I can hear Nessa breathing, see each cloud of vapour rise above her head then disperse into the chill air. Even with her there, ahead of me, I feel alone.

She must know where she's going. There are no more lodges now. Trees, wide and solid, gather around us, try to smother us with their claustrophobia. I find myself bending low, twisting my head to gain some impression of scale and perspective, but all directions seem the same. Only when I look back at our tracks can I sense that we've been moving.

The snow has disguised the terrain. It's smoothed the

hollows, but we only know this when we find ourselves up to our waists in drift. We wade through and feel the ground rise beneath our feet till we're on the crest of a rise, hard with glass-ice sliding us down into the next depression.

'It's going to be wet when this lot melts,' Nessa says. They're the first words she's spoken since we set off, and they warrant no reply. Even if they did, I'm conserving my strength. We keep walking and slipping, climbing to our feet, using our companionship to pull each other along. I've lost all sense of time. I could check by looking at my watch, but that's buried under layers of sleeve and glove. My body's been divided into zones; trunk and arms are warm, legs less so, feet and hands painfully cold; I've no feeling at all in my toes and fingers, and someone has stolen my nose when I wasn't looking. We come to a long slow slope down, and ahead of us the ground appears to rise sharply.

'Not far now,' Nessa calls softly over her shoulder. 'I think we should try to be quiet from now on.' I haven't said a word; she can't be referring to my laborious breathing, or to the noise of my passage through the deep snow. And why be quiet? From what she's told me, the way up to the quarry is quite easy on a wide, though sometimes steep, path. The track out of the quarry, however, is narrow and rocky, sure to be almost impassable with ice. So where can Eve Marton go even if she does hear us? What can she do? Shoot us? I try to control my breathing, tiptoe gently inside my boots.

There's a fence ahead of us, a stile straddling it. I'm impressed by Nessa's sense of direction. Just beyond the stile is a notice board dripping with icicles, its face peppered with hard snow. 'What does it say?' I whisper to Nessa as we pass.

'Something about the quarry being dangerous, that it's used for rock-climbing, that it's the possession of Forestcrag, and that people should keep out unless they have business there. Now will you please be quiet.'

The path from the stile joins what can only be wider path which clings to the side of the steep slope, then doubles back when it meets a steeper rock face. The rock is dark with stains, white with curtains of ice. That, I realise, must be the waterfall Nessa was telling me about. When I look closer I can see the darkness is a slow creep of gelatinous water, fighting gravity. The path rises, twists away from the waterfall; when the quarry was in use it could have been used for vehicles or ponies, now it provides me with a view back over Forestcrag. I can see the lights of the Tesseract over waves of white-topped trees, but anything beyond is lost in a grey haze. Perhaps there is nothing beyond. Perhaps the rest of the world has been lost and there's nothing left but the forest.

'Billy?' Nessa's whisper forces me to move again. She's not moving quickly, but I'm slower still. I'd thought I was reasonably fit, but the past few days have demonstrated the opposite. When I get out of this . . . Why does a voice warn me that thinking 'when' is presumptive, that 'if' might be a more appropriate word?

We climb higher and I notice more. The quarry has been cut into the side of a crag-topped hill in shelves. We're at the same height as the top of the waterfall, but the path climbs higher onto the next shelf. There are probably others beyond that. Nessa beckons me to her side.

'Are you okay?'

I'm breathing heavily. 'No. Does it make any differ- ence?'

'Not really. See, up there, the path disappears between those two rocks?'

I peer upwards, find two rocks which look as if they've been positioned by man rather than nature. I nod.

'When we get there we'll be able to see into the main part of the quarry. Just round to the left is the hut, it's beside a broad piece of level ground, that's where we go climbing. But away to the right the ground slopes then drops away vertically. There's a shelf below, then another drop to the quarry pond. It's deep, but even that'll be frozen. Be careful, it would be easy to go over.'

I nod again. I feel as if I ought to be in charge here, but what could I do? Perhaps when we get to the lip of the quarry, when we can see what lies beyond, I might have a greater role to play. Nessa sets off again, I follow; I'm becoming used to it.

It takes us ten minutes to reach the two rocks. The backs of my legs are crying with pain and cold. We collapse, lie in the snow peering into the cold of the quarry. Even if the sun had been shining it wouldn't have been able to reach into the quarry's depths. It looks preternaturally cold, the ice is blue, not white. I'm reminded that hell needn't necessarily be hot, and that this looks like the ideal place for the gateway to Hades. If the earth and stone had never been blasted away we'd be about halfway up the original hill. Towering above me are the black jagged rocks signifying the uppermost rim of the excavations. The ground ahead appears to be level; I can't see the dangerous drop away to the right, but to my left is a small cabin, its faded green paint rimed with white. It has a chimney, but there's no smoke rising from it. It has a window, but it's covered with a wooden shutter. It's pressed against, perhaps built into, the cliff face.

'Where's the door?' I whisper.

'Furthest side from us.'

'Doesn't look as if anyone's there.'

Nessa shakes her head. I feel an overwhelming relief. It'll be a pity if the journey, the effort, proves to be wasted. But if Eve Marton is there, even worse, if she's there and armed and keeping watch, I can't see how we can get at her.

'Now what?' Nessa asks. It would appear I'm back in charge.

'I suppose I ought to take a look.'

'In the hut?'

'Unless you can suggest another place where Eve might

be hiding? You stay here, if everything's okay ...' I think carefully, constructively. It feels good. 'If everything's okay I'll come and get you. If I just stand at the hut, wave you towards me, then there's something wrong. Just disappear, get back to the Tesseract, get the police up here as soon as possible. Okay?'

'Yeah.'

It's a relief to work with someone who doesn't ask questions. She understands what I mean without me having to spell it out. If Eve's there, if she has a gun, then she might figure out that someone has guided me up here. I could be forced to summon that person at gunpoint. I need a signal for that eventuality.

'Here I go then.'

'I'll be watching.'

It's impossible to creep forward, the snow's too deep. At the same time I notice there are no tracks leading up to the hut. I hug the wall of rocks on the left, and as the path widens into the quarry itself I can see the ground fall slowly to my right then disappear. I don't want to go too far in that direction. The closer I get to the hut, the less snow there is. It's as if someone has been out with a shovel and broom, but I assume the wind has scoured the rocks free of snow. Ice has taken the snow's place, lodged in the cracks and crevices, it lies on the ground in slab-like sheets. I take small steps, keep my centre-of-gravity above my feet, watch where I'm going; but at the same time I'm trying to keep my eyes on the wooden hut. If someone comes to the door, if that someone is armed, I have every intention of skating back to the comparative safety of the path back down.

I'm sweating. I reach the side of the hut, the one opposite the door, and press my head against it. I can hear no sound from within. I move quietly round the long side, duck beneath the window (there might be gaps in the shutter allowing my passage to be seen) then peer round the corner. The door's closed, but there's a padlock hanging from a staple, and the hasp is pushed to one side. That means the building isn't secure. But if someone's inside, why leave the lock hanging? If it was me, what would I do? I'd take the lock inside with me. But does that mean someone else would do the same? So what now? I know what I'd like to do, I'd like to choose indecision and stay just where I am, wait for someone to come and rescue me. But that won't happen. Do I open the door quietly, or do I fling it open?

I slide across the door to the hinge side. It has an aluminium handle, I lean out and pull it down, gently; it moves easily. I pull the handle towards me; there's no squeal of rusty hinges, just a happy smoothness. This is the point at which, if there had been too much noise, or if there'd been some movement from inside, I would have flung the door wide. I would have yelled something silly, something like 'Armed police! Come out with your hands on your head!' But there's nothing to make me do that. I pull the door wide and look inside.

The single room is cluttered but there's no sign of life. There's a table and a wooden chair, and the back wall, the stone wall, is hung with climbing ropes and harnesses and pieces of metal that look as if they hold ropes in place. I step inside. Under the table there's a rucksack, I hook it out. Inside are clothes, women's clothes, though there's nothing to say who they belong to, and a torch which – I check to make sure – still works. On the floor beyond the table is a small stove and several cans and packets of food, a half-full carton of milk, some pans; one of them is filled with ice. There are candles standing bold in jamjar lids. On the table is a guide book to Switzerland with several slips of paper marking pages. I open it at the first one; it's a street map of Zurich, written in the margin in pencil are the words *Banque du Crédit et Commerce, 17 rue des Anglais.* The other pages mark hotels. Inside the front cover is a name: Eve Marton.

In the far corner of the room is a crumpled sleeping bag. I

lift it up, shake it, but there's nothing inside. Beneath it, however, is a book, a novel, Eve's reading matter; she was planning on staying for a little while at least. It's obvious she's been here, but she isn't here now. Could she have heard us coming, seen us coming, and fled? And if so, where has she gone? That's when I notice the curtain hanging at the back of the building, languishing in the dark shadows. Nessa had mentioned the room beyond, built into the rock itself, but I'd forgotten about it. I keep still, listen for movement, for breathing; there's nothing. I reach for the rucksack, bring out the torch, switch it on and point it at the curtain.

'Come on, Eve,' I say, 'You might as well come out now. It's Billy Oliphant here, I know all about you. The police are on their way, you can't escape. Give yourself up, it'll be far easier for you if you do.' I'm tempted to make further noises to pretend to be extra men, policemen, Forestcrag workers, anything. But I overcome the temptation, I couldn't carry it off, I'd start laughing. Even now I can feel hysteria behind me, creeping up on me. I move forward to escape it, twitch the curtain aside and shine the torch-beam at the small room beyond. It's empty, cold, it smells of neglect. There's nothing there, only a bench carved from the rock itself and, above it, several drawings. I move closer. One of the drawings shows what appears to be the quarry in smudged plan and damp, peeling relief, it must be as old as the building. Others are more recent, less faded; they show unfeasibly well-endowed men having sex with women who seem capable of infinite pelvic rotation, whose mouths open ridiculously wide, and whose breasts seem pneumatic in a way even Monsieur Michelin could not have imagined. But they're nothing more than graffiti, signs of a juvenile mind, there's nothing to show that Eve Marton ever looked beyond the curtain, let alone stepped into the room. I check the floor and ceiling, shine the torch round the room once more, then pull the curtain aside again.

'Took your time, didn't you?'

I swear I take off, I didn't know adrenaline could hit so hard, so fast. Then I see Nessa sitting on the chair, feet on the table.

'I take it she's gone,' she says.

'What the hell are you doing here? I thought we agreed you'd stay where you were, wait for my signal.'

'I was cold. You've been ages. I came quietly, I couldn't hear anything, I peeped in and saw the light shining under the curtain. I knew it'd be you. Calm down, Billy, calm down Christ, you're nervous.'

'It's easy for you to say I'm nervous, you already knew I was here. I didn't know it was you. You could have been anyone.'

'Okay, okay, I'm sorry. I didn't mean to scare you.' It's the same 'sorry' Kirsty used to employ to make it clear she was far from sorry, that she really didn't give a damn about what I or anyone else felt. It makes me even angrier.

'She's not here, then? Course not, silly question.' Nessa looks around her. 'But she was here. So what's happened to her?'

'You tell me. You were clever enough to know, without the slightest shred of evidence, that she wasn't holding me prisoner here with a gun pointing at my head. So use the same process of divine guesswork to fill in the gaps yourself.'

This time she's contrite and means it. 'Really, I'm sorry Billy. I should have stayed where I was, I know that. But I'm here now, Eve isn't.' She hands me back the burden of leadership. 'What do you think we should do now?'

I could sulk if I wanted, I was once good at sulking; ask Sara. But that was a long time ago. I've grown out of that. So I start thinking aloud instead in the hope that Nessa might be able to fill in any gaps.

'There were no footprints leading down the path we climbed, she didn't go down that way. Could she have gone up the track through the quarry onto the moorland beyond? You seemed to think it was impossible, but Eve was reasonably fit.'

Nessa takes her feet off the table and goes to the door. 'That's the track, up there,' she says, points at what seems to be a vertical rock face. 'At least, I know where it is, but I can't see it properly. That's because it's covered in snow and ice, Billy. In good weather, in summer, I can climb it, but it's definitely a climb. Not graded, mind you, but something a touch harder than a scramble. You need hands and it wanders out over the quarry. I wouldn't try it in these conditions, and Eve wouldn't either. Anyway, look around you. She's left all her stuff behind. She didn't go up that way.'

'So where did she go?'

'Perhaps she left before the last big snowfall.'

I shake my head, 'That's illogical, she's still left everything behind.'

'She was going to come straight back? I don't know, can you come up with anything better?'

'Is there anywhere else she could be hiding?'

Nessa looks around her, holds out her hands. 'You've seen the facilities, Billy. This is all there is.'

'It looks as if she was interrupted. Nothing's been put away. If she went back down to the Tesseract with the intention of returning here, surely she'd at least tidy up.' I think of her room, so neat, almost sterile. 'No, there's no way she'd leave the place like this. There's something else.'

'Perhaps she went outside to piss, the wind was strong, she suffered from blowback and it froze her to the ground.'

'What does happen up here if you need to go to the toilet?'

Nessa shakes her head. 'You don't. When you're halfway up a rock face it does wonders for your bladder control.'

'But if she'd been here for a day she would have had to do something.'

'If it'd been me I'd have used a tin can, a pan, anything. Then I'd have thrown it out the door. Something more serious? A plastic bag.'

'I'm not sure Eve could have done that. She's too neat, too tidy.'

'So she went outside in a blizzard?'

'Perhaps.'

'She's be even more stupid than I thought, then.' Nessa looks around her. 'Well I can't see her at this level. And if she headed towards the rim, even by accident ...' She shrugs. 'Should we wander over?'

I don't want to go close to the edge. I've never been fond of heights and I'm becoming less fond as I get older. But Nessa's holding out her hand and motioning me forward. It appears I have no choice in the matter.

The ground is icy, it slopes away from us. I grasp Nessa's hand, but she seems fearless. 'It's okay,' she says, 'there's a walkway, a narrow path, before the big vertical drop.'

It doesn't feel that way. I've been fell-waking before, on forced marches, climbed those big green monsters where you think you can see the top but the curve of false horizon retreats ahead of you. This is the same, but in reverse. The slope gets steeper, almost forty-five degrees, and there's no sign of any walkway. I let go of Nessa's hand, lean back so my backside's in touch with the frozen scree. I slide myself gently forward in Nessa's wake, hands and feet and buttocks in contact with as much of the ground as possible. My knees prevent me seeing where I'm going, I have to peer between them every few careful, crawling, sliding steps. Nessa's unconcerned, I stop watching her while I concentrate on my own predicament.

'Well, if she did head this way in a blizzard, or even when it was just a bit icier than it is today, she won't ... Oh shit!'

I look to one side. Nessa's standing at the edge, the very edge. The world drops away entirely there, and the path she mentioned is only a metre wide, covered with snow. I creep towards her, an inverted double-jointed tortoise. 'What is it?' I ask. 'What can you see?'

'You'd better look for yourself,' Nessa answers.

When I reach the path I turn myself around, kneel, then lie at an angle so the whole of my body is anchored to the ground. I move my head gently over the edge.

The drop is about two hundred feet and it frightens me. I can feel my fingers become talons, digging into the rock. I have to close my eyes. But I know I have to open them again, to confirm what they saw. I cope better second time. Most of the area below me is taken up by an expanse of white ice, a frozen lake covered with virgin snow. But at the base of the cliff there's a small outcrop of rough rock and boulder. And wedged there, limbs at unnatural, swastika angles, is a body.

'Do you think it's her?' I ask.

Nessa's still standing, the toes of her boots overhanging the edge a little.

'Would you mind stepping back a little,' I add, 'you're making me nervous.'

She slides back a fraction. 'I can't think who else it might be. She looks very dead, though. I suppose I'll have to go down and take a look.'

'You'll what?' I scrabble back from the edge in case I catch whatever rash disease has infected Nessa.

'Go down. It's quite straightforward, Billy. There are plenty of ropes and harnesses back at the hut, plenty of places to fix them. I can abseil down.'

'Do you need to?' I've absolved myself of all responsibility for Nessa, for the body, for anything but myself. I have to look away from the drop and the body below, but the slope down which I've just been sliding looks too steep for me to make the return journey. I want to close my eyes, I want to stay where I am, I want a mountain rescue team to put me in a bag, fasten me to a stretcher and haul me away.

'Someone has to do it,' Nessa replies, 'after all, she might still be alive.' She looks over the edge again. 'Though I doubt it. And if it's not me, it has to be you. Are you volunteering?'

216

'I don't even think I can get back up to the top.'

'That's what friends are for, Billy. Just don't look down.' She helps me to my feet and pushes, pulls and persuades me back up the slope. Once I trip, fall to the ground and begin to slide back down. I scream, loud and strong in sheer, desperate horror, Nessa's feet are glued to the rock, she grabs me by the collar and hauls me upright again. 'Do you want me to carry you?' she says. She doesn't mean it, but I've no doubt she could do it.

The slope becomes smoother, softer, its threats are less to do with the violence of its angle than the intermittent ice embedded in its surface. I find I can walk unaided in Nessa's wake. I'm sweating, all my clothes are damp, the moisture on my face is beginning to freeze. I follow Nessa into the hut, launch myself, shivering with a mixture of fear and exhaustion, into the chair.

'This should do.' Her back is towards me, she's examining the coils of rope hanging on the wall. 'Or this, it should certainly be long enough.' She moves along the wall. 'And this harness fits me quite well. I've got gloves for getting down.' She turns to look at me. 'I was going to suggest you haul me back up, but ... You've never been climbing before, have you? No, daft question, forget I asked it. I can climb back, fasten myself to the rope, but there are lots of handholes anyway.' She selects her harness and straps herself into it, pulls a rope from its hooks on the wall and drapes it over her shoulder. 'Coming?'

'What do you want me to do?'

'Nothing. I'll fasten the rope, there are plenty of rocks big enough to support my weight. Then I'll abseil down, see how stiff she is.' She catches my grimace. 'Come on, Billy, we both know she's dead. This is a formality. Then I'll climb back up. We can go back to the Tesseract, get a stretcher and a few big lads who aren't frightened of heights to haul her up. If I get a move on we can get sorted before it gets dark.'

'I'm sorry,' I say, 'I didn't realise heights affected me as badly as this.'

'It happens, Billy.'

'I should be down there.'

'Why? You can tell me if there's anything you want me to look for. Do you think we should leave the body there until the police can get in for a look?'

'It might be wise. It's not as if she's going to suffer any more.'

'But I'd better have a look? Just in case?'

'Yes. If you don't mind.'

'Of course not. It's good to be in on the kill. Sorry, wrong choice of words, but you know what I mean. After all, it sorts things out, doesn't it? Us finding her here?'

'Yes, I suppose it does.' I'm surprised to find myself saying that, but the loose ends which have been rubbing the back of my neck like an embroidered label do seem to have been tied together rather neatly. There'll be no need for accusations, for long, tiresome questions, for the possibility of violence or retribution. Another problem solved. Why, then, do I feel no pleasure? Is it that Eve Marton's broken body is lying at the bottom of the quarry? Am I hurt by my own lack of physical prowess? I don't honestly know. All I want to do now is get out of the quarry and back to the dimly lit, overcrowded, warm, welcoming Tesseract.

Chapter Twenty-Six

I can only watch as Nessa clambers over the lip of the quarry and lowers herself down the rock face. Her rope is secure – she's checked that herself, knotted it to a boulder, had me haul on it to make sure it won't slip. Then she's gone. It's no use me walking round the upper level of the quarry to see her descent, there's no suitable vantage point. The only place I could watch from is the narrow ledge at the bottom of the steep slope where, only a few minutes before, fear cackled in my ears, squatted heavy on my shoulders. I don't want to go back there. So I wait.

I don't want to go back into the wooden hut, though the lowering clouds are threatening again. It's too dark in there. Eve Marton's body may be lying at the bottom of the quarry but she hasn't given up possession of the building yet. I tell myself this is nonsense, but I can't trust my emotions at the moment. I've never had any problem with heights before, beyond a thrill of dizzy pleasure when standing at the top of a high building. But my heart's still beating fast, and I want to breathe air that hasn't already passed through a dead woman's lips and mouth and lungs. I want to calm down, to feel I could – if I wanted – stride down the slope and peer over the edge at Nessa a few hundred feet below, just to make sure she's okay. The key phrase is 'if I wanted'; I don't want, under any circumstances. I've discovered a new weakness to add to the human frailties I'm developing with such innovative rapidity. Tomorrow there'll be another one. Bad breath? Impotence? Arachnophobia? Bring them on, Billy Oliphant'll have them, shelter them, give them a warm, comfortable home.

I find a rock and sit on it. I feel cold, but not as cold as I have been. Perhaps the thaw's on the way. I look at the lowering skies, but there's been no discernible change since we set off years ago, earlier this morning. All is grey and silent, not even a distant crow to blacken the air.

Nessa's voice echoes from the depths of the quarry, right on cue. 'She's dead, Billy.'

'Anything suspicious?' I call back in slow motion.

'Broken neck, back, legs, arms, I think. Broken everything. Hardly suspicious, though.'

'Is she cold?'

'Solid.' It sounds as if Nessa's speaking from a point in mid-air high above the frozen lake; it feels strange to be conducting a conversation with a formless entity, but I find myself talking to that point where, my ears tell me, she ought to be.

'Better come back up,' I say. There's no need for either of us to shout, the sound of normal conversation carries well.

'It'll take a bit longer than getting down.'

'I'll be waiting.' There's nowhere else for me to go.

After ten minutes I feel I'm beginning to lose some of the feeling in my toes. I march backwards and forwards for a while, throw my arms around each other. When that doesn't help I do a little dance on the spot. Then I wander over to where the rope is fastened, see how taut it is. I want to call down, ask if everything's okay, but I don't want to distract Nessa from her task. I head back to my rock, then decide that I might just be able to see Nessa climbing if I go to the quarry entrance. It might necessitate a little scrambling and scrabbling along the ridge of rock cratering the quarry, but I should be able to straddle the ridge and maintain contact with hands, legs and backside. It's all I feel capable of.

I don't make it that far. I'm almost there, perhaps twenty metres from the two tall stones marking the entrance, when a figure rises from behind one of them. I raise my arm in a salute, sure it must be someone from the Tesseract come to see what we're doing, perhaps help us out. My greeting brings no response. The figure is wearing a hooded coat, it could be a man or a woman. It reaches behind, over its shoulder, brings out what, at first, I take to be walking poles. But then it raises the stick-like shape to its shoulder. It's a gun.

I don't care who it is, I just turn and run in the sure knowledge that there's nowhere to run to. I'm trapped in the quarry. There's no way up, no way down, nowhere to hide. The only refuge is the hut, a dead end (an isolated, infuriating part of my brain notes the play on words) but I can hide in the cave and hope that the confined, dark space may alter the odds a little in my favour. I alter course, jig to the left as the first shot splinters the ice to my right. I tell myself to keep low, change direction again; this time I push off to the right. I sense the ice beneath my boot, I know I'm going to slip and fall, even as I'm going down I tell myself to roll over so I can rise quickly to my feet again. But I'm too slow.

I know I've been hit, but it's not pain I feel first. It's the sensation of the bullet hitting my leg, passing into the flesh at the back of my right knee, shattering bones and shredding ligaments. I have time to recognise that this isn't a flesh wound, that one shot has probably disintegrated my patella, broken tibia and fibula, that I won't even be able to rise to my feet. That's when the pain hits, when I scream, when I lose consciousness.

I don't know how long it takes me to come round; long enough for the figure to reach me, to be standing over me with the gun pointing lazily at my head. Even as I open my eyes I can see the trigger finger move slightly. I try to speak, but even the effort of opening my mouth causes jarring, scraping agony in my leg. But I have to say something, stop that finger squeezing the trigger. 'Who are you?' I hiss.

The figure makes a sound which could be laughing.

'Simpson? Harry?'

'You have to die, Mr Oliphant. There's no alternative.'

I don't recognise the voice. Why should I? I can't remember Harry Simpson's face, I can't recall how I arrested him; I can't even remember whether, during the arrest or afterwards in the cells, he might have fallen and hurt himself. That thought brings a smile to my mind, but on its way to my face it turns into a grimace of pain.

'You know too much, Mr Oliphant. You're quite intelligent, really, I didn't think you'd get this far.'

I feel myself slipping back into unconsciousness, but I know the words I'm hearing make no sense at all. 'Know too much'? 'Get this far'? Has the cold got to his brain? A simple statement would have been enough, something along the lines of 'I swore I'd get even,' or 'This is for all those years behind bars,' something short and dramatic and self-explanatory. I can come to only one conclusion.

'You're ... Not ... Harry,' I gasp.

'Harry? Who the fuck's Harry?' The figure reaches up with one hand and pulls back the hood of his coat. 'Who did you think I was, Mr Oliphant?'

The face is bruised, eyes framed with purple, nose bridged with yellow-black. There are cuts on his cheek and his lips are swollen.

'Phil ...?'

'You didn't know?'

I shake my head. This is madness. He's going to kill me because I hit him, hit him for ... I was going to say, for screwing my daughter, but that wouldn't have been true. I hit him because of what he said about her, and I'd do it again because what he said, what he did, was wrong.

'Well you know now. And before I kill you, I'd like you

222

to know there's no hard feelings. About this,' he raises his hand to his face. 'I deserved it. I'll even admit I was wrong. And I'll be there for Kirsty, when she hears about your death. In fact, if I time it properly, I might just be fucking her when the news comes through. Poetic justice, really. And you know what? Best thing of all is, it was her told me where to find you.' He puts his head on one side and looks at me down the barrel of his gun. His father's gun. The analytical part of me remembers that there was no sign of damage to his father's car when the gun was stolen. Hardly surprising when Philip Plumpton had access to the key.

'But ... why?' The question rises from genuine curiosity. If he's not killing me because I beat the shit out of him, then what are his motives?

'Why? Why what, Mr Oliphant?'

'Why ... kill ... me?' My voice may be incapable of transmitting information, but my brain is working.

'Because of what you know, Mr Oliphant, can't you see that?' He shakes his head. Beneath the bruises his face assumes a quizzical expression. 'Perhaps you don't know what you know. Now that would be amusing. But just as dangerous, I'm afraid, because one day you might realise exactly what you do know. That's why I have to kill you. And everyone will think it's that escaped criminal ... And that's who you thought I was! What's his name, you did mention? Yes, Harry Simpson. You thought I was Harry Simpson. That's good, because if you thought that, then everyone else will. That is so good!' He grunts a laugh at me.

I need time, but he doesn't want to offer me any. It's too easy for him. He's so relaxed he can't know about Nessa, but after he's killed me, then he's bound to find the rope, to see Nessa and finish her off. She can't escape, there's nowhere for her to go. What can I do? I can't understand ... That's all I can do. Ask questions. Hope he'll give long, drawn-out answers.

223

'But ... why?'

'Why? Oh no, Mr Oliphant, this isn't a cheap film or a trashy novel where the villain does a quick exposition, sums everything up neatly just before the hero miraculously escapes and uses the information he's gained to save the day. No, you'll die not knowing why I'm going to kill you. You'll die a failure. Good, eh?'

My right leg is my strong leg. No, get it right. *Was* my strong leg. I can't even try to move it now, but my tormentor's gun is, I reckon, just within kicking distance of my left leg. The trouble is, I need leverage. I brace myself, there can't be much time left. I tense the muscles in the top of my right leg, try to relax those lower down, almost cry with the agony. One kick, that's all I'll be able to manage. One kick to send the gun spinning out of his hands, to send it skittering across the ice, to send it sliding down the slope and over the edge into the quarry below. I take a deep breath and ... he moves, takes a step back. He's out of my range.

'Goodbye, Mr Oliphant.'

I want to close my eyes but I can't, and I'm pleased. I'm pleased because I can see, beyond him, Nessa's gloved hands appear over the lip of the quarry. I'm pleased because I can see her haul herself over the edge and creep towards us. I'm even pleased I'm pleased, because the smile of satisfaction on my lips, the smile that hangs there grimly despite the scraping of bones in my leg, puzzles my tormentor. He lowers his rifle to stare at me. He shrugs as my smile turns to wild, anarchic laughter haunting the echoing cliffs of the quarry. And as he raises his weapon once more to his shoulder, as I see Nessa unclip her ice-axe from her belt, he still doesn't understand why I'm so keen to die laughing.

Death isn't finite. It doesn't exist by itself, as a dark antithesis to life. Someone doesn't go along living, and living, and living and then ... stop living, and therefore be dead. No, death is gradual. It creeps and crawls, entwines itself around life, chokes it, destroys it by degrees. The movement from life to death is transitional. But the period of that transition, the time it takes to complete that journey (an irrevocable journey, I'd point out) is variable. Some people take a long time to die. But not Philip Plumpton. That's because Nessa's aim is good. The sharp point of her axe pierces Philip Plumpton's skull, anchors in his brain. He folds to the ground. His death is guaranteed. Only when that registers do I stop laughing and begin to cry.

I'm in too much pain; Nessa can't move me. Instead she brings whatever she can from the hut, finds blankets and Eve Marton's sleeping bag, packs them around me. She drapes a tarpaulin over me, over my body and my head, and sets off for the Tesseract to summon help. I drift into unconsciousness, wake once when an unfamiliar sound rackets the blue plastic of my temporary shelter. Rain is falling. The thaw has arrived.

Chapter Twenty-Seven

I do the old joke when the consultant comes round to see me. 'Will I be able to run a marathon when the plaster comes off?' He knows the joke as well, but he can't give the right response. Doctors aren't allowed to lie, he can't say 'Of course!' to let me say 'That's good, because I could never do that before the operation.' Instead he sits down on the bed – always a bad sign – and reaches into his pocket for his serious voice.

'We've had to make you a new knee joint, Mr Oliphant. It's a mixture of bone, metal, some rather expensive glue, and plastic. Then we've hidden it behind a new plastic knee-cap. There are more stitches in your leg than you'd find in a half-decent shirt.'

'I hope you took the pins and the tissues out, and those silly plastic clips that hold the collar and the sleeves in place.' It's not really funny, but it's the best I can manage. And I can see the consultant is an old hand, he manages to make himself smile.

'There *was* talk of a therapeutic amputation, Mr Oliphant. So I'd count yourself out of marathons for this year at least. Next year? We'll see.'

We're talking about different things. He's thinking of the heroic victim battling his way round the course; everyone who sees him goes 'Ahh!' Lumps are brought to throats, tears well in eyes, money is thrown into plastic buckets.

I'm thinking of running. Not good running, not efficient running, not even attractive running. I'm thinking of the even, measured tread that would take me through local parks on hot summer mornings, the entirely unreasonable, illogical feeling of fitness I'd tow behind me up steepening hills. I don't want people to sympathise with me, I want them to ignore me for my normality. I suspect I have no choice in the matter, and the consultant feels the same way. He should be telling me I'll be lucky if I can walk without a stick or a crutch. But he's too experienced for that. He composes his parting coda.

'If you want to run a marathon enough,' he says, 'you'll do it. With help, to start with. Physiotherapy. Perhaps even more surgery. But . . .'

He leaves me to fill in my own punctuation. Question mark? full stop? Exclamation mark? Perhaps even he, the most god-like of humans, doesn't know.

I have a room to myself and it's quiet, peaceful. There's a television high on the wall but I feel no need to reach for the remote and switch it on. I've had enough anaesthesia without resorting to daytime TV, and the news would only confirm that melted snow-water is still travelling down from the high moorlands to flood towns and villages on its way to the cold February sea. I could, I suppose, read a book. If the length of my convalescence is proportionate to the overall thickness of novels I've received from well-wishers, then it might be several years before I'm back on my feet. But only Kirsty is aware of my real tastes, she's the one who's ransacked the local SF bookshops for copies of *Heavy Metal*, some rather rude cartoon books by Manara, and what seems to be the collected works of Frank Miller. But I don't even have the will to glance through them.

Instead I feel under my sheets for the small, hardbacked notebook which is, for the moment, my only constant companion. Its first few pages contain a reconstruction of the days I lost; it begins at the end. I've noted facts and opinions garnered from Sly and Kirsty. I owe a great deal to Nessa.

It was Nessa who brought help back up to the quarry. She gave me the pethidine injection she'd begged and bullied from Cath Watson, supervised the long, tortuous journey back down to the comparative safety of the Tesseract. Kirsty told me that, when it became clear a thaw was on the way, Nessa commandeered a four wheel drive vehicle (probably Sir Charles Plumpton's Range Rover) to take her as far as she could drive to the main road. When even that could go no further she abandoned it, went on foot through the drifts to the nearest farmhouse. There she found a working phone and swore and cursed at everyone – farmer, police, RAF – until a helicopter was sent to ferry us (she came with me, held my hand throughout) away from and take police into Forestcrag. Apparently she came to visit me, though again I have to rely on Kirsty for that information. I was still in the operating theatre.

More information is passed to and from the police. There are two of them, one to ask questions and one to take notes. It shames me to say that I can't remember being told their names, and that their names aren't important anyway. The questioner is a DCI. He's young and he's polite, and that's something I'm not used to. My past and the reputation that accompanies it usually carry with them an inevitable abrasiveness when it comes to police interviews. Either the DCI has been well briefed or he's showing a great deal of sympathy with my situation; perhaps the consultant has spoken to him and told him the prognosis. It's clear he's spoken to Nessa, most of the time I'm simply required to confirm what is obviously her very accurate story. He needs a large amount of corroborative evidence regarding Philip Plumpton's death. That doesn't surprise me. After all, Sir Charles is a powerful man. But there are questions he doesn't ask me, important because of their absence.

The first involves motivation. I've given this a lot of thought, let's face it, there's not much else I can do at the moment except think. Philip Plumpton tried to kill me. At first I thought it was because I'd beaten him up, and if he'd confirmed that I would have believed him. But he didn't. He was quite specific. I can remember his words, I can remember them because they revisit me most nights and I wake up sweating. I'm lying there, his gun's pointing at my head, and he tells me he's going to kill me because of what I know. 'Perhaps you don't know what you know,' he says. 'Now that would be amusing. But just as dangerous, I'm afraid, because one day you might realise exactly what you do know. That's why I have to kill you.'

It must be something important if he felt it required such drastic action, especially since it was just insurance for the possibility of me realising one day what I already knew. But I can't think what it might be, and I'm worried that, if I say something to the police, it might prolong the investigation. They seem to feel that no motive other than the beating I gave him is required. I do ask whether they've looked into his background, found out anything about his mental health. Apparently he was a normal rich boy with a normal rich boy's bad habits – one count of possession of marijuana, drunk and disorderly twice, alleged (though not proved) GBH on one occasion, nothing to be ashamed of. An only child, spoiled rotten, bad-tempered though overflowing with social graces, with more money than sense, he was a typical example of his class and his upbringing. Though perhaps my leg was hurting particularly badly when I came to that jaundiced conclusion.

The second question I'm waiting for concerns Amy's murder. The DCI doesn't ask me anything. Now, I know I wasn't a witness. I wasn't even the first on the scene of the crime. But I'm bound up in her death, my responsibility extends beyond the boundaries of logic. I don't want to explain about the coat, about my leaving it behind when I went into hiding and Amy borrowing it. The DCI probably knows all about this, he's choosing not to mention it because he's a caring, responsible professional and he'd gain nothing from forcing me to exhibit my guilt once again. But I need to know what's happening.

'Is Philip Plumpton being charged with Amy's murder?' I realise, even as I ask the question, that I don't even know her surname.

'The coroner has already investigated her death and has confirmed a finding of murder.'

'That isn't what I asked.'

'The police investigation is ongoing.'

'And ...?'

'I'm not in charge of that investigation.'

I'd normally swear at this point. I'd make allegations of incompetence. That would upset the DCI, he'd stop co-operating, I'd get even more angry and we'd end up refusing to talk to each other. So I raise my eyebrows, wait for him to notice the gesture.

'But ...?' I add.

He takes the hint. 'But I hear – unofficially, of course – that there's insufficient evidence to prosecute the case.'

'That's a load of crap.' I tell him.

'I understand that there has been pressure placed at national and local level – political pressure, that is – to suggest that manpower and resources would be better used attempting to bring other criminals to justice. That is, to imprison those still at large and capable of potential further damage to individuals or property, rather than those who are, to state the obvious, dead.'

'Christ, where did you learn to speak like that?'

The DCI has a sense of humour. 'We go to a special school where we're taught to speak formal police. Embarrassing, isn't it?'

'What did it mean?'

'We know Philip Plumpton shot the girl, but we can't prove it. We might be able to prove it, but we've been told to prioritise elsewhere.'

'And the political pressure?'

'That's only my opinion. But Sir Charles isn't without influence.'

'The good family name?'

'Something like that. "Enough punishment already suffered," that seems to be the official line.'

'Hardly fair, is it?'

'Life isn't fair, Mr Oliphant. If it was, there'd be no need for policemen.'

We talk about other things as well. He sends his deputy out on some errand whenever he feels he's releasing information he shouldn't. I ask him about this, he says he's speaking as a friend and, if what he's telling me should ever be made public, he'll deny he ever mentioned it.

'Is this a policy decision?' I ask. 'And if so, is it your policy, your boss's policy, or the Force's policy?'

'I've discussed it with the Super,' he replies. 'We agreed we should keep you informed. It's a way of saying thank you, I suppose, a way of acknowledging that you did a good job. I've looked up your history, Mr Oliphant. I suppose that, personally, it's a way of recognising that, in the past, the Force didn't treat you too well. My opinion, of course. Entirely subjective. And others would disagree.'

I wonder what he's after, but I don't make any accusations. He's too fat and productive a cow to kill off just yet. I just sit back and enjoy the dairy products.

He tells me that the coroner has investigated Eric Salkeld's death and that it was undoubtedly accidental. His work computer has been checked, his internet record showed a large number of visits to sites dedicated to bondage and sado-masochism. On several he'd posted photographs of himself dressed in his basque and other, more revealing, items of clothing. There were traces of dried semen on his body, on the inside of the basque and on the carpet below the hook. The report will state that he killed himself accidentally, intent on self-arousal by constriction of the neck.

He had also been systematically defrauding the

Forestcrag employees. Records showed that he moved onto site every February. He said it was because he wanted to be present during the last few months of the financial year. He wanted to ensure that everything ran smoothly. It always did. The wages he stole were paid direct to several different bank accounts which themselves made regular payments to a single account in a Swiss bank. Swiss banks are, apparently, less reluctant to divulge information about their account holders than they were in the past. But this convivial willingness to help has, in this instance, come too late. By the time the police have found this information this account has emptied itself, and this time to an offshore bank whose clients pay large amounts for anonymity.

I remember the book I found at the climbing hut, the guide to Switzerland, but the DCI has already taken it into custody. He confirms that the name and address of the Swiss bank are those inscribed inside the cover. The link between Salkeld, the money and Eve Marton is therefore established. I suggest that this is at best a tenuous link, and the DCI is pleased to offer me more tangible evidence.

The police have been working well and fast. They've looked at all the dummy accounts set up to receive Eric Salkeld's false payroll payments. They were all in different banks, all in different women's names. But the signatures were remarkably similar to each other, and similar to Eve Marton's own signature. The accounts were all opened within days of each other; and within days of Eve Marton's appointment as Computer Manager at Forestcrag.

'Doesn't that suggest that the planning was Marton's rather than Salkeld's.' I suggest. The DCI hasn't finished yet. Salkeld was made redundant from his previous job, he'd been out of work for over two years and had retrained specifically to gain experience in computerised payroll and accountancy. His trainer on the Government-sponsored course? Eve Marton. The connection has foundations built into solid bedrock.

'We believe,' the DCI continues, 'that when Marton was

told you were a PI, she panicked. She thought you were there to investigate the fraud. She hadn't planned on staying the night, as you know, and she would have escaped if she'd had the opportunity. But she didn't. Instead she blundered into Salkeld's room while he was ... indulging himself. He may have already been dead. He may have been as startled by her as she was by him. Picture it, she bursts in, finds him trussed up in his costume, does a rapid exit; he's upset, slips and falls, kills himself.'

I could be feeling cynical. I could suggest that this explanation is too neat, it gathers together every available loose end and fuses them into a sublime and impenetrable Gordian knot which no one can be bothered to cut. I'm about to suggest this, but the DCI anticipates my objections.

'It could also be that Marton finds Salkeld *in flagrante* and decided to use the situation to her advantage. She's tall and strong, we know that, strong enough to unhook him, take his basque off and dress him in his pyjamas, then hang him up again. So it's conceivable that she might add her own weight to his. Pull down on his legs or kick them away. Make sure he killed himself. It doesn't really matter, she was the one wrote his "suicide" letter. She searched his room for any evidence which might counter that note, moved his boxes of softcore and his costume into her own wardrobe. Risky, but it worked. Almost.'

'But you don't have the resources ...'

'... to take the matter any further than that, yes, you're right. Does it matter?'

I shake my head. If Eve Marton had been alive then resources would have been found, investigations pursued. But she too is dead. The body count is as high as the last act of *Hamlet*, and the methods of killing equally diverse.

Eve Marton's own death is, of course, less controversial. 'She thought she had things covered,' the DCI suggests, 'but then things started getting sticky. She panicked again, decamped to the quarry. She slipped, fell to her death. It's that easy.'

233

The underling returns with sandwiches and tea, they offer to leave but I insist they stay. I have my own, more general questions.

'What's happening at Forestcrag?' I ask. 'I suppose they're suffering because of all the bad publicity.'

The DCI's eating, but his colleague seems pleased to be able to contribute to my education. 'Exactly the opposite,' he says. 'Never underestimate Joe Public's morbid curiosity. Four deaths in three days? One through sexual deviance, one accident, one murder and one self-defence? What more could they want? Apparently the place is packed out, they're planning murder tours and "Whodunnit Weekends". They're overjoyed.'

The DCI glances across, catches my eye. He says nothing, but his eyes apologise. 'He's got no tact,' they say, 'he doesn't know when to keep his mouth shut. Sorry.'

'David Morland still in charge?' I ask.

'Little bloke with a sweat problem? Yes, he's there, full of himself.'

'It's an ill wind . . .' I don't need to complete the cliché, the DCI and his friend nod their agreement. I want to go on. I want to point out that, when David Morland's selling his wares on the number of deaths at Forestcrag he's one short of the actual total. Danny Bateman was murdered just outside the site. But he doesn't count, he's just a poor copper killed while carrying out his duties. Perhaps I'll find the time (it looks as if I might have a lot of time to spare) to bring the matter up with Morland myself. I'd enjoy that. But for the moment I'm more concerned with the outcome than the events. I ask my next question. 'Whatever happened to Harry Simpson?'

The DCI assumes responsibility. He taps his fingertips together. That means the news isn't good. 'We don't know,' he says finally, and it's as if he's taking it as a personal affront. 'It was a confusing time. First the blizzards and the snow, then the thaw. And everything that was going on up at Forestcrag. Too much happening at once.'

'You mean he's got away?'

'Vanished. He's the one loose end we haven't tied up, and we're concerned.' It's almost a confession, the DCI is the sinner and I'm the priest able to offer absolution.

'Define "concern",' I suggest.

'Not as far along the line as "worried". When you were in Forestcrag we were worried. And that isn't as bad as "in despair". No, "concern" is worse than "anxious", and that's more serious than "thoughtful". Midway along the line, I suppose.'

'But you're still after him?'

'Mr Oliphant, he killed a policeman.'

That sums it up. Harry Simpson may have threatened my life, he may still be a danger to me, but that's not why they want to catch him. It's because he killed Danny Bateman. And I can understand that, even with my slightly different viewpoint.'

'I hope you find him,' I say. Ten Our Fathers and six Hail Marys if you don't.

I had other things to ask. I had a list, but they've covered most of the points or signalled that they have no intention of pursuing them further. They reassure me that Harry Simpson isn't around, if he was they'd have found him. Somehow that doesn't make me as happy as they are. They don't intend guarding me. But if I'm worried, if I'm suspicious, I'm to let them know. When it's time for them to go they seem genuinely sad. It could be that talking to me is, in comparison to the other duties they have to carry out, quite a pleasant occupation. Or they could be sad that I'm less enthusiastic than they are about their 'tying up the loose ends' of the crimes. It's not that I disagree with their conclusions, I just can't help feeling that they've arrived there too quickly. But I'm too tired to argue. I ask them to keep in touch if there are any new developments, they tell me they will but I suspect I won't see them again. They leave me alone.

It doesn't happen very often, being alone. In the physical

235

sense, that is; sometimes I'm at my most lonely when I'm surrounded by people. But for the first week of my stay in hospital there's usually someone visiting, popping in as they pass. Kirsty is a constant and welcome companion, though when I feel well enough to argue with her I have to insist that she spends some time back at school. Sly and Paula are looking after her, looking after me as well. Sly's flu has abated and he's working through some of the backlog of my work, trying to keep my customer relations good. He comes in at the end of every day to let me know what's happening. I think he's feeling guilty that he wasn't able to help me as much as he'd have liked, as much as he has in the past. Neither of us mentions this. Why are men so uncommunicative?

I don't find it difficult to raise my concerns with Paula, to have her confirm my suspicions of Sly's guilt. She'll deal with it, she tells me, I'm not to worry. Sly will soon be back to normal. I trust her.

Other friends call. Norm, ebullient as ever, suggests that, since I'm temporarily incapacitated, I might like to invest in his scheme to manufacture plastic sledges. He's picked up the presses cheaply, they're actually for making dustbins but they can be adapted easily and he's sure the inclement weather will return. He needs a quick decision. He isn't surprised or disappointed when I say no; the big sell is more important to him than the big sale. I find myself laughing aloud, the first time for weeks. I must be feeling better.

Me, Sly, Norm, it almost completes the old team. We complement each other – Sly's the strength, Norm's the technology and wheels, I'm the glue that holds us together. That's when Rak, the brains of our quartet, arrives; the sails of her coat unfurled, she blows and puffs into my room and sets about destroying the plastic chair simply by sitting in it. She's read all about my adventures in the local and national press but she wants to hear the truth from me, so I give her an edited version to keep her happy. She lets me know she's been promoted from the library, she's now in charge of the Council's website. 'So I'm my own boss, Billy. Unlimited access to the web, to Council databases, to information.' She rubs her hands together.

'How did the Council make such a mistake?' I ask her.

'I forged my own references. Told them how good I was, how cheap I was, how honest I was. Well, two out of three isn't bad. All I need now is a test, Billy. Anything you want me to do? Any impossible information to find? You know who to contact.'

I promise to do that. She hugs and kisses me before she leaves, that in itself makes me realise how ill I must have been; Rak doesn't show affection easily. I resolve not to put her in that position again, for my own sake. I no longer need imagine what it's like to be suffocated by a six-foot-wide amoeba.

When Sara gets back from her honeymoon she comes to visit me straightaway, though without her new husband. No one rang her to tell her what had happened, and that annoyed her. When she bustles in she's going to tell me off, but one look at me – my leg in the air, the machines I'm connected to, how thin I am – and she changes her mind.

'You're looking well,' I tell her, 'tanned. And the bump's developing.'

She preens herself. 'Look at you,' she says, 'you just go to pieces when I'm not around. How long before they let you out?'

'Another week. Though I might die of boredom before then.'

She thinks before she speaks. 'Don't do that, Billy. Life would be far less interesting without you.' She's close to tears. There are no recriminations, no telling me about the dangers I put her daughter into. I tease myself into imagining that, in a different place, at a different time, things might have been ... different. But they wouldn't, I remind myself. Put me and Sara together under any circumstances and we'll start to fight. She's better off where she is. And as for me ...?

'Have you heard from Jen?'

Jen. Have I heard from Jen?

I'm not sure who must have contacted her. Kirsty perhaps, more likely Paula. The first time she rang I wasn't all there, probably the results of the anaesthetic or trauma or simple lack of sleep. She must have been able to tell. She was calm, she told me she missed me, said she'd call back next day when I'd had time to rest.

The next call was different. I could talk, she'd had the chance to find out more – from Paula, from the press on the net, who knows – and she was in tears. She said she'd come back, I told her she'd do no such thing. It was an unresolved conversation, it stopped instead of ending when her bleeper – I heard it over all those miles – called her to some emergency.

We've spoken since but not resolved our feelings. She's looked into the practicalities of returning and they aren't easy to deal with. She has a contract, they have no one on hand to replace her, the financial cost would be great, the cost to her career even greater. I've told her again that I'm okay, that she doesn't have to worry. After all, the worst is long past.

We've talked about money. That was one of the reasons I didn't go with her to Canada, the need to make a living of my own. Apparently I may be due some type of compensation for my injuries, for the difficulty I may have in earning anything over the next few months. Or years. Oh yes, I'm aware of the problems I have to face. I haven't been allowed out of bed without the support of porters and fussing nurses. But if I'm due compensation then I'll use some of it, I tell Jen, to come and visit her.

We agree to correspond by email, we find it difficult to communicate on the phone. Paula's managed to find me a laptop computer and I can save my thoughts to disk; Kirsty sends them as an attachment without, she assures me, reading them; she returns Jen's emails to me in the same way. It feels hugely artificial. Letters have, at the very least, a sense of creation, of the analogue transfer of emotion from the mind to the page. There's a similar sense of distance, of travel, of time put aside, of effort put into the transmission of a fragile unrepeatable document. Electronic mail is, by comparison, impersonal. The product, the letter, is dwarfed by the incomprehensible complexity of the process. But we make do. Out of pure obstinacy I ask for a fountain pen and sheets of white, watermarked paper. I write Jen a long letter in my loping, untidy scrawl and have it posted in the knowledge that it will take at least a week, possibly two, to reach her. I write her a poem.

Every day I add my thoughts to my notebook. Every day I reach for the scrap of hospital paper on which Nessa wrote her own letter. It smells of her, her perfume and more. Not a long letter. But long enough. I've read it many times and I'm still not sure I understand it. So I read it again.

Dear Billy,

We could have been a hell of a team. I hoped there would have been a way of finding that out, of proving it, but it seems there's not going to be a chance to do that. I've been talking to Kirsty, she's a wonderful girl, you should be proud of her. She's the type of girl I'd be pleased to call my daughter. Or my sister.

On the way down from the quarry you were delirious. You kept on talking about someone called Jen. I know now who she is, what your relationship is. If she was around I might fight her for you, but I can't just take you in her absence.

You won't see me again. I won't pretend it's been an easy decision to make, but it would make things difficult for me – see what a selfish person I really am! Not thinking of you at all. Except I am, and it wouldn't work, believe me.

I'm not going back to Forestcrag. It was the wrong

239

place for me, but it took meeting you to make me realise that. I'm not sure where I'll go, what I'll do, but I'll probably end up somewhere warm – I've had enough snow to last me a lifetime. I have a little money saved up, enough to let me travel. I'll send you a postcard.

All my love, Nessa.

That's it. A fond goodbye, but still a goodbye. Not an *au revoir*. Some might even call it a brush-off. I wonder what Kirsty said to her. Was it a warning? After all, Kirsty and Jen do get on well together. I doubt it, Kirsty wouldn't presume to interfere to that extent. No, I have to assume that Nessa's taken time to think about what's important to her. I might have been on that list, but she's made her decision and crossed me off. I'm quite glad, really, that she's decided not to visit, it would have been awkward for both of us. But I regret not having the opportunity to thank her, and I smile when I think of her, because she saved my life.

My days aren't without interest. It helps when people call to see me, to talk about trivial things. But I tire easily. Most days I feel exhausted by the early evening, but I don't sleep too well. I have too much to think about.

Chapter Twenty-Eight

During the second week I'm given physiotherapy and crutches. People in white coats ask where I live, who can look after me. I tell lies about helpful neighbours but know that my friends will help out. So they discharge me.

Norm's snow hasn't returned, but the weather's still bad. Plagues of pestilence abound. Flood and famine walk the land. I sit at home and work my way through the pile of books I've brought back from hospital. None of them really interests me. I watch some videos but find myself falling asleep. I write polite notes to journalists and television producers implying I'm a recluse and telling them I don't want to discuss the Forestcrag deaths. Sometimes I see photographers waiting to catch me unawares; I usually limp to the front door and wave at them; they go away quickly, silent friendliness and approachability are new to them. I re-read my notes, try to interpret them, but they're too complex, they lead nowhere. My visitors develop regular schedules. Normality descends on everyone except me.

Walking is difficult but not impossible. My leg is in plaster and I have instructions not to use it for weightbearing, but it serves as a useful, weighty pendulum. The first time I use my crutches I reach the corner shop with difficulty and can barely make it back. Next day the muscles in my arms go on strike. But I persist. I get Sly to bring me some small plastic barbells, I use them regularly.

I look at myself in the mirror one night. The belt of fat round my midriff has disappeared, my face is almost angular.

My emails to Jen are becoming shorter, less frequent. I've nothing to write about. I'm not doing anything.

The weather begins to improve as March rolls into April and April gives way to May. I'm getting stronger. The plaster is removed from my leg to a round of applause from the watching nurses and student doctors. They're clapping for the consultant, not for me. My physiotherapy becomes more demanding, I'm allowed to use my leg to support my weight. I'm aware of the loss of muscle tone, it's thinner and weaker than my left leg. But I work on it.

'Labradors and Alsatians,' the consultant tells me, 'are prone to a hereditary disease called hip dysplasia. The socket of the hip joint is malformed, it isn't a full cup. The ball joint at the top of the dog's leg has nowhere to sit.' He holds his hands in front of him to demonstrate, one made into a balled fist, the other around it to make the socket. Then he opens the socket hand, makes it a plane, almost flat. 'See, the ball joint can just slip around wherever it wants.'

I'm not sure how relevant this is, but the consultant is a learned man. I let him go on. I have nothing better to do.

'But we aren't inundated with Labradors and Alsatians falling over each other because their back legs can't support them. What happens is that the dog's muscles compensate for this malformation, they grow stronger than they other-wise would. They cup the ball joint, augment the bony socket, so the end result is as if the ball and socket joint were fully formed. The dog has, for most of its life, no problems with movement at all.'

I don't need him to explain the analogy. My new knee will never be as good as the original was. Science and medicine haven't quite figured that out yet. But if I exercise, get up to strength, the difference won't be marked. Except for one thing.

'For most of its life?' I ask. 'How much of its life?'

The consultant gets down to specifics. 'I anticipate problems with natural loss of muscle bulk as you approach your mid fifties. By then the artificial joint in your knee will be close to the end of its useful life anyway, we'll have to replace it. In a few months' time your knee will be functioning at about seventy per cent of what it was capable of beforehand. Your second knee, the replacement when you get older, will only manage forty per cent. And there will probably be early onset of arthritis in associated joints in the right leg and in the left leg because of the extra work it will have to do.'

'Thank you for your honesty. I'd better arrange my round-the-world walk before then.'

'Use it, Mr Oliphant, while you have the chance.'

I do as he says. Within a week I'm down to a single walking stick which I carry mostly as insurance and to get young women to sympathise with me.

During the week before Easter I ask Sly to call round. I tell him I'd like to go out for a ride, ask him if he'd like to take me.

'Nothing would give me greater pleasure,' he says. 'Well, there are one or two things, but I'm not about to offer to do them with you. Where would you like to go?'

'This may sound silly, Sly.'

'I'm used to that.'

'I want to go back to Forestcrag.'

Chapter Twenty-Nine

It doesn't take us as long to get there this time. I have the opportunity to find out that Sly hasn't been called back for any reason. David Morland hasn't been in touch with him. Neither of us has received a get well card or a thank you note.

The countryside is almost beautiful. There's still snow sheltering in the grey temples of northern slopes, but with the van windows slightly open there's an air of freshness and greenery singing in fields and hedgerows. Even the sun is shining.

At the turn off to Forestcrag (the sign is visible this time) I see two or three dishevelled bunches of flowers where Danny Bateman's car had slid off the road.

'They might not let us in,' Sly says.

'Why not?' The thought hasn't even occurred to me.

'Well, neither of us became bosom buddies with David Morland, did we? In fact, I seem to remember hitting him. Didn't you do the same?'

'Literally or metaphorically? It doesn't matter, he hasn't suffered anything more than wounded pride. And besides, the place is buzzing because of us.'

'I still don't think there'll be a sign up saying "Welcome Back Sly and Billy".'

As we near the barriers they descend, blocking our way.

'I dare you to crash through,' I say. 'Bet if you do they

produce sub-machine guns from the guardhouse and start shooting. Barbed wire fences will pop out of the ground, a pack of Rottweilers will appear from nowhere, there'll be sirens and floodlights. Go on, I dare you.'

Sly declines the offer. 'Leave it to me,' he says, 'I'll have a word. I'm no diplomat, but I'm better at it than you are.'

'I know another way in,' I shout after him, 'we might have to crawl down a cliff, but we'll get there. Don't let them bully you.'

I wait. It's strange because everything is new to me, though I know I've been here before. Then it was dark and snowy, now everything is green. There are flowerbeds in front of the reception area, birds are splashing themselves in a bath in the middle of the lawn. There's little traffic, but that's because this isn't one of the changeover dates. Fridays and Mondays the site empties then refills. Three thousand people depart, another three thousand arrive. All trying to get away from it all.

Sly reappears towing a young man in his wake. He opens the door, makes the introductions. 'This is Dean Metcalfe,' he says, 'Head of Security.'

'Sam Ellis been promoted?' I ask, shaking the young man's hand.

'Mr Ellis is no longer with the company,' he smiles back at me. He's wearing a radio headset, miniature microphone and earpiece barely visible.

'Ah, Mr Stalin – sorry, Mr Morland – must have got rid of him.'

Sly decides he'd better interrupt before I become argumentative. 'Dean says we're welcome to come on site, in fact he'll come along with us wherever we want to go.' He has his back to the young man, he's grimacing as he speaks. 'He knows all about our adventures. Says he'd like the benefit of our professional opinions on the downfalls of the previous system.'

'Oh good.'

'He knows about your injury and suggests an electric wheelchair or a buggy would be useful if you want to go anywhere outside the Tesseract.'

'What a kind young man.'

'So what should our itinerary be?'

I look around Sly and beam at the new head of Security. He's younger than he ought to be for the job, probably a year or two out of university with experience as a junior in another arm of Forestcrag's parent company. This is his big chance and he's determined to succeed. I climb out of the van and exaggerate my limp.

'I'd really like to go up to the quarry,' I say, 'just to remind myself what it was like.'

He looks at my leg. 'Is that wise, Mr Oliphant? I've been up there myself, it's quite a steep climb.'

'Mr Rogers here has said he'll carry me if I have problems.'

He tries to stifle a grin; perhaps he'll survive the next purge after all. A few minutes later he's found a green golf cart and I'm sitting beside him (he insists on driving) with Sly folded into the back. Although he appears to know his way round and, when I query his directions, promises he's taking the direct route, I don't recognise the scenery. This doesn't worry me too much – last time I headed for the quarry Nessa was leading the way and I was content to follow in her wake. But everything becomes familiar when he pulls up beside a stile in a fence, beyond which a zig-zag path leads up a steep slope to a pair of tall rocks. I point them out to Sly.

'That's the entrance to the quarry. It's flat beyond there. Think you can make it?'

'Lead the way,' he says, climbs out of the buggy as if he's undressing himself.

'Are you sure you can manage this, Mr Oliphant?' the security man asks.

'Dean, do you want me to race you to the top? I can manage.' And I do. I'm fitter now than I was last time I climbed up here, my arms and chest are broader and my left leg is very strong. I've been exercising on steps and, although I always lead with my left leg, climbing the stile and mounting the slope isn't difficult.

By the time I reach the rock pinnacles I'm sweating and both my legs are aching, but Sly's taken off coat and pullover on the way up, stuffed them in his rucksack with the flask of tea and the camera I'd insisted he bring. Dean, I'm pleased to see, has stopped twice to admire the view.

'Okay,' he says as he reaches me, 'you've proved your point. You're fit.'

'No, I'm obstinate. What really happened to Sam Ellis? You can tell the truth, there are no microphones or hidden cameras up here.'

'You can guess,' Metcalfe replies. 'He made a handy scapegoat. He jumped before he was pushed. Morland would have gone as well, but there was a huge increase in bookings. If it continues the same way – and there's no reason to suppose things will slacken off this season – he'll be made a director.'

'What's he like?'

'I'll be honest, Mr Oliphant, because I can afford to be. There's been a reorganisation, security's now a head office function. So is payroll. David Morland isn't my boss. And I can tell you he's a very effective manager who does his job well by all the measurable parameters the company employs. The fact that I don't like him and think he's a shit is irrelevant.'

'That *was* honest. Thank you.'

'It's a pleasure. And I meant what I said earlier, if you'd like to comment on our security systems I'd be very grateful. There would, of course, be a consultation fee.'

'I never suspected anything less.'

I take the lead, pointing out the place Nessa abseiled down the cliff, the flat area where I was shot, the track up the quarry wall which would have led Eve Marton to her freedom. The hut is in the quarry's shadow, stubborn

247

patches of snow still cling to the hard rock above it. This time the door is locked and, when Dean Metcalfe unlocks it, there's a high-pitched whine inside from a burglar alarm. He punches a code into the wall panel and the noise ceases.

'Even up here,' he says, 'we've become more security conscious.'

Little has changed since the last time I was there. I'm surprised to find Eve Marton's sleeping bag, rolled and tied, filmed with dust that might be natural, might have belonged to a police forensic officer; I suspect the former, why waste time looking for fingerprints when there's no need to search for a culprit? The detritus of her brief stay there has at least been tidied away. The empty cans and bottles have been consigned to a waste-bin, and the police, I'm aware, have removed the incriminating tourist guide to Switzerland. I'm beginning to wonder why I'm here. The hut, the whole quarry, has a melancholy air. I'd been feeling optimistic during the climb. Without being able to say why – and the decision to visit the quarry had been impromptu, with no forethought – I had some ridiculous notion that by returning I might quiet the dull ache of suspicion that had been nagging me awake every morning. But there's nothing new here, no bolt of lightning to jar my mind into a new appreciation of old facts.

'What's behind the curtain, boss?'

'Graffiti,' I tell Sly, 'some of it rather rude.'

'Perhaps I'd better take a look.' There's a smirk in his voice.

'You'll need a light.'

'Here,' says Dean Metcalfe, 'I've brought a torch.' He hands it to Sly who disappears behind the curtain. I hear the click, see the flicker of light.

'It's cold up here.' I can feel an ache in my leg and I'm beginning to wish I'd brought some extra clothing. Sly whistles from behind the curtain.

'Boss, think you should have a look at this?'

Dean Metcalfe and I pull the curtain aside. Sly's bending down examining the stone wall carefully, but there's enough light splashing from the torch to show that the room is the same as when I last visited. The plan of the quarry is still there, so are the pornographic caricatures. It's the wall at the base of these that Sly is inspecting in some detail.

'Early Picasso?' I suggest.

'Right initial, boss, but the wrong artist. Come on, have a look.'

I hobble over, Metcalfe close behind. It's difficult for me to bend down, I have to extend my right leg sideways, but the light is bright enough for me to see that there's a signature on the wall.

'Infamous in posterity,' I say.

'Who is it?' Metcalfe asks.

'Philip Plumpton. And it's dated as well. If we can believe it, he drew these six years ago. Must have been about sixteen.'

'Before Forestcrag was built,' Sly adds. 'Must have been a precocious little bugger.'

Dean Metcalfe looks at the drawings and the signature. 'He was the one who tried to kill you?' he asks.

'Not too good at his job, thank goodness, he only succeeded in half-crippling me. But he did murder a young girl dressed in my coat. One and a half out of two.'

'He'd been up here before, then?'

'Not surprising, really. Daddy owned all the land round here. Junior must have spent his formative youth exploring the estate. When he wasn't hunting, shooting and fishing, that is. Must have spent many a happy hour up here with his softcore mags and his right hand working overtime. Drawing, I mean.'

'Think we'd better go, boss? Or was there something else . . .?'

Something else. Yes, there was definitely something else, there must be something else. I just can't think what it might be. 'I'll take a photograph of the drawings, just in case.'

The camera, I realise, is the one I was given to photograph Eric Salkeld, somehow it's found its way into my possession. It has a built-in flash, useful in the darkness of the rock room, and I make about a dozen exposures of Philip Plumpton's drawings, three of his signature alone. Then, to use up more of the film, I take snapshots of the inside of the hut. Before we return to civilisation I insist on having a cup of tea; Sly joins me, Dean Metcalfe prefers black coffee (which I haven't brought) and makes do with water. Sly insists on using the camera to catch me sitting on the uneven wooden chair, raising my plastic cup in a risible toast to good health.

The journey back down is tortuous. I slip and slide, even with Sly to help me the process is slow and painful. I'm pleased to reach the comfort of the buggy, decline Dean Metcalfe's offer of recovering in his office. I promise to come back to discuss security, ask him to pass on my best wishes to David Morland. He promises to do so with an enthusiasm as great as my own.

I dislike painkillers but that night have to resort to them. I don't sleep. My thoughts are of broken bodies.

Chapter Thirty

Sly's back again early the next day. 'You look rough,' he says.

I'm sitting in a stiff-backed chair (good for the posture) in front of my dining table, walking stick by my side. I'm pleased I was able to dress myself and, if Sly had seen the effort involved in reaching my chair, he'd probably be carrying me into hospital himself. But perhaps he does recognise how much of an invalid I am because he makes me breakfast, tidies up, runs round after me, fetches me a newspaper.

'Did you come to make sure I'm okay,' I ask as he washes the dishes, 'or is there a more devious purpose?' He's singing loudly, accompanying a radio station I don't normally listen to. This is, however, my home, my place of refuge, and I find it difficult to share it with anyone. Even with the well-meaning, ebullient Sly.

'Shit!' he calls from the kitchen, 'I knew there was something!' He hurries to join me, drying his hands on a tea towel. 'I completely forgot, boss.' He picks up his jacket from the sofa where he threw it (if I'd felt able to move from my seat I would have hung it up) and takes an envelope from the pocket. 'Thought you might want these. God knows why.'

The envelope contains the photographs I took the day before. I'd forgotten about them, it's almost embarrassing

251

that Sly should have had them developed and printed so quickly.

'I was in no hurry, Sly, they could have waited.'

'Yeah, I know. But my legs are sore with that climb yesterday, I thought yours would be worse. It was a good excuse to come round and annoy you.'

He knows me well.

'And I haven't even looked at them yet. Come on, let's see them.'

They're as I expected, nothing exciting or revelatory in any way, they look like bad copies of neolithic cave paintings. The prints of the hut itself are, because of the clutter, marginally more interesting. Sly spreads them out on the table.

'Reminds me of the old polar explorers,' he says, 'Scott of the Antarctic and all that. Mind, you'd need to grow a beard and develop a bit of frostbite to make them really authentic.'

I'm not really listening. I've spread the photographs of the cave room out over the table, overlapped them where possible. The perspective isn't quite right but, put together, they make a more impressive whole than individually. But what I'm interested in is not the Plumpton graffiti, it's the sketch to the side, the elevation and plan of the quarry. It's wrong.

'Sly, have a look at this, will you?'

He bends closer, moves his head from side to side to rid his eyes of the reflected glare.

'It's the quarry, isn't it?'

'I think so. It couldn't really be anything else. But it doesn't seem right.' I trace my finger over it. 'This is the path we climbed, yes? And at the top is the flat section, over to the right the pond, much lower down. And I think this is the path out of the top, just here.'

He follows my directions. 'Yeah, I'm with you so far.'

'But over the top here, where the path should head across open moorland, it looks as if there's another quarry. Or a pit of some type. The plan's faded, I can't quite see.'

Sly's as good with plans as I am, it's part of our livelihood. 'The elevation shows it better, boss, there's definitely another excavation of some sort. Not as deep as the main quarry, but it's there.'

I lean forward. He's right.

'So what does it mean?'

'I don't know. Perhaps nothing, perhaps something.' My leg twinges, it could be the beginning of an attack of cramp; I move it gently to one side. 'Sly, are you busy today?'

'What do you want me to do?'

'Be a messenger? A delivery boy? And could you pass me the phone?'

He does as he's asked, makes no comment as I dial.

'Hello, Rak? Amazing, this direct dial technology works. Remember you said something about wanting a challenge? Yes you did, you know you did. Well, I've some work for you. I need copies of Ordnance Survey maps for what's now Forestcrag Village – yes, I'm still working on that. In particular, there's a quarry they use for rock-climbing at the north end of the site, I want to know how far it extended, whether it's altered in size over the years, when it was started, who owned it, what was quarried there, when it stopped working ... What? I'm going too fast? You can't keep up? Rak, I'm disappointed, someone in your position of authority should be able ... Okay, okay, I'm sorry! Yes, everything you can get me on that. Sly'll be with you in an hour. Yes, an hour! You said you wanted a test! I love you too. Bye.'

I can feel the corners of my mouth curving upwards. Sly's expression is more enigmatic, he's not sure what's going on. Neither am I. But both of us have been in that position before.

'I'd set off now if I was you,' I say, 'just to put a little more pressure on her. Why should we be the only ones to suffer?'

Chapter Thirty-One

Sometimes, no matter how hard we try, things fall apart. Whether we're talking about relationships, businesses, games, or even lives, success doesn't necessarily follow the investment of large amounts of cash or time or energy or love. I seem, more often than not, to be a living example of that premise. But the other side of that coin is revealed when, with minimal effort, ideas or solutions or opportunities reveal themselves, begging to be used. I suppose that, when reckonings are made and the many small failures are balanced against the occasional huge success, humanity as a whole must benefit. Profit exceeds loss by a small margin, good manages to defeat evil (though only just), virtue and effort is rewarded and the generations roll onward. Despite the cynicism I carry as a shield, the melancholy I can't help displaying to all I know, I'm occasionally surprised when events conspire to convert me to optimism. This is such a moment.

Sly has disappeared to find Rak, the oracle, and return with her guidance, prognostications and hard facts. I'm excited, something is going to happen, though I don't know what. The photographs in front of me, laid neatly on the table, are hieroglyphs and Sly will return with my Rosetta stone. At one side are the other snaps, the ones of the hut. I do with them what I did with the others, arrange them in a panorama. They overlap, inconsistently, but the end result isn't displeasing. They would make a complete circle if I chose to join them that way, starting and finishing with the curtain. I place the odd one out, the photograph of me sitting down drinking tea, as best I can. But it doesn't fit at all. Sly was standing too close to me and he's used the telephoto lens; he was bending down while I, from necessity, was perched awkwardly in the hut's one and only chair. He's caught me with my right arm lifting my cup in a toast, a silly grin on my face. But my left arm, my elbow, is resting on the table top. And beside it, hidden by a cardboard box containing a coil of rope, is a book. I look closer, it seems familiar, but I can't quite read the title.

Somewhere in the flat there's a magnifying glass. It's not a large flat, there's little space to hide or lose anything. It still takes me half an hour to find it lazing at the back of the cutlery drawer (one day I must consider what logic made me put it there). I return to my seat, calm myself, and examine the photograph anew. I move the glass to and fro, do the same with my head. There's no mistaking the name of the author, Graham Greene; but the title isn't one I expected (although it's one of his best known works). Perhaps that's why my mind makes the ridiculous leap it does. The police have been working on the assumption that Eric Salkeld and Eve Marton were working together. They probably were. But why should a conspiracy be limited to two people? A tune rises in my head, a tune from a film. Harry Lime's theme. From the film *The Third Man*. Wasn't that one of the films Philip Plumpton particularly admired? Is that why he said I knew more than I realised? How could he have been involved in the fraud?

I think back to my first visit to the hut. I close my eyes, try to remember it as it really was. The sleeping bag in the corner, that was there, and a novel. Yes, I thought it was Eve Marton's, but ... Don't think, Billy, just remember. What else was there? A rucksack, but the police must have taken that away. A primus stove, she needed that to cook, and some tins of food. The Swiss guide, of course, candles, a torch, and ... Hold it. Go back. Food, what else was there apart from food? There was something else! I picture the line of things again, primus, tins of beans, sausages, a half empty carton of milk. Why? Why would Eve Marton want milk? She didn't drink it, she'd told me that once. In the offices when we were looking for evidence of Eric Salkeld's fraud, she'd said milk made her sick. At least I think she said that. But it's not enough.

Assume it's right, I tell myself. If the milk wasn't hers then someone else had been there. But when? It could have been during the summer, people climbing. Philip Plumpton knew about the hut, he could have been there. It could have been anyone. No! It couldn't have been anyone, it could have been one of a small number of people. I have to think. I have to eliminate possibilities. And to do so I have to make phone calls.

The first is to the friendly DCI whose name I've forgotten, but it doesn't matter. I'm suddenly *persona grata* at police HQ and he's found for me.

'I need to know something about Eve Marton,' I tell him, 'and although it sounds silly, it might be important. Is it possible for you to check her medical records and find out whether she was allergic to milk?'

Give him due credit, he doesn't laugh. He does ask why, and when I say I'm not sure, that it's a long shot, that it probably won't come to anything, he doesn't refuse my request. He isn't even fazed when I suggest he might like to call me back the same day. 'I know copies of the notes will probably still be with the coroner's officer,' I tell him, 'it shouldn't take too much time to look through them.' I'm at my most pathetic when I'm wheedling someone for information they're under no obligations to give me. 'And I know, strictly speaking, you shouldn't divulge such information to a member of the public. But this is a special case. I'd offer to come in myself and look, but my leg's really painful today ...' Beyond crying down the phone there's not much else I can do. It seems to have the desired effect,

I'm rewarded with the promise of a call as soon as possible.

My second call is a long shot, but at least I know the name of the person I want to contact.

'Hello, Dean Metcalfe? It's Billy Oliphant here. Yes, I'm okay, a little stiff after the walk yesterday. No, I haven't rung to make an appointment to see you, but ... Yes, I'll be pleased to come ... I really need to have Sly with me, I can't drive at the moment. No, the reason I rang is – I know this will sound a cheek – I left a book up in the hut yesterday. It's of sentimental value, would it be possible for you to send someone up there and pick it up? I know exactly where I left it. You'd go yourself? That's wonderful, would you mind ringing me to let me know it's there? Yes, it's a paperback copy of *The Third Man* by Graham Greene. Thank you *so* much. Bye.'

I feel tired but exhilarated by doing so much. I may not know which way I'm going, but it feels pleasant to be moving again.

Chapter Thirty-Two

It takes Sly over two hours to return, and he's staggering under the weight of material Rak's given him.

'I resign,' he says as he walks through the door, 'unless you happen to have a cup of tea ready made and waiting for me.'

'You can't resign, I don't employ you. At least, not at the moment. But I'm a kind-hearted sort of a bloke, so I'll make you a cuppa anyway.'

'Me as well,' echoes Kirsty's voice.

'What are you doing here?' I ask. 'Shouldn't you be at ...?'

'free periods, Dad, wonderful inventions. So I got the bus out here, thought I'd come along and cheer you up. What are you doing? I'll make the tea, you explain while I'm doing it.'

Sly's there before me. 'He's got me running round town collecting maps and books on Forestcrag and the surrounding area. Rak's hunted out anything and everything that has the remotest connection with the place over the entire history of mankind. Good job I've been weight-training.'

I'm about to explain properly when the phone rings. I'm the first to it. 'That's me. That was quick, I'm impressed. Yes, I'll tell you if and when I figure things out, like I said, it's a long shot. Yes, I've a pen handy. Go on.' I scribble information down on the paper I already have waiting on the table. 'Thank you, that might prove handy. Yes, I'll get back in touch as soon as I know anything for certain.'

'Who was that?' Kirsty asks.

'You know that old saying, "if you want to know something ask a policeman"?'

Kirsty and Sly both shake their heads.

'Oh. I must be older than I think. Anyway, it's perfectly true. I just did and he gave me the answer I wanted.'

'Which was?' Sly prompts.

'Yes.'

'Yes? Yes what? Come on boss, you're playing with us.'

Kirsty's looking over my shoulder. 'Dairy product in . . . you've got terrible writing, Dad . . . intolerance. That's it, "dairy product intolerance since early childhood". Is that right?'

'That's right. Eve Marton couldn't eat butter or cheese or eggs. Even more important, she couldn't drink milk, it made her sick.'

'So?' Sly's curiosity is cautious.

'So why was there a carton of milk at the mountain hut?'

'She was expecting visitors?' Kirsty suggests.

'Left over from the last time someone was there?' Sly's still being cautious.

'Either's a possibility. But more likely – at least that's what I think – is that another person went with her. Someone familiar with the ground for many years, someone who knew it would make a good hiding place. It could even be that this someone got everything together for her.'

'And who might that be?' Kirsty asks.

I don't want to tell her. She's spent a lot of time with me lately, yet I haven't dared mention Philip Plumpton. Neither she nor I have broached the subject of his death, his killing her friend, his trying to kill me. It might be difficult given her, albeit brief, attachment to him. The breezy, carefree innocent of the past few weeks has been the old Kirsty, the asexual Kirsty. But I know of the existence of a different Kirsty, neither worse nor better than the one

259

facing me now. She's in a state of transition, moving to and fro, being a girl one moment and a woman the next. I suppose I'm growing accustomed to this, so that too is a change. I want her to make her own decisions, but at the same time I have a desire to protect her. Protecting her means putting off a discussion of Philip Plumpton until she's ready for it, until she mentions it. So how do I cope with this now?

'I'm not quite ...' I begin, but Sly interrupts me.

'That could only be Phil Plumpton. He knew the place well, we've evidence of that. He was intelligent, he was associated with Forestcrag through his father, he could have ... What's the matter, boss?'

He catches my look of panic, my shaking head, but he doesn't understand. His kids aren't old enough. He has this to look forward to.

'It could have been Phil,' Kirsty says, her voice level and even. 'He told me he knew the place well, grew up there before the site was developed. But his family still owns the land, it's just leased to Forestcrag. In fact, they also own a sizeable part of the parent company as well. Not a majority shareholding, but his family forms the largest single minority group.'

I don't have to hide my surprise. 'I didn't know that.'

'We talked a lot.' She seems sad but not distraught. 'It might sound as if he was boasting – all that talk about owning land, shares and so on – but it wasn't really like that. We got to know each other quite well; at least that's the way I felt at the time. I would never have imagined he could do what he did. He seemed kind, thoughtful.' She smiles at me, pats my arm. 'Just goes to show, you can never tell from the outside what a person's like inside.'

'Did he say anything about me?'

'I've been trying to remember, Dad, whether he did or not. Whether I might have missed a clue, whether he might have given me some idea that he might do what he did. I don't think there was anything ... He asked if you were good at your job and I said you were, that you were very good, one of the best. I try to keep thinking objectively, remembering actual words. But it always comes back to the same thing, that he killed Amy but he was still prepared to ... you know.'

'Take advantage?'

'No, he didn't take advantage of me, Dad. He was actually quite polite, we talked about it first, we agreed we'd do it. It's just the fact that he knew what he'd done, he'd killed someone, but he could still go ahead and ... make love with me.'

'More tea anyone?' Sly asks, gets up without waiting for an answer and pretends to work noisily at the sink.

'It's always difficult to work out what people are really thinking, love. Phil killed Amy because he thought it was me. He tried to kill me later. There must be some pretty powerful reason for that and I'm keen to find out what that is. So if you do think of anything, anything at all ...'

'There's nothing, Dad, I've gone through everything he said to me and there's nothing. He was ... he was surprisingly normal. I mean, I said to him it must be great having a lot of money, being able to do what you want whenever you want. He said yes, it must be, if I ever find out I'll let you know.'

'What do you think he meant by that?'

'He was joking, obviously. It's the type of thing he said. He didn't make a lot of being rich or having a big house and lots of land.'

'So what went wrong?'

'I don't know, Dad, I really don't know. I don't even know if he went with me because he liked me or because I was your daughter.'

'That first night in the casino? He didn't know who you were, he didn't know who I was. I think he asked you to dance because you were so beautiful. But then, for some reason – and I can't tell when or why – it became so important for him to kill me. That's why Sly's been to

261

collect all this stuff. I think he may have been up at the climbing hut before he followed me up there. So we're checking everything there is to know about the place. We're looking for clues, motivation, anything.'

'Clutching at straws, you mean?'

'That's about it.' Perhaps not the words I would have chosen, but probably an accurate reflection of what I'm doing.

'Well, at least it keeps you off the streets. Anything I can do to help?'

'No, not really. I don't know what I'm looking for, so I really need to look through everything myself. I'm hoping for inspiration.' That much is true, but there's more than that. Kirsty seems to be coping well with the knowledge that she has slept with (ah, the euphemisms we use – as far as I remember she did very little sleeping) a man immediately after he killed her friend and just before he attempted to kill her father. But I don't know what, if anything, I'm going to find out by trawling through the pile of maps and books on the table, and it could implicate Philip Plumpton in further crimes. I don't want to put Kirsty under any additional pressure.

'I can give you a lift home,' Sly offers. 'Unless the taskmaster has any more jobs lined up.'

'Go on,' I say, 'abandon me. You come here, drink my tea, then leave me. But I'll manage without you. And when I'm rich and famous, you'll remember this day with regret.'

Kirsty grabs her own books. 'I didn't know you couldn't act,' she says, 'give me a ring if you want anything.'

'I knew you couldn't act,' Sly says, slings his coat over his shoulder. 'Seriously, boss, if there's anything you want just give me a buzz.'

'Thanks to both of you, but I just need time now. It'll probably come to nothing but I've nothing else to keep me busy at the moment. So I think I'll spend the evening reading.'

Kirsty bends down, kisses me on the cheek. ''Bye, aged parent,' she whispers.

'I'll just wave,' Sly calls from the doorway.

I hobble to the window and watch them drive away. I'm feeling a little better, moving more easily. I could probably manage a short walk to the corner shops, the sun's shining and I need the exercise. But the table's full and I've promised myself I'd work. I find another pen (best to have two in case one runs out of ink) and a fresh pad of A4, arrange the paperwork on the table in two neat piles. One is of maps, the other books, largest at the bottom. And then I'm ready to go.

Chapter Thirty-Three

I'm still working at ten. My pad's covered with scribbled notes and drawings. Lines run across the page, arrange themselves into boxes and circles, emphasise or cross out. There are three mugs lined up in front of me, none of them empty, the contents cold. I must have eaten because I don't feel hungry, but I can't remember what or when. I'm not sure whether I'm making any progress. I know more than I did, but little of it seems relevant. I decide to re-read my notes in an attempt to make more sense of them.

I know now that the Plumpton family once owned all the moorland for miles round the Forestcrag site. The quarry was worked until the late nineteenth century, and some of the high quality quartzite sandstone it produced was used to build the prison a few miles away. The maps show the way the land use has changed over the years. The present forest was nothing more than a few thickets of natural spruce in the early 1900s; and the quarry itself has also changed. From what I can see (and I'm looking at maps and checking leases, reading histories and biographies) the Plumptons and their ancestors concentrated on farming the lower, more fertile lands heading down to the sea. They kept the moors for shooting and let the grazing to tenants. They did, however, run the quarry themselves. Or quarries. The early maps show two separate areas devoted to this use, the smaller being dug first then, apparently, abandoned as the larger was worked more extensively. Both are still shown on maps up to 1902; but then, on the 1925 map, only the larger quarry is shown.

Nessa never mentioned the smaller quarry, though she said she'd climbed the path through the quarry to the moors beyond. It's not shown on the maps. It must have been filled in. Interesting, but not exactly relevant to my meandering investigations. I scrawl a line through it.

Rak has managed to find me copies of the planning applications for the Forestcrag site. They were submitted on behalf of Sir Charles Plumpton – obviously his involvement was crucial. I wonder whether the whole project was his idea. Who approached whom? Did he say to the Forestcrag parent company 'Excuse me, lads. I've got this great idea for a holiday village. And, funnily enough, I've got the ideal site for it.' Or did Forestcrag come to him, 'Chuck, you own a big bit of moor and forest and we just might have a use for it.' Does it matter? The application isn't detailed in the sense of having maps and plans with it, but it does use some emotive vocabulary. It speaks of the 'economic rejuvenation' of the area; it repeats the words 'high quality' with regard to the lodges, the facilities and, by implication, the clientele. But it also has a 'low environmental impact', with the lodges and the central Tesseract being 'invisible to all but the site users'. Forestcrag would place 'no unreasonable additional demands on local resources', that's one of the reasons David Morland didn't want to involve the police or contact the local authority for snow clearance. Clearly that extends to other areas as well: the new venture would make arrangements to dispose of its own rubbish, would install its own electricity supply and had 'a viable source of fresh water within the site'.

I'm already aware of the failing electricity supply; is that why I have little faith in Forestcrag's other areas of self-sufficiency?

This doesn't lead me anywhere. Nor does the information that the prison was requisitioned during the Great

War and turned into what sounds like a labour camp for the production of munitions. I'm similarly unimpressed by reading that the Plumpton estate has reduced in size over the years; that Sir Charles owns a flat in Westminster and a villa in Italy as well as the stately Plumpton Hall; and that he's a name at Lloyd's. But then I never did pay much attention to the interviews in *Tatler* or *Horse and Hounds*.

I am, it seems, nowhere near finding what I don't know I'm looking for. Yes, there's a loose connection with Philip Plumpton, but nothing specific. He lived in the area, knew it well, had visited the quarry and had drawn rude pictures on its walls. But there's nothing to say he was there at the same time as Eve Marton, nothing to suggest that he might have been involved in the fraud. Was I really expecting to find something in this ragbag of paperwork? Or was I clutching, as Kirsty suggested, at straws.

When the phone rings my eyes are closing, it jangles me back to life. 'Yeah,' I mutter into its mouthpiece.

'Billy Oliphant? It's Dean Metcalfe here.'

'Dean ...? Oh yes, from Forestcrag. Security. Hello, I'm sorry, I'm a little slow at the moment.'

'I hope I didn't disturb you.'

'No, not at all. Still up, still awake, ready to dance away the hours till dawn.'

He's not sure how to take me, there's that short silence when he considers how to respond, what to say. His decision is to bluster on, after all, he's the one doing me a favour.

'I've got the book,' he says, 'from the quarry. I went up myself this evening, it was beautiful. I could see all the way down the coast, the hut was in shadow, of course, but the whole site was bathed in sunshine. I must go up there more often.'

I'm jealous that he has the opportunity.

'Do you want me to send it to you, or will you collect it?'

It suddenly seems unimportant. The optimism with which

I began the day has evaporated. What can I prove by finding one of Philip Plumpton's books at the quarry? Only that he'd been there something, any time. 'Would you mind putting it in the post for me?' I say.

'No problem. It is the one you said would be there. Graham Greene. *The Third Man*.'

'I'm so pleased.'

'And there's a name in the front of it.'

Here we go. He's going to ask why I said it was my book when it belongs to Philip Plumpton. What can I say? But he goes on, and I find I don't need to make up an excuse.

'It says it belongs to Nessa Clifton.'

I surprise myself with the speed of my response. 'Tell you what, I'll pick it up tomorrow. I'm sure someone will give me a lift in.'

Chapter Thirty-Four

This time it's Norm I rely on. It means I have to listen to his plans for making easy money. I also have to make pleasant comments about whichever car he brings. Both are easy to do: so far as the first is concerned, listening is a pleasantly passive process and whatever Norm says I can safely ignore, secure in the knowledge that his ideas are inherently non-profit-making. The second is even easier. Even the most bad-tempered, recalcitrant vehicles will come up to Norm and purr, rub themselves against him, pledge undying loyalty to him. Providing, of course, he'll agree to take care of them, maintain them, smooth their bumps and bruises and tweak their moving parts. Norm is a motor mechanic without comparison and a compassionate, caring driver. He cares for his and other vehicles, for the road beneath their tyres, for pedestrians, cyclists and all road users. And he worries about me.

'I've been waiting for you to call, boss, I didn't want to impose, I know what it's like, I had problems of me own this time last year with me hernia, sheer hell it was. Mobility, that's the name of the game, you need to get out and about and me, well, I've got the time to take you, and the wheels. That Sly, he means well, but sometimes he drives like a madman and, let's face it, you don't want to be rushing about in a van, do you? Na, a smooth drive, a comfortable seat – yeah, you lean back if you want, have a snooze, don't mind me – next thing you know I'll have you safe at the door.'

Last year his favourite was an old jelly-mould Volvo. He'd tuned its engine to perfection, was working on its body for ages. Every time he took me out it was a different piebald mix of colour and bare metal. This time it's an eye-catching white-walled 1960s Vauxhall Velux with a column-mounted gear-change and bench seats. It smells of luxury.

'They're expecting me,' I tell him, 'I explained what I needed last night.'

'And what's that, boss?'

'Access to a room. Someone to answer a few questions. A buggy so you can drive me round the site. If you don't mind, that is.' I know Norm won't mind, even though I'm quite capable of driving a buggy myself. I find his chattering equivalent to a Buddhist chant, it's calming and reassuring. He knows I don't listen to him.

Dean Metcalfe is waiting for us. He's friendly, calls me Billy, I can tell he wants to know why I'm back so soon. He offers to accompany me and I accept. Though he's willing to give me keys for the places I want to visit, it's often easier to get things done if the person who gives out the keys is also there.

Our first destination is the staff accommodation block. I'd asked Dean to help me out with some information and he's keen to fill me in.

'Nessa Clifton is still, officially, on the books as an employee. She requested two months' extended unpaid leave and, given her role in the recent incidents, this was granted. We have a forwarding address and a mobile telephone number, but I've tried the number and it's not connecting. I had a quick look at the room she was using. It's a pigsty. I don't know if she came back on site to collect anything. You might be able to tell me when you have a look at the room.'

'Would I be able to look at her personnel records?'

'Normally, no. But in the circumstances ... That is, I'm not quite sure what the circumstances are, Billy, but I'm sure you'll be willing to help me out there.'

'Possible miscarriage of justice? I can't really explain more, Dean. And, as you know, I'm not a policeman. But I have suspicions, and if I go straight to the police they'll probably come in and turn the place upside down. I don't want to do that, it could be bad publicity, it would definitely be a huge inconvenience to you and your staff and your customers. I thought my light touch would be preferable ...'

'Of course. And I'm here to help. We can go to Human Resources as soon as we've finished at the accommodation block. I'll come with you in case you run across any problems.'

This can be translated as 'I'm here to keep an eye on you; if you find anything, I want to know what it is.'

I have a feeling that this weather won't last. It's too sunny, too warm. People are wandering around the site dressed in shorts and T-shirts. Dean has taken off his tie. Such behaviour encourages bad weather and brings out the pessimist in me.

I recognise the path leading up to the accommodation block. When Norm pulls up I'm already heaving myself out of my seat. Dean's at the door just as fast, he opens it and I lead the way down the corridor to Nessa's room. I have to wait for him to let me in and wonder what happened to the pass keys I borrowed from Nessa. It seems so long ago that we were trapped here on site, that we took refuge in her small gymnasium, that we spent so much time in each other's company. And that she saved my life.

The room is, as Dean described it, a mess Norm looks over my shoulder. 'Phwoah,' he says, 'something's crawled in here and died. Quite a few months ago, I'd say.'

Nothing seems to have changed or been moved since the last time I was here. The bed's unmade, the floor is strewn with clothes, the wastebin is still overflowing. Even the packets of pills are still on the bedside table.

'No one's been in,' I say. 'Is there no housekeeping done? You know, someone comes in to vacuum, to tidy up?'

'Only for short-term stays. Some people choose to live here all the time and cleaning is their own responsibility.'

'In that case I think we need to have a close look at exactly what there is in here. Norm, can you open the window? And we can chock the door open. If I tidy the quilt, then we can use the bed to put things on.'

We spend twenty minutes moving stuff around the room. We arrange clothes on the bed, not sure and not willing to find out whether they're clean or not; for some reason I start a separate pile of sportswear, shorts and socks and vests. Then there's a column of CDs and another of books. We line up her shoes, mostly trainers, against the wall. There are a few soft toys, some loose photographs of unknown people playing sports or swimming in the Tesseract pool. There is, however, a framed photograph of Nessa crossing the finishing line in some race. It's an upper torso shot, Nessa with her arms raised. The sky behind her is blue and she has a healthy tan. There's a number pinned to her vest but no advertising, no sponsorship, nothing to say where the race was run.

'Want me to look through the rubbish?' Dean asks. He's probably come prepared with rubber gloves.

'I don't think we need that,' I say. I sit down on the bed and begin to look through the books. Six of them are novels by Graham Greene. All six have Nessa's name written inside the front cover. I show the first few to Dean. The rest are Rough Guide and Lonely Planet books, well-worn. Nessa seems to have spent time in Nepal, Australia, the USA and the Greek Islands. But these are different in another way. The name written inside each of them, in what looks like Nessa's handwriting, is 'Rosie Sanderson'. I don't mention them, just leave them lying on the bed. 'Somehow I doubt Nessa's coming back to pick anything up.'

271

'Doesn't look like it,' he replies, 'I'll make an inventory and parcel this lot up, get it transferred somewhere safe for a while. That's probably a cupboard in my office. I'll wait a few months then have the stuff washed, send it off to a charity shop.'

I pick up a running vest and a pair of shorts, they look clean. I drop them on the four travel books. 'Would it be possible to have a look at Nessa's personnel files now?' I ask politely. Dean nods. I rise to my feet then push myself backwards onto the bed, shake my head from side to side.

'You all right, boss?' Norm asks. He's by my side, supporting me.

'Water,' I whisper, 'could I have ... a drink of water?'

Dean looks around. There are some mugs in the room but they all look in need of sterilisation.

'There are some in the kitchen,' I say. He nods and hurries away.

'Right,' I say to Norm, 'no questions. Take these ...' I pass him the books wrapped inside the running kit.' And this ...' The photograph joins them. 'And hide them. Plastic bag, stuff them down your trousers, anything. Our friend doesn't see them, okay?'

Norm nods. There's a bag on the floor, he puts them inside then pushes the bag down his shirt. Then he takes off his pullover and holds it across the resultant hard-angled bump. That's when Dean returns.

'Will you be okay?' he asks.

'Just had a couple of long days,' I answer, sip the water slowly. After five minutes I'm ready to be helped along the corridor. Dean helps me into the back of the buggy while Norm hides his package. 'I think I just needed some fresh air,' I say. 'I feel much better now. Good as new.'

Fifteen minutes later we're sitting in front of the same computer terminal I'd used to decide that Eric Salkeld had defrauded Forestcrag of a large sum of money. I'm almost sure we'll find nothing on Nessa, that the disk will have been wiped; but I'm proved wrong, the information is

272

there. Letter of application, date references called, copies of references, date of interview, letter of appointment, contract of employment. Everything is there. I begin to write down the address from which Nessa's letter was sent, but Norm interrupts me.

'The letter, boss, read the letter. "I am on the point of moving house; if I'm invited for interview please inform me of this by mobile." Sounds like an excuse to me. Bet the address doesn't exist.'

'What about the referees?' Dean suggests. 'They must know something about her.'

We flick back to the references, they're local addresses. But by then I'm suspicious. 'She was appointed before the place opened, three years ago. Unless my memory's failing me, that's when Eve Marton and Eric Salkeld started. Do you mind if we have a quick look through their records?'

We do so. Their home addresses are those given by Nessa Clifton as references. Marton and Salkeld give each other's addresses, albeit with different names, as places where references may be sought; their second reference is the same address in the City. My theory isn't original, but I'm the first to speak it. 'I bet you that's where Nessa Clifton was living, temporarily. Probably a holding address. Untraceable.'

'So they provided each other with false references?' Dean seems genuinely horrified.

'Looks like it. They were a team. Whether they planned on defrauding Forestcrag from the beginning I don't know. They could have just been after work together.'

'But they definitely knew each other beforehand.' Norm is keen to take part in the conversation. 'I wonder where they met.'

'We leave it to the police to find out,' I say, 'it's gone beyond anything I can do. We tell them what we've found out and they follow it up. They'll want to find Nessa, but I don't think they'll have much luck. They'll kick themselves for not being more rigorous. And if I talk to them nicely they might just let me know if they find anything. About a year in arrears.'

I contact the DCI straightaway and he tells me to wait there, he's coming to see me, to look at the information himself. While we're waiting for him I ask Norm if he'd mind taking me for a drive round the site. Dean passes this time, we agree to meet again in an hour. 'Just drive around,' I tell Norm, 'out towards the quarry first, I'll give you directions. I need to think.'

There's a great deal to think about. If, as appears likely, Nessa was involved in the fraud, then everything I've imagined had been done by Eve Marton could have been done by Nessa. Was Eric Salkeld's death in any way assisted by someone else? That someone could be Nessa. And that journey to the quarry, Dean Metcalfe led me along a shorter, easier route than the one Nessa used when she acted as my guide. Why? Nessa probably helped Eve escape to the hut, her book was there. Was she afraid I would see two sets of footprints? So why take me up there at all? There's only one possible answer. She knew Eve Marton was dead. But did she slip or was she pushed?

Of course, this is not evidence. It's supposition. But it fits the facts, it fits events. And Philip Plumpton's appearance, could that be tied in as well? That's more difficult. I can't think of any connection at all. But it might be there. It might come. What's needed now is evidence. That might come with the exhumation of Salkeld's and Marton's bodies. It might come with a more thorough investigation of the scenes of crime. Whatever it is, I'll play no part in it. It's beyond me now, all I can do is help the police. Why, then, do I have – tucked safely under my seat in a plastic bag – four or five of Nessa's books, books with the name 'Rosie Sanderson' written inside. I can't say for sure. But I know she saved my life.

Chapter Thirty-Five

I've asked Rak to visit me. I've chosen the armchair for her, I'm sitting opposite. The table's not as well-stocked with food as it was when she came in, she's on her second coffee (caffeine has no effect on her), and she's suspicious. But we wander round the subject first of all.

'Heard from Jen recently?' she asks.

'An email two days ago. A proper letter last week, with photographs.'

'She missing you?'

'Says she is. Says she's looking forward to coming back when her tour of duty's up. November's not far off.'

'Are you missing her?'

'Yes.'

'Yes? Come on, Billy, elaborate. Let me see you squirm a little.'

'Yes, I miss her. I miss her a lot, I think of her every day.'

'Good. You're not the only one she keeps in touch with, Billy, and she misses you as well. You were a pillock not to go with her, I told you that. If you'd gone, all this wouldn't have happened.'

She's right. But if I hadn't gone there would still be three (or perhaps two, depending on how you read the evidence) people working at Forestcrag stealing hundreds of thousands of pounds from the employees there. I'd be in

Canada, I'd be walking properly, and I would never have met Nessa Clifton. I would never have slept with Nessa Clifton, that's what I mean. Collecting guilt is something of a hobby with me.

'What do you want, Billy?' Rak's decided to come to the point.

'The same as usual, your help.'

She reaches for another sandwich. 'No, you don't invite me round when you want "normal" things. Normal things are, in your mind, your prerogative, you assume you can have them without any crawling or sucking up to me. Most of the time you don't even pay me for the hours I spend working for you. So this is more than normal. What's going on?'

She knows the outline of what happened at Forestcrag, but I have to explain a little more, keep her up to date with my investigations of the past few days.

'There have been some developments, Rak. The police believe a third person was probably involved in the fraud and may have been involved in the possible murders of Eric Salkeld and Eve Marton.'

'Woah, slow down Billy. That's not very objective. "Probably", "May have been involved . . .", "Possible murders . . ." Sounds like the type of thing the police like to keep to themselves, even if some of the leads have come from you. Am I right in this supposition? Don't answer, I'm right. So how does this still involve you? Why are you dipping your little snout in the trough when there are much bigger piggies in there?'

She never was very good at listening. 'That's what I'm trying to tell you, Rak. The third person is Nessa Clifton, the woman who saved my life. But she doesn't exist. She told me she was an ex-cop, said we'd met a few times. She was so persuasive she had me remembering when and where, but the police have checked and there was never a police officer with that name. She told me she was a tri-athlete with top five world-ranking; another lie. We've checked the photographs of the top fifty female triathletes in this country and none of them look like her. They've taken fingerprints from the room she used but they can't find any matches on any of the clothing worn by Salkeld or Marton. But it was winter, she was probably wearing gloves, and the whole thing shows such a degree of planning I can't imagine she'd let herself get caught with something as easy as that.'

'So you think she murdered the other two?'

'I don't know what to think, Rak. Murder? I'm not sure. Involvement? Looks like it, I'd go so far as to say it's almost certain. But she's vanished. No trace at all. That's why I want you to help me find her.'

'Oh, right, I see. The police can't find her with all their resources, but I can.'

'Yes. I have every faith in you.'

'Flattery normally works, Billy love, but it has to be within the realms of reality. How do you expect me to find her if the police can't?'

I take a bag from beneath my seat. 'Because the police don't have these, Rak.' I pass her the photograph and the books I removed from her room.

'Pretty girl. Strong looking.' She grins at me. 'Just my type.' She opens the first book, then the second. 'Rosie Sanderson. You think that's her real name?'

'Could be. The thing is, I don't know if this will work or not. If I tell you what I think, then your job is to tell me as many reasons as possible why I'm stupid.'

'I already know you're stupid. But go on.'

'Okay. This photo of Nessa, Rosie, call her what you want, it looks about five or six years old. It must have meant something to her, there was no other piece of memorabilia like it. So it's something special. Look at her, Rak. She's tanned, her hair is almost white. The sky behind her is blue, we don't get skies like that in Britain. And you can see the top half of her running number, she's number 531. That's a lot of competitors. So we're looking for runner number 531 in a fairly major triathlon. It took place some time in the past six – better make that eight – years, somewhere warm. Probably in one of these areas.' I flick my hand at the books. 'We just need to work these things out and we might be able to find her, Rak.'

Rak shakes her head. 'Not stupid, Billy, mad. And not just eccentric mad. You're downright lock-him-away mad, throw-away-the-key-he's-a-danger-to-humanity mad. You're certifiable. Jesus Christ, Billy, the things you ask me to do.'

'You mean you can't do it?'

'No. Did I say I couldn't do it? I could probably walk to London, Billy, but that doesn't mean that, when I calculate the time and effort involved, I don't conclude that it isn't anywhere near viable. I don't have the time, I don't have the resources, I don't even know where to start looking.'

'Okay then, rephrase that. You can do it, but you won't do it?'

'Did I say that? I don't think so. I just don't . . . Oh, fuck it Billy, I just don't know. Let me think about it, think about how to do it. I might be able to come up with something.'

'So I'm not mad after all.'

'Of course you're fucking mad! What excuse do you have if you're sane?'

I think that's a compliment, but it's difficult to tell with Rak. She picks up the photograph and the books. 'I suppose you've already looked through these,' she says, 'and I won't need this one.' She throws aside the book on Nepal. 'Not developed enough for large-scale racing, too difficult to get there. But these . . .?' She holds aloft the other books. 'The USA, Australia and half a million Mediterranean islands? I'd better go. Got a lot of work to do.'

She climbs to her feet and motions me back into my seat when I try to follow, blows me a kiss. Experience has shown me that being an investigator isn't about finding things out yourself, it's knowing who to get to work on your behalf. I'm lucky, in Rak, Norm and Sly I have a team who can help in most situations. But this is asking a lot.

I go to bed early but lie awake. There are sounds from the street, people returning from the pub, singing, whistling. There are cars slowing for the speed bumps then accelerating to the next. I identify distant sirens, distinguish police cars from ambulances. A man and a woman have an argument, she's screaming at him, he's apologising loudly, drunkenly. Cats fight and screech like banshees, ghost into secret shadows; dogs bark in wet-nosed backyards, keen to be off into the love-scented night. I hear all this and think of other nights. I think of Nessa, picture her dancing and angry in my underpants, shivering with cold, longing to be somewhere warm. I sit upright, suddenly awake. She said exactly that. She said she wouldn't spend another winter in Britain, she wanted to be somewhere warm with hills and the sea, cicadas and cheap wine. I can remember her voice, her words, so clearly I can see it myself. I reach for the pad I keep at my bedside and scribble the information down. It might help Rak. I'll ring her in the morning.

Chapter Thirty-Six

The phone wakes me. I've grown used to lying in bed in the morning, and the clock tells me it's only eight. Who would ring this early?

'Billy, it's Rak here.'

'Yeah? What's the matter.' I won't castigate her for the earliness of the call, she wouldn't ring unless there was something important.

'The matter? Nothing's the matter. I just want you to tell me how clever I am, what a genius I am. I want you to lie fawning at my feet. I want you to wag your tail when I tickle your tummy. Should I go on? I want you to procure delicious nubile young ladies for me, I want you to coat their svelte bodies in the finest Belgian chocolate. I want you to build me a special seat, electrically operated, so I can lick the chocolate away without having to exert myself.'

'Rak, have you been drinking?'

'Only the wine of exhilaration, Billy. What you're hearing is the intoxicating effect of triumphant sleep deprivation.'

'You've found her?'

'Oh, come on! I'm not that good. Let's just say I've found where she was. And that in its turn might reduce the number of places you have to look to find out where she might be.'

'So tell me!'

'Billy, why are you doing this? If she was involved in a murder shouldn't the police be doing this work?'

'Rak, I can do without the sermons. Just tell me what you know.'

'What is there between you, Billy? I know she saved your life, but think about it. Was it really altruism? She couldn't exactly shimmy back down the rope and hide. Once Plumpton killed you, she was next. It was the best, probably the only time when she could have attacked him and beaten him, after that he could have picked her off whenever he wanted. You're not stupid, Billy, but I know you well enough to read you and guess at your motivation. You're a sucker when it comes to women.'

'You included, Rak?'

'I don't count myself as "women", Billy. And stop trying to defend yourself.'

'I'm not. I agree with you. Women find it easy to manipulate me because I can't fight back. And I accept that Nessa may have done just that. But I have to find her myself. Regardless of what you say, she did save my life. She could have waited a few seconds, waited for Plumpton to kill me, it wouldn't have made any difference to her. But she didn't. That's why I'm here today, asking you to help me find her. I owe her the benefit of the doubt.'

I can't tell whether I've persuaded her or not. There's a long silence, neither of us prepared to speak. What it comes down to is whether or not she trusts me, and I have to wait for her to make that decision. Eventually she speaks.

'Billy?' she says.

'I'm still here.'

'Whatever you do, don't hurt Jen. She loves you, and I don't think you realise how much.'

Am I that transparent? She suspects my feelings for Nessa go beyond gratitude. That worries me, because even I'm not sure why I'm behaving this way. I've justified my secrecy in a way that satisfies my conscience, but it may

281

not be the truth. I don't want to know what I really think, what I really want to do. I don't want that confrontation, that degree of self-analysis. And she said Jen loves me. How does she know? Has Jen told her? Or is she employing the same Freudian divination on Jen that she's using to psychoanalyse me?

The silence is now all mine. I feel deeply for Jen. I enjoy being with her, whatever we're doing. I'm missing her company, her presence, the anticipation of her touch. I'm frightened she might find someone else, someone younger, better looking, better qualified. But is this love? I have great difficulty using the word. I can't say "I love you" without feeling I've devalued the concept. Hah! Look at the way I see it. Love is a "concept". It's not an emotion, it's not a mixture of passion and familiarity and excitement and appreciation and so much else; it's not the same for me as it is for other people. Do I love Jen? I don't know. Do I love anyone?

'Tell me, Rak,' I say, hoping the simple statement will speak all she wants to hear from me, because I can't say anything else.

'Okay, Billy, it's up to you what you do with this.' She pauses for a deep, asthmatic breath. 'First of all, I did what you should have done – I took the photograph out of the frame. It looked like one of those standard photos they take at things like the Great North run, keepsakes, a memento of the occasion. I looked on the back, it had some writing there, an address, a telephone number. Cyrillic script. Given the books, that means the Greek islands.'

'Sounds good so far.'

'Gets better. I faxed a copy of the back of the photo to the Greek embassy in London, asked for a translation. They replied straightaway. The photograph was taken by a company in Iraklion, Crete.'

'Crete? Hold on, Rak, just a minute.' I'm out of my seat, hobbling across the room to find an atlas. I lurch back to the table, flick through it until I find the island in question. 'Okay, Rak, go on.'

'The way this photograph thing works, Billy, is that the organisers of the event give – or sell – the competitors' race numbers, names and addresses to the photograph company. The company takes photos on spec, sends them out to the competitors' home addresses.'

'So all I need do is . . .'

'I've already done it. I rang them up this morning, Crete's a few hours ahead of us. I spoke to a nice young woman, speaks English better than you do, Billy. I think I've scored, but I won't be going to visit her, I wouldn't like to disappoint her with the real me. Anyway, I told her I was writing a book on triathlons and she didn't even ask why I was ringing at such a ridiculous time of day. I told her there were some top class British competitors who'd said they'd run in Crete and I was trying to find out when. I had her look through the archives starting four years ago, runner number 531, name Rosie Sanderson. She was there, Billy. Six years ago. And you know what? She was first woman home. My new friend gave me the address she was using at the time, somewhere in Khania. What do you think, then? Am I good?'

'You're the best, Rak, the very best.'

'Remember what I said, then. The warning. I know you Billy. You think you've got problems with your bad leg, fuck up on this and I'll break the other one so you never walk again. I'll send you the info by email. And remember, you owe me.'

'I'll remember, Rak,' I say. 'I owe you. And you needn't worry about . . .' But the phone has already gone down, I'm speaking to the dialling tone.

Chapter Thirty-Seven

I tell everyone I need a break. Rak knows, of course, but she says nothing. I say I'm going to Crete; I can use the advance of the compensation money I'm due to receive. I email Jen, tell her as well. She thinks it's a good idea, it'll be warm, I'll have the chance to lie in the sun and do nothing. What, she asks, will I take to read? Something by Graham Greene, I reply.

Kirsty comes to see me off at the station. Train to Manchester, flight to Khania, that's where I'm collected in a red car with rather a sad smile on its face. I'm staying in a small hotel just outside town. I chose it because the owners are English, long established on the island – I figure I'll need some local help – and because their son has agreed to act as my chauffeur for the week. My room is clean, small, it has a view of the beach and the sea beyond. On my first night, despite enjoying dinner with my hosts, I retire early and lie lonely on my bed. I can hear the waves and distant music and I want to be anywhere else but there.

My driver's called Nick, short for Nikos; he's usefully bilingual and seems impressed when he finds out I'm a private investigator. I do sometimes find it useful to let slip my occupation, it seems to have a standing far above the menial tasks it actually encompasses. Nick knows, then, that I'm on the island to look for an English woman who has lived there before – and I have only an old address – and professes to be a triathlete.

First stop is the address Rak found me. It's an apartment in a dusty, pot-holed backstreet and the tenant hasn't heard of Rosie Sanderson or Nessa Clifton or any other English woman. He doesn't recognise the photograph. Nor do any of the other tenants who are willing to open their doors to us.

Nick shrugs as he leads the way across the road back to the car. 'I think there must be a high turnover of tenants,' he says. 'This isn't going to be easy.'

'Hold on, just a minute.' An old woman is sitting at her window, watching us. She's dressed in black, white-haired, tobacco-skinned. Nick shrugs again, takes Nessa's photograph, walks across to the woman. They speak for a while, he motions me across.

'She says she remembers her,' he says excitedly, 'and I didn't prompt her at all. She says she lived here about six years ago, for a year. Used to go out running in the early morning, cycling in the evening.'

It sounds like Nessa. 'Ask her if she had a job, anything else she can remember. Did she live alone?'

Nick speaks again. The woman responds. Then Nick turns back to me.

'She thinks she lived alone, but she had visitors, men and women. They stayed for only a few weeks.'

'Sounds like friends having a cheap holiday. Anything else?'

'She used to go out in the morning, on her bike, then come back in the evening. She was never at home during the day.'

'So she probably had a job.'

'That's what the lady thinks too. But she doesn't know where.'

'Is that it?'

'That's it.'

It's better than nothing, but it's not enough. 'Okay. Thank her, say she's been very helpful.' I nod and smile my own thanks as Nick speaks to her. She says something back.

'What was that?' I ask.

'Oh, nothing much. Just that she always spoke to the old lady. At first it was "good morning", "good evening", "how are you"? But then the girl's Greek got better. Near the end she said she'd be moving out, that she'd bought an old house or a barn and was going to renovate it.'

'Yes? And where was it?' I hope the woman can remember. I hope Nessa told her. Nick nods his head and smiles again.

'She says she knows exactly where it is. "Up in the mountains".'

'"In the mountains?"'

'Yes.'

'Which mountains?'

'The mountains behind Khania.'

I walk back to the car. I groan as Nick joins me. 'I take it,' I say, 'that could mean anywhere in the west of the island?'

Nick seems as glum as me. 'That's the problem with an island that's mostly mountain.'

Still, it's a start.

Nick suggests moving on to the local athletic club. I feel this may turn out to be a dead end; I see Nessa as too much of an individual, unwilling to work with others, not a 'club' woman at all. But it gives us something to build on, and even if she isn't a member, someone might recognise her photograph.

I've told Nick and his parents that I'm working for a solicitor, that Nessa's been left a substantial amount of money but we don't know exactly where she is. This story appeals to all who hear it. The athletics club organisers are sympathetic, very keen to help, but they don't recognise Nessa. They give me the names of people to contact in other clubs in Rethimnon and Iraklion, Ayios Nikolaos and Sitia. But they're too far east and simply travelling to these other towns would take up a huge amount of time. I'm feeling discouraged, and not even Nick introducing me to his friends – all young, good-looking and tanned – lifts my spirits. But he does seem impressed when, in return, I show him a photograph of Kirsty.

I'd imagined someone telling me, within a few hours of my arrival, that he or she recognised Nessa. They'd give me her address, I'd call to see her. I haven't made plans beyond this initial confrontation, but even that now seems ridiculously optimistic. With my typical English naivety I'd underestimated the size of the island, the number of people there, the gargantuan nature of the task. Nick isn't worried. 'We'll find her,' he says, 'no problem.' It's his favourite phrase and it doesn't make me any more confident.

There is, Nick tells me, a very loose association of English expatriates on the island. 'We don't keep in with them much,' he says, 'we're almost naturalised ourselves. But newcomers usually need help to understand the way things work round here. If someone new comes, the first thing they do is find out which of their neighbours speaks English. If a neighbour *is* English, that's even better. So there's a sort of cell system, A knows B and C, C knows D and E, but A doesn't know E. We just need to pass the word round, see what we can find out.'

'And how long might that take?'

'A few days? A few weeks? I don't know, if we work hard we might find something soon.'

So we begin to work hard. The trouble is, I have little to go on. Nessa may have money, she may not. She could be travelling and living alone, she might have a partner. She could even have changed her appearance, cut and dyed her hair. But Nick's as good as his word, he begins work straightaway, telephoning, getting new names and addresses, telephoning them, working the chains. He gets me to buy two mobiles, they're cheap to use, they leave his parents' phone free, and we can use them from the beach. We have a map, we plot each new call to find out how far afield we're working. It feels good to be doing something.

At the end of the second day we find something. Someone in Kastelli, along the coast to the west, was visiting friends in Paleohora a few weeks ago. They went out to a taverna and there was an English girl working there, she fits the description Nick's been passing around Nick gets the name of the taverna, he says we can go the next day but I'm keen to go that evening.

Nick, like his parents, is very laidback. His favourite word is "tomorrow" and he employs it frequently. 'If she's there tonight,' he says, 'she'll be there tomorrow.'

It's occurred to me that this may be a false lead. There must be hundreds of women on the island answering Nessa's description, and the helpfulness of the locals might result in me meeting most of them. I have to be forceful. 'But more leads might come in tomorrow, and the day after, and I've only one week. And if she's working in a taverna she'll be up late tonight, she'll get up late tomorrow, and that'll be another day lost. Time *is* important. Please, I think we should go now.'

Nick doesn't really need much persuading. After all, I'm paying him, it's my car and my petrol. And I even let him choose what music is played on the cassette. That part is easy, since I have no tapes of my own and all his sound the same to me.

Paleohora is on the south coast, not far as the crow flies. The crow in question would, however, have to gain substantial altitude to cross the White Mountains straddling the island. Crete is a long rectangle, and travel along its northern coast, its widest edge where the land mostly drops gradually to the sea in a series of wide beaches and sheltered coves, is comparatively easy. But no broad carriageway runs along the rocky southern edge of the island, and the ribbons of single track road which cross the mountainous spine of the island climb steeply, cling to the sides of steep crags, twist and turn as they follow deceiving contours. Only goats, prickly scrub grass and vultures inhabit this rocky wilderness. That doesn't stop Nick driving as if he wants to add me to that brief list by using the simple means of overturning the car and throwing me out. He drives fast. I close my eyes, pretend to be asleep. My heart pumps to the relentless beat of his music.

Paleohora is a small town or a large village. It clings to a peninsula jutting into the sea, and its white buildings are beginning to shine in the reflected light of the warm, soft-breezed evening. It's early in the season, but everywhere is open. The main street is busy but not crowded, tables bustling out from a host of tavernas onto narrow pavements.

'It's packed in summer,' Nick tells me as he drives through narrow streets in an unfathomable and, as far as I can tell, ignored one-way system. 'This time of the year, though, it's bearable. And this, on the right, is our destination.' He drives past, slowly. There are several people eating but they're being served by a waiter.

'She could always have moved on,' he suggests.

'Let's find out, then.'

He parks a little further on, we get out and stroll back. I'm walking easily in the Mediterranean warmth. Perhaps this is what the future holds for me, a forced emigration to avoid arthritic British winters. Nick examines the sign above the taverna's blue and white striped canopy. 'Yeah, this is it.' We take a seat.

Both of us are hungry. Nick orders our meals in impeccable Greek, then we sit and look around. I'm becoming impatient. 'I'll ask if an English woman works here,' I tell Nick.

'Just speak English loudly,' he replies, following his own advice. 'This is the way it works. The taverna owner hires English or German speakers because he knows it will attract customers from Britain – and the States and Australia – or Germany. It makes ordering food and drink easier, it's possible to develop a good relationship, and people come back because of that. Anyway, we're going to find out now,' he points out. 'Dinner is about to be served by a rather good-looking woman.'

I have my back to her approach. Nick is smiling a welcome, but even as she moves past me I know it's not Nessa. She's too tall, too dark. Her smile, when she turns to face me, is beautiful, and I can tell she can't understand why I seem less than happy. She leaves our meal, hoping in Mancunian English that we enjoy it.

'No?' Nick asks needlessly. 'Pity.'

The evening passes slowly, I want to leave. There may be messages waiting for me back at the hotel, I feel I'm wasting my time here. I toy with my food. Nick understands but he's flirting with the waitress. As we're about to leave he takes her to one side and begins chatting to her. They laugh together.

'I wish you wouldn't use my time to chat up women,' I tell him.

'She's in her thirties, though rather well-preserved, and I'm twenty-one,' he replies evenly. 'She's also married to the owner, I saw the wedding ring, she mentioned it in passing. And I was asking her if she knew anyone of Nessa's description working in Paleohara. She gave me the names of a couple of bars. I thought we could have a look now.' In other words, he's doing the job I should be doing. He's investigating, reacting, asking questions, thinking. And he's still being polite, despite my rudeness.

'I'm sorry,' I say.

'That's okay.'

The evening passes into fruitless night more harmoniously. At the first bar the girl is a giggling teenager, at the second a hashed-out hippy in beads and dirty feet. But they listen to us, they give us other names, and these soon begin to refer to places we've already visited. It's after one in the morning when we decide Nessa's not in Paleohara and begin the switchback ride home again. But it hasn't been a waste of time, we've eliminated the place. At this rate it will only take a few years to do the same for the whole island. And then, of course, there's the possibility (in my mind rapidly becoming a probability) that she's not even on the island.

We stop beside a small whitewashed church to watch the moon rise. It's quite chilly on the heights, and quiet. Nick smokes a cigarette, we catch the strains of distant goat bells. He catches me pensive, staring at nothing, pats me on the shoulder.

'We'll find her,' he says.

I nod. 'Tomorrow.'

Chapter Thirty-Eight

Over the next few days we eliminate Kastelli and the tourist trap of Elafonisi, the south coast settlements of Ayia Roumeli and Hora Sfakion. We follow up leads at Platanias and Kalives. Nick distributes copies of Nessa's photographs to his friends, they arrange to visit every nightclub in Khania, looking, asking questions. We have no luck.

On my last full day I find myself in Georgiopoulis, to the east of Khania. There is, so Nick tells me, a large number of expatriate English here, in the town and in the hills behind the bay itself. He's trawling the bars, enjoying asking questions even when they bring no answers. And me? I'm sitting beneath a sunshade, yards from the beach, sipping a long, cold lemonade. My leg has grown more painful as the week has progressed, though I feel this may be a symptom of my increasing loss of confidence in my judgement and my ability to do anything constructive. I should be helping Nick; instead I choose to do nothing. It should be pleasant here, watching the world go by. I could pay more attention to the girls patrolling the waterside, topless and thonged, bodies the same even colour of youth and sun. I could watch the volley-ball match, the windsurfing, the water-skiing. But instead I hide behind sunglasses, stare at my fingers spread on the table in front of me. They're turning brown, I probably look fitter and healthier than I did when I arrived on the island six days before. Appearances deceive.

'Not going for a swim, Billy?'

I try not to smile as Nessa slides into the seat opposite me, but the impulse is too great, it feels so natural.

'Later, perhaps. How are you?'

She shrugs. She's wearing a broad-brimmed hat and sunglasses, a brief bikini top and a sarong slung across her hips. She stands up, unwinds the sarong, removes the hat, strikes a pose. 'How do I look?'

'Good.' Her hair is blonder than I remember. She's thinner, but more muscular. She has lines at the corners of her eyes, emphasised by the healthy tone of her skin. Her stomach is flat. I revise my opinion. 'Very good.'

'Thank you.' She slips back into her seat, crosses her legs. The waiter brings her a drink; either she's a regular or she ordered before she sat down. 'I heard you were looking for me. That is, I heard someone was looking for me, I was hoping it was you. I'm impressed.'

'Guesswork, Nessa. Or should that be Rosie?'

'Round here, neither. Rosie is my real name, but I changed skins quite a while ago. Nessa is probably better. For you, that is.'

There's an easy silence between us. Both of us have questions, but answers may spoil the illusions we've been building. I'm not even sure myself how much I want to know.

'How's Kirsty?' An easy topic, non-confrontational. I welcome the chance to talk about her.

'She's well. Quite jealous, really, when I told her I was coming here. I told her it was for a holiday, recuperation. She said she'd come to act as a nurse.'

'I can see that! She'd spend her days lying on the beach, her nights clubbing. She'd be very popular round here.'

'Yes, I can imagine.'

Nessa's reading me. 'Still finding it difficult, eh? She's a woman, Billy, not a girl.'

'I know. I can't help the way I feel.'

It's enough to satisfy her, to answer the question she

probably didn't want to ask in the first place. So we sit in silence, sip our drinks, look round when we hear screams of laughter or the screech of distant car brakes.

'Why are you here, Billy?' She's the first to flinch, to ask a direct, relevant question. I don't feel any triumph.

'Why do you think?'

She shakes her head. 'You're still a policeman at heart. Okay, I'll play the game for a while. First, you're definitely not here to recuperate, you're here to look for me. But why? It could be unrequited love, I suppose, but I doubt it. It might be that you feel you need to speak to me about Forestcrag, that's more likely. But which bits? The end, up at the quarry? Me getting you out, perhaps, you'll have heard about that. It could be unfinished business, things you want to say. "It was good while it lasted". Or even. "Thank you for saving my life". It could be any of those.'

'It could be,' I say. I pick up my lemonade, sip it again. It's a sign that I want her to continue, but she shakes her head. 'Your turn now,' she prompts.

'Okay. I do want to say thank you. You did save my life. And the fact that I can walk at all is probably due to you getting me to hospital quickly. So thank you.'

'You're welcome.'

'Other things? What did you mean by "unrequited love"?'

'A glib phrase, Billy, nothing more. I don't think we love each other, never did. Affection, yes, there was affection. And in different circumstances it might have grown into ... something else? Who knows? But not now.'

This is a fencing match. At the moment we're relaxed, there's no thrust for advantage. We're gauging each other's strengths. Nessa wants to find out what I know; I want to find out what she did. Neither of us wants to give anything away. We have different attacks, different defences. We know a little about each other, but not enough. Our strengths and weaknesses are suppositions.

'Where are you living?' I ask.

Nessa raises her eyes to the hills. 'Up there.'

'Nice place?'

'It will be, when it's finished.'

'Did you get all the money? Eric Salkeld's and Eve Marton's shares as well?'

She snorts, slaps the table, I realise she's laughing. 'Billy, oh Billy, that was a bit clumsy. Can't you do a little sort of dance round the subject first, out of courtesy? I mean, I don't even know if you're working alone here, or for the police. For Forestcrag? No, that's unlikely given the way Morland feels about you. Tell me, Billy. I'll be honest with you if you're honest with me, I promise.' She crosses her heart. 'Really, I promise.'

'Why should I believe you?'

'You have no choice.'

'I can tell the police where you are.'

'You can, yes, you can. But you haven't so far, why else would you be here on your own? And if you did tell them, you have no evidence I've done anything wrong. You have no evidence I'm anything to do with Nessa Clifton. In fact, I think you'll find that Nessa Clifton doesn't really exist.'

'I know that much already.'

'So tell me what else you know, what you suspect. And I'll tell you whether you're right or wrong.'

She knew what she was doing when she said I had no choice. I have ideas, proposals, theories, hypotheses. I can assume, make conjectures and accusations, I can speculate. But I have no hard evidence. So I decide to do as she says.

'From the beginning, then. You, Eve and Eric, you knew each other before you went to work at Forestcrag. You forged each other's references ...'

'I'm getting hot,' Nessa interrupts, 'let's go for a swim. Then we can't be overheard.' She's suspicious. That's good, to my advantage. It's easy to catch people out when they're on edge.

'Okay. But not too deep, I'm not a good swimmer.'

'Don't worry, I am.' She takes off her sunglasses. I remove my shirt and shorts, my briefs will double as swimming trunks. Nessa takes my arm. Her skin feels warm against mine, she smells of cinnamon. The sand is hot, the water warm and shallow. It's approaching midday and the sun is breaking the sea into shards of sharp light; we both have to squint. We wade in up to my waist then kneel, let the small waves wash us to and fro. Sometimes, by accident, we touch.

'I met Eve here, five years ago. She was on holiday. I'd spent most of my life travelling, bumming a living from wherever I could.'

'Australia, Nepal, the States?'

'You looked in my room. I should have tidied up before I left, thrown stuff away. But it doesn't matter now. I ended up living in Khania, helping out with a water sports company. I enjoyed it, stayed on, they promoted me to manager. It was going well. I bought an old farmhouse near here, up in the hills. I thought I'd renovate it, but then things went pear-shaped. I fell out with my boss, he passed word around that I was no good. I'd met Eve during the summer, she was good fun, said if I was ever in Britain I should look her up. I hitched my way across Europe, ended up on her doorstep. Trouble was, she didn't have a job either. She got occasional work freelancing, teaching computing and so on. I used to go along, first of all to learn and then to help. That's where we met Eric, on one of the courses. He was weird, he'd had psychiatric problems, his wife had run away with his daughters. He lost touch with them then found them again, but Eve and I could tell he wasn't well. It was really sad. He sort of latched onto us, treated us as his own family. It was his idea that we should all try for jobs at Forestcrag, and we got them. It wasn't difficult really, once we'd sorted each other's references.'

As she's talking Nessa keeps pulling her hair back from her eyes. She watches me all the time, she's learned that eye contact encourages trust. Why is it, then, that I keep glancing away?

'So when did you start stealing money?'

'Stealing? Yes, I suppose it was stealing, but it didn't feel like it. It as the end of the first month, Eric was doing the payroll using the figures he'd been given. The deductions were ridiculous. We had money taken off for uniforms, for tea and coffee, for transport to and from site. And the costs of renting a room, they were horrendous. He did it for a joke first, paid us extra. He said we could look on it as a loan, interest free. He'd explain it was a mistake when they found out, new software and so on. But no one found out. No one said anything.'

'So you kept going?'

'Yeah. Look, I'm getting cramped, all bent over like this. Do you mind if we go out a bit further?'

I look back at the shore. It isn't far away, and when I stand up the water's not far past my waist. I even feel comfortable with the weight off my leg, so I swim a few strokes further out to sea.

'That's better, thanks. Where was I? Oh yes, the money. We got together one night, had a few drinks, realised how much we could make if we did it properly. It was Eric and Eve really, they were the ones who sorted out the mechanics of it all. But I'd been around, I helped set up the accounts. It wasn't difficult.' She leans back, lifts her legs up and floats. 'Hold me up a little,' she says, 'then I can keep talking.'

I move closer, put one arm under her back, the other under her bottom. As the waves pass us her breasts and her pubis rise out of the water.

'We decided we'd give it three years. The three years would have been up in April. We just didn't get there. You came along instead.'

'I wasn't looking for you, did you know that? Morland didn't even guess there was any fraud.'

She jerks upright, treads water, spits. 'You what?'

297

'I never did tell you. I was there with Sly, just as a guest. Morland said his staff were being poisoned, wanted me to investigate. I said no, but he went ahead and made the announcement anyway. "Billy Oliphant, famous detective, will be passing amongst you. Beware!" Then things started happening.'

'Bastards! If only . . .'

'If only. If only I'd stayed at home four people would still be alive who aren't.'

Nessa reaches out and touches my cheek. 'That isn't true, Billy. Eric for one, he . . . He was strange, but he was getting worse. Eve and I were worried about him, he was withdrawing into himself. We didn't know about his habits, of course, his little vices. But we thought he might do something silly, give himself away. Give us away. So when we heard you were on site we told him to be careful. We told him to stay in his room. Eve arranged to stay as well, she'd come prepared, it wasn't just the snow. We'd arranged to meet in his room, talk about what we should do next. Eve and I arrived together, we found him . . . Well, you know how we found him.'

'Dressed in his fancy gear? Hanging from the wall?'

'He was dead. We didn't know what to do. We left him, went back to Eve's room. Then we talked. We figured out you'd be pleased to discover a theft. So we arranged that you would. We did the necessary, took him down off his hook, undressed and redressed him, put him back. Eve did the suicide note. She even put the bit in about blaming you, thought it might make you back off. We searched his room, hid the costume and his magazines. We thought that would be it.'

'But it wasn't. I began to think it wasn't suicide.'

'Eve was frightened. We decided I should make friends with you, try to find out what you were up to. So I asked around, Sam Ellis was helpful, he told me you'd been in the police, said you'd been kicked out. You were a bad lad, Billy.'

I need no reminding. Even now my past interferes with my future. 'You took a risk. You were never in the police, I'd never met you before.'

'I'd worked a similar trick in the past, if it went wrong I could always have claimed mistaken identity. But it did work. I knew exactly what was going on. It was me told Eve where she should hide.'

'You did more than that, you guided her up there.'

'How did you know that?' I've caught her off her guard for the second time. I'm pleased I still have the capacity to surprise.

'You left a book, I recognised it. And a carton of milk, Eve was allergic to it. I guessed.' I don't tell her I originally thought it had belonged to Philip Plumpton.

'Okay, you're right. She was frightened to go by herself, the weather was too bad. I took her up there, got her settled in. I'd planned to stay with her for a while, she was very nervous, but it took us ages to get there, even by the short route.'

'Yes, you took me the long way round in case there were any tracks.'

'You can be impressive sometimes. I stayed as long as I could but I knew I had to get back. She insisted she'd come out to see me on my way. She slipped, Billy. She slipped, she fell, she slid down the slope, over the edge. I knew she'd be dead.'

'You didn't check?'

She jerks upright again. 'Billy, there was a fucking blizzard blowing. I crawled down that slope, I lay on the edge, I couldn't see a thing. It was 200 feet down. She was dead.'

It's difficult to reconcile the two bodies, Eve's broken at the bottom of an ice-racked cliff, Nessa's bobbing in the warm sea a few inches away from me.

'I was so confused. I hadn't planned anything, things were just happening to me. That girl was killed. I was frightened. And when we were together, when we ... When we made love. It wasn't planned. I needed you, I think you needed me. We helped each other. Didn't we?'

She reaches for my hand but I pull it away.

'And the escape? Did it cross your mind when I was lying there with a bullet in my leg that I could just be your passport to a swift exit?'

'Billy, no! There was no power, no phones, you were delirious. I just did what I thought was best for you.'

'And for you as well. You were the first out of Forestcrag. I was the only one who knew any details about how the Forestcrag money was stolen or where it went to, and I was unconscious. Then I was under anaesthetic. That gave you time to move the money, make your statement to the police and escape. Isn't that the way it went?'

'No!' She dives away from me, begins to swim back to shore, but I manage to grab her foot. She kicks at me but I haul her back towards me, put my arm round her waist and pull her above the surface.

'No,' she cries again, 'you're wrong!' Her hands are beating the water ineffectually. I turn her around to face me.

'Why should I believe you?' I hiss. 'By your own admission you manipulated me and everyone else. How do I know you aren't lying now?'

She stops struggling but I don't loosen my grip on her, the water's up to my chest, it would be over her head if I let her go.

'You don't know,' she says. 'But for a while, a short while, I thought you might be the person who needed me. And I believed I needed you.' She puts her arm up behind my head and pulls our faces together. She tastes of salt and warmth. She raises her legs, hooks her feet round my back. I can feel her body against mine. And I push her away.

'You were the one who said it wouldn't work,' I tell her. 'You were right.'

She separates from me, floats a little distance away, stares at me. She looks hurt.

'If I believe everything you've told me,' I say, 'then you

had nothing to do with Eric Salkeld's death. You had nothing to do with Eve Marton's death. Even the ideas for the fraud were theirs. But they're dead and you've ended up with all the money.'

'It looks bad, I know. I can't help that. If I was really in control of everything do you think I'd have left it this way, with all suspicion pointing at me?'

'Nessa, if it hadn't been for a huge amount of luck and me spending a week searching for you, you would have got away with it.'

'Christ, Billy, I did! I got away with it. It was me found you, not the other way round. Think, man, why would I show myself to you if I wasn't innocent? Yes, I stole some money. But that's all I did. You won't believe me. That's why I ran away, Billy. We fucked each other, I saved your life, we've got something between us, and you *still* won't believe me. How can I expect the police to give me a fair hearing when you won't?' She stares at me, even when she's treading water I can sense the belligerence in her body. 'Right, come on. I'll prove it.' She grabs my hand, pulls me so hard towards the shallows I fall over. 'Get up, if you start drowning I won't save your bloody life this time.'

I can see Nick waiting for me, he stands up and waves as he sees us approaching.

'Wait here,' Nessa tells him abruptly, 'I'll have him back in two hours.' She throws my shirt and shorts at me, picks up her sarong and hat.

'It's okay,' I say to Nick, begin to hobble after Nessa. 'I'll be all right. I think.'

She opens the door of a small Japanese four wheel drive, it has no roof. 'Get in,' she says.

'Where are we going?'

'My house. I'm making it easy for you. If you don't believe me, you'll know where to come looking.'

I climb in, the seat is hot, even against my damp legs. I pull my shirt on and fumble for the safety belt. We're dripping water but Nessa doesn't seem to notice. Her lips are fixed in a narrow line, she's staring ahead of her. She drives faster, more carelessly than Nick. She takes me out of town, the road is metalled at first though it twists and turns a little and grows progressively narrower as we climb a steep hill. I look around me, determined that I should be able to recognise the route again. Then, without warning, Nessa turns onto a narrower road on the right, then left again onto a track between olive groves. Just when it looks as if the track stops, right up against a fence, she spins the wheel to the left. Up a steep concrete driveway there's a house being built or rebuilt. In its midst is a caravan. We skid to a halt in front of it.

'Here we are,' she says. 'This is where I live.' She opens her door and climbs out. There are red marks from the seat on her thighs. She has to hook her fingers in her briefs to pull them back into shape, then wraps the sarong around her breasts. When she speaks again her voice is calmer. 'Come on, I'll show you round.'

I pull my shorts on, I'm almost dry anyway.

'There used to be a small house here, a farmhouse. I wanted to keep it but it was almost derelict, so it had to come down. The state we're in here, with the framework up, has taken me five years. I'd add more when I had funds, do most of the work myself in the winter. It helped keep me fit.' She takes my arm, leads me round the front of the shell.

'When it's finished there'll be two ground floor apartments, one sleeping four to six, the other, smaller, for a couple. I'll have the first floor to myself but friends can come to say when they want.' She moves me further round, points to a small hollow. 'That's where the pool will be. There'll be a view down to Georgiopoulis, and up to the White Mountains as well. We can have wine on the terrace in the evenings, just here, and watch the sun set.'

'So this is where all the money will be going?'

'All? No, not all, Billy. This will cost about seventy,

eighty thousand when it's finished. Plus extra to get electricity up here. And water, there's a small spring just up the hillside, I've built a water tank, but local rules say it's got to be filtered to keep it pure. I've got to put in a filtration system. Even worse than being at home. Good God, even Forestcrag didn't need a filtration system. Anybody could piss in their bloody stream. Probably did as well. Anyway, I'll use the balance of the money for investment. Something local, something for tourists. I might even have enough time to train again.'

'Get back in the top five? You tell me I should trust you, Nessa, but I keep on coming up against the brick wall of lies you've told in the past.'

'That was no lie, Billy.' She takes my hand again, leads me back across the building site to the caravan. She opens the door, nothing round here is locked. It's as I expect, untidy, a copy of her room at Forestcrag. There are clothes everywhere, books strewn on seats, a quilt lying dead on a dishevelled bed. She doesn't excuse the mess but dives into it, swims across to a cupboard above the window (a window which is staring at a block wall). She brings out a trophy, a silver cup. 'There you are,' she says, 'proof.' But I don't take it from her. Instead I pick up a photograph from the shelf above the cooker. There are three people in it, one of them is Nessa. She's much younger than she is now, the photograph must be about ten years old. She tries to take it from me but I pull it back.

'That was just after I finished university. Before I started travelling.'

I move away to the door so I can examine the photograph more carefully. I wipe the glass with the door curtain.

'I should have noticed the likeness,' I say.

'Yeah. My Dad. And my sister, though she was taller than me even then.' She thrusts the trophy at me. 'See, I was going to tell you.' I read the inscription. '1991 World Youth Triathlon Championships' it says. 'Third Place – Rosemary Salkeld.'

The faces in the photograph are all familiar, there's Nessa, of course, and her sister, whom I know as Eve Marton, and her father, Eric Salkeld.

'Now do you believe me?' she says.

An hour later she drops me back at the beach. We embrace. She cries. Both of us promise to come and visit each other, and both of us know we're lying. Then she gets back into her car and drives away.

Nick is all questions. 'Was that her? It looks like her, she's a bit younger than the description, but it could be her. How did you find her? What did you say to her? Where have you been?'

I'm getting used to lying. 'I've never seen her before,' I say. 'We got talking. She invited me back to her place. We spent some time there. And that's all I can say.'

I don't know if he believes me or not. It doesn't really matter. I'm going home tomorrow.

Chapter Thirty-Nine

I find I can walk more easily now, though my leg still hurts at night if I've done a lot of walking or standing during the day. I begin to start work again, with Norm's help. My regular clients seem pleased to have me back, new customers comment on how bronzed and fit I look.

I find I use sub-contractors more than I have done, certainly for straightforward security installations. The other work, the PI work, I still keep to myself. It's mostly routine stuff. Nothing exciting. I'm getting better at managing my life, I decide, I have more spare time than I used to. I spend it wisely. I see Kirsty regularly, I even visit when Sara's at home and comment on the beautiful volume of her pregnancy. I email Jen two or three times a week and anticipate her return with relish, talk to her live once a week. On one such occasion I propose marriage to her. She's flustered, says I can ask again when she can see my face looking up at her as I kneel on the floor. I accept the delay.

I read more. Mostly local history.

One day in summer I make a telephone call to a senior Environmental Health Officer from one of the local authorities. I don't know him, he doesn't know me, but I invite him to a meeting the next day at Forestcrag. He's reluctant to attend, but I tell him Sir Charles Plumpton will be present, and David Morland. Neither of them know, at that time, that there's a meeting. But they'll be there, I've found out that much, for the opening of a new slide in the Tesseract. I'm pleased to hear that it's called 'Missing Bodies'. Doors open and close within it at random, diverting the slider to different parts of the pool.

I ring Dean Metcalfe and tell him I'm coming to see him to discuss security. He says it's inconvenient, but I press a time on him well before the opening of the new slide.

I prepare my paperwork.

On the day in question my meeting with Dean goes pleasantly enough. I feel sorry I've used him as a dupe to get me on site, but not very sorry. When we finish I chat to the security guard at the main gate and I'm there when the Environmental Health Officer arrives. I greet him like an old friend, vouch for him and he is, as I expected, allowed to enter. I'm the only one knows his job. I commandeer a buggy and give him a tour of the site.

David Morland and Sir Charles Plumpton finish their scheduled duties on time and retire to the managerial suite for a celebratory brandy. That's where the EHO and I find them when we march in, despite the flustered flapping of arms from Morland's secretary. Give him his due, he waves her away as I make the introductions.

'What on earth do you want?' he asks wearily.

'To finish my job,' I reply from the depths of my armchair. I haven't told the EHO everything, but I've told him enough to keep him there with me.

Morland grins at Sir Charles who is, I'm pleased to see, slightly less sure of himself. 'I wasn't aware you had any unfinished business here at all,' he says.

'You gave me the job yourself,' I counter.

'I did? I can't recall any offer of employment to you, Mr Oliphant, and given your record here, your involvement in and, I dare say, wilful exacerbation of the recent unfortunate incidents, I don't feel I would ever be in the position of wishing to offer you a post.' He leans back plumply in his seat, overjoyed that he's managed to wrestle such a complex sentence into submission. He raises his eyebrows and waits for me to reply. I wait as well, until the silence is about to become embarrassing.

'You wanted me to investigate a case of suspected food poisoning. Long-serving staff, you said, were suffering from stomach upsets, headaches, nausea and diarrhoea. Now do you remember?'

'I remember that you turned the offer down, Mr Oliphant.'

'Are you sure? I believe there are witnesses, some of them still working here despite your high staff turnover, who can testify that you informed them all of my employment. Without specifying exactly what I was to do, of course. But you did mention this in front of a large number of people.'

Before he can reply I take a tape recorder from my briefcase and set it ostentatiously on the table in front of me. He glares at it, willing it to break down.

'I offered you a job. You turned it down. I informed my staff that you would be working amongst them, that you were a private investigator. I would have to take legal advice on whether a contract exists between us.'

'I already have done, Mr Morland. There is a contract, and I have fulfilled it.'

'Oh, I'm so pleased. Then why don't you let me have your findings and leave.'

'I'm here to deliver them personally.'

Sir Charles twists in his chair, addresses Morland. 'If you don't mind, since this appears to involve the day-to-day workings of the company, I think I'll disappear.'

'I think you ought to say,' I say. 'This does involve you directly. And your son.'

Morland is on his feet. 'Don't you think you've done enough damage already, Oliphant, without coming in here and twisting the blade ...'

'No, David, it's all right.' Sir Charles motions Morland back into his seat. 'I don't mind staying. Mr Oliphant is quite within his rights to request me to say.' He looks across at me and I can see the sorrow on his eyes. Love for a child is unconditional.

'Get on with it,' Morland says ungraciously.

'Thank you.' I reach into my case again, bring out my maps and plans. 'I've done a little research over the past few weeks and months. I believe that Forestcrag's water is taken directly from a reservoir constructed in the quarry to the north of the site. Is this correct?'

'You know it's correct. The quarry pool is our reservoir, but the water's filtered, it escapes over the waterfall and then it's treated thereafter. There can be no problem there.'

'How does the water get into the pool?' I ask.

Morland's face twists. 'How should I know? I'm not an expert in engineering, if you'd told me I'd be expected to answer questions of a technical nature then I'd have made sure someone was here to answer them.'

I look across at Sir Charles. He nods wisely.

'I have no claim to expertise,' he says, 'but logic would dictate that the pool is filled by water filtering through the high land above and around the quarry.'

'Sir Charles, I agree entirely. Now then, some more questions. Some of the stone from the quarry went to build Garthdale prison, I believe.'

'Yes, I think that's the case.'

'But the prison hasn't always been used as a prison?'

'No, during the Great War it was used by the War Department. It and the land around it was sequestered; I believe experiments were carried out on new forms of munitions and explosives. I'm not quite sure ...'

'Scientists and explosives experts from a company called AWP Limited were billeted there. And workmen. There had been problems, I believe, with drunkenness in the factories and the War Department believed that a degree of isolation from those temptations would be welcome. AWP is, of course, Armstrong Watson Plumpton. Your great grandfather, Sir Charles?'

'Yes, I think you're right there.'

'And do you know the type of munitions they were developing?'

'Yes.' He adds nothing. He's nervous.

Morland decided he's had enough. 'Look here, Oliphant, what are you getting at? If you think you can . . .'

'I think I'd like to listen to the captain rather than his parrot,' I say. 'Would you mind telling us what type of munitions they were developing?'

'You know, don't you?'

'Yes. I'm curious to know whether you do.'

'I'm not sure of the specifics. Shells with gas in them, that's what I heard. Mustard gas and so on. Unpleasant stuff.'

'That's what my information says.'

'Hold on,' says Morland, his manner suddenly avuncular. 'I know exactly what you're getting at.' He smiles, shakes his head in the manner of a schoolmaster who's discovered that his worst pupil's sudden and surprising intelligence is due to him reading answers copied from another. 'Oh dear, Oliphant, what a waste of time. Do you really think we haven't checked everything out. Oh dear, dear, dear, all you're doing is making a fool of yourself. We knew, you see, we knew about the dump. Have you got that in your paperwork? The dump? Yes, the shells, waste material, it was all dumped in the quarry, then earth was shovelled in on top of it. We found it all when we carried out our viability exercises. There was no waterfall then, no stream. But we knew what we wanted. We cleared the site in its entirety, took away all the topsoil, all the waste, not to mention tons of rock underneath. The quarry's clean, Oliphant. Now if you don't mind, you've wasted our time too much already.'

I lower my voice, I want the others to be paying careful attention. 'Philip found something new,' I say.

Morland harrumphs, Sir Charles leans forward.

'He knew the place well, didn't he?' I continue.

Sir Charles nods wistfully. 'He spent all his childhood here.'

'All?'

'He went to the local primary school, local secondary school as well. We always believed it was important to support the local community.'

'Really?' I shuffle the papers in front of me. 'Are you sure? Nothing to do with cashflow problems?' I've checked the records. Philip Plumpton did attend local schools, and I can remember Kirsty saying something about his claims that he wasn't rich. Though I've found nothing definite to confirm this, it's worth pushing to see what I can find. And Sir Charles doesn't know I'm fishing with a fake worm.

'It was quite a while ago, Mr Oliphant, my memory isn't too good these days. But . . . it may have been that we were short of cash at the time. It could have been a contributory factor.'

'There's no shame in that, Sir Charles. Most people can't even think about the option of private education. But what I'm trying to confirm is that Philip knew the quarry and the moorlands very well.'

'He did.'

'He knew about the history of the site, then? The prison, the munitions, the dump?'

'I never asked him directly, but he did have an interest in local matters.'

'Let's assume he knew, then. You see, there's a small artificial cave behind the climbing hut. Philip knew about that, he drew some interesting pictures on the wall. But he will also have seen there a plan of the quarry. Or quarries. At the time of the munitions experiments there were two quarries, the ordnance survey maps of the time confirm this. And the smaller of the two quarries was nearer to the prison than the larger.'

'What are you suggesting, Mr Oliphant?'

'I'm trying, Sir Charles, to imagine what your son was thinking. You've told me that the quarry, the *larger* quarry, was cleared of all contamination. I have no reason to doubt this. But I'm trying to get into the minds of those who

310

disposed of this material in the first place. They can have had no real idea of the toxicity of their waste products. They would, I feel, have looked around them and thought of all the possible places they could bury the stuff. And where was nearest? The small quarry. But the volume of waste was too great, they filled that small quarry. So what next? They covered it in, then moved on to the large quarry. Now, it was easy for anyone to see that the large quarry had been used as a dump, even seventy years afterwards. But the small quarry had by then disappeared under a natural cover of gorse and grass, bracken and bog. The records were hidden in secrecy. Who could guess what was there?'

I wait for someone, anyone, to say something. Sir Charles sighs.

'Philip would have known,' he says. 'He studied geology at university. He carried out an investigation into the water tables in the area. He would have known.'

'But he didn't say anything. Why not?'

'I don't know.'

'Are you sure?'

Sir Charles stares at me. 'You've made your point, Mr Oliphant. Do you really need to go on? My son is dead. He can't harm anyone now.'

'But he could, Sir Charles, he killed an innocent girl and he almost killed me. Do you know why?'

He refuses to answer.

'Let me make a suggestion, then. He knew, as many people know, that you are in financial difficulties. You have problems, I believe, with gambling. I don't condemn you for this, I sympathise with you. But perhaps you ought to seek some help rather than try to disguise or hide your addiction. Your gambling is financed by the income you receive from your Forestcrag shares. Philip knew this as well. Now then, Sir Charles, had Morland told you that he was having the staff illnesses investigated?'

'I don't know. I can't remember, possibly he said something.'

311

'Yes,' says Morland sulkily, 'I did mention it.'

'And you, Sir Charles, in all innocence, probably just in passing, mentioned it to your son. And even though I initially declined the job, Philip assumed, wrongly as it happens, that I was close to finding out the truth. If that truth had come to light, what would have happened? Perhaps we do now need some expert opinion, some expert advice. From an Environmental Health Officer?'

The EHO clears his throat. 'From what I've heard,' he says, 'from what I've seen, it's likely that the site water source is contaminated with several unnamed toxic substances. Blood tests on those suffering from exposure to these substances would, on account of the unusual nature of the substances, probably show nothing. Given the fact that water does not, until recently, appear to have had a natural overland escape route, it is possible that the water table may also be contaminated. It is essential that further investigations are carried out. I would recommend to my employers, the Local Authority who have a statutory obligation to consider safety in this area, that the site be closed pending these investigations.'

Morland is on his feet again, he's shouting. Sir Charles is dabbing his eyes with a handkerchief. I want for quiet.

'Philip Plumpton was aware of all this. Closure would mean his father's financial ruin. But he thought I knew more than I really did. He decided to kill me and, when it went wrong, when he killed an innocent girl instead, he showed no remorse. He continued to pursue me. He tried to kill me.' I pick up my paperwork and put it away in my briefcase. 'I won't make any public announcement about this, others will do it for me. The Forestcrag share price will undoubtedly go down. Forestcrag will be closed for a considerable period of time. I have the greatest sympathy with the innocent employees who will suffer because of this.'

I feel no satisfaction at my pronouncement. It brings my investigations to a neat conclusion, but one that's far from satisfactory. I've made a decision to tell the world about my suspicions (and, despite my confidence that I'll be proved right, they are just suspicions). As a result of that decision people will be hurt. Innocent people will lose their jobs, their livelihoods, perhaps their self-respect. It's a wonderful thing, the passive tense, it takes away responsibility so easily. Let's put it right. It was my decision; my action; and so it must be my responsibility. *Mea culpa, mea maxima culpa*. And the other side of the coin? I could have said nothing, done nothing. After all, I've already demonstrated that I have the capacity to ignore facts, to ignore the law, even, if I want to. No, even that's not really true. So far as Nessa's concerned I looked at the information I had and I acted as judge. But as a result of that decision no one else was hurt, no one suffered. Well, perhaps I suffered; I still feel like a policeman even if I'm not one, and I know what I ought to have done. I chose not to do it. I have to live with that decision. The difference here, at Forestcrag, is that someone might become seriously ill if I choose not to make my findings public. Will that work as a sop to my conscience? I'll find out tonight when I'm lying in bed, thinking lean and hungry thoughts. If I can get to sleep I'll be okay.

First I have to get through the rest of the day. I'm sweating, I feel faint, my knee is hurting. The EHO is at my heels.

'How did you guess?' he asks.

'An accumulation of evidence,' I tell him, 'that meant nothing until I had the catalyst.'

'And that was . . .?'

'A friend. She was talking about something entirely different, and she said something which helped me make a connection. She used to work here. She told me Forestcrag didn't need a filtration system. She said, and these were her exact words, "anybody could piss in their bloody stream. Probably did as well." And it was true. Somebody had pissed in their stream.'

The End

Summer on the high moorlands. Skylarks dot the sky with crotchets of sound. Curlews like kites sail on soft melodic breezes. Cotton grass crowns tussocks of wiry grass, small flowers of blue and yellow hide in their shade. A dog barks, follows the shepherd's wide whistle of command, leaps walls and circumnavigates the flock of wary black-faces. The shepherd watches closely. He's counting, checking, making sure every animal is healthy. This year, more than any other, it matters.

'Git doon,' he yells. The dog crouches. The farmer lifts his hand to shield his eyes from the sun. They're tired eyes, a tired man. It was a bad winter, a worse summer. The men in white overalls are still working up at the quarry. Forestcrag is still closed. No one visits the farmhouse to buy cakes or slake their thirst with tea and lemonade, he can't even sell his stock until the tests are finished.

He whistles again and the dog's off, over a slight rise and down the dip beyond, then . . . Then nothing. No dog. The shepherd curses, convinced he should have left the beast at home. The other dog may be older, almost infirm, but at least it knows its way round and does as it's told.

'Where are yu, stupid fookin animal!' He stalks off in the direction the dog took only a minute before. It could have hurt itself, cut its leg on some hidden barbed wire, but it's more likely to have found a scent or a dead fox. The

315

shepherd crests the rise and looks down as the dog looks up, guiltily. 'Coom 'ere,' the shepherd shouts, but the dog curls its tail under its legs and refuses to move. The shepherd reaches for his belt. The dog will suffer for this.

He gets closer, the dog is whimpering now, the belt is raised and ... falls limply to the shepherd's side. The shepherd pushes the dog to one side. 'Holy Jesus,' he says.

He's looking at a man's body. The shepherd is old, he's lived with death and life for year after year. He pokes the body with his foot, moves it slightly. Its flesh is still visible in places, but putrefaction has long passed. The skin is leathered, the fabric of shirt and trousers eaten away. The shepherd looks around, notes the lie of the land. He'll have to come back with a policeman.

'Coom on lad,' he says to the dog, and this time it obeys. Man and beast head down into the valley, into the welcome of the cool farmhouse. He lives alone. He picks up the telephone, checks a list scribbled on the wall and dials. He doesn't use the number given in the directory for police, that would merely get him through to a distant office who would contact a policeman out somewhere in a car. This way is far better.

'Hello, Davie? Aye, Tommy Waugh here. I knaa thoo's off duty, lad, but I thowt th'd want to knaa. I've just been on t'tops. Found a body. Reckon it's that lad got away in the storm, what's 'is name? Aye, that's it. Simpson. Harry Simpson. Daft bugger, got what 'e deserved, eh? Paid back for 'is crimes, 'e was, nee doubt. Aye, see yu soon, I'll put t'kettle on.'